half irish

Half Irish

First Edition

Copyright © Peter J. S. Waugh 2015

Peter J. S. Waugh has asserted his right under the Copyright, Designs and
Patents Act, 1988, to be identified as the author of this work.

First published by The White Signature 2015

A CIP catalogue record for this title is available from the British Library.
ISBN: 978-0-9575900-4-5

Published by The White Signature
www.thewhitesignature.com

Edited by Siobhan Dignan
www.siobhandignan.com

Cover artwork by Aly Harte
www.alyharte.com

Printed in the UK using only FSC® and PEFC approved products.

For Kerry.
Always follow your dreams.

half irish

PETER J. S. WAUGH

PROLOGUE

I wait
For you
To come
And sit
With me
And tell me all the things that make your soul so sad.

I'll listen to all you have to say
And the way it makes you feel
I hate the way the world has made you disappear.

I want to hold you and tell you to show yourself
Your beautiful self
To show the talents that you have inside
The smile that brings life to all who are captured by it

Allow the beauty you hold to come alive.

A girl.
A boy.
Strangers.
Friends.
Soul mates.
She quickened my heart.
She arrested my mind.
She awakened my soul.
All thanks to the flick of a wrist one beautiful day in a Belfast park.

I could tell you many tales about my early years, and for a while, I will. After a few babbling noises resembling Mom and Dad, my next words were *up* and *apple*. A few weeks later I created controversy amongst my family. According to my cake-shop-owning *Mom*, the next word I uttered was *cake*. My sports-loving *Dad* says it was kick and my diaper would say it was *kaka*.

The first and only fistfight I have been in was with Dylan Fielding in the 4th grade. I made his nose bleed with a sweet uppercut. I still plead it was an act of self-defence after Dylan tried to cut my hair during an art class. I thought he was going to take our cut and stick lesson to a new level so I stopped him in his tracks.

The highlight of my dating life, until the summer I lost my heart and fell in love with Tabitha, my Belfast girl, extends to a single defining moment when I wooed and kissed Alice Pinkerton in the tunnel of my kindergarten play corner. Even though I have emerged from my awkward early teenage years of pimples and growth spurts with relatively good looks, my teenage years have been lean in the romance department. I was too busy hanging with the guys to have a girlfriend, plus I didn't want to get my heart broken like they do in rom-coms!

As far as sporting prowess goes, it's impressive. I'm a classic all-rounder. In Junior High I had a 22.4 ppg average shooting hoops for the mighty Village Dunkers. Le Bron James, I'm coming after you!

Yet these stories are inconsequential (that's a big word for a Tuesday morning) in light of the journey I'm about to take you on. My name is Tyler, Tyler Sontoro. I live in the Village area of New York City. The best city in the world. I'm the product of my Belfast-born mom and my Italian descended dad. For the last few years I have been educated at a great public high school in the Village. Soon I will take a few more classes in life, dorm-rooms, fraternity traditions, laundry and English Literature at a college a few states away. But before that happens, I need to bring you into a fairytale and share with you the ways in which my life has been redefined over the last few months. To tell you about all of these wonderful moments, we need to travel back to a cold, crisp November evening in my magical city.

I hope you enjoy my tales of love and longing, destiny and design.

I hope you laugh until you cry, and cry until you are left with a dream for your life so daring that it makes your soul tingle with excitement.

Thanks for being my guest, a fellow traveller passing through.

This will be beautiful.

Tyler Sontoro

PLATE TECTONICS AND SHAKESPEARE

My mind was dominated by the finer details of plate tectonics and the literary musings of a certain William Shakespeare on an otherwise mundane November afternoon. After finishing a sketch of a diagram about the Earth's core, I began to make some comments on a few sonnets of arguably the world's finest writer. But I was bored, so for at least twenty minutes I sat and played with my pencil, trying to make it do that helicopter thing between your thumb and forefinger. I managed a few stalled take-offs before my stomach let out an earth-shattering rumble.

Mom had work that morning, and after lunch and yoga with the girls, spent the afternoon at home reading magazines and picking up after her two men. Now she was in the kitchen speaking to her sister on the phone. I could tell it was my Aunt Beth as Mom's accent changed, the speed of her speech quickened and she used Belfast words like 'wee' and 'aye' a lot.

1

It's been over twenty years since Mom moved to New York, but Aunt Beth and Mom remain really tight. They Skype a couple of times a week and text all the time. Our families are pretty close. Cousin Patrick goes to Queen's University in Belfast (Not Queens NYC unfortunately!) so he's been giving me lots of tips about college life. I have visited Ireland twice. Once for vacation when I was a kid. The last time was for my Granda's funeral when I was thirteen. That was a flying visit and a pretty difficult trip.

I abandoned the books and made my way towards the hub of our home in the hope that a wonderful aroma would waft towards my nostrils. As I peered round the kitchen door my mom greeted me with a thumbs up and with her other hand motioned a five-digit-flash. In other words 'I love you, but get out and give me 5 minutes.'

I stood and waited at the door for a few minutes, listening to Mom's side of what sounded like an intense conversation. *What was up?*

'It's just so terrible Beth ... How has he been since? ... and now?'

There was a long pause.

'Don said he thought it would be a great idea. I'm sure Tyler will be thrilled too ... We'll work out the dates closer to the time.'

What was I gonna be thrilled about?!

'I know it would mean so much to Patrick ... yes ... of course ... How's Mommy handling it all?'

I walked away from the door. A funny feeling came over

me. I knew I shouldn't have listened in on the conversation. Now I had more questions than answers. Was Patrick in some sort of trouble? He seemed to be OK on Facebook. His statuses weren't depressing and he hadn't mentioned anything on our recent Skype conversation.

Confused and slightly worried I made my way to see Dad, who had been home for half an hour. I heard gunfire and cuss words coming from his den, so I knew he was trying his best to catch up with me on *COD*. Bless him. Running intel missions was his way of relaxing after a busy day at the office. I knew I shouldn't disturb him, but I was so hungry!

'Dad.'

Nothing.

'Dad.'

Nothing again. The volume was up too loud in his headphones.

'DAAAADDDDD!' I shouted as I jumped in front of the screen. He took his headphones off and tried to kill one last insurgent.

'Hey Tyler. What's up? How was school?'

'Yeah it was fine thanks.'

'Did that physics teacher give you any slack on your project?'

'A little. But I still have tons to do for it.'

Dad was staring at the screen, reading the analysis of his last game.

'Are you on dinner tonight?' I asked.

'Yeah. But your mom's speaking to Beth so I can't get into

the kitchen.'

'Do you know what they're talking about?'

Dad instantly went silent and awkward. 'Ermm,' he bumbled. 'Ermm no.' He shook his head and curled up his front lip. 'Do you know how to get past this level?'

Dad is a terrible liar.

'Yeah. But I'll let you figure that out for yourself.' I walked towards the door. 'Call me when dinner's ready, yeah?'

'OK son.'

I carried my hunger and rejection back to my room and began to research the history assignment I was a little behind on. *Man I've done enough work tonight* I thought as I sat down at my desk. I searched for my cell, which was hidden under my textbooks, and sent a text to my pal Alex.

Tyler:	*Bored!*
Alex:	*Me 2. Wot u up 2?*
Tyler:	*Waitin 4 dinner - hungrrrrrrry. U?*
Alex:	*Math n still struggling wit physics.*
Tyler:	*Got my diagram finished – yeeeeoooo! gtg. Mom's rushing 2 my room. Wot did I do?!*
Alex:	*No idea. Let me no.*
Tyler:	*L8rs!*

Faster than a volcanic eruption, Mom scurried down the hall towards my bedroom. In the seconds before she burst in, I tried to recall anything remotely mischievous, dangerous or semi-illegal that I had been up to lately. The last time I got in trouble was for running my phone bill up, but that happened before the summer, and I've been relatively good since then. We also had #spliffgate last year, but I don't want to talk about that. (I didn't inhale.) The news Mom brought taught me that messengers aren't always the bearers of bad news. She just came straight out with it.

'Your aunt wants you to visit them in Ireland on your summer vacation.'

'What? You serious? But I thought they were going to France next year?'

'They changed their minds and want you to spend three weeks with them. Isn't that a fantastic idea? Or will I tell them you're too busy?'

For a few seconds I stared at the tired schoolbooks strewn across my wooden desk and then couldn't hide the smile that broke out across my face. My cheeks scrunched up into two gerbilesque balls of delight. I had one question: 'So what's Patrick doing over the summer?'

'He's your tour guide,' Mom said nervously.

'Man this is so cool! They didn't mention anything about this when I spoke to them last week.'

'I know. But some things changed for them, so they want you to come visit. Stop over-thinking it and get excited! It's a wonderful opportunity for you.'

Immediately I scrolled through my iPod and planted some gravity-defying old school hip-hop beats into the airspace of my bedroom. The beat was phat, the lyrics leapt out of the speakers; the mood the music set was the definition of excitement. Mom began to tap her suede moccasins off the wood floor, which sent a message to the rest of her body and within a few beats she was busting some exquisite moves from *The 1984 How to Dance and Create a Revolution Rulebook.*

My dad, a rarely reserved man, caught the vibe pulsing out through the house. His feet scurried towards my room and 10 seconds later he bounced over the threshold with a version of the wiggly worm that tested the flooring to the limit. The Sontoro family spent the next few minutes busting moves like never before. After our very necessary dancing session we caught eye contact. Dad drew breath and uttered one beautiful word, 'Cosalá's.'

COSALÁ'S

We used to justify our frequent trips to the best Mexican restaurant in Greenwich Village as a way to practice our Spanish. But after working our way through the menu extremely quickly and still having a poor grasp of the language, our educational justification for visiting Cosalá's faded as quickly as a banshee at the sight of a Ghostbuster. Our visits were now a tried and tested family tradition. Cosalá's is littered with neon signs, collected by the owners during the various road trips they have made. My favourite is the *Jesus hearts tacos'* sign they bought in Southern Texas. Only in Texas, right? That night we sat under a flashing electric blue sign with the words *'Park Rangers are heroes. Buy them a beer.'*

The chili in Cosalá's is hotter than a midsummer's day in NYC. Mom ordered the Chameleon Quesadilla, Dad had some Culiacán Chili and I tackled a Steak Taco Trio. We started with guac 'n' cheese covered nachos #obvs. The food tasted better than it had in months. A flavour of expectancy filled the air. In between spooning 'sides' of beans and salsa onto my food, my mind drifted towards my trip to Ireland. *I wonder if there are any good Mexican diners in Belfast?*

As she finished the last bite of her quesadilla, Mom was nudged by Dad. An obvious signal to spill the beans! She wiped her mouth and spoke up, 'Tyler, we want you to try and pay for this trip by yourself.'

The news startled me. With my attention grabbed by this life-changing news, I lifted my spoon, scooped up something green that I thought was guac, but in reality was a big helping of Cosalá's notorious 'Green Death' chili sauce (made with green chilis so hot the staff have to wear gloves and eye goggles when they whizz it up in the blender), dumped it on my taco and popped the taco into my unsuspecting mouth. I thought my folks were playing good cop bad cop, but then Dad piped up, 'And your mom and I decided we'll take a trip to South America while you're in Ireland. We feel ready for a long break and to see a few new places. You can have your adventure and we'll have ours.'

Long before Dad finished talking my mouth was already on fire! I couldn't speak. My parents were waiting for a reaction, but I couldn't give them one! I fanned my mouth for a few seconds and in between finishing off all of the soda on the table, I managed to croak out a response, 'Oh, OK. That sounds cool. Took too much Green Death,' I gasped as I tried to swallow the news and quell the fire in my mouth.

We ordered dessert (cooling ice cream for me), and for the rest of the evening my mind was somewhere between Buenos Aires, Belfast and part time jobs. I've never been away from my folks for more than a couple of days. Now we'll be at opposite ends of the world. And then there's the money thing. Mom is a successful businesswoman and Dad has made a nice bit of coin working as an attorney. My parents have been so kind to me. They have provided me with everything, and more, a nearly 18-year-old guy needs to navigate from the cradle to the cusp of college life. From love to laughter, new threads and gadgets, they have spoiled me with everything I have taken for granted. This was the first time they set me an economic challenge.

Mom went on to explain they could afford to pay for my trip, but because I'm doing so well at school and they're helping out with my college, they thought it would be a good chance for me to gain some valuable life experience. Plus she wanted me to have money to spend during my time in Ireland and to chip in a bit to take the burden off Aunt Beth.

'It will be good for you to channel your time and energy to raise the money for your trip,' she said.

A quick bit of arithmetic on my salsa and guac-splashed napkin showed the following:

Flights: $900ish

Spending money: $1000ish

Target $1900 in the 28 weeks remaining (give or take a few to find a job and for vacations) = $67.86 per week. But let's round it up to $70.

I currently spend most of my weekly allowance on transport, new music, food and hanging with friends. I could live like a monk to scrimp and save off that allowance, but not buying music and donuts for a few weeks would barely get me out of NY State, never mind across the Atlantic. As we finished our dessert and squared up our bill, I realised that getting a job was my only option. I had been nervous when Mom and Dad told me about my challenge, but when I saw the generous tip dad left our server I had a feeling that earning my way to Ireland might just be do-able. Unfortunately the restaurant didn't have any slots for waiters. I asked on my way out!

JOBS FOR TEENS

It was a cold, cloudless evening. I love strolling round my city on nights like this. On the walk home we threw some thoughts about my job prospects into the night sky. My ideas ranged from the ridiculous to the ridonculous and then to the realistic - from getting a job as a street performer, or a posh pooch walker, to engaging in medical research, or seeking out espionage missions for any willing party. We stopped a bullet's length short of seriously entertaining the idea of me working as a hit man - it was only going to be for a few months! I think the *Bourne* trilogy we watched on our last Friday Film Night had a profound influence on that part of our conversation.

The job ideas were hazy, but as we rounded onto Perry Street it was clear that this teenage lad was being sent out to work. Mom and Dad viewed it as, and I quote, 'critical to the development of my character ... an opportunity to learn new skills and meet wonderful people.' Oh, and of course it was going to help me to 'appreciate the value of a Benjamin. They don't grow on skyscrapers you know'. Thanks for that folks.

An only child, living in Manhattan with wealthyish hard-working parents, I should have been the last person in the city looking for a part-time job, especially during a recession. But my parents have always told me they got to where they are through hard work, networking, creativity and the guts to say the wrong things to the right people. Now they were giving me the chance to try my hand at this life experience called work. We grabbed a coffee on Bleecker Street and sat on a bench, (it was just about warm enough to sit out), and my parents laid down ground rules for my moneymaking efforts.

1. Don't sell any of your stuff.
2. Don't sell any of our stuff.
3. Don't steal and sell anyone else's stuff.
4. Be proactive and creative.
5. If you haven't got a job by February we will reconsider how you pay for the trip, but that's no excuse.
6. You can't exchange your 'Santa/18th birthday' present for cash. (I've asked for a wicked guitar).
7. Nothing illegal or slightly shady.
8. Have hope.
9. Don't give up!

Arriving home I made a beeline for my bedroom. My chi-li had barely settled by the time I reached for my tablet and entered *'Jobs for Teens NYC'* in the search engine. The nightly pre bedtime crime drama TV fix was on the back burner, as it would be criminal if I didn't raise enough money to visit Ireland in the summer! Come on Google, do your business and create some promising, dollar producing links for me!

As I waited for the search results to appear on my screen, I was reminded of something Mom had said to me earlier that evening. The final words from Mom's rallying inspirational speech on the front steps of our apartment building came to mind before I scrolled through the results: *'Use your imagination, and if that fails, then be prepared to work damn hard.'*

The search engine returned the following:

'Do you see yourself in business? Start a franchise with us. Make money overnight.' Total lack of capital to invest just might be an obstacle!

'Be part of the future of medicine *and* earn money. Join a medical research team near you.'

Although with this type of work there's always the fear you may never live to enjoy the money you earn. Or that you may have extra limbs to clothe. This was never a serious consideration.

The search engine also returned a few more realistic results. A couple of blocks from my refuge in the city, a fruit shop was looking for a part-time assistant/juice bar operator. Further afield, the jobs that caught my eye included a sales assistant in a toy store, some seasonal retail jobs on 5th Ave, and a 'business information distributor'- otherwise known as a leaflet dropper! Before the lights went out in our crib that evening, I showed my research to my folks. Dad's face suggested he'd rather just give me the cash. No questions, no paybacks, just a one-way deposit of bills.

But Mom knew what he was thinking and spoke up, 'All looks exciting. You'll have plenty of stories to share if you get any of these jobs.'

'Yeah I know,' I replied. Without my brain knowing, my mouth continued to speak, 'I'm strangely excited about earning my way to The Emerald Isle.' I tried to say it in an Irish accent. Note to self - work on the accent. 'Think I'm gonna go on a job hunt tomorrow after school. Find some more places with openings, but for now, my food baby and I need some shuteye. Night.'

'Night. Say a prayer to St Joseph. He'll get your career started.'

'Sure thing Dad.'

The Catholic side of my faith came out that night as I whispered some of my job desires towards the Saints and trusted in the Good Lord to provide for me. After all Ireland is God's Country, so He would definitely want me to go there. Right?

Hey God. Hey St. Joe. Just wondering if you could sort me out with a job. It's a little prayer but it would mean a lot to me. And, if it's not too much to ask, can you keep me away from anything greasy, smelly and cold? I don't want to wear a hairnet or wear a funny coloured uniform! Oh and I'll promise to get my school projects finished in time. Dealio?'

I slipped into bed and wondered what Patrick was up to. I made a mental note to get in touch with him. As my head eased onto the pillow the snippets of Mom's conversation I'd overheard drifted into my mind and I wondered what it was that she was keeping from me. Hopefully Patrick would shed some light onto it. But it didn't sound like the kind of thing I could just ask him straight out. I tried to put such thoughts out of my mind and began to picture the green fields and black cabs of Ireland. Then, as I fell asleep, my dreams ushered in the as yet invisible stories I was to live out over the next few months.

MONEY MAKING IDEAS

'What happened to you last night? You never replied to my text message!' Alex asked.

'Oh yeah. Sorry man. I wanted to tell you both in person.'

Rodriguez brought his head out from inside his locker. 'Tell us what?'

'I'm going to Ireland for my summer vacation! Well … Northern Ireland.'

'What?! That's so awesome,' they both reacted.

Rodriguez and I high-fived the news before Alex chest bumped me.

'Northern Ireland. Man that's gonna be so cool,' Alex enthused before asking, 'Northern Ireland? Is that like in the north of Ireland?'

Rodriguez shook his head.

I explained, 'Northern Ireland is the northern part of the

island, but it's part of the UK. There was conflict there for like 40 years, but it's safe now.'

Alex still looked puzzled.

'United Kingdom. You know, England and Scotland and Wales.'

Alex gave a fake nod of understanding. Then he asked, 'But there's still leprechauns in Northern Ireland. Right?'

Rodriguez and I looked at each other before we gave a simultaneous 'yes' to Alex's ridiculous question.

'My Uncle Richard and Aunt Beth are hosting me and my cousin Patrick is my tour guide.'

'That sounds awesome. Beats my trip to the Lakes,' Alex said. 'How long are you going for?'

'Ermm ... three weeks.' (really it was going to work out at about three and a half, but the guys didn't need to know that at this stage!)

'THREE WEEKS!' Alex shouted. He turned to a group of girls who were walking past and yelled, 'Tyler's going to Ireland for three weeks in the summer!' They looked at him and laughed.

Alex is one of my zany friends who has no sense of personal space! One of the girls started talking about her relatives that visited Ireland and gave me a list of things to visit. I turned back from chatting with the group of girls to see that Rodriguez's face had dropped. We have been best friends since kindergarten. Inseparable for so many years. I think Rodriguez thought we were gonna have one last summer hanging out before college. I probably should have texted him last night to break the news. Alex was still shooting the breeze with the girls as Rodriguez finished packing his schoolbag.

'I'm so happy for you Tyler.'

'Really? You seem a bit bummed out.'

'It's just with what's been going on with me lately, I guess I've just been used to having you there. Then with going off to college, I thought we were both gonna be around all summer.'

'I know man. But three weeks will fly by. Plus I think something's up with my cousin Patrick. Mom and Aunt Beth were talking in code on the phone last night. I could sense that something's wrong from their tone.'

'That's just their funny Irish accent man.' Rodriguez always tried to turn the conversation into a joke to dodge talking about any serious issue.

'LOL. I'll have to get used to that brogue.'

'I'm gonna miss you bro.'

'Ditto, but they have WiFi in Ireland so we can still chat!'

The bell rang and we made our way to Mrs. Bennett's math class where I blamed the excitement of the previous evening for totally forgetting to start, never mind finish, my algebra assignment. I hope St Joe hadn't noticed! I managed to avoid her wrath by discussing the subject of Ireland with her - apparently she's 11/16th Irish. I didn't know you could be 11/16th of anything. It felt so good being able to legitimately tell her, 'I'm Half Irish'. I told her of my plans for the summer and, prompted by her sweet sweet memories from a trip she had made to the West Coast of Ireland a few years back, she burst into glorious, cringeworthy song. I'm pretty sure I won't be as far west as Galway, but she didn't need to know that. My plan succeeded and she gave me an extension on my work. Boom!

I was living for the shrill sound of metal clanging against metal when the bell would free me to hit the streets and search for businesses that were seeking a guy like me to make their profits skyrocket. It was another cold day in the city. The cloudless, starlit sky from last night had been replaced with a big grey rug of snow-filled clouds, but the surly weather failed to check my upbeat attitude as I leapt down the front steps of our school and hit the sidewalk with a bounce.

For the next ten blocks I found out that it's bleak out there. I stopped by businesses that looked like they would hire a teenager and heard phrases like, 'I wish I had enough trade to hire people', 'Sorry man not today', 'I can give you a two week unpaid trial?', 'Maybe next year', the odd abrupt 'No', and countless blank stares. By the time I made it to Madison Square Park, I needed a sugar boost. After a couple of donuts and a Coke, I weighed up my options and started to fill out a few application forms I had downloaded the previous night.

With the forms half complete, I people-watched for a while. Most applications required a résumé, which for a somewhat sheltered, middle-class 17-year-old high school, everything-handed-to-him-on-a-plate guy is pretty much a non-event. I noted down my favourite subjects, sports achievements and exaggerated my extra-curricular activities. Reading it left me empty. I wouldn't employ this guy! Aside from the obligatory details found on all application forms and résumés, I decided to bring my personality to the desks and inboxes of managers up and down Manhattan by creating an Irish inspired piece of literature. It had started to rain. The depressing weather matched my fruitless afternoon. I was now desperate. I think it's called 'Pulling the Irish Ace out of the pack'.

Two hundred years have nearly passed, since the Irish came to town,
Their crops had failed, their joy had gone, their smiles were but a frown.
My mom descends from that fair Isle, Belfast does make her smile,
I hope to spend my summer there, but the cost is proving a trial.

With my Irish charm and a hard working attitude,
I'll make your customers glad that you hired such a dude.
So help me raise my airfare, make sure I pack my case,
I'm asking for a part time job, please reply with haste.

Not exactly a limerick, and some dodgy rhymes, but I hoped they would get the gist of what I was trying to do. After sending off the necessary forms all I could do was sit tight. So, during the days of waiting for my words to work their magic, I thought of a few ways to save money:

1. Choose the 'Eat-out' option in cafés.

Or even cheaper, pack a lunch and picnic! Eating on park benches is free!

Upsides - I will be able to see more of the city and by saving 40 cents here and $1 there I will gather together a few helpful dollars.

Downsides - NYC can be super cold in the winter and I run the risk of my sandwich gaining additional dressing from a pigeon's butt.

2. Walk/Cycle/Fly everywhere.

Upsides – Save money on subway fares. Increase my fitness. Tone my calves.

Downsides – I would always be late and I may need a new pair of sneakers, a jetpack, a new coat and an umbrella to make it work. Jetpacks cost a lot of money, plus I would miss seeing some of the characters that use the Subway.

3. Look for change down the couch.

Upsides - Unexpected earner, potential goldmine, sitting on couches is a great thing to do.

Downsides - I might find some gross things down there: used Kleenex, old food or worse. I will also look like a weirdo if someone catches me fondling the dark regions of their sofa.

4. Lay off the soda and start drinking tap water.

Upsides - Soda is not great for my teeth and water is definitely better. Lower dental bills.

Downsides - Forbidding my mouth to taste the sweet bubbly nectar will be hard! Missing out on the competitions some drinks companies offer.

5. No new clothes until the summer.

Upsides - I checked out my wardrobe and I think the clothes I have will do me until the weather gets a bit warmer. I will need a pre college shop, and maybe some new shorts for my vacation. Correction: I'm going to Ireland, I'll need a raincoat. But the swag I have should last me until the summer.

Downsides - I will no longer be able to walk the corridors of high school in the latest fashions. I will be a season behind. #shame

6. Dog walking

Upsides - I'm sure there are a few dogs that need walking in our building or next door. I'll get a bit fitter and might meet a girl if the pooches I'm walking are really cute.

Downsides - Picking up dog poo. The freezing cold winter weather. Picking up frozen dog poo!

For the next week and a half I became the thriftiest teenager in the city and was able to save, find and collect $89.02 by the following methods:

$8.50 – checking vending machines for change. It's amazing how careless hungry people in a hurry can be, and what you can find when you begin to look in different places - and are slightly desperate!

$9.80 – drinking tap water and not soda.

$7.10 – I skipped my regular after school donuts.

$13.20 – Walking instead of taking public transport. I also thought that when I get my new guitar for my birthday I can start busking in the Subway.

$30.42 – I made a point of visiting a lot of stores and cafés that had couches. I don't know if this is classified as stealing, but it's in the past now. $30.42 was a surprising amount of cash to find down the back of couches. I think I'm gonna branch out into armchairs next week!

$20 - Dog walking.

On the downside, I walked right into one disgusting expense. I had to spend $45 on a new pair of sneakers after I stepped in some dog crap! I had put an ad up in my building's lobby next to the mailboxes and bingo! Little Miss Lambert from across the hall asked me to walk her dogs. All six of them. They weren't exactly cute or toilet trained. It was a complete disaster. I had to stop every five minutes to pick up doo doo from one of the dogs that must have had some stomach problem, and then spend another five minutes untangling the leashes from around my ankles. A few cute girls walked past me on the third poop stop. I was trying so hard to act cool and casual, but I tripped over Deputy Dawg's leash and stood straight in his little smelly present. I'm not sure if it was the smell or the shame that was more embarrassing. No amount of scrubbing could remove the stench, and the poop had gotten onto the suede, so my Converse quickly found a new home in the trash and I had to go and buy some new sneaks. In the sales, of course! The $20 I had earned from walking the dogs turned into a $25 loss! So by the 29th November my travel fund looked like this:

$89.02 – $45 = $44.02 saved and earned. (26 weeks to go)

As the week, and my new career in 'Adventurous Saving' progressed, the need for a constant, reliable stream of income became a stark reality.

MON AMOUREUX SECRET

Esther Sontoro, a.k.a. 'Mom', is really special to me; hilarious and embarrassing, all rolled into one cool 5ft 7-inch woman.

Before gap years were a rite of passage for many teenagers, Mom took a trip and made a few decisions that changed the direction of her life. As her peers were taking off for college, Mom and her bestie, Nancy Robinson, cashed in the wages from their summer jobs, threw on their loaded backpacks, and took off on a hitch-hiking trip through the parts of Europe that were open for business - pre-fall of the Berlin Wall.

From the châteaux of France to the breathtaking fjords of Scandinavia, the girls ventured around Europe in search of the next piece of mind-blowing architecture or inspirational scenery that made their hearts skip an extra beat and their friends insanely jealous. After a couple of months of travel they arrived home to a snowy, yet still tribally divided Belfast. The

80's in Belfast were a difficult time. Northern Ireland was in the middle of a violent conflict that was tearing people and communities apart, with bomb scares, shootings and security checkpoints very much a part of daily life.

I'm pretty sure Mom edits the content of some of the travel tales she tells me, but one thing she can't edit is the passion that emanates from her soul when she recounts the diverse culinary delights and dodgy dangers sampled on that trip. Aside from a few pounds and the ability to ask 'ou est la toilette?' in nine different languages, Mom gained something extremely valuable on her expedition. When she stepped off the plane, she brought with her the one thing she wanted to devote her life to. Having been inspired by the pastas of Italy, the pastries of France and the daily coffee 'n' cake ritual of *fika* in Sweden, her soul was set alight with an unwavering passion to discover more of the culinary world. At school she had studied Home Economics as well as taking a cooking night class in the local college. On the weekends and during vacations she had worked in a neighbourhood bakery; but a career selling coconut fingers (yeah I know, how can coconuts have fingers?!) and sausage rolls (this ones easier to imagine!) wasn't enough to satisfy this girl.

Keen to build on her field research, my mom spent the next few months volunteering and working in Belfast's then limited restaurant scene, gaining experience anywhere she could. Then, by a wing and a prayer and a strategic recommendation from one of Ireland's best chefs, she gained entry to one of the finest culinary schools in Europe - Festa del Re (The King's Feast). Situated in the bustling streets of Rome, this place was the ultimate destination for aspiring chefs. Those fortunate enough to gain a place were taught the fundamentals and the secrets of gourmet dining by some of the world's top names. The students were immersed in a world of experimentation, opportunity and colourful ingredients.

After her time at Festa del Re, Mom decided to specialise as a pastry chef, which released another dream - living in the heart of Paris. During the 18 months she spent in Mon Amoureux Secret, she devoted her time to playing with chocolate and cream, sugar and crème pâtisserie, tarts and all kinds of breads. The winding streets of Montmartre provided the perfect backdrop for Esther as she developed her skills and gained respect throughout the college. Her hard work, enthusiasm and creative nature helped her win over the hearts, minds and palates of her tutors.

Through the encouragement of her tutors, Mom sent her résumé off to a select group of pâtisseries and fine dining establishments in the US. She received a few offers and rejections. One NYC high-end pâtisserie, who boasted several prestigious 5* hotels and restaurants on their client list, spoke with Mom's tutors and offered her a job, if her grades kept up.

As the rays from the winter's late morning sun danced through the shutters of her Parisian attic bedroom, Mom opened the envelope that would direct her future. She often tells me she wore a smile for the next week as she reflected on her final Mon Amoureux Secret grade. Distinction. She skipped to the nearest payphone in Montmartre, made a quick call across the Atlantic to tell her new employers to get her visa ready and then broke the news to her proud, yet reluctant parents.

Mom returned to Belfast for Christmas before she flew to New York to begin a new year and a new American chapter of her life. One thing I'm glad she didn't leave in Belfast was her love for breads and cream buns. Mom makes the best soda bread, pancakes and chocolate éclairs I have ever tasted!

Her scuffed leather suitcase had barely disturbed the dust on the floor of her extremely modest NYC shared apartment before she was whisked to a small, beautifully-decorated uptown pastry emporium. Chatty and lively, Mom soon proved to Gloria, the owner, that she had the skills to pay the bills. It didn't take her long to introduce new bakes and amazing cakes to the pâtisserie's already impressive list of temptations.

But it wasn't only Gloria who was impressed with Esther's golden locks and mouthwatering creations. A rather loud and lively Columbia graduate showed a particular appetite for sweet treats and this cute Irish girl. After a few weeks of commenting about her coffee éclairs, Donato (yes my Father is called 'The Don') plucked up the courage and asked Esther on a date.

The safe bet of the dating world since the 1950s - dinner and a movie - wasn't for Dad. He went all out to impress Mom with surprise dates up and down the city. What a guy! He thought of no better way to introduce her to NYC than to take her skating in Central Park, people-watching in Times Square and to some of the best nightclubs in Manhattan for weekend cocktails. And once they started going steady, they spent their time together exploring the epic museums, endless restaurants and famous comedy clubs of the city as they set free the ghosts of relationships past and dreamt about what the future might look like.

Their blossoming romance was as natural as the morning sunrise and gridlock in NYC. In between earning his own cases and working nights in his great uncle Giuseppe Piccolo's pizza parlour, Don saved enough money to visit *that* store on 5th Ave and splash out on a ring that is still as sparkly as the day he got down on one knee at the top of The Empire State and surprised her with it.

After their wedding my parents made their home in the Village, where they enjoyed 4-and-a-bit years of child-free newly wedded bliss. During that time Mom set up and established her own pâtisserie a few blocks from the apartment and Dad grew in stature and reputation in his law firm. Aside from working hard, they enjoyed leisurely weekends exploring New England and date nights taking in jazz clubs, legendary gigs and Broadway shows before this bundle of 7lb 9oz joy bounced into their world and changed everything.

The beautiful thing about love is that it can strike the heart with more power than a hurricane, yet feel as soft as a summer's breeze.

ORANGIONATION

The city is a lot brighter. The excitement is building. School tests are rolling in, and between basketball practice, music lessons and school projects my schedule is piled as high as The Chrysler Building, but it all points in one direction - the wonderful holiday season is upon us.

In our house, Jesus and Mother Mary are celebrated and cherished throughout the year, but at this time our expressions of reverence are propelled into overdrive, thanks to that one special night in Bethlehem and the imminent arrival of Santa's sleigh. Excessive carol singing, way too much food, an abundance of festive decorations, sentimental old movies and ridiculous amounts of Christmas cheer and hearty ho-ho-hos mean that December is a month filled with exciting surprises and life-affirming rituals. I can't resist those once-a-year aromas, heartwarming sounds and colourful lights, plus a few hazelnut cinnamon frankincense flavoured lattes thrown in for good measure. I hope you can understand why the Sontoro family goes all out for Christmas! The Sontoros heart Christmas. Like we love everything from the religious traditions to the glittering store windows on Fifth Avenue to the Macy's Thanksgiving Day parade which kicks off the season - every magical element, especially the build-up to it.

Today, December 3rd, is the day when the lights are turned on at The Rockefeller Centre. Mom gets totally stoked as she joins with the rest of the city to mark the start of the festive season. From now until the big day she will re-read the Bible entries about the journey to Bethlehem, culminating on the famous night when there was no room in the inn. She says it helps her regain her focus for Christmas and the year ahead. But just in case you thought she was a religious nut, it's also the time when Mom adds generously to her extensive collection of Christmas DVDs, ornaments, lights, sweaters, decorations, wreaths, gingerbread recipes and holiday themed cookie cutters.

By carefully selecting a playlist brimming over with festive spirit for Le Petit Papillon, her pâtisserie, Mom believes she can create a little winter wonderland for her customers and staff. Every year she goes all out with traditional seasonal and sweet goodies from around the world. That cinnamon aroma is the real deal. And let's not forget her window display! This year the stores in the Village have created works of art that would make Santa's elves green with envy and even make The Grinch crack a smile.

So this morning, I was briefed army-style:

'Get straight home from school and layer up. Your dad and I are leaving work early to give us enough time to bump our way to the front of the crowd at 30 Rock. After that it's Bean Station for a hot chocolate and window shopping before we walk home. Yes I said walk home.' Mom had created a plan to welcome in the holidays and was hoping to exercise it with military precision.

Family nights like this are precious. As an only child such times always come with a bit of pressure. I feel it is my responsibility to always be 'on' for these nights. My parents love me a lot, and after being a grouchy Baa Christmas Humbug when I was 12, I realised how much being happy and upbeat for evenings like this means to my parents. So I don't linger on my way home, I wrap up like a snowman and cheer extra loud when the lights are switched on and begin to blind me. Now I actually enjoy this family occasion. Having little traditions like this is pretty cool, and makes families, well, families.

In some semi-unrelated news I casually bumped into Jay-Z and his entourage when I was walking home from school last week. Instantly star struck I hustled my tablet from my satchel, handed him a Sharpie and now I have his signature on the back of my iPad! I see celebs quite regularly in NYC, but Jay-Z, that's off the scale. All of these things, minus the tests and homework, are super exciting, but one other thing trumps them all. I GOT A JOB! Well actually I GOT TWO JOBS! Tyler Sontoro has entered the world of paid employment! Ireland in the summer is onnnnnn like Donkey Konnnnnng!

A few weeks back I made you aware of the job prospects for a teenager in NYC. A couple of interesting developments occurred after my initial research. I wrote to a toyshop. They wrote back two days later. Two days. I know. Very fast!

Dear Tyler,

Thank you for your application for the position of Action Figure Consultant. We were overwhelmed by the interest in this position. We don't normally write letters of rejection but I was just so impressed by your limerick that I thought I should write to you.

Thanks for the holla,
We hope you earn enough dolla
To pack up your suitcase, because
Ireland's such a beautiful place.

Unfortunately we are unable to offer you a position in our store but we will keep your details on record for any future openings.

Many thanks,
Charles Huston
Deputy Manager

But don't shed any tears of disappointment for me. When every door closes another opens - right? Well yes and no. About 14 other doors closed, namely the Turkish kebab shop, local pharmacy, hardware store and leaflet distributor, to name a few. Three doors are possibly still open - or in other words I haven't heard anything back from them. But most importantly, two doors opened and I walked straight through both of them into the wonderful land of employment ... until I realised there's only so many hours in the week and with school, B-ball and my social life I had to choose one of them.

Job No. 1.

The first job was a temporary holiday gig in a well-known clothes store (that old people think is too dark.) I had hoped to blow my pay cheque on loads of new threads (I know this goes back on my other statement about saving money, but technically I would have been saving money, as the clothes would have been cheaper!) Yeah right. They said it might be made permanent part-time when the holiday season finished, but I couldn't take the risk, so I passed on Rodriguez's name and they gave him the opening. I had argued with Mom and Dad about keeping the two jobs, but they were pretty adamant that I didn't need both, and they were right. I was being greedy! Deep down I knew it was the correct decision. Rodriguez could do with the money after his dad got ill and lost his job. Suddenly there was a big question mark over him going to college.

Job No. 2.

The second job is the one I'm excited about. A permanent part-time Saturday gig that will take me right through to June, when I board the plane and fly to Ireland. It's kind of a random job. I will be spending Saturdays earning my dollar in a hipster fruit and veg/healthy living store.

I like to think I was headhunted for this position. Last week a smiley dude called by our apartment. When I answered the door his first words were, 'Are you the kid with the limerick thing?' From the funky logo on his black T-shirt I quickly realised he was from Fresh & Juicy. He introduced himself as James Marcus, founder and proprietor, and explained he was on a delivery on my block and wanted to find out if I was all I said I was in my slightly bigged-up résumé.

Mom invited him in, and over a cup of coffee he realised I knew my broccoli from my banana and offered me the evolving position of juiceologist at Fresh & Juicy. The conversation was simple and to the point. He wanted me to start right away and even gave me a few extra shifts after school in the lead up to Christmas. We lingered in small talk and discovered one another's plans for the holidays, and importantly Mom and James made the connection that they were both local business owners obsessed with good food.

'Right Tyler I mustachio.'

'Huh?'

'I gotta bounce.'

'OK. Sure. Thanks so much for dropping in. I can't wait to meet the whole crew.'

I walked James to the front door of our building. He'd started down the steps when he turned,

'Tyler.'

'Yeah James.'

'I have big plans for growth over the next 6 months, big

plans. We are gonna go places. Looking forward to having you as a valued member of family Fruicy.'

'LOL. Fruicy. You have some dope words man. I'm really excited to be part of the team. It sounds like an amazing job!'

We both smiled, high-fived and said our goodbyes. Just before I closed the door James called after me and threw an apple in my direction.

'Get used to seeing a lot more of these Tyler.'

'Awesome man! I love oranges!'

We laughed.

'See you Thursday for orangionation!' he said. James unlocked his bike from the front of our block and I hurried inside and Skyped Patrick to tell him the good news. He did a little dance in his room! Then we chatted for a while about how college was going for him - really I was trying to pick up on any clues that something might be up. Any time I talked to him over the past few weeks he seemed his usual upbeat jokey self, but I got the feeling he was trying not to give anything away. You know when someone deflects any questions you ask them about their personal stuff? I still sensed that there was more to the trip than Mom let on.

PETER J. S. WAUGH

SNOWY NEW YORK CITY

It decorates the balconies of the skyscrapers that keep guard over the streets of my city. It hypnotises office workers, providing a welcome distraction from their screens and makes a coat over the top of Washington Square Arch. It dodges Building Control and Customs, brings mayhem and disruption for some, and smiles and excitement to others. From Queens to Brooklyn, Staten Island to the Bronx, this week the first snow of the season fell on the city. The concrete jungle is now covered in a white blanket of cold fluff.

During a snowy lunchtime I walked past a group of kindergarten kids who were mesmerised by the drifting snowflakes. I watched them spend part of recess spinning in circles, with their mouths open and their tongues sticking up in the air, hoping to catch some snowflakes. When the bell sounded, these mini snow people plodded back to their classrooms and began counting the minutes until school was over and they could run outside and make snow angels. Many, many snow angels, all sporting perfectly formed wings and finger drawn halos.

Through the Twittersphere a snowball fight was arranged at Central Park. When my crew arrived, little snow statues and sculptures had sprung up all over, like a pop-up exhibit from The MOMSA - The Museum of Modern Snow Art. The snowball fight was an epic battle. We marked out a zone, picked teams, laid out a few ground rules, and went into snow-ball fight overdrive. Alex brought his A-game and was crowned king of the white stuff. Afterwards we played a game of capture the flag, made a gigantic snowman, and when the lack of light brought our games to an end we warmed up in a diner on the Upper Westside that makes some of the best *pasta fazool* in the city.

A few of us from my math class had gathered with the dual purpose of winning the snowball fight and tackling a looming class project. The fact that we had all failed to bring our books showed that we only cared about the snow and stuffing our faces! As we ate we made some notes, agreed on a time for a Skype conference later that night, then forgot all about the school project as we ordered dessert. Riding the sub home I wrote a little poem as a tip of the hat to the city. It's pretty terrible but hey!

PETER J. S. WAUGH

Central Park
Covered precisely with
Carefully placed
Cold precipitation as
City people
Curiously ponder
Creating paw prints in the
Park's canvas

Quick. Listen to what comes from Queens. The snow quietly
Usurps
Everyone
Even
New York's
Sassiest people

The snow has power
Holds your eyes, changes your wardrobe
Everyone go get your snow game on

Believe
Receive
Only love
NYC forever y'all. Peace out.
X

I heart NYC in the snow.

MAMMA MIA, IT'S CHRISTMAS

Christmas was amazeballs. Let me bring some substance to the use of such a ridiculously awesome word.

Christmas Eve. 2pm.

The lights were bright.

The cash registers were ringing.

All my favourite Salvation Army peeps were bell ring a ding dinging.

When I walked out from my final shift at work, the city was on Christmas overdrive. I made a last minute dash around the Village to buy a few gifts for my folks. Later that evening the wider family met at Pusco's where we had an awesome feast to wish everyone a *Buon Natale!* We do Christmas Italian-style which means, for us, it's all about *la famiglia, l'amore e il cibo.* Normally we meet in Uncle Antonio's where everyone who is even semi-related to us comes to eat and hang out. But this year we decided to have our Christmas Eve meal in Pusco's and saved Uncle Antonio's for Christmas Day.

We still kept on a few of our fave customs. All the kids were stoked - so excited and hyper of course. Especially me, the biggest kid of them all, even if I am turning 18 very soon. We all wrote letters which we placed under our parents' plates for the mammas and papas to read after dinner. That could be a while - the meal was a banquet of over 10 fish dishes. The Italians make a big deal of Christmas Eve, but keep the meat for our Christmas Day feast.

Afterwards we all went to Midnight Mass (which was at 10pm!). Then home time, where we ate Mom's amazing homemade chocolate chip Panettone (a secret Sontoro family recipe) and Christmas cookies from every part of Italy, and posted some Christmas selfies online - complete with ridiculous hashtags. That meant that it was only after my parents went to bed that I had my traditional, even later, late night, last-minute gift-wrapping session. I must remember to buy my gifts pre-wrapped next year.

Christmas morning is always a blur of excitement. Even though it's only the three of us, we have the festive music blasting from 6am. Dad had prepared a carefully chosen playlist for us as we gathered round the twinkling tree to swap gifts and then rustle through every drawer in the place in search of batteries to power some novelty gift. This year it was air drum drumsticks! In my Christmas Eve rush to buy Mom and Dad some presents I ended up getting Mom a mishmash of gifts - a potato peeler, socks, a USB mug warmer in the shape of Manhattan, a remote controlled candle set and I saved a Christmas present disaster with a voucher for a local spa. I got Dad a new game for the X-Box, a 2ft Statue of Liberty figure filled with candy and a voucher for his favourite restaurant. Dad made our Christmas breakfast - this year it was waffles and pancakes - basically loads of bread and sugar! Sometimes he tries to make an Ulster Fry (popular in Northern Ireland) but no one can make it like Mom.

After Mom unwrapped her random assortment of gifts, we Skyped our Northern Irish family.

'MERRY CHRISTMAAAAASS!' we shouted.

'HAAAAAAAAPY CHRISTMAAAAASS TO YOUUU!' they sang back.

'It's snowing over here!' Patrick was pretty excited about this.

'Aye. It's a bit unusual for Belfast to have a white Christmas,' Uncle Richard piped up. 'Look!' He carried the laptop over to the window and we saw the flakes falling and snow-topped hills behind houses.

'Wow!' Dad and me said together.

'Have you eaten yet?' Mom asked.

'The bird just has an hour left,' Granny said. 'So we still have to see what it tastes like.'

'I'm sure it will be delish,' remarked Dad.

Granny chuckled. 'You weren't the one picking up a greasy 20 pound turkey from the kitchen floor at 7 this morning!'

'What?!' Mom spluttered.

'We had a bit of a fowl incident this morning.' Aunt Beth

paused. 'A combination of too much grease, a shallow tin and Richard's lifting skills meant the turkey tried to make a dash for freedom.'

The Sontoros gave out a collective laugh. Granny rolled her eyes as only grandparents are allowed to do.

'It's extra seasoning,' said Uncle Richard.

Everyone laughed some more.

'Esther, is that what I think it is?' Aunt Beth asked Mom.

'It is! My boys were good to me!' Mom flashed her new bracelet in front of the camera.

'Hey Patrick, what did you get for Christmas?' I spoke up.

'I did OK. Some money and clothes and a new smart-phone.' He didn't seem too excited about his gifts.

'Finally came into the 21st century?' I asked. Until then Patrick had used what could only be described as a 'dumb-phone'. I was excited that I could now text him on a few free apps instead of only our Skype calls.

'I might join you on Twitter now. See what all the fuss is about.'

'Awesome.'

'We better let you guys go and make sure the turkey hasn't escaped while you were busy talking to us. Careful lifting it out of the oven!' Dad warned.

'Great talking to you,' Granny said.

'I'll call you later Beth. Say hi to David for me.' David, Mom's brother, was coming round for lunch with his family.

'Will do. Enjoy your feast!'

We 'donned our gay apparel' and walked through the snow to Uncle Antonio's crib in Little Italy - not too far away - where we hung out all day. The Italian side of my family knows how to do Christmas bigtime! *Il Pranzo* is always a wonderful, mouthwatering event. The table was set with fine china and silverware for eighteen people, plus a table runner the length of Appian Way. Weeks and days of preparation came to a delicious end as Papa blessed the food and we tucked into our antipasto of dried meats, olives, breads and cheese. The courses last for hours as we chat and laugh and the adults drink a lot of red wine!

After our pasta course, *Pasticcio al forno* (think the ultimate mac 'n' cheese), we move onto the meat course. Papa usually carves the beef and chicken. By the time we tuck into Granny's *Amore di Natale*, we are stuffed like cannelloni, but you can't resist the cakes and sweet treats she has made. I see Granny Caterina a few times every week. She lives a few blocks away from us and is the sweetest old lady you could ever meet. She tries to fatten me up and always asks if I have a girlfriend. She usually grabs my cheeks and says, 'How could someone not fall in love with this beautiful boy. You are too thin. Eat some of my cannolo.'

Post feast we played a few board games and then the night finished with a karaoke battle. It was such an incredible day. I love Christmas with my Italian family. From the fantastic traditions to hanging out with my cousins, and let's not forget about the food! We left Uncle Antonio's a little earlier than usual (it was still late, around 12.30, not the normal 2 or 3 in the morning!), because the next morning we were going on a vacation trip. Mom and Dad had managed to get a few extra days off.

Bright and early, we drove out of the city convoy-style with a few families to New Hampshire, where we skied and partied until the 31st when we made a mad dash back to see the Ball Drop and ring in the New Year with tens of thousands of other New Yorkers in Times Square.

On our way back Mom used words like refreshing, rustic and exhilarating to describe the trip. But I had only one word - awesome! The powder was fresh, the halfpipe pumping and one of the chalet girls was B-E-A-utiful (not that I did anything about it. She was a few years older than me and I thought there was no way she would fall for a doosh like me - even though Dad kept telling me she was '100% into me'. It's #totesawkward when your dad points these things out for you.)

And that was it! A whole 'nother year to wait for Christmas again. And here I am, back in my room, organising my backpack, searching for my sports gear and planning to get an early night due to my return to school for the final five months ... ever! But, I just can't help but be distracted by the new Brazilian Rosewood handcrafted guitar that's in the corner of my room. I replaced my beat up Yam with this joint Christmas/18th birthday present and it has helped me write a few songs over the holidays.

I love being a muso. My passion for music comes from my dad and my Granda, Mom's father. Granda was a renowned musician in Northern Ireland. He played with his combo, The Forevers, throughout the showband era - a time when over 500 bands travelled up and down the country to entertain towns and villages at nightly dances, often in very remote rural areas where the bands were the only thing happening for anyone under 30 for miles around. Many couples would never have met and got together without Granda's band – including my grandparents!

Granda and his band played in all the top venues - from The Boom Boom Rooms in Belfast, The Floral Hall in Newtownabbey to The Strand and The Arcadia up north. They came up with their own version of soulful rock 'n' roll, which sometimes slipped into pop-inspired songs with a country twist. For special shows and TV performances they brought in the unmistakable sound of a big brass band. The Forevers always stunned the crowd when they changed into colourful suits during the intermission and did their polished dance moves in perfect syncopation. In Belfast, there's a word for people like Granda – legend.

Granda loved playing in his band, until one tragic night when The Miami Showband Massacre changed the meaning of music. As gunmen were smuggling a timebomb onto the unsuspecting Miami Showband's minivan, it went off early, killing three and wounding two of Granda's closest friends. Suddenly 'the music died'. Touring and enjoying the freedom of the open road was no longer safe in '70s Northern Ireland. The Forevers, like so many other showbands, were over.

For a few, the music played on, but Granda felt the weight of the massacre in a different way. He began to support his friends through the worst of The Troubles and focused on raising his family. He hung up his electric guitar and poured all his energy into building a career in accountancy. He still enjoyed listening to music with Granny on lazy weekend afternoons and going to live events after normal nightlife began to return to Northern Ireland; after all they owed their relationship to The Forevers. Granny had caught Granda's eye one night from the stage and he chased through the crowd during the interval to get her number. The rest, as they say, is history.

Granda passed on his love of music to the next generations. Every time we chatted he was asking about music and telling me stories about the bands he loved to listen to as a kid. My mom gets her love of music from him too; she always has music playing and is an accomplished violinist.

I guess you could call me the epitome of my click and buy generation, because, by December 26th I had already spent $125 of music vouchers on fresh new sounds. I have been listening to the man that is John Mayer, The Boss and a fresh new band called Matrimony, simply wishing I had written some of their amazing lyrics.

And thanks to my beasty new wireless headphones from my Irish relatives, I passed the time on the long car journey to New Hampshire and back, listening to the evocative sounds of Foy Vance, Bethel's driving melodies and the unmistakable beats of David Guetta. Inspired by the powder and the wide-open spaces of the White Mountains, I wrote a few songs there. My style landed somewhere in between teenage-angst-driven indie, power pop and the lyrical madness of Kanye. If you want to know what that sounds like, you can buy my EP when it comes out! I don't claim to be a great songwriter, but you gotta start somewhere.

I mixed my time on vacation by playing in the snow, racing down the slopes, breathing in the fresh, bracing air and just sitting in the stillness of the mountains. I had space and time to think about the exciting possibilities of the future and reflect on what has been a pretty pleasant nearly 18 years. Writing an album wasn't my goal, but creating the space to write down notes of self-reflection was a welcome opportunity the ski break provided.

So for the few days of my trip, I took a journey into the unknown. I embraced silence. Listening to the sounds, voices, words and whispers, wind and birdsong, snow crunching underfoot or falling off a branch, that emerged from a time of silence was freaking scary. I inhabit a world of noise - news coverage, advertising, radio, music, everyone else's opinions and cellphone chatter, plus the constant background noise of the city. All these things drown out the place of tranquility in my life. Silence is something I'm not used to. There's always car horns, garbage trucks, people, sirens, shouts, breaking glass. In NYC silence only happens as you sleep, and even then, your dreams speak.

Such rare times of silence and reflection have helped me to think about the massive changes that I am about to go through. Graduating high school, my first trip without my parents, moving to college. The words I'm writing and thinking are helping me to process so many impending transitions. Maybe too I will meet a girl and find out what love is all about.

Sitting on the balcony of my chalet, just, you know, looking, listening to the breeze, allowing my pen to move without effort was weird. Words rose, some fell, some landed on a page. Writing songs has helped me to notice things. Take in the world around me and offer my opinion to all who will hopefully listen.

Now that I'm back in the city, I have been spending all of my time singing sweet lullabies to myself in my bedroom. I have found myself noting words and phrases on every scrap of paper I can find. I'm writing down all of the things that evoke my senses and cause passion to rise in my heart. It happens as I ride the subway and listen to the people of my city. The heat and shades of colour, the intricate tributaries that love pours into and spills out of, the noise and rhythm of the tribes that inhabit every space of my wild and beautiful city.

All of these things are contributing to my first No.1 record. I hear they put plaques on walls for that sort of thing. I can see it now - 'Tyler Sontoro penned *Incredible* while studying for his high school diploma. A man of true genius.' But for now, I leave you with these words. Please be kind.

Incredible

My heart boasts of your love
It sees your face
It loves your beauty.

My heart pounds.
Can you feel it?
We will discover

HALF IRISH

The incredible sounds of my heart.
Together

Into the night
Into the night I run
Hold me
Come into my heart
It's incredible

Into the night
Into the night I run
Hold me
Come into my heart
It's incredible

I wanted to have two hearts
For the day that you break mine.
But if I had two hearts I wouldn't know what one to give away
Give away, give away

Don't break my heart
Don't break my heart
Don't break my heart

Come on heart, look at the world
De-fib don't tell me lies
Bounce my heart back into the wild.
For some time now it's been deader than dead

So bounce back to life
Life revive me
Life lift me
Heart of hope don't dare leave me.

Into the night
Into the night I run
Hold me
Come into my heart
It's incredible

Into the night
Into the night I run
Hold me
Come into my heart
It's incredible

Life revive me
Life lift me
Heart of hope don't dare leave me.
Life revive me
Life lift me
Heart of hope don't leave me.

Into the night
Into the night I run
Hold me
Come into my heart

FRESH & JUICY

During my informal job interview, James Marcus found out that Mom owns a pâtisserie, the antithesis of the philosophy of Fresh & Juicy. I thought he would slap me with an out of date banana and banish my job prospects to the compost pile. Instead, his pout gave way to a wry smile. With the security that no one else could hear him, James said, 'Everyone, even me, needs a sweet treat now and again, my friend!'

Smiling is part of the uniform in the store. I have been working at F&J for a month now and really get off on it. I get to align onions and arrange limes in lines (which helps my slight OCD tendencies). Placing pineapples and arranging apples ain't that sexy, so, to understand why I enjoy work so much, you have to get the vibeosophy (vibe & philosophy – it took me a while to get used to that word!) of our store.

We blend sustainable living and delicious fresh produce

together, as well as awesome smoothies. Our produce is eco-friendly and comes from NYC rooftop plots, community gardens and organically cultivated, ethically-driven farms upstate, plus some great organic growers for all the stuff our state can't provide. We work closely with the farmers and other suppliers to make sure our produce is as fresh and good for local communities as possible.

We do seasons, we do flavour, and we think peculiar looking is the pick of the crop. Some of our peppers look like footballs and our cucumbers could be used in a game of ultimate boomerang, but, in my opinion, our organically grown produce tastes ten times better than the genetically pumped stuff you find in the big impersonal supermarkets.

But our vibeosophy extends beyond zucchini and beets. All possible waste is composted and used to fertilise the farms and urban gardens. Any produce that is close to going out of date is either blitzed into superfood smoothies or donated to the local shelter. A few Village residents have even had work experience in the store, gardens and allotments. James continually reinforces that we aren't just selling fruit and vegetables; we are providing our clients with the pathway to a tastier, healthier and more fulfilling lifestyle. So we want them to buy into our vibeosophy and like to help them live better lives.

Alongside the traditional function of selling fruit and vegetables to NYC residents and restaurants, we sell the best smoothies in the Village. Yes, they are officially 'The Best', confirmed during the second week of January, or De-toxuary as James Marcus calls it. We nutri-blitzed the opposition in the

17th Annual Village Smoothie Olympics with our fantastic super healthy veggie smoothie of kale, Manuka honey, oats, spinach, walnuts, carrot and - wait, I can't tell you all of our secrets! Our smoothies are something out of the ordinary. Blastberry, TriBeCa Tipple, Village Five-fruit Fave are some of the more popular ones. James is so proud of them.

So you can see why I love going to work. Not only do I earn green stuff for my trip, but being part of the Fruicy crew is a blast. I get to exercise when doing my deliveries, have made new friends and I also help people to understand the benefits of a good and balanced diet. People including yours truly. I have earned 260 dollars in a month. That beats flipping greasy burgers and wearing a cheesy uniform complete with hair net any day of the week. Nice work St. Joe!

MY TRIPPLE DIPPLE A+ GAME

After a few weeks of the new school term and several solid shifts at Fresh & Juicy, tiredness hit me like an avalanche of fresh powder crashing down the side of Mount Washington. I have crawled through to this, the last week of January, burnt out from frantically juggling homework, sports stuff, partying with friends, working in Fresh & Juicy, practicing on my guitar every spare minute and, of course, writing and singing when I have any energy left. But I have a plan to put the jump and jive back into my life for February. A conspiracy to unleash joy on the city is creeping out from my sticker-clad guitar case.

There was one welcome piece of relief during January - my 18th birthday! Yes, mid-January brought one of those marking moments of my life, symbolised by lots and lotsa cake. My family in Northern Ireland sang to me over Skype and my parents threw me a surprise party, filling our place with my friends and my American family. It was pretty cool to be the centre of attention.

18 is officially an adult, in Ireland anyway. But in the US, you're still kinda ¾ grownup, meaning you can now do everything - join the army, get married, drive, be a dad, vote, have a job and buy your own place - except have a beer!

So Mom made a big deal of my birthday. Probably too she wanted to make the day special because I'd already gotten most of my gifts at Christmas time. But Patrick had kept his gift until my birthday and surprised me with tickets for a gig when I would be over in Ireland. The gig was on Friday 13th June so I was going to leave for Ireland on the 12th.

I have always laughed when normal people said they were focusing on their music career. That phrase made me think of 45-year-old men who hadn't lost hope of one day making it in the music industry. Working low-end jobs in between touring crummy bars, they were slaves to their endless dream. But now, I get it. Over the last few weeks I have turned into one of those guys, only a few decades younger, as I put the finishing touches to my mountain-inspired melodies.

During a daydream in chemistry class I made a note of all the cafés I knew of in the Village who would be into my music. Then, in between work, assignments and basketball practice, I sang to some café managers, most of whom invited me back to play in their coffee houses. I booked in four gigs for late February and early March. My payment was the tips I earned and as much soda or coffee as I could drink! And my parents were happy because it was safer and warmer than Plan B - busking in the subway. But I gotta tell you what happened in The Bike Factory.

Wandering and playing my way around the Village, and one gig in TriBeCa, I marvelled again at these great neighbourhoods with their exposed iron fire escapes, weathered brickwork still bearing faded traces of old fashioned painted-on advertising, decal-clad shop windows, fresh graffiti and abundance of eateries with funky light fixtures. If Times Square is a glimpse into the non-stop inner workings of a frenzied mind, and Central Park the green lung that helps people filter and breathe, then the Village is the soul of the city, a place set aside so you can begin to make sense of life.

After a genuine 'non merci' from a French café (it has put me off going to Paris), I plucked up the courage to hit The Bike Factory, long ago an actual cycle workshop, but now a place that holds mythical status in the Village coffee shop scene. I was a bit hesitant about entering, but I knew if I turned my back at that stage of the journey it would say a lot about my vision for my future. I stood on the sidewalk and sipped a lukewarm latte. Taking in the street I made some mental notes about my quest:

1. I need the bathroom.

2. I can't believe that I already have a few bookings! Score!

3. I need to hire someone to do the artwork for my EP *Songs From The Mountain.*

4. I feel like Frodo approaching Mount Doom.

5. I wonder what's for dinner.

6. I love my city.

7. I REALLY LOVE my city.

I turned and looked through a window of a BBQ joint, caught my reflection and ran my fingers through my hair. I was wasting time, so I procrastinated even more with a nervous tweet: 'My gig quest has proved successful - 4 bookings so far! #awesome #gigging #nyc #thevillage', fixed my scarf and then just stared at the café for a few minutes. I scanned the street. Two friends embraced and one of them began to peel clear Saran wrap from his arm, showing off some fresh ink on his half sleeve. A businessman slammed his briefcase on the top of a trashcan, yelled and then tried to jam his briefcase into said trashcan. Four nannies strolled past, pushing baby buggies. A delivery van pulled up in front of me and blocked my view of the café.

More minutes passed. I was still staring at the café like a creep from a horror movie, when an obese guy strolled by its entrance. At the same time its door opened and the sound of 90's Brit-pop emerged from the sound system, warming the cold streets of the city.

I imagined the pep talk Will-I-Am would give me, 'Man go and bring it to that place. Bring your triple dipple A plus game. Bring your attitude, your magnitude, your soundatude and you will leave with a record deal, never mind a few gigs.' I tweeted him. '@iamwill Wish me luck - trying to get a few gigs in #NYC to earn money for my summer vacation to #Ireland - heading to @thebikefactory now'

To understand the reason for my nerves, you need to know that The Bike Factory is a coffee shop famed for hosting secret performances from genuinely mega-talented world-renowned musicians. It has tens of thousands of followers on Twitter who don't need any excuse to take an extended lunch break or hang out in the venue before they head back to their loft apartments. The café is also a leading voice for the emerging talent that lives in the city. It's every young songwriter's dream to play here, with the hope that they will get spotted by the coolest music industry game changers.

Ok, here goes nothing.

Audrina (Black/35ish/Half Shaved Head/Stylish/Tattoos) greeted me when I walked in. Her smile was wider than the Hudson and her teeth were whiter than my mom's Crème Chantilly. With my guitar in tow, I knew she could tell what I was after, but she patiently listened to my spiel. After my garbled introduction, Audrina said, 'See that guitar?' She pointed to a beat-up red vintage acoustic guitar in the corner of the room.

'Yeah,' I replied.

'Make my Tuesday a tuneful one pretty boy.'

'OK.'

Wow. Panic. An instant audition. I threw my duffle coat onto a scuffed leather couch (the couch had denim stitched into the arms - so cool) and walked over to the guitar. The pick up was broken. There were hints of a once-vibrant red stain around the edges of the guitar. It was now a faded Saharan sunrise. I took a minute to compose myself. I was really nervous. I wondered what famous musicians had played riffs on this old, yet beautiful instrument. I glanced over at Audrina as I tuned the guitar up. She smiled. It put me at ease.

'Yeah it's probably older than you are,' she said.

I played a little upbeat country tune I had penned, then broke into a remix of Matrimony's *Obey Your Guns* to show my range before finishing with a tribute to my city, thanks to Alicia Keys and my new friend Jay Z! Audrina was up and grooving as I rounded off my mini set. I think that meant it went well.

'Sign him up,' a guy shouted across the café. A group of hipsters, who were sitting near Audrina, gave me a round of applause. It felt weird!

'Hey Tyler,' Audrina's voice was like velvet. I had an instant crush on her. I think she could tell. But it's probably an every-day experience for her.

'Yeah,' I replied.

'You free next Thursday night?' In that split second I thought she was going to ask me on a date and forgot all about the purpose of being in the café, and the age difference.

'Uhhhh yeah!'

'OK - you're in. Be here at 7. Show starts at 8. You got 20 minutes.' She gave me a playful wink

I began to blush and thanked her a million times over.

'Thanks so much Audrina. I won't disappoint.'

'You better not. You're my wild card.'

I couldn't hide my delight and gave her a hug before I gath-ered my coat and case. Audrina made some small talk which I was too ecstatic to even hear, but I made sure to listen carefully as she filled me in on the details of the gig. As the café filled up with after-work regulars, she walked me towards the door.

'See you then Tyler. Just come and enjoy yourself. You'll

be great.'

'I can't wait. Adios Audrina.'

A few people stared at me as I walked out the door. It was unusual to be beaming ear to ear like an idiot on a chilly winter weekday. When I was a block away from the café I stopped and did a little dance to express my excitement. That night it was my smile that was wider than the Hudson, all thanks to the wonderful Audrina.

THE BIKE FACTORY

The next week went by in a blur. I practiced my junk off any spare minute I could grab. My set was only twenty minutes, so I wanted it to be super tight. There was no room for error. The audience was literally going to judge me, and their judgment would go a long way towards my trip to Ireland. As Audrina had explained, I was going to be paid $50 for just turning up, which was cool in itself, but after the $50 it got interesting. The café run a dollar tip section where during gig night the customers tip the musicians, as well as the café staff. Then the customers text in their fave, and the tips, usually a couple of hundred dollars, are a prize for the winner. Power to the people and all that.

After restructuring my set list a few times and with my falsetto polished, my rapping 'spot on' as Mum would say and my swagger A-1, I headed out for my Thursday night gig in The

Bike Factory. It may sound pretty old-school to gig in a coffee shop, but it works. As I walked through the wooden doors of The Bike Factory, with their logo of a bicycle leaning against a lamp post created in colourful stained glass above the doors, I was wired with excitement.

After all, I had messed about on the guitar for a few years, but it was only over the last six months that I had started to write my own music and take it seriously. Now I was playing a gig! Not just any gig, but at a venue that was a HUGE DEAL for even the professionals to play at. A few friends from school knew I was playing. Over lunch they joked with me that *American Idol* was too low key for me. Rodriguez came to my house after school for dinner and walked with me to the gig, giving me a pep talk all the way.

The set-up inside The Bike Factory was a little different from a normal day. Tables had been cleared away to make a stage area, while the couches were pushed back to make way for some scruffy tall bar tables. A solitary brown leather Chesterfield sofa was reserved for the judging panel, while a coffee table made out of a few pallets sat in front of the couch. On the panel were a couple of prominent stars from NYC's music scene and two other people that I had to Google when I went to the men's room. I tuned up, taped my set list to the floor, grabbed a drink and chatted with some friends who had turned up.

Set List

Van Morrison - Brown Eyed Girl
Two Door Cinema Club - This Is The Life

HALF IRISH

Matrimony - Obey Your Guns
Tyler Sontoro - Incredible
Bruce Springsteen - Born To Run
Snow Patrol - New York
The Undertones - Teenage Kicks

My set was at 8.25, so at 8.15 I went to the makeshift 'Green Room' to compose myself. I had chosen a Northern Irish inspired, New York sprinkled list of songs. I knew I wasn't the best singer, so my song choice had to stand out. Patrick and I regularly swap tunes from the hottest new artists on either side of the Atlantic. I love that we have a common interest in music, passed down to us from our Granda. And it's nice to download a few bands that haven't made it over to the US yet, or aren't quite so well known over here. Makes me feel a little bit ahead of the game.

A few minutes later I heard my name announced and I emerged with a confident wave and smile to the crowd even though my legs felt like Jello. I think the judges could tell I was nervous, so I took a few seconds to compose myself and allowed the smiles of the crowd to soothe my terrified pounding heart. But in a flash, Granda came to mind and my nerves began to fade. I could imagine him in his element playing to audiences across Ireland. He always wore a huge smile when he told me about his adventures as a musician.

Despite more than enough bum notes on *Brown Eyed Girl*, it went down a storm. *This Is The Life* lifted the crowd, before *Obey Your Guns* rocked the life out of the place. Then I had a classic 'go big because you're going home anyway' moment.

Before I rolled out *Incredible* I gave the crowd an introductory rap:

Uh,
Yeah,
Let me see your hands New York.
Clap for me,
Slide for me,
Throw your eyes to the front and your problems to the back.
They say I'm a man boy but tonight I'm your joy.
It's my job to make you laugh,
It's not my job to make you cry,
All I'm doing is trying to live and love so don't be shy.
Fall into my beat and if you're on heat,
Here's my number - say wahhhhhh.
Some say I can't sing, but wait until they are blinded by the bling that
my songs bring,
Then the haters can give me a ring, or a call,
I sure hope pride don't come before a fall,
Cause right now I'm having a ball.

Send the haters to Marseille when they hear what I have to say.
They say Nice is nice this time of year,
With their boats and wine and fresh sea air.
But New York City you're the one for me,
Nice may be nice but NYC is a million times as nice - you're my vice.

The lights,

The sights,
The men in tights,
Stars are born everyday - from Harlem to this stage right now.
I may be 18 but 18 years from now you'll still remember tonight – the
night you tell your kids you met a star.
So clap for me,
Slide for me,
Sing for me,
New York City,
Uh,
Uh,
Uh.

With the rap word-perfect and the crowd in the palm of my hand it hit me. I felt amazing. I was on a high! Being on stage was the biggest blast of my life. Not just fun, but exhilarating. For the first time I was feeling what Granda used to feel, and it was epic.

I unleashed the opening notes of *Incredible*, fell into one of The Boss' big anthems, played the legendary *New York* by Snow Patrol and ended with *Teenage Kicks* - everyone in the place loved that song. I didn't play it perfectly, but my enthusiasm carried me over and above my ability!

A few friends had skipped band practice to see this mind-blowing experiment. Rodriguez and Alex smiled and bopped throughout my set, which flew by quicker than the express to Queens. Not that it was a perfect performance; there were those dodgy notes on *Brown Eyed Girl*, I got my timings wrong and had to skip a few verses in *Born To Run*, and I'm sure

I made up a line or two in *Teenage Kicks*. But it was all good. The crowd gave me a generous round of applause when I left the 'stage'.

After me there were three remaining acts, before Audrina called all five contenders back onstage. Together, we listened to flattering comments from the panel. A couple of big names were among the judges, so I listened up extra hard to what they had to say.

One of the judges, a guy in his late 30's wearing a leather jacket told me, 'Your song choices and arrangements were awesome. Keep working on your technique. Especially your finger picking.'

Another judge, a blonde in her 20's, who looked very familiar, (probably from MTV?) said, 'You are gonna be a star! You owned the stage tonight. But you need to focus on your breathing.'

When they were finished and everyone had put their hands together for the celeb panel, Audrina spoke: 'Tonight we have heard from some amazing emerging artists. So give it up one more time for our fantastic, brave contestants!'

With a sweep of her tattooed arm, she indicated all of us and the crowd erupted into cheers and applause. When the whoops died down, she announced, 'but there can only be one winner.'

Audrina created a dramatic pause. She stared at each of us on stage, then back at the audience, then back at our nervous faces before she gave the nod to a guy at the bar and the results of the text vote came up on screen.

'The winner is ... Shannon Cortez!'

I hadn't won. But I wasn't too shabby either. The incredible Shannon would have been a hard act for anyone to beat.

The judges had noticed my nerves and my off-key moments. But they had encouraged me too. A couple of them came up to me afterwards and told me not to give up, to keep playing, keep gigging and getting experience to work on my confidence. I was a mixture of emotions and just caught snippets of their comments. While I didn't go into a venue like The Bike Factory expecting to win, and Shannon had been a virtuoso, the news was hard to take and the money would have been a great help for my trip to Ireland. But hey!

Before I left, I texted Mom and Dad an update of my night, made one last trip to the john and said goodbye to my friends and thanks to Audrina. The tiled walls of the men's room were covered in graffiti, inspirational sayings, lyrics, toilet humour - and phone numbers. I added one of my lyrics from *Avalanche*, a song I had written on vacation, to the dryer on the wall, *'You'll never find another like yourself.'*

On the walk home I hummed/whispered some lyrics to a new song, *Always create, Always creating.* Before I rounded the corner into my block I had a moment under the stars. Lyrics from *Avalanche* struck me all over again:

Unique. Me. Myself.
Take the moment.
Seize the day
Make it a monument
Create it your way.

You'll never find another like yourself.

I walked on and pondered. Maybe it's because I have been engaging in way too much self-reflection by writing my own songs, or the reality of looming adulthood, leaving school and leaving home is edging closer, but over the last few months I have thought more about life, what it means, and how we express what we love. Despite not having 'loved a girl', I have found so many other shades of love and I have discovered that I have a lot of it to give.

During my time in the mountains I was visited by an uncontainable desire to explore, expand and use the gifts and talents that lie beneath my daily routine. I realised that I stand on the cusp of adulthood and this overflowing barrel of endless possibility lies before me. My interior, real self is hidden amongst the fancy structures I build around my life. And I am becoming aware that there can be drama in the monotonous. Deep, ehhh.

Since Christmas, thoughts about life and death, heaven and hell and everything in between, sometimes scary, have entered my mind. Then last week, Rodriguez invited me to his hip and trendy church. The pastor sat on an armchair facing the stage and told us how, that week, he had preached his life. The singing was incredible - like being at a concert. I never expected anything like that in a church! Musically it was awesome. I was blown away. And for a church service, it was actually quite fun, yet totally emotive. Certainly different. Whatever has been happening over the last few months I know that my soul has definitely been stirred. Rodriguez is big into his church. He hits up youth group every week and his pastor has been really helpful since R's dad got sick.

But now this taste of defeat. A knockback, maybe a reality check, but-

Mom was waiting for me at the front door of our building.

'Do you need a bed? I used to have a son who lived here but he became a musician and has gone all rock and roll on us. I hope he comes back to visit his parents someday.'

I laughed. She gave me a massive hug.

'I'm so proud of you.'

'But I didn't win Mom.'

'It doesn't matter,' she said. 'You played that gig. You have really taken to your music and we couldn't be happier.'

'Thanks Mom. I really tried - but I guess I just have to practice a lot more.'

'Listen to yourself!' she gently scolded. 'Only 18 and you're performing at The Bike Factory! That's impressive!'

Dad walked towards the door and bear hugged the life out of me.

'Hey Mick.'

'Mick?' I said.

'Yeah like Mick Jagger.'

I shook my head at him. Dads are so corny.

But he wasn't done with the cheesefest. 'You know, now that you're a famous musician I have to give you a songwriter nickname. What do you want it to be? Bruce. Noel. Freddie. Paul. James. Stevie. Otis. Bob. Johnny. I could list them all day long.'

'You're cray cray Dad.'

'Maybe you want Britney. Beyonce. Kelly. Lady. Alisha?' he said.

We didn't agree on a name. I guess he is just going to call me whatever cheesy thing comes into his mind.

'Let's go inside. It's freezing out,' Mom said.

When I walked through the front door of our apartment, I pointed to the steaming hot chocolate that was sitting on the sideboard and looked at Dad.

'Is this *yours*?' I asked.

'Yeah,' he grinned. 'But there's gallons more! Grab a mug and tell us all about your gig.'

For the next twenty minutes I was once more the centre of attention as I talked them through the gig and my plans to hit even more cafés and raise a few more dollars for my trip. Dad usually only makes his special hot chocolate with extra whipped cream on special occasions. So they must have been proud of me.

OSCAR SCISSORHANDS

Late February (after another romance-free Valentine's Day, sigh) and work introduced a new all singing, all dancing rewards promo. Our customers, after every cumulative $200 spend in the store, received a 10% discount, complimentary delivery and a smoothie of their choice. It meant I scored a 3-hour delivery shift, usually on a Tuesday afternoon, when I got to cycle around the neighbourhood (on ice-free days) and race up and down apartment buildings delivering produce to our wonderful customers. Fresh & Juicy fixed me up with some neat wheels. A designer came out to the store and we worked up a fly-looking black and yellow fleet of custom bikes. My ride was complete with side and front panniers, Fresh & Juicy decals, a fluttering flag, pristine white rims, finished off with spinners, just like the rappers have on their pimped-up transport. Oh yeah!

The extra shift (including tips) was a helpful boost to my

savings account. But the money I earned by gigging was going to definitely change my trip from being a good time to a totally awesome adventure. Speaking about gigging, I haven't told you what happened since my spot at The Bike Factory.

I was gathering my leads together after one of the gigs I had scored at a venue near school, when a really pretty girl came over and started chatting to me. She was a little smaller than me and was wearing a shocking pink snood. Like a 'shocking pink' snood, not a 'shocking' pink snood. Get me? Just before she started talking to me I began to feel the onset of a cakehead (a combination of the noise & excitement of the gig and too much coffee & cake (I started using a lot more mash up words since hanging round James Marcus), so I was hoping to make a quick getaway. But the girl who had caught my attention? I knew her from school, Susan. And let's just say you never turn down the chance to hang with Susan.

Susan is the type of girl that should always pass you by in the corridor. She was born to breeze through school without any bullying, self-esteem, acne or academic problems. You know those people exist, right? She has no need to say hi or engage me in conversation, but she does. She always smiles and laughs at my jokes, listens to the music I put up online and likes my Facebook statuses.

Is that what constitutes 21st Century flirting?

I must ask my mom, or Google it.

There's bound to be a meme about it somewhere.

She looked exceptionally pretty, (her standard look is pretty). It felt more than cool that she was talking to me. I sensed a tingle running through me; she kept playing with her hair, which I thought was a sign that she was nervous, and when she touched my arm I felt all giggly and silly.

After a few compliments about my set and some other small talk about school, the gig and Facebook friends we had in common, she launched into a conversation about her Nana Ling's 80th birthday party that was coming up in March. Eventually she asked me if I would play at her Nana's birthday (a roundabout way of asking me on a date perhaps?!) Amongst other things, Susan explained that some of the members of her family were a bit crazy and LOVED to sing, so I wasn't to be offended if people came up, took my microphone, and began to sing along with me as I played. I told her that I had never played at a birthday party before, so the thought of being responsible for the music on such a meaningful occasion was pretty daunting. Anxiety intensified when Susan revealed the cash incentive for the party was $400. My eyes nearly popped out of my head when she mentioned that amount! I was nervous, but I knew I couldn't turn down a gorgeous girl and $400!

Having recently watched *Spiderman*, I left the conversation thinking, *'with a great appearance fee comes great responsibiliteeee.'* I also wondered if I was her *Peter Parker*, with the guitar my mask and the barrier between me conquering, or even just communicating with the female race.

In the run-up to the birthday party I tried my hand at busking in the subway. I convinced Mom and Dad that it was a good idea by telling them the judges at The Bike Factory told me to build my confidence by performing anywhere and anytime I could. It was cool to see people dance in front of my open guitar case and I earned about $150 in three weeks!

Oh, and there was a brief snowfall, but before you could say 'snow people selfies', the sun reduced the snow people that appeared across the city to piles of coal, carrots and unwanted Christmas scarves.

Two weeks before Nana Ling's birthday celebrations, I met with Susan and her family at their restaurant. We discussed the *Michael Jackson* covers and some epic power ballads they wanted me to play at the party. I also inherited the role of DJ during the times when I wasn't playing guitar and a third role of technological wizard. Susan handed me a pen stick full of music, photos, videos and some instructions for putting together the type of presentation her family wanted. The video presentation was to encompass the 80 years of Nana Ling's life and was going to be played just before they gave Nana her cake and presents. I guess they wanted to get their money's worth for $400! No pressure then. After spending a few hours being tourists in their own city, Mom and Dad joined us for a chowtastic chicken satay and were introduced to Susan's crazy family.

Schoolwork definitely suffered in the week leading up to the birthday bash. But on the Wednesday before the party I proudly showed Susan the progress I had made on the video. Over some pretty gross mac and cheese and a raspberry yoghurt in the school cafeteria, she gave me a few helpful pointers and some family in-jokes, to make sure the house would come down in a mix of tears and laughter. With her dark brown eyes, cheerful comments and beautiful smile, Susan was my angel in the cafeteria.

After lunch she walked me to my locker. Other people stared at us, trying to figure out if we were together. I did my best to give the impression that we were. I opened my locker. She put her hand on my shoulder and gave me a parting hug, 'See you Saturday dude. Don't be late!'

I walked to English class thinking of all the famous love interests in literature. Maybe people would write about Susan and me? Maybe I had a chance? After fantasising my way through English I skipped to the men's room and checked her Facebook profile before math. Oh no! Shock of my life! She was Facebook official with some punk from a school a few blocks away. This news was fresh. I wondered why she hadn't said anything? How had I missed the signs? Susan hadn't mentioned anything about this Darnell guy. My chances with her had long disappeared down the sewers.

The news put me in a terrible mood and once more made the gig all about the money and only the money. $400 would go a long way to pay for my flight to Ireland. Money, not kisses, was now the main motivation.

On Friday I put the final touches to the set list during Miss Farrow's English class. Then, on inspecting my hair in a conical beaker during chemistry lab, I decided to get my hair cut on the way home. I wanted to look slick, sleek and presentable for any gig and family photos I might photobomb for my FB music page.

Living in the same neighbourhood all my life, I know most of the local business owners. And, having a mom who runs her own business and a business studies teacher who thinks 'small independents are a crucial model to strengthen our economy,' I support local, family enterprises; in this case, Oscar's Barbershop. Over the last 18 years I have gladly moved from Oscar's booster seat to barber's chair. When big name, big bucks salons have appealed, I have remained faithful to Oscar and his sterilised combs and slick wet look gel.

But, this thrifty-emotional attachment to my local barbershop doesn't always yield the best results when Oscar downs tools and circumnavigates my head with a mirror. Oscar has given me a few dodgy styles and unintended mullets over the years. My hair technician is an ex-Colombian miner who ended up, quite accidentally, as a barber in NYC. So Oscar tends to take creative license when I present my flowing locks before him. On this occasion his imagination extended a little too far, and for the first time, Oscar totally butchered my hair.

'A little trim, shorter on the sides, you know like how the cool kids are wearing it,' were the instructions I gave him. Then Oscar took to my locks like an electronic *Edward Scissorhands*. By the time the razor finished its path of destruction, I could see way too much scalp on both sides of my head, but then behind my ears he had left this longer mullet thing going on. My eyebrows were longer than the hair on the right hand side of my head, with the left-hand-side bearing the indent of a couple of speed stripes.

Oscar, are you drunk? I thought to myself as I tried to keep my composure in between gasping and gulping at the mirror. I had long and floppy hair on the top of my head, bangs, and no hair on the sides! I looked like a goofy gang member wearing a branded raccoon on his head! You might ask why I didn't speak up and interrupt this barbershop massacre, and that would be a fair question to ask. Let me explain. Oscar is a 74-year-old, young at heart city legend. One of the TV channels did a real life-documentary about him; you know those *NYC's Real People* shows. So when he heard I was playing some gigs, I think he wanted to give me a unique look that would be interesting to the people I was entertaining. His heart was in the right place, even if his razor wasn't. As for his eyesight? Don't even go there.

So I need a bit of life advice. What do you do when the barber goes left field and makes you look like the bullied sheep in the pen? Should you make a huge deal of it, or simply place $15 into your barber's hand, utter a few words of thanks, accept his best wishes for your gig and head straight to the nearest thrift store to buy a new collection of hats? With the buzz of Oscar's razor still ringing in my ears, I searched through the local St. Vincent de Paul's selection of headwear and found a new baseball cap, a flat cap and a woolly hat - complete with a fantastic bobble. My trip to Oscar's had clipped $31 from my shavings account!

$12 for City Clippers

$3 tip for Oscar

$4 for a flat cap with leather trim

$3 for an old Padres baseball cap

$2 for a woolly hat that definitely needs a trip to the washing machine

$7 for major comfort food on my walk home

Dad was out of town for the night with work, so when I arrived home Mom called him and provided him with a 360-degree tour of my haircut. Her hysterical laughter was a frightening backing track to the video call. But by the end of our conversation I was making jokes about it too. I had hoped Mom could do some damage-limitation trimming, but she did not trust herself with the scissors and figured she would just make a bad thing even worse. Later that night Mom brought out the family photo albums and showed me her hideous 80's perm-bob thing. I don't know if I laughed at her shoulder pads or her hair more.

While we were sharing this moment of embarrassing confidences, I told Mom about Darnell and my zero chance with Susan. Mom has always been interested in all two seconds of my love life. So this news didn't seem to bother her. Some of her friend's kids have the perfect relationships, which she always tells me about and shows me on Instagram. Gag! Secretly I think she would love me to have a girlfriend so they could chat about girly stuff together, never having had a daughter of her own. But she doesn't pressure me, plus it's kind of her fault, as she banned me from having girlfriends until I was 16. Puberty is difficult enough to deal with! Instead Mom always says that one day I will meet someone and when I do I will know. I wonder what that feels like? Knowing. The One. Falling in love.

Anyway, with the haircut hysterics over and the heartbreak hangover from Wednesday dealt with, I settled down to a Friday night movie & takeout with Mom - romantic or what? But before the Thai food arrived, I decided I would treat Patrick to a cheap laugh and Skyped him to show off my new rock star image. I realised, with Patrick, this is letting myself in for some serious 'slagging' (teasing which he is expert at) and potential blackmail. But inspiration struck. They have some pretty out-there fashions in the UK, so I thought I could fool him into thinking my haircut was the latest thing all the NYC hipsters were rocking. Maybe he'd want an 'Oscar' for himself.

Chuckling at the idea of being the practical joker for a change, I pulled on my new woolly hat and switched on my laptop. No reply. Was he out? Probably. It was Friday night for him. Seconds ticked by. I'd give it five more rings. I was about to give up when Patrick's face came up on screen - a dark circle in an even darker room. It was hard to make anything out. He switched on a desk lamp. He was sitting in a bathrobe and looking very grubby too.

'Heya Tyler,' Patrick sounded deadpan; not all that thrilled to be talking. His voice didn't have its usual energy. Was he home with the flu? 'Look, now's not a good time, but-'

'Sure, OK,' I hesitated, then remembered my webcam was still off. 'I'll be quick.' I turned it on and as the green light appeared, whipped off my woolly hat.

'What the-!' Patrick dissolved in laughter.

'Like it? It's the latest hipster look over here.'

Patrick was laughing too hard to speak. Tears rolled down his cheeks. He wiped them away with the sleeves of his grungy terrycloth bathrobe. I ranted for a while about my haircut. He was helpless with laughter. And the hysteria went on for at least five minutes. My joke idea went out the window. Every so often I would try and interrupt with a 'Wow, I knew it was bad but-' or 'Maybe I should ask for my money back?' But after a while I stayed quiet and just wondered if Patrick was OK, especially when he covered his face, his shoulders shook and breathing seemed to come in gasps between the guffaws.

Eventually Patrick got control of himself. He took a few deep breaths, blew his nose loudly on the robe (yuchhhhhh!), wiped his cheeks with his fists and gave me that big Patrick smile. 'Oh man! Thank you for that Tyler. I needed that. You have *no* idea. Whew!'

The laughter had exhausted him. Yet it seemed to have perked him up too, because for the next twenty minutes we had a very entertaining discussion about how to rescue my haircut. Go for broke and dye it bright blue, get extensions put in, go bald and tattoo my scalp, part it down the middle and go for a 1920's greaseball look. Soon I was laughing until tears came out too.

Patrick thanked me again as he hung up. 'Cheers Tyler! You are a lifesaver! And Oscar too.'

I had to wonder again.

In the morning I put new strings on my guitar and made my way to the restaurant. I was ready for some off the chain Chinese food and epic 80th birthday party banter - a word I picked up from my weekly Skype chats with Patrick. He's told me it was a boring time of year, nothing 'strange or startling' going on, but he was doing a lot with some of the sports societies at

Queen's. I still felt a bit weird about the hysterical laughter, but in the light of day, I decided I must have been reading too much into it. Anyway I told him about Susan. Patrick had no advice to offer. In fact he confided he was still trying to figure out Northern Irish girls, who probably have the world's best radar for BS and bad pick-up lines; never mind figure out American girls! He reminded me that we had plenty of time to practice flirting with girls when we were together and was excited that I was saving so hard for my trip.

NEON SNOW

It was the most random way I earned money to get to Ireland. Wait - I just remembered that scavenging week at the start of my fundraising efforts! What was I thinking?! I managed to swap my days and swing an easy Sunday shift in Fresh & Juicy to allow me to play at the gig. Not only had I been rehearsing for Nana Ling's party, but it was playoff season and our b-ball coach was making us sign up to extra practices. I was knackered as Patrick would say.

I opted to walk to the birthday bash, not because it would save me a few dollars on the subway, but because it was a beautiful late winter's morning. My urban trek took me through a few neighbourhoods I wouldn't normally venture into. Exploring my city is always a learning experience. From people-watching to checking out the constant transformation of the landscape, it's amazing to see what's springing up, getting a refurb or what's new in canine fashion! Plus I wanted to take in as much of NYC as I could before I headed off to college, as I knew I would miss the bright lights and sheer magnitude of my hometown.

The restaurant was at the corner of Canal and Louis Faketon Street. A neon sign a few doors down from Susan's claimed: 'Every bite take U2 Beijing and back.' I smiled at the unintentional music reference and patted my pockets for my cell to take a photo. I'm told New York's Chinatown is quite like parts of Shanghai, crammed with people and commerce and bustle, except the money smells different, the lights are dimmer and the plain-clothes cops stand out like the bright neon signs sprouting from nearly every building.

The area around Canal Street is full of places to eat, mini markets, handbag hustlers, and Tai Chi practicing, Mah Jong playing, iPad reading elderly people. I was early, so I grabbed a tea and sat and watched life unfold in this wonderful part of New York. Previously I had only popped into Chinatown for dinner and hadn't stopped to appreciate the district. But today I felt like I was in another country. Everything around me was so different. For starters, the neighbourhood is loud. Loud in colour. Loud in decibels. Loud in motion. Compared to the Village, Chinatown's colours are clashing and in your face. In the Village we have tastefully exposed, understated 'minimalist' brick shop fronts, but in Chinatown I noticed nearly every building wore a cluster of blinding neon and plastic signs full of bright Chinese characters. And wherever I turned there were exchanges, business transactions and conversations going on. I looked on as a store assistant hung up Peking duck on a hook in the window of their deli. A group of young teens walked past with upbeat Chinese pop music blasting from their phones. I stopped outside a fruit and vegetable shop and, despite having worked in Fresh & Juicy for a few months, stared at exotic produce that was new to my eyes.

Still sipping my green tea, I made my way to Susan's restaurant; the aroma of five spice hit my nose about five doors up from the place. Passing a row of street stalls selling knock-off watches - I bought a 'Rollex' for 10 bucks - and arrived bang on time (well I hope the watch was telling the correct time!) at Ling's, where the chill of the March air made way for blissful warmth.

Susan was waiting for me just inside.

'Hey.'

'Hey. You all set?' she asked and threw her arms around me.

'Yeah. I feel great. A little bit tired from the walk.' When I first saw her all the feelings I had for her flooded back. But I knew I had to resist them and just get on with playing an awesome gig. Epic fail was not an option. Or dating Susan.

'You walked over? How crazy are you?!'

'Yeah it's a nice day.'

'Yeah if you're an Eskimo,' Susan said.

I laughed at her joke and pulled the hood of my coat up. 'Do I look like an Eskimo?'

'You look like a dork!' Susan hit my arm to show me that we both knew she was kidding. 'You want to bring your stuff upstairs?'

'Sure.'

We tramped upstairs and Susan showed me around a surprisingly large room custom-designed for parties. There was a wall somewhere behind the enormous 60-inch flat screen that hung at the far end. Dotted round the place was a wireless 32-point speaker system, networked into the hallways, kitchen and the bathrooms. And a small stage had been set up with a mic and decent sound equipment ready to go. The venue was a technological dream! After my tour, she left me to set up a few pedals and re-tune my guitar as the cold had played havoc with my strings.

When they said it was going to be a family party, I had thought it would be on a small scale. However by family, they had to mean anyone who had ever shared the same bus as Mrs. Ling. There must have been over 100 people there by the time I got up to play some background music while the buffet was brought out. I was a little on edge, but when Susan walked towards me with a glass of water, my dry mouth and nerves faded away.

'Tyler,' Susan whispered to me as another one of her family members stared at me.

'Yeah.'

'Take your hat off.'

'Ermm I can't.'

'What do you mean you can't?' Susan asked. 'It's respectful.'

'I got a really bad haircut yesterday. Like catastrophically bad.'

'Why did you do that?'

'I didn't do it on purpose!' I reacted.

'It can't be all that bad.' Susan insisted.

'Oh. Oh it can. Imagine a hipster Kim Jong-un! See.' I removed my hat to reveal my presidential hairstyle and Susan burst into laughter.

'It's cool Tyler. In a weird kind of way. You can pull it off.' She giggled at her own pun.

'You sure?'

'Well ... kinda! You're an artist!'

One of her uncles came over to me and inspected my hair. He tousled it and chuckled before he made a few comments in Cantonese to Susan, which she didn't translate for me! Another one of her aunts pointed and laughed at my haircut! But after blushing for a couple of minutes, I got down to the business of being the party entertainment and soon forgot all about my hair. The day was a complete blast, stretching from late afternoon into the evening. Nana Ling's party was onnnnnn.

I was about to put my guitar away when some of the men, who had polished off way too much firewater, started throwing money at me to persuade me to play their favourite songs. I was like a real-life jukebox and dropped hit after cheesy hit as long as the money was being stuffed into my pockets! An hour later, with the skin on my fingertips turning rawer than a T-bone steak, someone hit the lights, my presentation came up on screen and then a birthday cake, complete with sparklers, was wheeled into the room. The room burst into song.

Nana Ling's face was a dream. She looked so happy! It was a beautiful sight. After that I became DJ, rested my fingers and pumped some funky beats through the sound system.

People started leaving around ten. If they thanked me once they thanked me a million times for playing and 'DJing' at the party - (little did they know my awesome mixes were just a playlist and a very handy little app).

While some of the guests made for home and others helped the staff to clear up, Susan and I took a seat at a table to catch up. Thoughtfully, she had put together a plate of all the nicest dishes from the buffet, with extra helpings of the Peking duck and spring rolls. I was starving!

'So who's this Darnell guy?' I jumped in without thinking and immediately remembered so many other things I shoulda and coulda started the conversation with, like, 'Did your Nana enjoy the party?' 'What are you doing tomorrow?' But no. I decided to ask straight out the question that had been bothering me all week. She looked a little embarrassed, even when I started spluttering some 'sorrys' and 'my bads'.

'Oh, he's just a guy.'

'Just a guy?' I said. 'He has to be more than a guy ... you're Facebook official.'

'He kinda sprung the Facebook official thing on me. I was mad with him for a while about it but we're cool now.'

'Why weren't you sure about going official with him?' I asked.

'Well there were a couple of things. My dad doesn't really like him.'

'But your dad likes everybody!' I said. We both looked over at him sharing stories and enjoying a beer with his friends.

'He's in a good mood today. Trust me, he doesn't like everybody!' Then Susan continued, 'the other thing was, I thought you were going to make a move.'

My jaw hit the ground. I couldn't believe what she had just confided.

'Yeah. I mean I liked you and flirted with you real hard in the café and then in the cafeteria that day. But you didn't take the bait. Or I guess I should have just came straight out with it.'

My hopes soared. 'Maybe we-'

Susan interrupted me before I could finish. 'No Tyler. I couldn't do that on Darnell.'

'But your dad would be happy. He likes me!'

She gave a half laugh. 'That's true. But no, I'm happy with Darnell and I'm not a cheating type of girl. If we'd become friends a little earlier, then who knows.'

There was a lull and as I munched on a spring roll and thought about what might have been, a welcome distraction arose in the form of some awful Chinese dance music and an argument between Nana Ling and the rest of the family. Susie translated and told me her Nana was trying to pay for her own party! The bickering summed up the Ling family. Kind, energetic and passionate. Generous too. The family had welcomed me, fed me and had provided me with half my flight (when you include tips) to Ireland. A fantastic result for a day's work. Certainly a day to remember.

Realising it was nearly 11 o'clock, and with the snowflakes

starting to make a quilt on top of the neon signs, I said my final thanks and goodbyes to the family. Susan walked me to the door and put her hand on my arm. She gave me a lingering hug, thanked me again for the day and told me to check my Instagram on the way home as she had put up a few funny photos from the day.

'See you on Monday, Tyler. And can you forget about what I said upstairs? I still want to be friends with you. It's been fun getting to know you.'

I looked over her shoulder and out the window, before I looked her in the eyes.

'Yeah I think so.' Then I switched my focus to the floor, really hard. Linoleum has never been so fascinating. 'It's just. It's just I've never had a girl say that to me before ... and ... well ... you are totally pretty and smart and we get along so well and ... I just wish Darnell didn't exist! Damn you Darnell!' I exclaimed before we both laughed nervously.

Susan came forward to give me another hug, and as she did she hit her head off my guitar case that was hanging off my right shoulder.

'Oh I'm so stoopid!' she said.

I held her head and made her look into my eyes to make sure she was OK. My heart skipped a beat. She moved towards me, kissed me on the cheek and ran back upstairs.

With the kiss still fresh on my cheek I made some pointless comment about the amount of snow that was falling. But Susie was gone. Then I opened the door. Yep, still snowing. Before it closed I turned and shouted back up the stairs. 'Hey Susie, thanks for today. It was fantastic. Even better than I could have hoped for.'

On the cab ride home I tried to process what had just happened and all I came up with was #kickingmyself #majorcrush #loadsacashinmypocket

SENIOR PROM

After that last snowfall melted and spring finally hit NYC, my trip to Ireland seemed closer than ever. The second half of March kicked things into place for my summer trip for two reasons:

1. St Patrick's Day. Cousin Patrick - not the snake chasing, Jesus loving, Christianity spreading, long haired shamrock-wearing St. Pat - thinks Yanks love Paddy's Day more than the Irish do. He's probably right. With around 40 million people claiming Irish heritage in America we do go crazy for it. Heck the peeps in Chicago even dye the river green! Maybe because I knew I would soon be in Ireland, I got even more involved in the celebrations than usual - like pretending to be sick so I could ditch school and sneak off to the huge parade that is one of the biggest events of the year in NYC. I think Mrs.

Bennett, the math teacher who claimed to be 11/16th Irish, read through my sore stomach, but she let me leave school early. Well, not before she told me a few traditional customs of St. Patrick's Day.

'Tyler, did you know? The farmers begin to plant their potato crop after the celebrations, as St Patrick's Day marks the middle of Spring and the promise of better weather. February is traditionally the start of spring in the Emerald Isle. *(Who'd have thunk? That's still mid winter here!)* And the men wear caps with a sprig of shamrock tucked into them when they head to the pub to drink the 'Pota Pádraig' after mass, as the rest of the family prepares the traditional feast.'

'Ehhh no. I didn't know that.' I didn't think even Mom knew that one.

'Oh and I'm glad to see you're wearing green.' I was wearing a green snapback ball cap Patrick picked up for me at a golf course he goes to regularly - so it is the real deal - plus lime socks (reject Christmas present that comes out every March 17th). Mrs. Bennett's lecture was not over. 'Because traditionally, if you didn't wear green on St Patrick's people were allowed to pinch you!'

Now I do happen to know for a fact that this is a custom they *don't* practice in Ireland. My Mom was a bit surprised by the pinch-o-rama on her first March 17th in the US. But it does not pay to contradict a math teacher as it raises the risk of extra homework.

'Thanks for the heads up. Can I go now? I need to get to the nurse.'

She raised her eyes and gave me a wink that made me realise she knew I wasn't sick. 'Don't worry about the nurse. I got your back!'

I turned and began to walk down the corridor. Mrs. Bennett shouted after me, 'Make sure you eat all your cabbage and corned beef Tyler! Guaranteed to sort out your sick stomach.' That's another 'traditional Paddy's Day custom' my mother had never heard of until she arrived on these shores.

'Will do!' I shouted back.

I stopped by Mom's pâtisserie on my way to the parade. She had made a major tribute to Irish baking, with soda bread, potato cakes, wheaten bread and brack all arranged in a special display - with some green éclairs thrown in just for the luck of the Irish. I set a few delicacies aside for Mrs. Bennett as a thank you for 'believing' my pretty lame sick stomach excuse.

2. Plane tickets. After months of hard saving and the $400+ from the birthday gig, I was able to book my ticket to Ireland. Yes! It all became real to me once I took a screen shot of my ticket and sent it to Patrick. I was leaving on Thursday 12th June, arriving in on Friday 13th June and leaving from Belfast on Tuesday 8th July - about 3 and a half weeks in total. He insisted I fly into Dublin so we could hang out in the city for a night and go to the gig he had bought me tickets for. Throughout April he gave me tonnes of attractions to research to help him put together a packed tour itinerary for my stay.

Ever since the bizarre laughter after my haircut, my weekly chats with Patrick had been pretty normal. Same old same old even. The usual stuff about music, sports and the summer trip. As for the out of control hilarity, I didn't like to ask, or even speculate. Patrick seemed OK now and stoked about me coming.

Of course I had probed Mom a couple of times about what her and Aunt Beth had been chatting about the night they told me I was going to Ireland, and I still had my suspicions that something wasn't quite right. Or hadn't been right, but maybe was OK now. Anyhow, over the months leading up to the trip, Mom didn't let anything further slip, so stuff in Belfast kind of took a back seat in my mind. Maybe because there was so much else going on.

And then ... seemed like before I knew it, Senior year was almost over, it was hot out, flowers were blooming in window boxes all around the Village, people were wearing shorts, eating outside and buying Italian ices from street stalls. All of which could mean only one thing - Prom was just around the corner.

What do *She's All That, Napoleon Dynamite, Twilight, 21 Jump Street, 10 Things I Hate About You, Mean Girls, American Pie* and *Never Been Kissed* all have in common? Yeah you guessed it - awkward prom scenes. Senior Prom, arguably the all-time greatest teenage rite of passage, was off the hook.

Filled with fake tan. Selfies. Breath mints. Retro shoulder pads. Updos. Dodgy dos. Pastel suits. Topped off with plenty of pink lipstick, OTT aftershave, false lashes, hair extensions and raunchy dance moves. It wasn't quite *Clueless*, but some of the girls in school did dress as if they had just stepped out of the 90's - apparently it's fashionable. Or was that the 80's? There was plenty of parent-sponsored, designer chic on show too. A week before prom, Mom took me out with a couple of her friends to get me suited and booted. They picked out a wicked suit, shirt, a matching trilby, a bow tie and some hipster-tastic brown suede shoes. The outfit was epic, but hopefully not an epic fail when I look back at the photos in years to come.

On the night itself Dessie T forgot to get a wrist corsage for Alisha G, which just ruined her night. I'm told the limos were longer and blingier than the previous year. Francesca's group performed a not so secret flash mob (so 2010) to *I Got A Feeling*. After their moving tribute to *The Black Eyed Peas*, we danced the floorboards off. Others spent the rest of the night with their arms wrapped round their significant others, making declara-tions of undying love and fidelity that would last long after the final bell of our high school career had echoed in our ears.

Or not.

I made no such statements.

If you are wondering who my date was, well, it's a funny story.

Throughout April I'd been sorta dating a girl called Holly. After a great start to the year, my gigs in coffee shops dried up, so I hid out in the subway until better weather made it possible to busk above ground. A few Sundays ago, as heavy winter overcoats were replaced with spring jackets, and families and walkers suddenly emerged from hibernation, I made my way to the High Line - the city's newest walker's hangout. It's pretty impressive; an old train line above street level that was abandoned for years but has now been turned into a high-rise linear park full of plants and walkways and cool cafés. Even running water to cool tired tootsies! It was a great place to share some of my songs that I had squirrelled away and refined over winter.

The first time Holly passed by she stopped to listen for a few songs before she dropped a couple of dollars in my cup. The following Sunday she brought a friend and the third Sunday she waited and started talking to me.

I had finished writing most of my EP back in February, but didn't record it until April. I wanted it to be good enough to justify charging for it. After all, the judges from that night at The Bike Factory had strongly encouraged me to work on a few areas. So I took their advice, and also in an attempt to forget all about Susan, I packed the rest of March with practice. But she kept popping back into my mind. It was hard to accept what I had let slip through my fingers.

So Holly just came along at the wrong time. Or maybe not. Because I was mega busy with the EP. Recording the final tracks, finalising the artwork and then making preparations for the launch. Holly was really cool, but after an initial flurry of texts it just didn't take off. It was probably my fault. Around the time I realised Holly was into me and vice versa, I was trying to grab any spare shift in Fresh & Juicy I could get, I had to give all my free hours to riding the wave of my EP, and spend whatever was left over to see friends and family before heading off for the summer. History will record that my pursuit of music and money trumped Holly's advances. Story of my life. Always too busy to fit in romance. I made myself a pledge -

that would have to change.

James Marcus let me hold an EP launch night at the end of April in the store as a way of bringing his vibeosophy and my *Songs From The Mountain* to a new generation. It was such a cool night. The audience really put their hands together for my original work. And, after my gig, I had my New Hampshire-inspired music on limited edition USB sticks to hand out.

Holly came along to the gig and we hooked up afterwards for a coffee. Things looked promising again, but only for about a week. Then I ran out of time again. More hours at F&J and on the bike making deliveries, more family stuff, and after the EP launch, more gig requests, so I gave up on the whole dating game. I guess that's what college is for? #teenagedrama

Anyway, it all meant that next thing I knew, it was May and Senior Prom was here before I knew it and I was completely unprepared. No date and no plan. In stepped Rodriguez. Some people my age love to use apps to try and match themselves up with other people in their area. My app is called Rodriguez - who hooked me up with Chelsea, who turned out to be a friend of Susan - yes Susan. But that's OK.

Chelsea had an interesting story, which she shared with me over a burger and fries. Basically her boyfriend of 7 months and his family had just moved to Alaska. Like a month before prom. His father was a marine biologist and took a new job, which meant he had to move to a town that had fewer people than my building. I joked with Chelsea about the lengths people would go to avoid being her prom date. She squirted mustard onto my burger. I hate mustard. We laughed and then thrashed out our pre, during and post prom protocol.

Back in early March one of my teachers spotted me at a gig - cue awkward social chat - we got talking about music and he asked me to perform a few songs at Senior Prom. The bad news; the school had zero money to pay me. But they agreed that I could sell my EP at lunchtimes in the week leading up to the big night. The sales paid for my outlay on prom, so I didn't eat into my savings for Ireland. Handy. But what reeeeaaally made me jump at the chance to play at prom was I knew my friend Maisy's dad was in charge of organising the music for the night. If my Mom is one of the éclair fairies of NYC, her dad is one of its music moguls. He owns his own label and has some of the hottest new and established artists on his roster. As a result, and what a result it was, he managed to snaffle two quality bands to play exclusively for our Senior class. It meant some amazing musicians heard my tunes. Even better, I had an encouraging chat with Maisy's dad who promised to give my EP a listen with his creative team. I had to hold back from doing a little dance of excitement.

I played a small six-song set filled with some love songs and some lust songs. During riffs I watched Chelsea doing her thing in the dance-off circle which looked so much fun, until Olly started putting the moves on her. I could tell she was feeling uncomfortable, so I caught her attention and waved her onto the stage to play my kick-drum for my last song. We had an absolute blast. #promrocked

Most of the kids I hang out with went to an all-night af-ter-party in Shakers where the dancing was unbelievable. When we were finally kicked out of the club, seven of us grabbed some Lebanese takeout on our way to my place. We devoured tabbouleh, falafel and shish tawookas, then showed my parents pictures of the night as they ate their breakfast. For the rest of the day we all slept and lounged about the living room. I thought Senior Prom was going to be a non-event, but it was the bomb. Tiring too, zzzzzzzzzzzzzzzzzzz.

TYLER'S GUIDE TO IRELAND

Rodriguez:	*Wanna hang later?*
Tyler:	*Sure. Wot u wanna do?*
Rodriguez:	*Dinner?*
Tyler:	*RU asking me on a date?*
Rodriguez:	*No! I have something 4u*
Tyler:	*???*
Rodriguez:	*I'll explain l8r*
Tyler:	*Usual?*
Rodriguez:	*Yeah*
Tyler:	*7?*
Rodriguez:	*Perfecto*

I threw my phone onto my bed and just lay there, staring at the ceiling. So much change was about to happen. Mom and Dad were getting ready to go to South America, I was about to finish High School, leave a job that I loved, go on an epic summer vacation and then head out of state to college, without my best friend Rodriguez. I hadn't felt like this before and I didn't know how to deal with it. There was a mixture of excitement for the journey, fear of the unknown, reluctance to quit my job, tingles of expectancy about college. When the whole mess settled in my stomach it was a big mix of *uuughhhhhhh*. I picked up my To Do lists which were growing by the day.

PACKING LIST

Clothes - Socks, jeans, chinos, shorts x3, sneakers, t-shirts, hoodie x2, flannel shirts x3, jacket, swim shorts.

Belt

Sandals

Toiletry stuff and zit cream

iPad

Camera

Chargers, adaptors

Guitar

Ear plugs, Kleenex, lip balm

Headphones

Passport

Cash

Notebooks and pen

ORDERS FROM PATRICK'S FAMILY

iPad Air

iPod Shuffle x 4 Green, Blue, Pink, Red

Giants tops x 2

Columbia Lions t-shirts

GIFTS

NYC baseball caps x 2
FDNY & NYPD t-shirts for Uncle Richard & Uncle David
Times Square Snow Globe for Granny
I Heart NYC mugs x 3
Key rings x 4
Fridge magnets x 6
Cheetos Xtra Crunchy
Milk Duds and other movie candy

I stacked a couple of things I intended bringing and figured out when I'd have time to go and buy the gifts over the next couple of weeks, before I realised I needed to get a move on and meet R. He was waiting for me inside our usual burger joint and stood up to give me a back-slapping guy hug.

'Hey man.'

'Hey Tyler. Started packing yet?'

'You mean started thinking about it? I threw a few things into piles before I came out. Hey, maybe you could check my list to make sure I remembered everything?' I tossed my crumpled list onto the table as we sat down.

Rodriguez laughed a little as he read. 'Hope they sell underwear in Ireland, otherwise you're in trouble.'

I laughed too. 'Knew I'd forget something important!'

'That's a lot of gifts. You sure you have room for all of that?'

'Probably not, but dad keeps telling me to bring tons of NYC stuff to give to 'random people that I meet.''

'Your dad is so cool.'

'Most of the time.' Since Rodriguez's dad had gotten sick, I realised how lucky I was to have my parents and made a point of not griping about them, even when I felt like they were giving me a hard time.

He reached for his bag. 'You might want to make sure you have room for this too.'

'What's that?! For me? You couldn't wait till we'd had the food? Wow, it must be something!'

'It's your gift.' Rodriguez passed it over the table. A hand made book - *Tyler's Guide to Ireland.* The front cover was a map of Ireland with a few famous sights dotted around it.

'Yeah. I didn't tell you, but I did one of my final art projects on Ireland so you could have your own personalised guidebook.'

'Man this is awesome. Like, wow. I feel bad, I don't have anything for you. I'll bring something amazing back.'

'Anything for me?!' Rodriguez exclaimed. 'Come on! Don't you remember everything you helped me through this year?'

As his best friend of like 15 years, I guess I had spent a lot of nights listening to him talking and venting. He'd had to take on so much more responsibility with his Dad sick and his Mom working overtime to make ends meet. R had a lot less time for fun, or just for being young. Plus I convinced James Marcus to give my job to Rodriguez this summer so he could earn some cash for college. It would top up the clothes store job which had lasted after Christmas but was only for a few hours per week.

'That's what amigos are for.'

'BFFs forever!' we chanted and then did an exploding fist-pump and laughed.

We hadn't realised our waiter was standing at the end of our booth. He started laughing at us and after joining in on a second fist-bump, took our order.

Over burgers 'n' fries, Rodriguez helped fill the gaps in my packing list. Besides underwear, I had forgotten my phone, and most important - something for the rain! Then Rodriguez talked me through the book. I was so impressed by the amount of work he had put in, with different sections including The Best Stuff To See, Belfast, Dublin, Slang Expressions, Food & Drink and even a few sections that were left blank so I could scribble some of my trip memories and add my fave discoveries onto the pages of his project. On a second look through the book when Rodriguez was in the restroom, I noticed some Mini Rodriguezs that he had placed in different photographs. Standing outside Dublin Castle, on top of the Cliffs of Moher, outside Belfast's City Hall and at The Giants Causeway eating a hot dog! Hilarious! I also recognised some of the places from Patrick's proposed itinerary that he had sent through. It was all starting to feel so real!

On the opening page Rodriguez had noted: *At 13,843 sq km Northern Ireland is about the size of Connecticut, yet has half the population of the Nutmeg State. For a NYC resident it's easier to look at it this way - more people live in the 251 sq km of Brooklyn than in the whole 13,843 sq km of the province of Northern Ireland. More people live in NYC than in the whole island of Ireland!*

Rodriguez returned to his seat and took another bite of his

burger.

'Love these Mini Me's you put in, bro. I guess you're gonna get a vacation after all!'

'I thought I would gate crash your trip!'

'This is such a cool gift. Thanks buddy. This is amazing.'
Lump in the throat time.

'It's stupid and kinda like a Junior High project - but I got an A from my design teacher so I'm happy!'

'So weird to think graduation is next week, and then … that's it.'

We both did a big scary 'Urghhhhhhh.'

'Yeah, like I really want to graduate but school has been so good,' I said. 'I'm kinda scared about college, but I'm hoping to get some good tips over the summer from Patrick. Though he's still living with his folks.'

'If he remembers to pick you up from the airport!'

'True dat. What about you?'

'Never thought I would say this but I will actually miss some of our teachers,' Rodriguez admitted.

'Mrs. Bennett,' we both said at the same time.

'Like you, excited and nervous. But I can't think too far ahead. Mostly I'm focusing on finishing school and getting started in Fresh & Juicy.'

'You're gonna love the vibeosophy! I can't wait to train you in at orangiontation!'

During our walk home I gave R the lowdown on being a member of the Fruicy crew and we practiced his veggie-tastic sales patter and customer service technique.

Then it was graduation, which was awesome. Throwing that hat with the tassel in the air and walking our school corridors for the last time was emotional, and there were lots of tears, even from parents. Mostly from parents. After a couple of weeks of over-thinking that moment when I received my high school diploma, it just felt right. I was even asked to sing at the commencement ceremony which was such a great honour. My love for music was something the school had invested in through countless music lessons, choirs and concerts over the years so it was a great way of repaying them. For many of us school had been our harbour. Now we were being pushed out from our place of safety to a never-ending adventure on the high seas.

My friendship group, together with all our parents, went out for dinner. Rodriguez's dad came along. Hopefully it was a sign that things were looking up for the family. His dad ate all the food and had dessert too, which has to be promising. After food with the folks, Maisy's dad had booked a VIP night for everyone in our homeroom in one of the hottest clubs in town open to under 21s.

We boogied till way past closing time, and I even managed some dance-floor time with Susan. She was still with Darnell, but because it was only people from our school that were allowed into the private party at the club, I got my chance. As I was dancing with Susan I began to think about what the girls in Ireland would be like. If their smiles were half as inviting as Susan's and banter as good as Chelsea's, then it would be an unforgettable trip!

FLYING SOLO

Do you have packing rituals? When I should have been stuffing my suitcase, I took note of a few traits common to the Sontoro family. We eat the fridge. We eat the freezer. Yes, we literally eat everything until the shelves are bare. Waste is unthinkable. This ritual always results in some interesting dinners in the week preceding our trips. A hamburger with cinnamon and raisin bread instead of a bun. Grilled cheese and jam sandwiches, squash and lime stir fry, and on the final night a homemade pizza with anything that's left in the cupboard. It's the only time of the year that Mom's cooking sucks and I wish we had our own dog. In preparation for the last meal, which I knew was going to be disgusting, I managed to convince Mom that I had to dog-sit one of our neighbour's designer pooches until they were back from work. Let's just say that Lady Coco was well fed that night.

Before we leave for a trip Mom triple checks the taps, thermostats, window locks, the taps, sockets, the trash can, the laundry basket, the stove ... and did I mention she checks the taps? She lays out newspapers and a few clean dishes to give a *Home Alone* inspired illusion that people are still in the apartment. Dad watches Mom check all of the aforementioned things (great word Tyler), gets his gadgets together and splits up the spending cash into manageable wads. I simply do as I'm told.

· The apartment had been turned upside down in the search for luggage, swimsuits and eye-masks, but we were nearly there. Since January Mom and Dad had also been nailing down their South America trip. Realising they could not see it all, the big challenge was to decide the must-see places that were also do-able within three weeks. This was sorted over loads of visits to Cosalá's where my parents also got the opinions of the staff and most of the regulars. Dad wanted Chile, the Andes and the Galapagos. Mom had her heart set on Machu Pichu and the Inca Trail, with maybe Bolivia and Lake Titicaca if they had time. But they both wanted to camp in the Amazonian Jungle and experience Rio. So, with the guidance of a travel agent, they decided on an eco tour, including a few days in Brazil and a quick trip to the Iguazu Falls. Ever since, Mom and Dad had been running around getting vaccinations and picking up everything from mosquito nets to water purification tablets!

'Tyler'
'Yeah Mom.'
'Have you packed your sneakers?'

'Yeah Mom.'

'Are you sure?'

'Yeah Mom.'

'Have you packed your washbag?'

'Yeah Mom.'

'Have you-'

'Mom, I'm not going to Outer Mongolia! My headphones are round my neck. I have my passport in my carry-on and I have squeezed all of the gifts in, but I will double, triple and quadruple check for you.'

Yes, it's the day of our departure and we are all leaving on the same day, #seemedlikeagoodideaatthetime - Mom has stepped up about 3 gears. So as I quadruple checked my suitcase and carry-on backpack, I watched Mom prowl our place and disconnect every electrical appliance, just in case they decided to get all *Toy Story* on us when we were away. She even pulled out the power from the fridge. It was that serious. But Dad plugged it back in without telling her. Last time we went on vacation Mom ended up defrosting a prime rib of beef that was in the back of the freezer and we arrived home to a really gross smell.

Earlier that morning, I had caught Dad acting sus over breakfast. He confessed, as Mom was getting ready, that he had forgotten to buy travel insurance, so I helped him arrange some online. He slipped me a 20 and swore me to secrecy!

One of my other tasks is to keep watch for the cab. I create mass hysteria when I holler that the cab has pulled up, and get a well-deserved pull on my ear when Mom realises I'm joking.

After I had, by now, quintuple checked my stuff, and Mom had packed and repacked her hand luggage, we realised we were 10 minutes early for the taxi, but Mom chased us, then locked us out of the apartment. Sitting on the front step of our building, I realised my only job had been taken from me! During those 10 minutes Mom reminded me of the many branches of her family tree. I wasn't listening to her. I was too excited. Months of saving and dreaming had finally paid off. I had enough money and then some, and I was only a few hours away from seeing the green fields of Ireland.

We made casual conversation in the cab. Dad asked the normal cab questions to which the driver responded in song. Random. It felt like we were about to flash up on a TV show. Which we did! This kind of thing happens in NYC. And, because we joined in the singsong, we received our cab ride for free! Luck of the Irish I guess.

When we pulled up to the international terminal at JFK, the excitement immediately drained and the reality of not seeing my parents for the next 3 and a bit weeks hit. I wasn't too thrilled about saying goodbye to them and it's always nice to leave on a good note. So I apologised for giving Mom a hard time while she was in manic packing mode. We're super tight and this would be the longest we had ever spent apart. I told myself it would be good preparation for college, but I was nervous. I could tell my parents were anxious too, so I broke the ice and started to talk about their trip. I gave them stern warnings not to eat anything from the carts on the side of the road and cautioned them not to post any swimwear shots on Facebook.

Nobody wants the whole world to see their parents like that. I stepped out of the cab. Mom and Dad grabbed my bag and guitar from the trunk. We hugged. We hugged again. At one point I thought the cab driver was going to join in!

'Whatever you do, enjoy yourself. Be polite. Don't get arrested or anyone pregnant,' Mom said before I grabbed my bags. I told her to have more confidence in the 87% I gave her last year for her parenting skills. (Yes it's a real thing we do - Mom read it on a lifestyle blog and it's now an annual feature of my life.) One last hug and Mom and Dad split for another terminal. I gulped, waved them off before I put my headphones in, pressed play on my travel playlist and pulled my suitcase towards the check-in desk.

Waiting for the plane to board I flicked through *Tyler's Guide to Ireland* and sent out a few last minute texts to Patrick, R, Alex and Mom and Dad. From my seat on the plane I finger waved goodbye to what I could see of the Manhattan skyline. An architectural wonder, backdrop to so many movies. Iconic. Home. I gulped again.

'First trip away from home?'

'Yeah.'

'You'll be fine kid. I was your age when I first left home too. For 'Nam.'

These words of comfort came from Old Man Chris from Ohio. Turned out he was an ex-jumper for the US Air Force and a complete hero. He had jumped 76 times - literally a master of his trade - and he had the medals to prove it. On three occasions he had been separated from his corps deep in enemy territory in Vietnam. All three times he made it back to them; once via a village of friendly locals where he joked that he may have a son. I knew it wasn't a joke. He showed me his old photos. The guy had been a babe magnet. Even now, Chris felt like a Viet hero. His tired eyes came alive when he told me his stories; the gravelly tone of his voice echoed an illustrious history and when I saw the way he shuffled to the bathroom, I felt the weight of every landing that his now shot knees had absorbed. And to think he was my age out there!

Before he told me his war stories, he had given me his lengthy health history. A cancer survivor, Chris now had one lung, and was taking numerous meds to stay alive. He knew he was going to die soon and as a result was flying without insurance. But this was his last chance to say his goodbyes to a lifelong family friend who owned a castle on the west coast of Ireland. The friend had paid for his flight over. The castle was in a place called Dun-nay-gaul or Dongle. I couldn't make it out.

For all I knew he was going to Dublin for a jolly, getting jacked up on all things Irish, before flying home with a suitcase filled with everything green. I didn't know what part of his story to believe until he asked me to reach up and get him his pills. Chris opened his little daily box and threw a handful of them into his mouth. Then I believed his entire story. I listened to his rasping breath and thought about what I would do if he stopped breathing. So I decided not to snooze on the plane journey. I didn't want to wake up to a Cold Old Man Chris resting on my shoulder.

Somewhere over the Atlantic he showed me the wrinkled tattoos on his forearms and told me the adventures that came with them. He was an expert storyteller and filled our time with tall tales and laughter. While we ate our plastic airplane food, he told me one thing that really stuck with me.

'You know, son, I've lived a really interesting life. But that was a choice. I could have lived a boring life. I could have joined the rat race. I could have simply existed, you know, as a meaningless ghost. But when I joined the Air Force I had to decide to live every day, as I knew every time I faced combat it could have been my last on this beautiful messed up planet. Live your life son.'

I knew he hadn't heard of *Rihanna*, so he wasn't quoting the pop princess. I let him listen to one of her tracks. He liked it. He showed me another tattoo, Live your life, *vivet anima tua*, inscribed in Latin on his forearm. Gauging by the wrinkle coverage and faded nature of the ink, I knew these words had been inked onto his skin long before Rihanna had been born.

Chris was so interesting that I skipped watching one of the inflight movies, *Iron Man*. Sorry *Tony* but I was sitting beside my own superhero! At baggage claim I helped Chris grab his suitcase. We said our goodbyes and gave each other manly backslaps. I was worried about slapping him too hard in case I wrecked his good lung, so after one heavy slap I gave him a little pat on the shoulder. I waited for my bag and guitar and watched this legend of a man shuffle away, knowing that he was going to live to fight a few more days. *Dongle be kind to him*, I said to myself.

FROUSINS

I *was hoping for Bono but Tyler Sontoro will do*

Patrick popped his head out from behind this larger than life sign that greeted me as I came through customs at the arrivals section of Dublin Airport. It was some welcome! The bright red sign, complete with hand painted shamrocks and an American flag caught everyone's attention. Patrick (brown messy hair/stubbly beard/grey hoody/blue eyes) was wearing a mischievous grin that took over his face.

'HEYYYYYYYYYYYYYY Tyler!'

'HEYYYYYYYYYYYYYY Patrick!' I ran towards him. We hugged it out.

'That sign is amazing!'

'Cheers. It's the edited version! Come on, we gotta shift or we'll be charged for an extra hour's parking!'

Patrick grabbed my suitcase before we power-walked to the

car. Semi-jogging across the skybridge that connected the terminal to the parking garage, I indulged in some people-watching and listened out for Irish accents. And I also started to think about what the un-edited version of the sign read! When we got to the car, a beat up VW, we jammed my luggage and guitar case into the trunk, or boot, as Patrick called it, and screeched out of the parking garage.

Sitting in the passenger seat, tired and a little smelly from travelling, I couldn't believe that after seven months of saving, thinking, researching and trans-Atlantic chats with Patrick, I was finally in Ireland. I was journey-worn and bleary-eyed but, even at 8am Irish time, I was alert enough to know that Patrick was going the wrong way.

'Patrick, the sign says Belfast is that way.'

'Sure does brother, but remember we aren't going to The Shaft just yet! We have our gig in Dublin to enjoy!'

'Sorry man, it's been a long journey. I totally forgot!' I said.

'By the way, I like your hair. Glad to see Oscar has redeemed himself.' Patrick said before he laughed.

'Yeah he gave me a good vacation cut!'

Driving on the left side of the road felt strange. Also strange, as we got close to downtown Dublin - there weren't any tall buildings! But the place definitely had a city vibe; the streets and sidewalks were busy, there were cabs and cyclists weaving in and out of traffic and I could see a few fellow tourists holding maps up, trying to figure out where they were. With Patrick by my side I hoped I would be an incognito tourist over the summer.

We ditched the car in a parking garage and checked into a 12-bed dorm room of a newly opened hostel right in the centre of everything. The old brick building looked well worn and shabby outside, but inside was a surprise. The place had been furnished in a minimalist style, and decorated with glass bottles and exposed concrete. Ultra cool.

The rest of the day was our own. I had researched The Fair City and my findings directed us to the coolest coffee shop in Dublin, where we sipped the flattest milkiest flat whites you could find in the city, admired everyone's beards (should I return home with one? Could I even grow one?) and planned out the rest of the day.

The city was buzzing. From the cobblestone squares of Trinity College to the Gravity Bar in the Guinness Storehouse we walked, ate and drank our way round Dublin. But the main reason we were there was my 18th birthday present from Patrick - a gig in the happening Temple Bar area, a big nightlife destination. One of Patrick's favourite artists was over from the US. Granda's influence has rubbed off onto Patrick and, just like me, he is a massive muso, so we were excited to see how the Irish crowd would take to this little-known star.

After our pre-gig dinner of BBQ pulled pork and fries, we made our way to the venue. I'd forgotten the legal age for getting into bars and having a drink is 18, not 21 like at home, when the burly bouncer laughed at the picture on my driving licence and then let me into the packed club as the support played their last song.

Earlier we had discussed gig etiquette. Patrick told me his

one golden rule. 'Don't talk to me during the gig. If I want to say anything I'll speak to you.'

I replied to his selfish statement with loaded questions, such as, 'What if I want to buy you a drink?'

'Easy. Guinness all night.'

'What if someone wants your number?'

'You have it, so you can give it to them.'

'What if someone can't see past you and wants you to move?'

'They can wiggle past me. Or find somewhere else to stand!'

Experiencing the gig was a blast and a half. It was a rowdy crowd. After the opening few songs most people put their cell phones away and joined us dancing. The set went by with a blur. The encore turned into a mess of singing, jumping bodies, a shower of drinks and a crowd yelling their hearts out to one of their Internet idols.

With the gig a memory, we hit Temple Bar in search of some late night revelry. It was weird that it was still light out at 11. We pub-crawled and managed to avoid the macho-looking stag parties and the groups of tourists who had sampled way too much of the local hooch. We settled in one of the clubs along the cobbled main drag. Returning from a trip to the men's room, I found Patrick in the middle of the dance floor, surrounded by ladies who were on a hen party. Patrick used his prize possession and talking point - his American cousin - and brought me into the conversation.

'Hey!' one of the girls shouted at me.

'Hey. What's your name?'

'Shauna. You?'

'Tyler.'

'Where you from?'

'New York.'

'Coooool - so am I!'

'You serious?' Her fake Noo Yawk accent was pretty terrible.

'No, I'm pulling your leg!'

So I tested out a local expression: 'You're taking the mick, right?'

'Aye! Just having you on!' she laughed. Turns out she was from Belfast.

We yelled small talk at each other over the music and swapped slang. I asked her to translate some expressions I noticed Patrick using. She told me that 'wee buns' means 'that's easy', a 'slanging match' was not what we were having, but actually an argument or 'row' and 'melter' means 'someone who puts your head away.' I had to Google to translate her translation. Despite Mom's Irish roots there were some phrases that I just couldn't understand! We awkwardly danced with these ladeeez until they found out our ages. But instead of being a turn-off, the women started cracking jokes and teased me about my young looks. Shauna told me I would be a heartbreaker on my trip and kept saying I was *as cute as a button.*

At around 2.30am, exhausted, and having enjoyed my crash course test on the meaning of the term wingman, we stumbled back across the ornate, iron Ha'penny pedestrian Bridge which spans the Liffey River. By the time we got back to the hostel, dawn was already starting to break! But that would not stop me falling asleep to the sound of other people snoring, sniffing and two people, errr, awkwardly getting it on. In case you ever wondered - people can always hear you. Only 24 hours earlier, I had been sitting on my front step, waiting for the taxi to arrive. Now I was lying on a mattress in a Dublin hostel drifting off as Pedro from Brasil snored his head off and Olivia from the Czech Republic and Carlos from Argentina whispered sweet nothings in each other's ears.

During this trip I have planned to write something down at the end of each day. You know, a highlight or a thought that I could write a poem or a song about at some stage. I even bought a new notebook to record the memories of my trip. Fighting to keep my eyes open and realising my notebook was in the car, I made a note on my phone, partly inspired by Old Man Chris:

Throw away any idea that you know what each day will bring. Enjoy the surprise. Live for the unknown.

On my first night in Ireland I fell asleep fully exhilarated by the conversations I had enjoyed, Dublin's history, the creamy Guinness and the lyrics from the gig. I nodded off with a happy heart, tired, and for the first time in my life, feeling a slightly fuzzy head.

WE'LL BE GRAND

By the time I rolled out of bed, Pedro had packed up his stuff and left for France. Olivia and Carlos were still sharing a bed and some Asian ladies were getting changed right in front of my eyes. Like right in front of my eyes! I can honestly say I had never slept in a room like it before.

After checking out of the hostel, we devoured one of Dublin's, sorry man's, finest fries. It was my first, but definitely not last 'Full Irish' of the trip. The fry consisted of white toast, wheaten bread, two fried eggs, baked beans, mushrooms, bacon, two sausages, a grilled tomato and black and white pudding, served with bottomless tea. They love tea over here. I couldn't see my feet after polishing off the monstrous amount of food. Well not quite, but I was really stuffed!

We took a mid-morning stroll through St Stephen's Green and enjoyed the efforts of the incredible street performers on

Grafton Street. Mimes, musicians, magicians, soloists and bands, some attracting a huge circle of onlookers. I was wondering how much money these guys made on a busy Saturday, but Patrick seemed anxious to hit the motorway. I was sort of annoyed. We had nothing to do for the next 3 weeks and he was rushing us out of one of the greatest cities in the world. Once we got our gear from the hostel, we headed for the car and were on our way again.

'Patrick.'

'Yeah.'

'I don't mean to be *that* passenger, but you're going the wrong way ... again.' I pointed to a sign on the opposite side of the motorway that was now a blur in the distance.

'I know,' Patrick replied with a laugh. 'You're an inquisitive wee cousin aren't ya?' I joined in with an unconvincing chuckle before he explained himself.

'I thought we could do a whistle-stop tour of the island. Just a few days. That OK with you? Or do you have other plans?'

'No, I have no plans.'

'We're gonna have to work on your sarcasm.'

'Ehh, yeah, sure man. Is Aunt Beth cool with it?'

'You're not used to total freedom are you? You're 18 now! Enjoy it! Besides, work is mental for Mum and Dad ATM, so they will appreciate the space. Even they know you can't come to Ireland and stay up north all summer. There's so much to see down here.'

'Have you done this trip before?' I asked.

'Ehhh sort of.'

'What do you mean, sort of?'

'When I was small, we came to a few places down here on a summer holiday.'

'So you know your way around then?'

'Yeah for sure. We'll be grand. I mean I was only about seven, but sure things will come back to me. Sometimes you just have to be spontaneous. That's when the craic is best!'

Unconvinced of his answer, but happy to go with the flow, I reached into the glove compartment and found a battered, tea-stained road map. Patrick asked to have a jook. It was barely in his hand before he chucked it out the window.

'We don't need that my friend. Intuition, road signs and the spirit of discovery will be our guide for the next few days!'

I tried to grab the map. Americans don't do throwing trash out of the car. But my efforts were useless. Through the rear view mirror I watched the map flap helplessly at the side of the road. 'We're going to have to pull over and go back and get the map. It's littering.'

'OK maybe I shouldn't have thrown the map out. That was daft. But I can't stop on the motorway. Tell you what; I'll sponsor a tree to make up for it. Make that two trees and a large shrub.'

'Deal.' I reached for my iPod, scrolled through a playlist and hit play on my *Rap Diddly Brapp* playlist before I asked, 'By the way, what's a shrub?'

Awesome tune after disturbingly awesome tune pumped through the sound system for the rest of this beautiful early summer's day as we cruised the coastal road to Cork. Taking the long way, we stopped for lunch in Wexford, sipped tea from crystallllll cups in Waterford, and took a selfie beside the sign for Youghal - 'cos the name of that place is something else.

We pulled into Cork city that evening and, tripping with tiredness, found somewhere to eat. The previous night's partying on top of the long drive, flight and jetlag had caught up with me. So we decided to have a cultural evening. After splitting a seafood platter for two, we sat in a 'wee' bar and had the craic* with the locals. We attempted Céilí dance steps (badly) to a trad band. I tried to do rhythm section on the bodhrán and played some of the other strange instruments during one of the band's breaks, before we said our goodbyes and fell asleep in our makeshift bedroom (the car).

After the most uncomfortable night's sleep I have ever had, we woke up to a beautiful sunrise and a knock on the window from the Gardai. The nordy licence plate and the steamed up windows were enough to raise suspicion amongst the cops. They gave us a stern telling off for snoozing in a no parking zone and then sent us on our way. I honestly had no idea what they said; their sing-song accents and rapid-fire speech were indecipherable to my American ears. Patrick had problems understanding too.

Making the most of our unexpected early start, we rallied over the country roads, round part of the Ring of Kerry, before we arrived at Killarney National Park. We walked around the park, scrounged dinner off some German campers and set up Patrick's tent amongst the birds, the bees and some really tall trees. Then we hung out round the fire with our new friends until the sun disappeared at nearly midnight, which was so strange for me - it gets dark by 9pm at the latest at home. On my walk to the tent, I was still trying to process the Germans' inspirational travel stories. Over the years they had chalked off 67 countries; slept everywhere from railroad carriages to high rise penthouse suites and eaten everything from tarantulas to alligator burgers. #travellife

With another sunrise wake-up call, courtesy of a few noisy birds, we embarked on a breathtaking early morning hike in the forest park before we took The Wild Atlantic Way coastal route up to Galway. Our bashed up VW passed through quaint little villages containing little else than whitewashed cottages, a pub and a church. Along the way we saw spluttering tractors carrying bales of freshly cut hay and to my delight I even spotted a horse and cart and a thatched roofed cottage! A couple of times cows and sheep blocked the road and we had to wait for the sheepdog to herd the animals along to the next field. Such experiences all made for awesome Instagram posts. I couldn't get over how beautiful Ireland was turning out to be. The narrow, twisting roads and the dramatically different views around every bend raised the hairs on the back of my neck. Patrick took the stunning scenery for granted, but my heart was awakened every time I caught a glimpse of the sea or a new mountain peak.

The West of Ireland is wild, beautiful, rugged, wave-and-wind-lashed. Standing on The Cliffs of Moher, with the sea crashing against the rocks below and the salty Atlantic breeze fanning my face, it was like nothing I had ever experienced. I felt like I was perched on the edge of the world. Home was over three thousand miles away, but in that moment I realised that, for the next few weeks, home was wherever joy bubbled up from my soul. That was when, in a flash of inspiration, I came up with a name for my next EP - *Songs from The Island*.

Walking back to the car I burst into laughter as I remembered this was one of the places that Rodriguez had placed a Mini-R. I ran and grabbed the book from the car and got Patrick to take a photo of me pointing to Mini-R on my travel guide!

We managed to make it to Galway by around 8 where we experienced the famed friendliness of the people of this city, and free pints of beer (we played the American card and I played a spontaneous set which got us in good with a pub owner). Patrick now thinks he is my agent. After listening to hilarious stories and for the first time, the Irish language, we moved on to a jazz bar, where, hearing our plans to snooze in the car, one of the staff let us sleep in his spare room in exchange for a bed/couch/floor if he ever came to NYC. Apparently couch surfing is a great way to see the world!

Next morning though, the party was over. Patrick was slumped over, sitting on the edge of his bed staring at his smartphone.

'So where to next, Patrick?'

'Ermm. Belfast. I need to get home.'

* craic. Not crack (cocaine) but craic (banter, fun, laughter, joking around). It's an Irish word that they use a lot.

GREEN GRASS UNDER MY FEET

It wasn't until we were back in the car and on the road before he let me in on what was going on.

'Didn't want to tell you earlier, but today is the day I get my exam results,' Patrick began. 'I failed two modules.'

'That is a bummer!' I exclaimed, unable to hide my surprise and feeling I had to say something, but whatever I said was probably going to sound stupid. The family was always going on about how bright and high achieving Patrick was. He was studying medicine at one of the top schools in the UK and the course was almost impossible to get accepted into.

'Too much partying?'

'Something like that. I'm so so sorry Tyler.' Patrick looked devastated.

'Sorry for what?'

'You know, cutting this trip short … and everything. One fail would be OK, but two means I have to get back.'

'Never mind that! You didn't say you were finding medicine tough.' I realised this was the first opportunity Patrick and I had to talk since I arrived in Ireland. We'd been so busy meeting people, getting lost on the narrow twisty roads, having a laugh and thinking about where we would sleep next, that there was just no space to have a heart to heart. Who would have ever thought Patrick was going through so much suspense and anxiety all this time? Maybe that was what Mom and Beth had been talking about?

'Yeah … I didn't want to put you off coming over. I thought I'd get through my exams,' said Patrick. 'Well I hoped I would. Can't say I'm surprised, really. I was sure I'd fail Anatomy. But *two*!' He rubbed a hand across his forehead.

'What does that mean? What happens now?' I asked.

'I don't know. Failing one module happens all the time but two, that's a problem, a big problem.' He was lost in thought. 'I knew I'd be in trouble if the gall bladder came up, but I thought I'd breeze through Disease and Treatment.'

I couldn't really comment, knowing nothing about either topic.

'I guess that changes our plans for the summer.' I said.

Instantly Patrick's face fell even further.

Oh no. I had said the wrong thing and tried to rescue the situation. 'But that's cool! I'm OK! Don't worry about me,' I spluttered. 'I'll find plenty of stuff to do.'

I glanced across at Patrick. He was focusing on the road.

He looked broken.

The journey from Galway to the north was a quiet one. Patrick had planned to take me to Enniskillen and a few other places on the way home, but we stopped only at the 'Welcome to Northern Ireland' sign at one of the border crossings for a much anticipated yet not so smiley selfie.

To break the silence, I played some music that I thought he wouldn't have heard yet. Patrick only spoke a couple of times. One of the times was to ask me not to mention his exam results around his parents. The poor guy had to be dreading returning home to his folks with the bad news. I shared his discomfort. The family had been so thrilled and proud when he got accepted into med school. Eventually Pat picked up a bit and asked me about my college course - I'm hoping to major in English Literature. I knew he was being polite and I tried to stifle the excitement I had about college life.

Pat had turned off his phone, using the excuse that he was driving, but I think he wanted to avoid any phone calls from friends and classmates who had passed all their tests. His only call was to his folks, to say we were going to be home a couple of days early. I could hear their excited voices over the phone.

We arrived safe in the arms of Aunt Beth and Uncle Richard that afternoon. Five days and 745 miles later and I had made it to suburban Belfast, my home for the next 3 weeks. As we parked the VW in front of the house, we saw Pat's parents' cars already there. Patrick put on his game face and walked up to the front door.

I hadn't expected Aunt Beth or Uncle Richard to be home when we arrived, but Richard had been able to get out of work early and Aunt Beth teaches little kids so she was just in the door herself. Pat used me as an excuse for our early arrival back in Belfast – something feeble about jet lag and not packing enough underwear to last the week. It wouldn't have convinced me, but my aunt and uncle were too excited to care.

Telling me to consider their place my home for the summer, Beth gave me a tour of the house. Coming from an apartment in the heart of Manhattan there was so much to get used to. Stairs were the first thing! Then they had a garage, a sunroom, a garden and patio. Their own private outdoors! An identical house was attached to theirs side by side. They called the arrangement a semi-d. A duplex to us Americans. It might sound silly, but that summer I loved being able to walk barefoot from the kitchen to the garden. Aunt Beth explained the house was in a very handy location, just a couple of miles from the city centre so it would be 'a doddle' for me to get around by bike, bus, or even 'shank's mare'. Translation: walking!

Over the rest of the afternoon Uncle Richard kept joking around and would periodically hit me on the arm as he said, repeatedly, 'It's so good to have you here! Can you believe he's finally here?' Aunt Beth was busy in the kitchen and on the phone probably telling all my relations I had arrived safely, but every so often she would come over to me and give me little squeezes on the cheek. It was cute, but kinda sore.

I unpacked and familiarised myself with the house and garden, before I heard the doorbell and ten seconds later a choir of voices. I walked down the stairs and was greeted by a big

'SURPRISE!' from loads of my relatives (some that I didn't even recognise!). I hadn't realised it was dinner time - a family BBQ in my honour. Aunt Beth had managed to rustle up the food and the whole clan at short notice, which was pretty impressive, as the family party was supposed to be a couple of days from now – our original arrival date. She'd prepared a great spread of your typical cookout food - burgers, corn on the cob, chicken and lots of different types of salad. They like their mayo here! And their desserts! Every guest seemed to bring a different cake!

As the night went on, Granny and what seemed like several dozen other relatives would come over and examine me and then have big discussions among themselves about how much I looked like my mom, or some Great Uncle. Yes, I did feel like a zoo animal, but it was fun to see them all and they didn't stare at me for too long. Very soon we were chatting and joking together just like my Italian extended famiglia.

The highlight of the evening has to be when Uncle David (Mom's brother), tried to run away from a bee, tripped over a bucket, and in an attempt to save himself, reached out, grabbed some washing that was on the line and pulled the whole thing, clothes and all, down. He ended up flat on his back in the middle of the garden with all sorts of sheets and underpants around him.

More hilarity came when I shared some of the crazier moments of the trip, such as running out of diesel just outside a little town in The Burren.

Picture this: Patrick and I are in the middle of an isolated stony moonscape in the middle of rural Ireland. Thanks to Patrick's map malfunction on the outskirts of Dublin, we had no idea how to get to Galway and we ended up on what must have been Ireland's longest gas station-free route. Chug, chug, cough, shudder, dead. In the middle of nowhere! Our only option was to try and flag down the nearest farmer. Two hours later Patrick, a friendly farmer and I were all squeezed into the cab of his mud-splattered 1980's Massey Ferguson tractor. Instead of bringing us to the nearest gas station, he brought us back to his place, where he filled up a plastic container with his special diesel and fed us a massive helping of ground beef and potatoes that could have satisfied an entire NFL team. After many cups of tea - with cake - Brendan and his wife Eileen fixed us a travel package crammed with edible goodies for the rest of our journey. I think we could have sailed on a 2-week voyage across the Atlantic on the amount of grub she gave us.

Then there had been our German campsite friends. Or Campsite Gerta, as Patrick had nicknamed the lady who told us about her experiences dining on bugs on toast, and rôtisserie guinea pig in Peru. I told Aunt Beth about meeting Slaggin' Shauna in the Dublin bar and our dance-off at a Dublin chipper in the early hours of the morning with a group of guys who had just finished their 'school leavers' exams. I had to ask them what that meant because my high school never had final exams like that. A couple of weeks of 3-hour tests? That sounded pretty intense and I considered myself lucky to have escaped that kind of stress.

The banter around the table was fun, everyone seemed really relaxed, and the nice weather helped. I had stopped thinking about Patrick's exam results until Tommy, one of Beth and Richard's lifelong neighbours, asked us why we hadn't stopped in Enniskillen.

Patrick was getting another burger from the grill. 'Oh. Ermm we just wanted to get home to see you guys! There's a festival later in the summer so, uh, I though, uh, like, we'd save Fermanagh until then.' I knew Patrick was lying, but did anyone else see through his awkward body language and spluttering response?

My favourite guest at the cookout was Granny. We were so happy to see each other. She had brought round a selection of sweet treats, including her famous homemade lemon drizzle cake. As dessert was being served, I disappeared to my room and came back laden with presents for the family. Those extra key-rings and mugs Dad had told me to get turned out to be handy for the surprise guests at the cookout. Despite everything, Patrick could not help being a little bit excited about his iPad Air. Everyone left around 11.30pm - an early night for an Irish family gathering, even on a Tuesday!

I started to help tidy up but Beth told me to go to bed.

'Thanks. I'm totally bushed.'

'Oh I'm sure. Plus Patrick needs an early night. He gets his exam results tomorrow.' Beth tapped her finger on her wall calendar. Neatly written in the square for Wed, June 18, was the reminder: *P's Results*. She'd gotten the day wrong! Today, Tues, June 17 had been results day. I didn't know what to say.

'Ehhh I'm sure he will do great. He always does,' I managed to stammer out before I made for the bedroom.

Despite the house being a generous size, Patrick and I were sharing a room over the summer. Granny had been sleeping over a lot more lately. Being on her own and not as able as she used to be, it was easier for her to stay with the family a few nights a week. So the old spare room had been turned into a space for Granny, and when she wasn't there, an office for Patrick to study in peace and quiet. As two only children it was going to be an experiment, but we looked forward to the kind of goofing off we'd missed out on, not having brothers. But that night nobody was in a horsing around kind of mood. Patrick turned in pretty much right away without much comment.

Very quietly I changed for bed and worked out that we had driven the equivalent of NYC to Chicago - give or take a few miles. Now that's a whim I wouldn't have entertained in the good ole U S of A. So I grabbed my journal and wrote the following in my nightly notes:

> *It was billed as a 1200 km detour, but when you stand on the top of a cliff, climb a mountain, play a gig and get lost in the wild rural Irish landscape it's not a detour, but a life-tour!*

The smell of the fresh clean sheets and the bliss of a comfy mattress combined and as my head hit the pillow, sleep simply happened.

HOW NOW BROWN COW

Patrick's In No Particular Order Top ~~30~~ 31ish Things
To Do In Northern Ireland

1. Cycle along the Lagan
2. Make candy at Aunt Sandra's
3. The Ulster Museum
4. Game of Thrones tour
5. Belfast City Hall & Stormont
6. The Northern Trinity - The Giants Causeway/Carrick-a-Re-de/Bushmills Distillery
7. The Other Northern Trinity - Beaches/Surfing/Barry's
8. The Crown Liquor Saloon
9. The view from the top of the old Library at Queens (don't ask how we get up there)
10. The Ulster Folk and Transport Museum
11. A round of golf

12. Titanic exhibit

13. Lean against the Albert Clock & dance through the fountains

14. Go To Church - St Anne's Cathedral, St. Malachy's Church & St. Peter's Cathedral

15. Belfast Zoo

16. Say hi to Nuala with the Hula

17. St George's Market

18. Carrickfergus Castle

19. Rathlin Island

20. Camping in the Mourne Mountains – Silent Valley, Tollymore and Castlewellan (get lost in the maze)

21. The Glens of Antrim

22. The Tayto factory

23. Black taxi tour of Peace Walls & murals

24. Crumlin Road Prison

25. Strangford Lough, especially the ferry

26. W5 with our younger cousins

27. Caving in Enniskillen

28. The Walled City

29. St. Patrick's first church and grave

30. Fish and chips at Long's & java in a few trendy coffee shops

31. Sunrise at the top of the Cavehill

Patrick was hyped the next morning. It wasn't long after Beth and Richard had left for a Pilates class before work when Patrick announced he had a surprise for me. So we quickly got ready and went out for a morning bike ride on a path alongside the banks of the River Lagan. Then over a bear-sized break-fast in South Belfast, he showed me his surprise - the list.

Having eaten half of a double egg soda with a side of beans, Patrick laid out his *'Top 30 31ish Tourist Attractions In Northern Ireland'*. As he talked me through all the stuff we hoped to cover in the next 2 1/2 weeks, he mimicked his dad's nagging soundtrack from the months of April and May: 'Tyler has saved a lot of his own money for this trip, so you better make it worth his while. I will be so embarrassed if Esther finds out Tyler hasn't had a good time with us. You better plan a great summer for your cousin.'

As a result Patrick had compiled an amazing itinerary, which would take us on another crazy race, or three, around the island - the Northern part of it anyway. We had talked in the spring about things to do and I had given him some thoughts about the places that were top of my list, but Patrick had really done his homework. This time he was hoping to hit all of the best tourist attractions (according to him) in Northern Ireland. The list ranged from visiting the spectacular - Mourne mountain range, to the thirst quenching - drinking the finest milkshakes available in Belfast (I did remind him us Yanks invented milkshakes so I was doubtful his faves would even come close). But I was stoked that food and drink were going to be a big part of the plan. And I was really looking forward to tasting some Irish foods.

Even though Northern Ireland is not huge, I had to wonder how we would squeeze so much into my vacation, but Patrick was confident. He said we might not have a lot of time in each place, but we needed to *hit it like it was hot*. That's when I knew the impact of failing his exams hadn't hit Pat yet. I didn't know what happened when a student bombs out on major tests, but I was guessing there would have to be some meetings to try and work it all out. And maybe a lot of hitting the books if he was allowed to retake the tests. And before that there was telling his folks! So I was expecting to visit a few of these attractions by myself. Not that I would tell Pat that.

Yours truly still trying to figure out what some of the more bizarrely-named attractions were, we crossed the road, chained our bikes up and walked through the front doors of the Ulster Museum at around 10.30. Brutalistic 1960's architecture had been given a new lease of life after a multi-million pound re-furb, and the result was an amazing museum that wouldn't be out of place in NYC. We found Pete the polar bear, a really old airplane, a taxidermist's heaven, stones and rocks from another galaxy and tags and sprays from a visiting graffiti artist. And a mummy. During the visit I also picked up many interesting facts about the history of Northern Ireland and noted a few minor updates to *Tyler's Guide to Ireland*.

The trip to the museum was as much an excuse to use and abuse their air conditioning (it was actually sunny and hot out!), as it was an opportunity to check a couple of places off our list. The exhibits were sweet, and I was so glad the heat (not the cops) had forced us inside. But if the morning had been about the past, the afternoon was all about the future.

We met a few of Patrick's college friends for a picnic lunch on the grass at Botanic Gardens; an oasis for students and residents of the University area. Colourful flowers and shrubs line the walkways and fill the beds and borders of the park. Daisies are sprinkled across the lawns. There are amazing historic greenhouses, over 150 years old, including a steamy tropical ravine! And the museum overlooks it all. Handy!

Patrick played it cool with his friends when they asked him about his results. He dodged giving a definite answer and told the group that he, 'needed to have a wee chat with a couple of lecturers.' Some of the guys raised their eyebrows to indicate they knew what he was being so cryptic about. But then, in a ploy to change the direction of the conversation, Pat began to tell the group some of our travel stories. It worked! A couple of his friends were heading off travelling for the summer and were so relieved they didn't have to repeat any exams and cut their adventures short. Patrick was surprisingly good at hiding his failure.

Sunshine meant the park was crammed. Office workers hid in the green nooks, stealing shade and a few extra minutes for their lunch break. Pensioners and professors were lining up at an ice cream van to buy 99s. 99s? The guys told me that 99s are ice cream cones topped with a mountain of soft serve vanilla ice cream, raspberry sauce and a flaky chocolate bar. They said that learning how to eat a 99 before it thaws and drips all over your clothes is a rite of passage that every kid in Northern Ireland has to master before their 10th birthday! Pat also had me believing I only had 99 seconds to eat the thing before meltdown!

As I unsuccessfully tried it out for myself, school kids wearing Harry Potteresque uniforms sat near us in groups on the grass eating their lunch. Back home, school had already been out for the summer for a few weeks, and most schools don't have uniforms, so it was weird to see kids in blazers and ties, and in June!

Students had taken part in a sunshine-inspired coup d'état of the large open grassy space in the middle of the park. For many of them Botanic Gardens was a place of carefree laughter - celebrating passing exams and getting the grades they wanted. For others, graduation and the stomach-churning thought of job hunting and entering the big bad world of employment, was an imminent reality. And probably among all the laughing students were people like Patrick, pretending everything was OK and trying to hide their bad news from their happy, relieved friends.

All morning I had been trying to cheer Patrick up. He'd tried to fake it, but had been in a terrible mood since we had arrived back from our road trip. I kept telling him it was only a few exams, but his downer frame of mind wouldn't shift. And what did I really know? I hadn't started college yet and this was a different country with a totally different system. Plus he was a medical student; there was massive pressure and expectation on him, from school, family and himself.

So we hung out at the park for a few hours. Tyler keeping up the happy face. Patrick keeping up the fake-happy face. Chilling, kicking a soccer ball around, eating ice cream and playing a rather noisy and rowdy game of Ultimate Frisbee.

And that's when something happened that changed the direction of my trip. Call it fate, call it design, call it a misplaced Frisbee, a sunny day, a bungling boy and a gorgeous girl. Whatever ... I'm going to call it a game changer.

'Tyler, go long!' Patrick shouted. A park packed full of people; I should have read his play. Patrick had his strong arm on and launched the Frisbee miles over my head. I sprinted after the slim plastic circle. My eyes were focused on snapping the thin bit of yellow plastic out of the air.

'I got it! I got it!' I shouted as I launched myself into the air and made a solid attempt to snatch the Frisbee. It was just out of reach and skimmed my fingertips. I crashed to the ground with a rib-cracking thud and lay flat on the grass. I closed my eyes for a few seconds before I rolled over and brushed off my pride. When I opened my eyes I realised I had landed in the most intimidating circle I had ever been in. I looked up and counted them. One, two, three, four, nine. I had crash-landed in the middle of a group of *nine* college girls. They had been enjoying a sunbathing-gossip-magazine-reading-fruit-eating picnic until I spectacularly dived into their midst, knocking over two water bottles and flattening a bunch of bananas.

I spent what felt like a century, but in reality was a few seconds, plotting my next move. Should I get up, rescue the Frisbee and act like nothing had happened? Make some sort of semi-funny joke to cover my embarrassment? Or answer the question that interrupted my inner train of thought:

'Hey, is this yours?'

I'm sure my cheeks were as red as some of the roses in the park. When I looked up to see who had asked the most obvious of questions, I was spellbound. The girl before me was beautiful. Not for the first time, I thought of my life as a movie. It was *The Meet*. The scene would pan out to record the reactions of onlookers as they witnessed my slow-motion over-enthusiastic dive. The group of guys would be pointing and laughing. The director would capture the girls' reactions as I crash-landed in the middle of their group and spilled their lunches everywhere. Then the director would catch the most important interaction of the day. The camera would zoom in as one of the girls flicked her hair off her shoulders, removed her oversized sunglasses, smiled, made eye contact with me and asked, 'Hey, is this yours?'

Then a long gap in the soundtrack as everyone waits for my reaction.

A high-pitched 'Ermm yeah' came out and brought my film thoughts back to reality. #totesembarrassing

One of the other girls spoke, 'Ohhhhh, you're not from round here are you?'

'Ehhh no. I'm from New York.'

'New York you say.'

'Yeah. In America.'

'As opposed to the other New York in Pakistan?' she said.

The whole group laughed. I didn't know what to say. Had she just made a joke? I had a feeling they were laughing at me. The girls continued to talk a mile a minute. Some of them adopted New York accents for words like *coffee, hot dawg, Central Park*, and named other landmarks in my native accent. Then they added in references from TV shows. I just sat there feeling somewhat confused but patiently waiting for it to end, trying to clean up the mess I had made and trying not to correct the *Chuck Bass* quotes they were murdering. In reality I was flattered they would liken me to a hunk like *Chuck*. So at first I faked some spontaneous laughter. But their dodgy accent routine was starting to get old, and I was feeling pretty damp too from all the spilled water. I gave it five minutes before I interrupted their impression reel.

'You girls need to work on your accents! Sorry about the Frisbee.'

A girl who sat behind me replied, 'No worries. Just tell Patrick to be more careful next time.'

'Patrick. You know him?'

'Yeah I know him.' She sounded unimpressed. 'Don't tell me you're related to him?'

'We're cousins.'

'I knew perfection had to have a flaw.'

Her friends laughed. I joined them. There was an awkward pause when I should have said goodbye, but I lingered, and finally, with a burst of courage asked them to join us in our game of Ultimate Frisbee. They agreed; some more eagerly than others, I noticed.

If my face showed pure fear when I entered the group of girls, the reaction of the guys was one of total astonishment when I walked towards them with the Frisbee and nine girls in tow. Now the summer had started!

The two groups became one and we spent the rest of the day together. One of the Irish clichés of clichés is that everyone knows or is related to one another. Rodriguez highlighted this to me in a series of memes in his guidebook. But, there is truth in the memes. Belfast being Belfast, the guys and girls recognised each other from the corridors of university and the dance floors of the local clubs. These free spirits were semi-strangers one minute; then had cousins and copious amounts of friends in common the next.

Later in the afternoon someone suggested we head to Shaw's Bridge for a cookout. Some of the group cycled over and others crammed into two cars, stopping on the way at a supermarket to grab meat, bread and drinks. We met at Freddy's Steps before finding a spot where it would be OK to have a BBQ. Then we grilled up and talked into the night in one of the most beautiful parts of Belfast, until dusk meant lights out.

I was getting along well with the girls and got my revenge on them mimicking my accent by asking them to say, 'How now brown cow.' Honestly their attempts were hilarious. Their accent made the words sound so different!

By now Patrick was worn out from the effort of acting like everything was normal and had given up trying to do the happy face thing. He seemed less interested in mixing with the girls and more comfortable hanging with his mates, but that was OK. But when people started comparing exam results, he took off by himself. One of the girls asked me why he had vanished and seemed down. I made up a lame excuse, figuring the less information, the more believable.

'Bike lock hassles.'

'You never know with Patrick when he disappears,' smiled Conor, who seemed to be his best friend. 'He could be planning a prank!'

Not this time I thought as I laughed along with the group.

But let's get down to the really unforgettable thing (for me anyway) about that night! From the park to the forest, my mind was captured by one of the girls – let's call her Frisbee Girl. She was like 5ft 6' with wavy caramel hair, a summer sprinkling of freckles across her nose, and these deep blue eyes that had flecks of green and hazel in them. She was stunningly pretty and had a wicked fashion sense.

By the time I crashed into bed that night, she was one of a whole pile of new 'friends' I confirmed on Facebook. And I got all stupid and giddy just looking at Frisbee Girl's profile. At the cookout we had sat side by side on a log. We flirted a little (I now knew how to pick up the signs) and caught eye contact a lot during the day. I hoped I had made a connection with her. After we ate I tried to impress her by copying the other guys in lifting rocks and throwing them into The Lagan. I know, guys are pretty sad!

Frisbee Girl had a name. Tabitha. She had been kinda quiet and left early. I hoped I hadn't scared her off.

Patrick hit the lights and we avoided sleep by recapping the day.

'Who was that girl who knew you Patrick?'

'Jess,' he said sternly. Odd because he had not even said hello to her all day.

'You got history with her?'

'Yeah. Kinda.'

'What do you mean kinda?'

'Ermm I don't wanna talk about it tonight. Maybe another night. Today was too much of a good day to spoil it.'

'Oh, OK. You had a good day? You seemed like you were hating every minute of it,' I blurted, before adding, 'But I really appreciate you taking me out, and everything.'

There was an uneasy ten seconds of silence before Patrick threw his covers off, jumped onto my bed, pinned me down with his knees and just licked my face.

'Night cuz, thanks for a great day.'

'Ewwww! What the heck man?' I struggled to say back to him.

He looked me in the eyes and we both began to laugh.

'All you need to know is that Jess is a long story and I don't want to ruin your trip by boring you with the details.'

'Sure thing Pat. I'm always here to be bored by your story.'

Patrick laughed a little.

'Cheers.'

'Night.'

'Night.'

Patrick was soon snoring his head off. I was staring blankly at the ceiling, thinking of how to sum up another awesome day. My eyes were beginning to close when my iPad lit up. A notification from Tabitha!

Hey Tyler. Hope ur arms aren't 2 sore from trying 2 lift all those rocks! Today was brill. I normally don't do this. I have never done it before. Just wanted 2 say hi and see if we could maybe hook up 4 a coffee? Sorry had 2 leave early – had 2 check in on things at home. Anyway let me know.
Speak soon
Tabitha
Xx

OMG. Seriously. OMG. I wanted to wake Patrick up and ask him what to do, but I knew he needed his shuteye. Tabitha made me feel like how I'd felt with Susan, only different. Better different. A million times better different. I fell asleep smiling, thinking about Tabitha's message and trying to figure out how they had suspended that dinosaur from the ceiling of the Ulster Museum.

MURIELS

'Patrick.

'Yeah bro.'

'She wants to go on a date! Well, I think she does.'

'Am I still dreaming? Is it morning yet?'

'No and yes.'

My answer had puzzled him. He stared at me as I invaded his personal space and plonked myself down on the edge of his bed.

'OK. First of who is she? Secondly, why does she want to go on a date with you? And thirdly, what do you mean you think she wants to go on a date?' Patrick motioned the words you think with his fingers, sat up on his bed and stared out the window. Then he rubbed his face as he pondered my situation or possibly figured out if he needed the can (or loo in Pat's lingo). I read out the short message Tabitha had sent.

Patrick shifted his bleary morning eyes away from the grey day out the window and fixed them on me.

'Oh Tabitha. She's cute. And yeah man, she's keen. Stop faffin about!'

'How do I play it? What does 'faffin about' mean?' I asked.

'You know. Just go with it. Don't over think it. But play it cool. It's not as if it's gonna be anything serious.'

Patrick grabbed his phone and began to play some game. His interest in my love life lasted all of sixty seconds. But he was right. I was over-thinking it. I needed to take it easy and just see what happened. He got up and went to the bathroom. On his return I fished for more advice.

'So do I ask her where she wants to go? Or do I make the decision? Do I wait a few days before I reply?'

He laughed at my lack of dating experience. 'She's quite sporty from what I can remember. Maybe you could go for a walk by the Lagan?'

'Do you mean where we cycled yesterday?'

'Yeah.'

'Cool. I'll think about it. No I won't. I'll just do it!'

Patrick slowly shook his head at me and made a horse noise with his lips. 'You really don't have a clue about girls do you?'

I smiled and joined him in shaking my head.

He plugged his phone into the charger, sat down beside me and looked me in the eyes before launching into a pep talk. 'Put it back in her court. Say something like, 'Sounds cool. I'm busy for a few days with family stuff - you know how it is - everyone wants to see me - I'm the cool new kid in town! Maybe we can hang out after the weekend?' I think that gives a balance of confidence and enthusiasm but still leaves room to keep her guessing. By the way, just joking about the cool new kid bit. Don't use it. Seriously.'

'Good. I had my doubts about that line.'

Patrick was calculating a strategy. 'Let's see, today's Thursday. Leave it like another 24 hours. Keep her waiting for a reply. It makes you sound like you're not too keen. No one likes an eager beaver.' Pat stood.

I did have a twinge of doubt. She was gorgeous, but could I afford to waste four precious days and then only have two weeks left for anything to develop? But Pat seemed to have more experience in these matters so- 'Great advice man. I mean what do I have to lose?'

'You're such a dork,' Patrick said, before he punched me in the arm, reached to the end of my bed and grabbed a towel.

'I'm getting showered first,' he announced. He walked towards the bathroom before he popped his head back round the door

'Here Tyler.'

'Yeah.'

'I was thinking-'

'That's a first,' I interrupted.

'Touché. Anyway it just occurred to me, you probably shouldn't go on that walk at the Lagan after all. I mean it will just be the two of you and if it turns out that she's a bit of a psycho, then, well, it's just the two of you, alone, by the riverside. I mean, there are plenty of bushes to hide your body in!

Or that deep murky water!' He said it with a conviction that his imaginary sensationalist story was the next big news flash to come out of Belfast!

I just laughed at him. 'Your mind is a dangerous place.'

'If only you knew,' he winked.

That morning we toured a candy factory where we got to make our own sweets with weird & funky flavours like rhubarb & custard and blackcurrant & mint – surprisingly tasty! We chewed the results as we walked the historic streets of inner city Belfast.

Along the way I stopped to check out some paintings on the sides of people's houses. These were nothing like the fading old artwork on the sides of NYC brownstones advertising soft drinks and foods from the olden days. Instead there were old guys with long hair wearing clothes from a few hundred years ago riding white horses, soldiers carrying machine guns, illustrations of the Titanic, sports heroes, World War I stuff, faces of people I wouldn't recognise, slogans and symbols I could not figure out. Patrick said these murals, sometimes called 'Muriels' for fun, are a real Belfast tradition. They sure gave the ones in SoHo a run for their money.

Before we knew it, we were back across the Lagan River and 'downtown'. Patrick had booked us in for a tour of Belfast in the city's famous black taxis, so for the next couple of hours we sat back, enjoyed the ride and listened to the sometimes illustrious, sometimes illicit history of my mom's hometown. We saw more murals, on the peace walls built to separate neighbourhoods in conflict, and on the sides of pubs, shops and houses, covering all kinds of subjects - from machine guns, to Irish dancing, more people I wouldn't know, and the situation in the Middle East. Patrick also explained about the flags flying and the different coloured kerbstones (green and orange colour combo and red white and blue) and how they marked out the different communities, national identities and heritage in Belfast.

As I tried to understand the broad accent of the tour guide, my mind wandered between the political statements on the murals that decorated the walls of the city and the dilemma of where to go on my first Irish first date. Still wondering, as we polished off a late lunch and a latte in the trendy Cathedral Quarter (this particular coffee shop being one of the items on Pat's list).

Next stop: we found ourselves looking at a wonky clock tower. Patrick explained the history of the Albert Clock (thanks Wikipedia!). Construction on the 113ft clock tower began in 1865 as a memorial to Queen Victoria's husband. But it became more famous as Belfast's take on The Leaning Tower of Pisa, as it had a 4ft tilt due to being built on wooden piles on reclaimed land from the River Farset. Legend has it that one 'wee lad' climbed up the tower to watch the launch of the Titanic.

Pat also pointed out the large square nearby and made me promise to dance in its fountains before I left Northern Ireland - maybe at the end of a night out in one of the clubs in the nearby Cathedral Quarter!

The skylines of Belfast and New York could not be more

different. First off there are hardly any high rise buildings in Belfast and the fact that Samson and Goliath, the cranes from the dock area, feature prominently in Belfast's skyline, shows how 'short' the city is. The city also felt really small. From downtown I could see mountains, sea and even farms and fields on the hills beyond.

And our entire day-trip from Patrick's house in the south of the city to the east, back into the city centre, out west on the taxi tour and back into town again, then down along the docks, only covered a few miles.

But I thought Belfast and its setting was beautiful. I loved the old red brick buildings and City Hall. Absolutely the view of the day was when I stood at the docks, looked down the mouth of Belfast Lough to the Irish Sea and then back at the rest of the city. It was so strange to see views of mountains and countryside, church spires and streets of houses, instead of skyscraper after skyscraper.

After a selfie with a 20ft pottery fish, I discovered who 'Nuala with the Hula' really was. Also known as the Belle on the Ball and the Thing with the Ring, it's a cool steel and bronze sculpture of a woman standing on a globe holding up a ring of thanksgiving. I found out Nuala's official name is Beacon of Hope and she is starting to become a symbol of the city. After 'The Balls on the Falls' - don't ask - it's the second tallest sculpture in Belfast. I circled the globe and as my finger pointed to New York, the thought suddenly struck me. Today is June 19th, I'll be outta here on July 8th! With so little time, is it really such a smart idea to play cool and hard to get with Tabitha?

Patrick was leaning against the railings, staring up at people zip-lining across the river.

'Cuz,' I said.

Patrick looked over at me.

'I'm going to go for it. There's no point wasting time.'

'You serious?' he replied.

'Yeah. Life's too short man.'

'You're mad! Does your travel insurance cover it?'

'What?'

'Like if the line were to break and you ended up swimming for your life in the Lagan, would your travel insurance cough up?'

I was puzzled. 'Hang on. Are you talking about that?' I pointed at the zipliners.

'Yeah. Why? What are you on about?' Pat was even more confused.

'Tabitha.'

We laughed.

'Glad you grew a set!' was Pat's response.

I didn't know what that meant, so I just laughed along and joined him in staring out over the river, until exhausted, we called it a day.

After two long days in a row running around Belfast, we planned on chilling out and watching Youtube videos for the evening when we got back to the house. But a letter from the university was waiting for Patrick on the hall table. And once he read it, he knew he couldn't put off talking with his parents anymore. They had to have spotted it when they got home from work and left it on the table for him, but Richard and Beth were giving their son the space and privacy to open it himself. I respected them for that.

In language that was very formal, Patrick had been called to explain his grades at a panel interview on Friday 27th June.

Luckily Granny popped in for a visit – I'm guessing Beth had phoned and asked her to come over and keep me entertained. Anyway, she brought warm scones and we had a proper 'natter', while Patrick, Beth and Richard had a conference in the kitchen for over an hour. I guess this was when the reality finally hit Patrick.

Later Patrick filled me in on everything. Driving home from Galway, Pat had thought, or maybe hoped, that he would just have to go and talk to one of his tutors and then do his resits in August. He admitted he wasn't totally surprised he hadn't exactly aced his exams. But he was totally unprepared for bombing out so badly. But when no letter appeared right away, he thought maybe just maybe he would be OK.

No such luck. As Patrick finally explained to me, the letter spelled out the seriousness of his situation and the steps he would have to take to ensure he could stay in the university and continue his course. He showed me the letter and it was scarily businesslike!

First year students got some leeway, but as a second year medical student, it was different. So he now had to sit in front of a panel of lecturers and explain why he had flunked his exams. He also needed to provide evidence that he was a serious student, genuinely interested in the subject and that normally, he could handle the workload and the difficulty of the course. By evidence, Pat said that could mean personal references from his professors, a doctor's note if he had been sick or under stress, or proof of some sort of personal or family crisis.

But I was still totally blown away by what had happened. Did any of these things, sickness or stress, apply to Patrick? I mean, the guy is pretty spontaneous, so maybe he had blown off revision for sports or partying one too many times, but that didn't explain how he had totally failed two modules. I did have to wonder if any of this had anything to do with Aunt Beth's invitation to me all those months ago and her coded phone calls with Mom, which always left Mom looking concerned and quieter than usual.

But I didn't feel I could ask. If Pat wasn't volunteering the information, I wasn't going to start with the awkward questions. So instead I just told him if he needed time to get his stuff together, I could explore Belfast solo or get Granny to take me 'for a wee dander doyne the toyne'.

Beth and Richard were in the kitchen. I stayed in the living room, channel surfing. Some programme about teenage millionaires came on and I remembered that after my bravado that afternoon I hadn't replied to Tabitha to chat about our date.

> *Hey,*
> *Don't worry I'm not freaked out. Still up 4 going out soon? Am free 2mo (short notice I know). Tyler.*

I could see that she was online. Immediately she started to type a reply.

Tabitha:	*Hi. Have 2 work in the morning, but cud meet after?*
Tyler:	*What u wanna do? Maybe head 2 Stranmillis 4 a walk.*
Tabitha:	*Need a ride?*
Tyler:	*No it's cool. I can cycle over n leave my bike somewhere.*
Tabitha:	*Meet u at the coffee shop with stripy canvas beside fruit and veg shop?*
Tyler:	*Great. Say 1?*
Tabitha:	*1's good. What's ur number? So I can text u if running late.*

Let history note that she asked me for my number first. I gave her my digits.

Tabitha:	*Looking forward to it*
Tyler:	*Same here*
Tabitha:	*Night x*
Tyler:	*Night*

Then I heard shouting coming from the kitchen. What was going on?

CODE WORDS

'Patrick! Tyler! Kitchen!' Richard bellowed.

I met Patrick in the hallway. His eyes were red and puffy. I opened the door of the kitchen. Beth was sitting at the table, staring into a cup of tea.

'Tea?' Richard said.

'Yeah,' Patrick replied.

'Ermm I'll just have some juice please.' I needed a tea break! We all took our seats at the table.

'So. Let's address the elephant in the room,' Richard announced.

I stared at Patrick.

'What are you going to do on your date with Tabitha?' Richard asked.

It caught us all off guard.

Even Patrick managed to crack a smile.

'I'll tell you, that lad didn't waste any time!' laughed Richard.

'We've arranged to go for a walk tomorrow.'

'Oh, that's nice, but that's not a real date is it?' Beth asked.

Patrick looked confused.

'I thought it was?' I said.

'Well what if Tabitha thinks you guys are just meeting up? You should plan something for after your walk, just incase you are getting along really well. Like dinner or something like that.'

Richard piped up and advised going for the big impression. 'Take her to The Merchant for Afternoon Tea.'

'What's The Merchant and what's Afternoon Tea?' I asked.

The family laughed, before they explained the ins and outs of Afternoon Tea and 'the bomb' (probably shouldn't use that word to describe something in Belfast), of a hotel that is The Merchant.

The doorbell rang. Beth got up from the table to answer it. *Who was calling at this late hour?* When she came back into the kitchen she was carrying two pizzas. This late night pity party turned date night discussion was now a late night pizza party.

Aunt Beth suggested we keep it simple. 'Just go for a casual walk around the shops. Maybe call into one of those new museums or pop-up shops in town. Just casual. Ask her what she hasn't visited in Belfast and go from there. A new experience for the two of you. You know, keep it light and casual.'

'Then you could have casual sex at the end of your date,' Patrick said.

I let out a belly laugh. Aunt Beth threw her napkin at Patrick and told him off for being rude. Patrick picked the napkin up from the floor before he added, 'Man, chicks love the cinema. Non-committal, maybe get some casual dessert after.' He winked at me. 'But seriously get dessert after, not before. If you get dessert before then you're stuck around a table of small talk. But if you get some dessert, say chocolate fudge cake, after you have watched the movie, you have something in the bank to talk about.'

Strangely, his plan made sense.

But Patrick wasn't finished. 'I mean if you do it my way you can open up a whole new can of first date chat such as your favourite films, your guilty pleasures, your top three film stars, your weird film cartoon crushes. A whole Hollywood Boulevard of conversations.'

We stared at him.

'What? Why are you creeps all staring at me?'

Uncle Richard acted as our counsel, 'the slight matter of your weird cartoon crush confession.'

Patrick looked at me for support. I shook my head in disbelief.

'For a guy who doesn't talk much about his love life you seem to be the all-knowledgeable first date guru,' I blurted out.

Silence.

Beth and Richard stared at each other.

Awkward.

Patrick didn't speak.

I pretended not to notice the change in the mood.

The silence stretched out.

Something definitely wasn't sizing up.

From Patrick's consistent avoidance of discussing the female species dating right back to our Skype conversations. Then this moment.

Uncle Richard broke the tension and brought us back to my first date dilemma.

'What if she is zero banter?' he said.

'Well, then I'll just make up some excuse that I need to leave,' I answered.

'We could do that thing you see in the movies,' suggested Patrick, glad to have the focus switched back to me. I could text or call you halfway through the date and see if you need an escape plan. You could have a code word and we could make up some excuse for you to leave!'

'LOL. Yeah I mean there's no point in wasting time with her if it's gonna be boring.'

'We can work out our code words later.'

'Oh you boys,' Aunt Beth said. She had been quiet, her head buried in her tablet. I thought she was bored with my teenage angst, but when she spoke I realised she was actually very concerned and was taking her duties as my Summer Mom very seriously.

'Here's a solid backup plan for you Tyler,' she said. 'I've been Googling the most effective first date conversation starters.' And she started listing them all before everyone shouted, 'No! Stop!' and began to try and guess them. Favourite pet, band, film. Favourite places to visit. Family background. Career plans. Free time.

'You'll be fine,' she reassured me. 'Besides you're so cute she will probably just giggle and stare at you the whole time you're together.'

I didn't know how to reply to that comment. Patrick's groan said it all. We sat around the table for another hour. Having the banter, as they say, munching pepperoni with extra cheese, and listening to Beth and Richard recalling their first dates and their worst dates.

PAPER BOATS

Patrick planned to spend Friday making calls and setting up appointments with his lecturers, tutors and various other 'bods', to get his story sorted for the panel. But before he went to the Student Union offices to get some expert advice, he very kindly drove me, plus bike, over to the Titanic Museum.

He was so keen to get to the Student Union that when he left me off at this incredible exhibit, the doors weren't even open yet! So I wandered around the docks, being amazed by the view out to sea, exploring the exact place where the famous ship was built and launched, oh and dodging swooping seagulls.

I was the first person to board the Titanic that morning. From rivets to rowing boats, first class cabins to *that* night, the interactive museum is something else, especially for anyone nuts about nautical stuff. I thought I would have to fill in time walking the city before my date with Tabitha, but Titanic took me most of the morning to wander round. It takes up six floors or something! But I did have a half hour to spare so I popped into the Dock Café for a coffee and homemade apple pie. The café runs an honesty box system and has mismatched furniture and a chilled out vibe. It was the perfect place to help me relax before meeting up with Tabitha.

Being early was my theme for the day. Patrick had wildly overestimated the time it would take me to bike it from the Titanic Quarter to the 'wee row of shops at Stranmillis', or I had used up all of my nervous pre-first date energy and pedalled way too quickly. Either way, I was early.

I grabbed an apple and a pear from the local fruit and veg store and smiled at the irony that if I was still back in New York I would be working right now in Fresh & Juicy. Maybe James should call his place a greengrocer's shop from now on? That would be cool. He'd go for the mash-up name. *I wonder how the guys are surviving without me?*

Resisting the urge to jazz up the shop's ho-hum displays out front, I snapped a selfie with one of the fresh produce stands in the background, put it through a filter, tagged the Saturday crew from work and sprinkled in a few funny hashtags with in-jokes they would appreciate.

Either way I was way too early. Watch check. Yep, still very early. With midday sunshine on my back, I tried to chain my ride to a bike stand that was outside a charming coffee shop. People enjoying a lazy lunch sat under the cover of a striped awning. Other customers were inside enjoying lattes, teas and a tempting selection of cakes. I was making a really simple job very difficult, getting grease from the chain all over my hands, and had just about given up on locking the bike when I heard a voice that sent goosebumps all over my body.

'How many Americans does it take to chain a bike up?' Tabitha laughed at her own joke. 'Looks like you need a hand.'

I stood up to say hi and shook her hand. Yeah you heard correctly. I shook her hand and got grease all over her too!

Great start.

Earlier that morning I had reviewed all of Tabitha's photos on Facebook, twice, but nothing could have prepared me for seeing her again in person. Even in her sweats and hoody she was a babe. *What would she look like in her going out clothes? Probably out of my league.* We both stood and stared at the bike. I wished the awkwardness of the oily handshake would pass. I knelt down beside the bike, fiddling with the lock and managed to wipe some of the grease from my hands.

'Sorry about the greasy hands. Don't want anyone to steal Uncle Richard's wheels. I know what you Belfast people are like.'

'Nice try you loser.'

We both laughed. Nervous laughter. But it was laughter, which I took as a good sign. With the bike chained and secure (oily fingers crossed) we set off on our walk. It was a beautiful setting for a first date, well if this was even a date. We strolled along the tree-lined riverbank of the river Lagan, part of which was a former canal route that meandered through quaint old locks and under bridges.

For the first half hour we filled the air with getting to know each other talk, I used some of the family's suggestions from the previous evening, before we reached another café along the route. The café and outdoor seating area were packed with families, cyclists and dog-walkers all taking a well-earned rest from their afternoon adventures and enjoying the good weather. As we approached the café, Patrick's words came to the front of my mind: 'Don't sit down at a table with her. It could get boring, and then you're stuck there!'

He must have had a really bad dating experience that involved him being stuck at a table. In fact a lot of his date warnings seemed to revolve around being trapped in boring situations. Unless he suffered from claustrophobia! I suggested we just grab a drink and keep walking. I also took the opportunity to clean the rest of the grease from my hands. Tabitha seemed OK with my suggestion, so we sipped on soda and shared potato chips as we followed the river on past Shaw's Bridge (choosing Cheese and Onion was a bad idea!).

I patted my pockets for chewing gum or mints. Negative. Uh oh! As we walked, Tabitha told me about her part time job in her dad's friend's newsagents. She worked some weekend days and mornings when she was in college. She was 19 and going into her second year of university - studying English and Drama at Queen's. Her brainy science nerd brother Jack lived in Manchester, England, and was studying for a PhD in Zoology. I also learned she had been to Florida more times than I had! Irish people seem to have a thing for Florida I discovered. She hadn't mentioned a mom. Was she dead? I showed her some photos of my parents, so I talked about them for a while to try and fish for clues about her mom.

A couple of miles upstream Tabitha passed me some chewing gum - score! We crossed the river via a wooden bridge and began the walk back. *Nothing major has happened so far. Is this good or bad? Normal? Is our first date going well?* We had small-talked about the usual stuff like college, the summer, Patrick, box sets, embarrassing dads, and then she got me talking about music. I didn't mention anything about my EP, until she called my bluff and quoted a few of my lyrics at me. It caught me totally off guard. She wasn't the only person who had spent their morning checking Facebook! My cheeks went the colour of a fluffy red squirrel's tail.

But after awhile I took a few sheets of crinkled paper from my pocket.

'What's that for?' Tabitha asked. 'You gonna write me a song?'

'If I had a dollar for every time a fan asked me that.'

'Let me guess, you would have $2?' Tabitha laughed way too hard at her own joke.

'Well I was going to say $1, 'cos I don't have any fans, but $2 sounds better!'

We laughed again.

'Do you know how to make a paper boat?' I asked.

'Ermm nope.'

'OK. I'll show you the basics and then we can race our boats back down the river.'

'Sounds fun!' She actually sounded enthused about our mid-afternoon craft activity.

We perched ourselves on an overhanging branch, and as the river rushed beneath our feet I showed Tabitha the basic folds required to make a paper boat. I had Googled them the previous evening, but she didn't need to know that! She seemed impressed. As we sat on our pew in the tree and made our boats, a few older people passed and smiled at us. Copious folds and one paper cut later and we had a mini fleet, ready for the inaugural Lagan T&T Boat Race. Careful not to crush our boats, we clambered down from the tree and found a place to launch. Tabitha stood in a daze as she watched the gentle current take the boats downriver. We watched until they turned a bend and went out of sight. She ran ahead of me and shouted,

'Come on captain! We need to go before any pirates seize our boats.'

'Or dogs.' I said. A passing collie looked ready to jump in and snatch my lead boat. Or sink it. I smiled. I think our afternoon craft session had been a winning move and for the first time ever I could say - Tyler 1, Dating Disasters 0.

By the time we made it round the meandering corner, our boats were long out of sight. So we took a slight detour from the main path. By detour I mean we walked round a field; it's what Irish people do for fun ;0. Before our change of course, Tabitha had checked a sign and worked out we must have walked around eight miles. My legs were starting to feel it, so after another few steps, we lay down beside the riverbank for a rest.

Even though we weren't doing anything spectacular I was having an amazing time. I felt relaxed. Calm. Comfortable in

Tabitha's company. It was easy. Natural.

Watching the branches sway in the afternoon breeze I noted a few things.

She was funny.

She was easy to talk to.

Her hair turned gold in the sun.

Making a paper boat whilst trying to keep your balance up a tree is difficult.

Her smile was infectious.

We seemed to have made a connection.

Those eyes.

I thought first dates were always supposed to be about small talk and having a laugh, and this one had been - up until now. But as we lay on the grass Tabitha caught me off guard as she began to spill about her parents and their messy and long-drawn-out divorce. She obviously felt at ease around me, or maybe she was just an open person. She seemed really cut up about the split. And no wonder!

It wasn't all that long ago. Plus, I couldn't believe that she had been put in a position where she had to choose sides. When Tabitha decided she wanted to live with her dad, her mom totally cut her off. This was right when Tabitha was doing school exams! Her mom still had not forgiven her. Tabitha went through the whole of her first year of university without speaking to her mom. In fact they had only been in contact three times in the last two years. And one of those times had been through a text message.

To make things worse, the guy Tabitha was dating when

her parent's breakup happened dumped her just as she needed someone to rely on. Since then her friends and her blossoming acting career had been her support. But, Tabitha admitted, the ongoing cold shoulder from her mom was not something she could just ignore. Even though she knew it was 'daft', Tabitha couldn't help blaming herself in some way.

She was finding it harder lately to have the confidence and energy for her acting - turned out she had acted in a few productions at The Lyric. When I looked blank, Tabitha explained it was a highly rated theatre in Northern Ireland and getting into its youth company was a really big deal. Often it led to amazing opportunities for young actors.

Throughout, her dad had been her rock, but it wasn't enough. Sometimes.

I listened to Tabitha telling me about how her trust in people and her own faith in herself had slowly ebbed away. She had passed up on a few auditions, as her self-confidence was pretty low, and had to pull out of one play when things got really bad at home.

Tabitha finished. We sat. I watched as two birds danced before us. Tired from their performance, they took rest in a nearby tree. I tried to take in what she had just said. She broke the silence.

'OK, I know I'm talking too much, but when I saw you in the park, something in me just felt good. And then driving home that night I started to feel happy for the first time in a long time. It's been hard to get excited over the last few years. I don't expect a lot of good things to happen to me. But I couldn't fight the excitement I felt when I saw you,' she looked up at me then down at her lap. 'I hope you didn't think I was a weirdo 'cos I messaged you? It's just . . . when we made eye contact, I knew this was different. Besides, there were so many other girls at the park that day, I wanted to be first in line!'

'What other girls? You're the one I noticed. I'm all yours.'

Yeah I heard it.

Whoops!

Tabitha was taken aback. 'Oh really. All mine?' she said curiously.

Our conversation had turned into a blushfest. I broke the awkwardness.

'I felt something too when I first saw you. I'm not that good around girls. I've had a few disappointments, as well as a few embarrassing stories! But you . . . you're cool. All that stuff that's happened to you sounds really rough. I don't really know what to say.' With Patrick's exam results and now Tabitha's revelation, this was beginning to be the most used phrase of my trip!

'You don't have to say anything. I'm sorry for dumping on you. My friends are great. I can talk to them, but they probably get sick of me rabbiting on. They've got their own stuff to deal with. And Dad. Well. He tries to be so strong for me. But he's hurting too. And I know how difficult things have been for him over the last wee while.'

She looked up at me.

We gazed at each other for a couple of seconds. What I felt when I had first caught eyes with Tabitha in the park came rushing back, but stronger. It was weird. I was scared. I wasn't supposed to feel like this, especially not this quick. I broke eye contact by looking at the river, then back at her shoes, her knee, and then her eyes again. There was just something about her eyes. The way she looked at me was captivating. Her eyes invited me to fall into them. They were bright, clear, pure. Blue like the oceans, green, like the leaves on an oak tree, with these hazel flecks. Guarded by really long lashes that made my heart turn every time she blinked. And those freckles scattered on her nose! But even though I think this was the moment I was supposed to kiss her I had to shake it off. I couldn't kiss her. I couldn't fall for her. My brain told my body to kiss her, but when I finally summoned the courage to move towards her, huge golf ball-sized raindrops began to fall from the sky.

We hadn't noticed the storm clouds coming over the mountains from the west of the city. Instead of kissing her, I pulled Tabitha up and we ran towards a nearby tree. Only a few steps from the riverbank, but by the time we reached the shelter of the dense canopy, we were drenched. Under the shelter of the branches we noticed the tree was carved with inspirational words. The trunk had a tattoo sleeve! I took a photo as Tabitha ran her fingers over the intricate carving. Waiting for the downpour to pass over, I described the thunder 'n' lightning summer storms we experience on the East Coast.

'We're still a good couple of miles from the car. Do you want to wait it out under here?' Tabitha asked.

'Yeah. But it could be awhile. That rain doesn't look like it's going to stop anytime soon.'

'Whatever you think. You're the one who's cycling home,' she reminded me. 'But I might give you a lift. If you're lucky.'

Just as we were about to leave the shelter of the tree I realised this was the second perfect opportunity of the day to kiss her. I didn't want our first kiss to involve clambering over a gearstick in her car with my relatives staring at us out the living room window, or a hurried peck at the shops in front of everyone. So I took her hand, put my other hand on the small of her back and, even though it was our first date, and against everything the sensible side of my brain was telling me, I kissed her. The setting was perfect. An empty field. A summer storm. The drum of the raindrops pattering off the leaves drowned out the sound of the nervous pounding heartbeat of young love's first kiss. The rain fell harder as we kissed for what seemed like ages. I'm glad the downpour was there to cool us down. We came up for air and didn't know where to look.

'Shall we?' I said.

'Ehhh what?' Tabitha looked startled.

'Oh I mean run for the car!'

Scurrying back to the car, we didn't hold hands, we didn't even try. That's what couples do. We were just two kids having some summer fun. Thankfully my bike, completely soaked, was still there when we got back to the café. We went inside and dried off over a hot coffee. Sensing the date wasn't over, I suggested that we grab some food at a nearby restaurant. She ran to her car, came back with a bag, and went into the bathroom. Girls are always prepared for these things. As Tabitha changed, I messaged Patrick.

Tyler:	*Things going awesome. Just back from walk - going 4 dinner now. What u at? We kissed.*
Patrick:	*Not much. Panel stuff all day. Bored. Will let mum know ur bailing 4 ur new BFF GFF.*
Tyler:	*Lol*
Patrick:	*CU later stud*
Tyler:	*Stud? Seriously??!!*

I was about to put my phone away when it buzzed again-

Patrick:	*Can't believe u kissed her!!!!!*
Tyler:	*Too much on the first date?*
Patrick:	*No but #doesourbromancemeannothingtoyou?*
Tyler:	*#awesomehashtag*
Patrick:	*Let me know when your coming home so I can get the X-Box on. Xz*
Tyler:	*Xz?*
Patrick:	*Xx. Enjoy ur food.*
Tyler:	*nps*

Then, one of life's little wonders happened. Tabitha emerged from the restroom looking like a million dollars. I was wearing standard-issue versatile (now semi-damp) boy clothes of shorts and a shirt. Tabitha had been wearing sweats and a hoody and was now glammed up in ripped jeans, a pretty coral top, sandals and had her hair half up in gypsy/hippie style. How do girls transform themselves like that?

If Tabitha's ability to disappear into the smallest restroom known to man and emerge looking like a million dollars impressed me, she was equally impressed at how I managed to fit my bike into the back of her ridiculously small car. We made our way into the city and spent a couple of hours eating chicken, fries and dessert, which they call pudding here. Even though we had been together for ten hours straight, the conversation flowed right until she pulled up at the sidewalk of the house. Patrick leaned out one of the bedroom windows and wolf-whistled in our direction. I told him to clear off as we shared a little hug and a peck on the cheek.

When I stepped into the house, Beth, Richard and Patrick were sitting on the stairs like the Von Trapp family, looking all innocent but bursting with curiosity. Before I had even closed the green front door with its stained glass panels, they threw a hailstorm of questions my way.

'So . . . how was it?' Beth asked as she raised her eyebrows.

'Is she a good kisser?' Patrick added.

Uncle Richard stared at me, awaiting a reply,

'Well,' I paused. I broke into a wry smile. Smiling had been a favourite activity of my day.

'Well . . .' I was milking their attention, and they knew it.

Sensing there was a story to tell Aunt Beth cut in. 'I'll stick the kettle on.'

'Family meeting in the lounge in five!' Uncle Richard declared.

We spent the rest of our Friday night discussing dates: first dates, awkward dates, horrible dates, romantic dates and spontaneous dates.

'Just take it easy with her OK? Remember you're away from here soon!' Beth advised before we all went off to bed.

'Yeah I know. Can't get too involved. I'll just take it as it comes.'

I knew keeping some emotional distance was going to be difficult, as every time I thought about Tabitha my heart started beating 'a mile a minute.' Already I noted that this phrase was one of Uncle Richard's favourites. Later, Patrick 'schooled me' at *GTA*. Before we crashed for the night I sent Tabitha a message:

> *Hey! Just wanted 2 say thanks 4 today. I hope I wasn't 2 forward in kissing u but I just caught the vibe. It would b cool if we could hang out again. Now I'm the eager one. Lol. I'm busy the next few days but maybe something later in the week? Thanks again. Night x*

She replied by the time I had brushed my teeth.

> *Hey T. U def. weren't 2 forward. Just awesome. It was a really cool day. I didn't have 2 think about whether I wanted 2 kiss u or not. Sorry again 4 dumping all that stuff on u. It's just that ur someone who is detached from here. A different view. Besides you have 2 listen to me. Remember I'm all yours! ;0 Had a great day. Would love 2 hang out soon. Let me know when suits. Night x*

THE COASTAL

Cutting a narrow path between the hillside and the shore, the stunningly beautiful coast road had its white-knuckle moments, but the views across to Scotland made it worth every hairy twist and turn. I considered closing my eyes and pretending to be in a road-hugging Mustang, but that meant I would miss out on the incredible scenery of mountains, cliffs and ocean. Easy to see why this rugged place of steep valleys backed by mountains was cut off from the rest of Northern Ireland for centuries and had such close links with Scotland.

I even noticed the local accent had a Scottish burr, as we stopped a few times on our way round the Glens of Antrim coast. The first was for gas near Ballygally, where Pat pointed out the haunted castle hotel! Next a 99 in the quaint little village of Cushendall. We made good time to Torr Head where the Irish Sea becomes the Atlantic – now that's a wild place!

Patrick pulled over in a little parking area and we managed to snap some amazing photos around the abandoned coast-guard building. Not to miss out on our morning cup of tea, he unpacked his duffle bag and poured two steaming cups from his Thermos flask. He even brought gravy rings (doughnuts and no gravy) to munch on as we sat on the roof of the lonesome structure. The vista was one of the most sensational I'd ever seen. Like, ever. Right up there with the California Coastal Highway. With the cliffs to my back and the sea air on my face, I was reminded of the summer Mom and Dad took me on a road trip through California on Highway 1. Whenever I watch re-runs of *The OC* I smile at the memories I have from that time. Sure the weather is colder in Ireland, but the views are just as spectacular.

With Scotland's Mull of Kintyre only 10 miles across the sea, we took it in turns to look through the binoculars to make out the coastline of our Celtic cousins. The views were so clear; even without the binoculars I could see fields!

Patrick explained that this headland used to be a lookout post for transatlantic ships, but centuries before that, the ancient Celts had a castle on this spot that doubled as a lighthouse. 'See this wall? Right here, in the 6th century was the citadel of the chieftain Barrach the Great, not to be confused with Barack the Obama. Dunworry!'

I dropped the binoculars. 'Why would I worry?'

Patrick was laughing so hard he had trouble saying 'that's the name of the castle!'

Back in the car I recalled some of the information about the area that I'd read in The Ulster Museum beside their display of finds from shipwrecks all along the Northern Coast. Some of the gold coins even came from ships of the Spanish Armada that got blown off course way back in 1588! That's before the first Europeans came to live in America. For the rest of the drive I allowed my mind to wander through the seas of history, where Spanish galleons sailed through the waters of my imagination.

It had been an early start, so when we arrived in Ballycastle at brunch o'clock we 'tucked into' a fry-up in a friendly little diner. Patrick had warned me to keep room for an epic dinner, so the hearty brunch was to tide us over until then. I opted for The Coastal – 4 'rashers' of bacon, 2 sausages, 2 eggs, 2 soda bread, 2 toast, 2 potato bread, beans, tomato, mushrooms and a cup of tea. An ocean of food, enough to feed a small family for a bargain price of £5.99! Between bites we discussed pirates. Patrick's new pirate name was Patrick Silverhook McGaw. I chose the imaginative Tyler the Terrifiarrrrrrr (go on, say it with a pirate voice!)

Filling our stomachs with a fry had been an excellent idea, until we started walking over the Carrick-a-Rede Rope Bridge - a 20 metre long rope bridge over a 30 metre chasm with huge waves crashing over jagged rocks far below. The swaying bridge links the mainland and Carrick Island, basically an oversized boulder with grass and not much else. These days the bridge is safe and sturdy, though it does move around. But when you see the pictures from the not-so-olden days, you wonder how anybody crossed that thing without losing their lunch and fertilizing the vegetation on Carrick. Patrick assured me it's 1000% safer than what it used to be, but that didn't convince my fry from nearly saying hello as I made my way across – not looking down of course!

Working our way further along the coast we stopped at Bushmills Distillery where *The Water of Life* has been distilled since 1608. I'm not a whiskey fan (I say that as if I have years of drinking experience to back up my opinion), but this place was incredible because you actually see the whiskey being made – not a video or a reconstruction but the real deal. What was even better was the chance to buy Dad a personalised bottle of a variety that can only be bought at the distillery itself. He was gonna love it!

Distilled and chilled we pretty soon found ourselves on the rocks - millions of years old granite rocks. The Giants Causeway, a UNESCO World Heritage Site, is such a cool place to visit. It's totally unique in the world, and so impressive. To try and explain the mysteriously perfect hexagonal columns, the ancient Celts came up with wild legends about battling giants. But really, volcanic action should get all the credit, not Finn McCool (that's the Irish giant). I could go on and on and on, but the only way to get the picture is to go and see the place. #finnrocks

We cruised round the coast to Portrush, a seaside vacation place that people in NI just love; probably because Barry's Amusements, Ireland's largest theme park is there. OK, so compared to US theme parks, it's pretty rinky-dink, more State

Fair than Six Flags. Actually Barry's reminded me of the old time boardwalk fairgrounds at Santa Cruz. Small, but big on personality. But in a funny way, there's something incredible about the place. It's authentic for sure!

After spending all our small change on the penny arcades, we bumped a few peeps on the dodgems and threw our hands in the air like we just didn't care on the rickety Big Dipper.

With our adrenalin at an all-time high we walked to the harbour where I experienced a big helping of culinary heaven. Patrick ordered for me, and we swapped dishes half way through like two indecisive lovers. On a middle-of-the-meal bathroom trip I caught a glimpse of the desserts. OMG! The slices of cheesecake were as tall as The Causeway Cliffs, the profiteroles the size of local hero Finn McCool's fists and the meringues were as colourful as the dodgems in the amusement arcade. Boy do they love their cream here!

Rolling out of the restaurant we went on a post dinner stroll and played some more arcade games. After another ice cream (I don't know where we found the room), we made our way to a local surf spot where we set up our refuge for the night. Which took all of 5 seconds – thank you whoever invented the pop-up tent. We hung out with a few surfers and arranged with two of them to borrow their spare boards the following morning. They wanted us to join them in the water that evening, but my stomach was larger than *Shamu*, the Killer Whale, so there was no way I was going into the water.

With the Atlantic our TV, we built a campfire on the beach and spent the rest of the night watching the surfers, sipping on a few brewskis and developing our pirate fantasy.

'Back in a minute cuz.' Patrick said.

'Cool.'

I thought he was going to answer a call from nature, but he returned holding a blanket, two forks and two take out boxes. A fine display of bromance!

'Got us some pudding.'

'Pudding?' I puzzled. 'That's not pudding.'

'Yeah it is. It's from the restaurant we were at.'

'No, pudding is gloopy. You buy it at the store in a little cup, like yogurt. It's usually one of the more gross things in the school lunch canteen.'

'Over here, this is pudding.' Patrick corrected me, revealing two massive slices of cheesecake.

'You sure have funny names for things! Even though you speak English, some days I need an interpreter!'

Patrick laughed.

'Well whatever this is, I have one word for it-'

We both said the word *AWESOME* at the same time. Patrick passed me my box of pudding and I dived in.

Having made a great start on Patrick's ambitious *'Top 30ish list'*, we talked about what the rest of my visit could look like, now that he had to study for his resit exams (provided he was lucky enough to get the go-ahead from his panel). Patrick seemed pretty upbeat after a productive previous day of meetings and phone calls. We still had some day trip things like Rathlin Island and The Walled City to take in, and a camping trip to The Kingdom to blow off steam the weekend after Patrick faced the panel, so we sketched out a bit of an itinerary for the next couple of weeks.

Business done, we finalised our pirate boat names. Patrick went for The Destroyer, I called my boat The Emerald Raider. Patrick asked me loads of questions about life in New York and we compared notes about our voyages through teenage life. He told me what it was like to grow up as a peace kid in Belfast, the first post-conflict generation in decades. We shared our boyhood dreams and our manhood aspirations. We laughed about our Prom v. 'Formal' experiences, and Patrick gave me some much-needed advice about college. But it was growing up as 'only-kids' that was the crown of our conversation.

With the sun hovering on the horizon and our toes buried in the sand, it felt like we were in a Jack Johnson video, minus a few tanned surfer dude and dudette friends and a chubby Hawaiian playing the ukulele. The sound of the Atlantic lapping at the shore was the perfect soundtrack to bring a busy day to a peaceful end. The only cloud, Patrick and what was going on with him. Which made me wonder about Patrick's love life. He must have one. But anytime I brought it up he always changed the subject. I couldn't help but think something was going on. During our Skype chats all spring he hadn't mentioned anything about girls. Maybe there wasn't much to talk about, or maybe this was another thing he was trying to avoid sharing with me. Yet I needed some advice about what it's like to date a Northern Irish girl. I had to try and get him to talk! So I did.

I tried sounding casual: 'so Patrick, any girls in your life?', and 'and what about your love life then?', but that got me nowhere. Silence. Or a change of subject. 'Hey, check out that sunset.'

Eventually, after possibly a few too many times dodging my persistent questioning, Patrick jumped up, stamped out the embers of the fire and marched to the car.

Oh crap. Now I've done it.

He came back with a few golf clubs. My cousin truly was the master of diversion. And because the campsite was beside one of the best courses in the land and it was still light, even at 10pm, we decided to take advantage of the free green fees.

'Rory McIlroy watch out!' Patrick roared as he sunk a 20-foot putt, turned the club and used it as a bazooka and blew the pin apart (not literally!) We messed about on one of the greens until a cloud covered our floodlight - the moon.

We were turning back towards our tent when Patrick suddenly asked, 'Do you remember the girl from the park?'

'What one?'

'You know the one I said I wouldn't talk about.'

'Jemma. No Jessica. Yeah Jess.'

'Yeah her.'

'What about her? You got the hots for her? I knew there was something you weren't telling me, you dark horse! Is that why you haven't talked about girls yet? You want my advice on what you should do?' I gabbled then stopped before I spoke again, 'Shut up Sontoro and let the man speak!'

Patrick was laughing at my outburst.

'Sorry!' I made the zipping gesture across my mouth.

'I wish I only fancied her.' Patrick paused. 'We have a history. It's pretty baisée.' From my love of all things indie I knew he had just said a French four letter word.

He sat down on a nearby rock. The tone of the conversation was suddenly a lot more serious than I had anticipated. I stopped staring at the stars above and the waves below and gave Patrick my attention. Clearly I had touched a nerve and now he was ready to talk about it before I said any more stupid stuff.

'I don't even know where to start,' Patrick said.

'Start where you're at.'

Patrick poured his heart out for close to an hour. Turns out his girl problem was big. Much bigger than I could ever have imagined.

Patrick and Jess had been dating since their mid-teens. Childhood sweethearts who once walked the school corridors hand in hand, they split for a couple of years when Jess started hanging out with a different crowd. Patrick always thought that group was superficial and 'up themselves' - into labels and everyone looking like clones and all that. Now he knows it was just a teen phase, but it was too much for easygoing, 'do your own thing' Patrick to handle. Anyway, they got back together at the end of their first year of college when Jess was Jess again.

Things were going good, not super serious yet, but definitely good, until they found out that Jess was pregnant. Patrick had just came back from a summer Eurailing round Europe when she told him the news. A few roller-coaster weeks followed as they tried to 'figure something out': how to tell family, how to 'get their heads round' the whole change in their lives and how they would manage to raise their baby and do college.

The implications of the pregnancy, the possibility of having to quit education, the loss of freedom and the reality of parenthood - so many huge things at once, but together Jess and Pat gradually began to sort through it all, tell parents, make a plan and become more at home with the idea. And as family showed their support, Jess and Pat even began looking forward to a baby in their lives. Especially once they saw the first scan!

'Seeing the child actually moving made it so real. We were so excited we went out and bought maternity clothes that day, and even some baby stuff! Everything was proceeding normally, the morning sickness, the food cravings, the tiredness, the first wee fluttering kicks. Textbook signs. But Jess had to hide them all, because we had decided to wait before spreading the news beyond family.'

Both sets of parents had advised the couple to hold off until 14 weeks, when the worst danger of miscarriage had passed. At last they could tell their surprised and shocked friends and deal with the huge mix of reactions. And just when things were settling down, and Jess was starting to wear the maternity jeans, she was rushed to hospital. Complications, which Pat did not want to go into.

'We lost our little girl at 21 weeks.' His words pierced through all the banter of our trip.

As Patrick confided in me, I did the calculations in my head. Mom must have told me I was coming over to Ireland for the summer just after they had lost the baby. It felt weird that no one had said a word. Not Mom and Dad who never keep anything from me. And not Patrick, even though we spoke on Skype most weeks on the lead-up to my trip. But were there clues? Or had I been too focused on raising travel money and my own stuff that I hadn't noticed anything was wrong and hadn't been so great about asking Patrick about his life?

It all made sense. The reason for this trip, bombing out on his exams, the false bravado, the joking around, the manic travel and always keeping busy busy busy. Not to mention changing the subject whenever I got too close, or the serious, strictly private conversations he had with his mom most days. Everything began to click into place. I guess a summer hanging out with me was a strategically planned distraction for Patrick.

He talked and cried. I listened. I wiped my eyes and blew my nose on my hoody sleeve. I tried to give reassuring nods and comments. But I had very little to offer apart from my presence. Tumultuous wouldn't even describe his year. And his dark valley wasn't over yet, now with this totally understandable exam meltdown.

'I'm still up and down. Some days it's a struggle just to get out of bed. And the day in Botanic seeing Jess brought it all back. That and the exams. Just too much.' He shook his head. 'After everything we went through, Jess and I couldn't really handle it. Being together, or anything. Losing the baby, and other stuff, drove us apart. Since then we have been off and on. Mostly off lately. I didn't know she was going to be in the park that day. It's hard seeing her because-' He broke down.

'Sorry man. But you know, it must have been fate she was

in the park that day. You would have avoided seeing her and dealing with stuff all summer if I hadn't caught that frisbee.'

Patrick stared at me.

'A problem shared is a problem halved.' I added, just to fill the tense silence.

'First off, you didn't catch the Frisbee, and, I know I'm having a serious moment here, but what are you, a ninety year old man coming out with phrases like that?'

He seemed annoyed, but then we both realised how ridiculous and actually funny what we'd both said was, and we had to laugh and apologise. Then we looked out at the sea. The moon was reflecting off the surface, making it silver and highlighting the shifting waves that covered the murky depths.

'So are you guys together now?' I asked.

'No. But some days yeah. I don't really know what we're doing.'

I made a sympathetic noise, not really sure what to say. How could I? I couldn't begin to imagine what he was going through. But somehow I knew that just being there for him was going to have to be enough to help him. Ever the comedian, Patrick ruffled my hair and began to tease me about Tabitha. Joking. Patrick's never-fail defence mechanism.

'Thanks for the chat cuz.'

'Always here for you bro. I mean I don't have a clue about . . . you know, but I hope you guys can work it out. And if I can do anything to help you this summer just ask.'

'Thanks man. I will.'

We stood up, stretched and hugged it out before we made

our way to the tent. I tried to fall asleep, but the sound of the wind blowing against the canvas walls, and a chorus of intermittent pungent farts (thanks to the brewskis we drank!), quickly followed by a round of childish giggles, kept me awake.

I didn't know how to take the revelation from Patrick. I'm not used to drama. Well, apart from Rodriguez's in school. But that's not really drama. More like a tough time for his family. Lying on my back I realised that in school I had been something of a sounding board for my friends – when Rebecca came out of the closet and Darius was caught cheating in his exams. I'm the default guy that people look to for answers. Me, with all my worldly experience! Most of the time I have no idea what to say. I just listen to them.

I lay awake trying to find an answer for Patrick's problem and wondered how his revelation would affect the rest of my stay and his summer. I only had 16 days left and now had this emotional bombshell to deal with. But I was glad he had confided in me. It had to help. Even though other people knew about the situation he told me things he hadn't even said to his Belfast friends.

Tabitha's riverside first date disclosure and now Patrick's beachside revelation, made it clear that my trip to Ireland was going to be about a lot more than taking in the sights and sounds this wonderful island had to offer. Instead, I was there to tend to the troubled souls of two of its most beautiful people.

'You guys coming?'
'Surf's pumping lads. Get out of your pit.'

Our surfing buddies had arrived and were stoked for us to join them in the water. They shook the tent.

'All right! All right!' we both shouted.

'See you in five.'

'OK.'

The morning breeze carried the conversations of the surfers into our ears as we wiped the sleep from our eyes. We stared out of our portal, crawled from our sleeping bags and met the guys at one of their vans. I had two crash course lessons. First: how to put a wetsuit on. Second: how to surf. One of the guys handed me his spare longboard and when we walked down to the (bracing is an understatement) water he pushed me out onto the endless bobbing expanse. After a few bails I caught a wave and rode into shore (on my knees). It was a start.

Two hours later and I had managed to complete a couple of rides in with both feet kinda on the board. Enough to know I loved it!

Patrick and I packed our pop up tent (which took a lot longer than setting up) and made a quick dash to Portstewart where we joined our new friends for breakfast. Cruising the strip Patrick showed me where he usually partied during university term time when he came up to visit his mates. As we stuffed our faces with two bacon sandwiches each, the gang shared a few, probably exaggerated, stories about nights out in the local haunts. Patrick seemed to be in a good mood, despite (or because of?) last night's revelation.

After a brisk walk from the harbour to the Barmouth we were ready to hit the open road again; well, after I riffled through and purchased a selection of some old cowboy books in a second hand bookstore. On our way home we stopped off at Dunluce Castle, the eerie ruins of a medieval castle, with half of it just clinging on to the edge of a cliff, the rest long gone, and then the quaint Ballintoy Harbour, before a squall (check me out using nautical terminology) blew in and forced us inland.

Next stop Ballymena. Patrick wanted to show me one of his favourite bakeries where they sell pancakes stuffed with chocolate. Fabuloso deluxe! That's me being Italian. When my dad loves a food he makes all these flamboyant hand gestures while eating, kissing his fingers and waving his arms in the air, like a TV chef or something. But I didn't want to drop the crepe-like yumminess.

Our trip north was all about the Bs. Ballycastle, Bridge, Bush, Basalt, Beach, Ballintoy, Bakery. And the B to beat them all - Barry's. I was beginning to doze off dreaming about fairground rides and those amazing desserts, when a text from Beth directed us to Green's Pizza. The pizzas and milkshakes she'd ordered for an alternative Sunday dinner would be ready for us to pick up on our way home.

DATE CRAY CRAY

We went date crazy. My two new favourite people, Patrick and Tabitha, told me the story of their homeland through trips to haunted castles and dark dungeons, ancient ruins from the early Christian days, nights at the theatre and trad music bars, and many places only the locals know about. For the next few days, in between Patrick preparing for his daunting meeting with the head of his faculty and some other important peeps, we managed to knock a few more things off 'The Top ~~30~~ 31ish Tourist Attractions In Northern Ireland'.

But Patrick was increasingly too preoccupied. He'd come along, but his mind would be somewhere else, or he'd be busy on the phone, or have to leave early for a meeting. He had a lot to do before Friday's panel! Getting letters from his doctor, meeting his tutor who would be coming along to the meeting to help make his case for staying on and repeating the exams, getting support from the advisors in the Student Union to get 'the head's up' on the whole process and what to expect. Pat also confided that he had been talking to a counsellor over the past few months and she would also be providing a letter explaining his stressful year and episodes of depression. Probably he was seeing other folk too. Anyway, with all that going on, by the end of the week, Pat just could not summon up the energy or interest for sightseeing. But that was fine. There was no way I was going to pressure Pat into coming along. Just me and him was one thing, but if Tabs was there, would Patrick really want to play third wheel and tag along with a couple? 'Not on yer Nellie!' Gran would probably say. And it was good, just the two of us.

Although Tabitha was very eager to step in and cover some of the things on the list to free up Patrick, I played it semi-cool with her and visited a couple of the attractions by myself (Belfast Zoo and Crumlin Road Prison), and went to W5 (a kids' interactive museum) with Beth and our younger cousins. Mostly though, Tabitha and I explored by night. We passed these endless bright summer evenings with walks by the shore, milkshakes and movies, drives (amazing how you are out in the bright green countryside in just ten minutes. More like 2 hours from Manhattan!) and putt putt golf. But I'm jumping ahead.

Have to admit I was glad to be out of the house too! As the panel date loomed Patrick was increasingly stressed and moody. His flashes of humour and liveliness were becoming more rare. The house was tense. I couldn't wait for this Spanish Inquisition to be over so I could enjoy the last few days that I had in Norn Iron with him. After the panel I would only have 11 days to go before plane time.

I learned more about the ins and outs of the panel Patrick was preparing to face on the day I went to W5 with Beth and the kids. On the way to pick them up she explained that, for a medical student, it was a big deal to fail so spectacularly. The rest of his college life was riding on this meeting. In fact his college life could be over! Even after the panel, he still would have to wait a few days to learn the outcome.

While we were alone in the car, I brought up the delicate subject of the baby. Patrick had shared with me that they had agreed to call her Ella, after the phenomenal Ella Fitzgerald, one of Grandad's favourite singers. Maybe I shouldn't have, but I hadn't been able to tell what I knew to a soul - I didn't know how much Tabitha was aware of - so it was good to talk it over with Aunt Beth. And I think she appreciated being able to open up about Patrick's problems too.

Beth apologised for keeping me in the dark and didn't try and make any excuses about it. 'Perhaps Richard and I should have told you, but we felt it was up to Patrick.'

We pulled up outside my Uncle David's house. Beth switched off the engine, and before we got out of the car, she turned to me, 'I know you probably don't realise it, but Patrick has been different since you have been here.'

I raised my eyebrows, 'Like better different? 'Cos he's been pretty grumpy at times.'

Beth smirked. 'Yeah. Better different. Happier, a bit more settled. More his old self. Until just the last few days that is. This wretched panel has really been getting to him. I cannot wait for it to be over. I am sure they will understand his situation and let him do the resits, but there are no guarantees!'

I just nodded. I got pretty good at that during my time in Belfast!

Aunt Beth sighed and gave a big shrug. 'It's been a difficult year for all of us. And the Jess business of course. Still unresolved. I just wish he would sort things out with her. She's a lovely girl, but I don't know if it's right. Or if it was ever right. Pat and I talk all the time, and that's a good thing, but I can't tell him what to do or what is best. Their future is his decision.'

I nodded again.

'I do think though, that for now, the pair of them should take a break from each other. All these ups and downs and off and on, it is just upsetting him and not what Patrick needs right now with so many academic pressures. I have tried telling him. But I don't know how much he listens to me. Maybe he'd listen to someone his own age?' My aunt looked right at me, and what could I do but nod?

'Uhhh sure. But he hasn't mentioned a whole lot about Jess. Just bits here and there. So I don't really know what's up.' I shifted in my seat.

'No wonder his studies- '

We were interrupted by our little cousins running out to the driveway and slapping their hands against the door.

'Just keep an eye on him would you?' Aunt Beth quickly said before opening the car door.

The rest of the conversation would have to wait until after we had entertained the little monsters.

Up until this point I hadn't pushed Patrick too much about how things were with him and Jess. But I had walked in on him a couple of times while he was on the phone, and from the tone of some of his calls and the way he sometimes threw his phone in a temper at his pillow I knew that things weren't great. He could fool himself, but he couldn't fool me. I tried telling him I was sure things would work out, but what did I know really?

That evening we made our way into the Cathedral Quarter. Pat assured me he had done all he could for the panel and needed a night off. The next day, Thursday, was his last day before P-day, so he planned to spend it chilling, having fun and trying not to think.

For a change, it was me making the plans, because, while I was in prison (Crumlin Road tour, that is!) I'd picked up a flyer about an open-mic night in this cool new old-school pub in the Cathedral Quarter. I registered to play a thirty-minute set, just for the craic, and in between the sightseeing and date nights with Tabitha, practiced as hard as I could for my first gig in Belfast – and first performance for Tabs and Pat. Even better, it turns out that Northern Ireland being Northern Ireland, Patrick knew the guy who was running the open mic night, Gareth.

We decided to make a night of it, so Patrick invited some of the lads I had met in the park and Tabitha brought along a few of her girlfriends. Aunt Beth wasn't digging that Jess was going, especially as Patrick needed to be focused and confident with the panel just round the corner.

I needed to be focused and confident too! So I decided to play a couple of the crowdpleasers that went over so well at The Bike Factory - This is The Life and New York - before I let loose with Incredible, followed by an acoustic version of one of the summer's pumping dance tunes - Seasons. And I finished off with a couple of tunes from my Northern Irish repertoire. The crowd really went for it and I could see Tabitha, Patrick and their friends were pretty 'gobsmacked' – in a good way.

Afterwards I got chatting to a few of the other artists playing, some of them regulars on the Belfast busking scene and pretty amazing musicians. It was cool of them to welcome me onto their turf. The night was more for the fun of it rather than prizes, which made it all more relaxed. We got a couple of drinks for free and the audience fave - a guy called Steve - won a restaurant voucher.

'Hey Tyler. Great effort tonight.'

'Thanks Gareth. It was cool to play.'

'Good call playing the Northern Irish songs.'

'Yeah I was sucking up to the crowd but hey!'

'I loved that other song you played.'

'Seasons?'

'No. Incredible. Who's it by?'

'Oh.' I laughed, 'It's one of mine.'

'Wow. And the boy can write!'

I gave him a smile. 'Thanks man.'

'It was really good. I mean it. Here - I run a little festival that happens later on in the summer. Let me check and see if we have any more slots left. I would love you to play. We have a few international artists coming, but we haven't had someone from NYC on the lineup before.'

'You serious? That would be awesome!'

'Absolutely. I'll e-mail you the deets later.'

We swapped contact info before Gareth had to go and chat to some of the other artists.

'You finished being a superstar yet boyo?' Tabitha asked.

'Haha yeah. He just asked me to play at a festival. Can you believe it?'

'Gareth is kinda big deal on the music scene here. You must have impressed him.'

'Serious?'

'Yeah.' I went off into one of my daydreams where of course I am in the starring role, on stage at the festival in front of a crowd who are just loving my music. And while it was great Gareth was into my sounds, what a huge disappointment the festival would be happening without me! Yes, I Googled it right away and was devastated to find out it was happening only a few days after I got back to NYC.

I pushed that thought to the back of my mind as we moved onto another venue and danced the night away. I hadn't been watching P – my bad, Aunt Beth! But Patrick left early with Jess; they seemed to be getting on well. We partied on with the rest of the crew, including some of the guys I was going camping with later in the week. Tabitha drove me home just after 1.

'See you tomorrow?' Tabitha asked as I struggled to get my guitar out of the back seat of her tiny car.

'Yeah sure Tabs. I'll call in the morning!'

'Sure thing. Or I can always give you a shout. Night.'

I stood on the sidewalk and watched the stars collide. I hadn't closed the car door. I was lingering. We had enjoyed a couple of nights of dates (yes they were definitely dates!), but we hadn't kissed since that first time. After being so forward at the beginning I was being a gentleman. But tonight I could feel this sense of expectancy. All night Tabitha's eyes had told a story of delight and joy. Her comments to me about the gig had been super complimentary. Against Beth's advice to take it easy, I knew if I hadn't already, I was totally falling for her. I took a long look at her eyes gazing up at me, shining in the moonlight, then I sank back into the passenger seat and we kissed. All of the 'will we won't we kiss again' thoughts vanished in that moment.

When I got inside I made a cup of tea, and, inspired by the night, wrote a song for Tabitha. I hadn't told her how I felt, but by the words that flowed so easily from my mind, I knew that things with her were starting to get serious.

No, seriously serious.

PINGING WINDEES

Picture this:

2am on a beautiful midsummer's night.

I'm standing in Tabitha's driveway.

My guitar is hanging over my back.

The bike is propped up against a cherry blossom tree.

It's a promising picture, but instead of serenading my girl with wonderful lyrics, I was stuttering to explain to Big Graham (Tabitha's dad), Steve (her neighbour - who was holding a base-ball bat) and a slightly flustered Tabitha, why on God's green earth I had just smashed her bedroom window.

It was the worst way to introduce myself to her dad.

I got everything wrong.

After a wonderful evening together, I decided to end it with a big, surprise, romantic gesture.

Anyway, I hatched Plan Romeo pretty much as soon as Tab's car had pulled out of the drive. I grabbed my guitar, wheeled out the bike, but on the ride over to Tabitha's, my phone battery had died. So giving her a wake-up phone call was out the window. Probably a smarter dude would have turned back. Not me! When I arrived in Tabitha's driveway I grabbed a handful of bark chips from one of the flower beds and threw it at what I guessed was her window, expecting the wood to gently tap the glass.

I had been looking forward to Tabitha opening her window, delighted and overcome with emotion when she heard me serenading her from the garden below. Then I would come to her front door and add to the romance of the scene by giving her a kiss and telling her I had written a song just for her. Well, that was one scenario that definitely didn't happen!

Blame it on a hidden stowaway stone that totally smashed the pane, set off the intruder alarm and signalled all the house security lights to come on. Boy did I ever underestimate my incredible throwing arm! Must be all the B-ball!

Instead of moonlight bliss and Tabitha's delighted smile, I got me in the spotlight surrounded by broken glass and her face through the shattered window wearing an expression of pure horror - of the 'what on earth just happened?' variety.

Though totes embarrassed, a part of me still thought it was a great romantic idea, in theory. And I still do, if things had gone right. I just got the 'how' all wrong. But let's just say it was a one-off that I probably would never repeat again! I learned a few lessons. For starters, now I know what daft means.

And raging – as in Tab's dad, a big guy and pretty scary when riled, which he was when he threw open the front door, swore blue murder and called me a 'tube'. The neighbour came running with the bat, a Boston Red Sox souvenir from a recent trip to Beantown. Then Tabitha came out to the driveway, hands to her face. Scundered. A NI word for 'let the earth open and swallow me up embarrassed.'

Despite his anger, Graham did laugh when Steve said 'och, he's only pinging the windees. You know what lads are like! Clean daft! Don't tell me you never pinged a few windees in your time Graham?'

But mostly he was fuming. And rightly so. He ordered Tabitha back to bed. Then, so we would not wake any more neighbours with Graham's tirade, he brought me inside where he mocked my attempts to sing about love to his daughter at 2 in the morning. I stood in the hallway taking the blast. Our conversation lasted all of one minute, ending, thankfully, when I rather shakily introduced myself and explained that yes, I had been out on a few dates with his wonderful daughter, before apologising profusely and promising to pay for the window. Graham agreed, opened the door and walked out into the driveway to start picking up the glass.

That's when I noticed Tabitha had been watching the whole thing from the stair landing. As I turned to go, I caught her eye, hoping for a bit of sympathy, but she gave me this look of anger and contempt that I knew she had perfected in her acting classes. You know – the could you be more stupid? look. I was about to say my good nights and walk out the door when she just let me have it. Both barrels.

'Tyler you just don't get it! I can't fall for a guy who does stupid stuff like that. You of all people should have learned how much trouble impulses can get you into. Just look at Patrick!'

'Ehhh-'

She was Big Graham's daughter all right. 'And my dad really really did not need this. Do you know how much he worries about me? He's got enough stress in his life without a looper boyfriend who is living in some sort of rom-com fantasy land!'

Now that was a bit unfair!

She didn't hold back.

'Like what have you had to deal with? Making smoothies, finding a Prom date, playing your guitar in the subway, hoping your shirt matches your hoodie. Big deal. Some of us have had our lives turned upside down. We have real concerns to think about, not that stupid teenage stuff. You haven't a clue!'

Woah! Where did that come from? OK I did a dumb thing, but come on-

Even her dad must have thought so. He stepped into the hall. 'Tabitha, that's enough.' His stern tone interrupted the flow.

'No Dad. It's not.'

She stared at me. I stared back. It couldn't be any more awkward.

'I think it's time for you to go Tyler.' Graham's voice was gentle but worried as he ushered me towards the open door.

'Mind yourself on the bike.'

'Yeah, go write a song about it or tweet some celebrity. Hide away in your superficial online life. Some of us have had to deal with real crap Tyler. Hashtag go figure that one out.'

'I . . . I'm sorry,' I gulped.

'Tabitha. Apologise.' Graham ordered. Tabitha ran up the stairs.

I just stood there in the hallway. Graham put his hand on my shoulder and squeezed.

'Don't worry about it son. You weren't to know, but she got a bit of news this evening when she came in. It wasn't the easiest for her to hear.'

I just nodded.

'The last few years have been hard on our Tabs. And now that some of her friends are going through the same thing, she's been living through it all over again. It's just the two of us so we can be a bit overprotective of each other. That's dads and daughters for you.'

I nodded again and had nothing more to say. As I climbed on my bike, I restated my promise to Graham to pay for the damage and apologised once again.

The cycle home was slow. The first pink streaks of dawn were beginning to colour the sky. At 3am! Crazy! I wondered what Tabs' bad news had been? Ireland was beginning to bite. Never in a million years did I dream that I would be faced with so much big, real, serious stuff.

In a way, Tabitha was right. I thought about what I had just tried to do. I played her words over in my mind as I crossed the Lagan and watched the river flow beneath my feet. The same river that had hosted the T&T boat race. The butterflies of our early romance had just been replaced by a killer stare and cutting truths that destroyed all sense of my summer romance.

I wanted Patrick to get an undisturbed sleep on this last night before his big meeting, and I promised Granny I wouldn't abandon the guitar, so I spent the rest of the night, well early morning, writing a few songs about my time in Ireland, before I fell asleep on the couch. In my journal I had made a note of lines and thoughts that had popped into my mind since I had been on The Emerald Isle, but hadn't devoted time to sit down and pull them all together. Plus my pledge to note down some thoughts each night had been pretty sporadic. More than I had ever dreamed had happened over the last few months. So when I should have been sleeping, my creativity came alive.

Down by the river

We sat down by the river.
You took my hand
You held me tight.
Walk with me into my land
How can a stranger feel like such a friend?
Take my words to the fire
Cause I don't want to burn you with what I have to say
You're my summer sky
Turning grey to blue
I see everything through you

Life becomes new
Two kids playing with the idea that love might come to town
Come and fix this broken heart.
My beautiful American friend . . .

The City

Here I go
Here I stay
On the sidewalk of your city
I will walk another way.
Listen as we sing
A new song over you
A new start for every boy and every girl.
So say goodbye to yesterday
Every morning is a brand new day.
So bring your smile
Bring your inner child to everyday . . .

I finished these songs and outlined a couple more in my note-book. I posted some of my fresh new lyrics to Twitter and thought about sending @iamwill a tweet, 'Hey what do you think of this - 'Here I go. Here I stay. On the sidewalk of your city. I will walk another way. Listen as we sing. A new song over you', but then Tabitha's words about living in a fantasy came into my mind and I threw my phone onto the floor.

MY WEE GRANNY

I fell asleep for like three hours, until a smartly dressed Patrick leaned over my face and began to read some of my lyrics to me.

'Here I go
Here I stay
On the sidewalk of your city
I will walk another way.
Listen as we sing
A new song over you ...'

'Man you're deeper than you look.'

With only a couple of hours sleep after the shenanigans last night, I had been looking forward to lazing about until Patrick came back from the panel. So his presence was really annoying. Embarrassing too. Until I sing them to other people, my lyrics are private. To me, other people reading my words equates to taking a bath with a stranger. You just don't do it. Plus I was still feeling the shame, shock and hurt from the previous night.

All I could think though, was that my romantic ramblings were probably the lift Patrick needed. He was wearing nicely ironed chinos and a buttondown, had combed his hair and shaved off his stubbly beard. I would tell him about my previous night's disaster after his meeting, and boy how he would laugh!

'Good luck P. Call me later when you're finished, yeah?'

'Sure man.'

I couldn't tell him he would be fine or that we'd celebrate, and he probably would laugh if I promised to send a prayer to St. Joe for him (Joe being pretty helpful to me!). But I sent one anyway.

Richard was already at work, so when Beth left the house for her final day of the school term, I managed to get another couple of hours shuteye before I cycled over to Granny's. I'm sure she would have some great advice, and great food for me.

During my stay Granny seemed to visit just about every other day. Usually she dropped in with a freshly baked sponge cake or similar goodies she had rustled up in her kitchen. On other occasions she left us eggs from her neighbour's chickens. Agatha's eggs were the talk of the parish, the yolks 'as golden as a North Down sunrise' as Granny would say. She always brought milk for tea, cos if you haven't realised, they love to drink tea over here. And to go with the milk; still-warm scones, pies, biscuits, or 'a wee nibble' to help you through the morning, afternoon or evening. That summer I experienced firsthand the primary source of my mom's love for the culinary world.

Granny stayed five minutes or five hours (usually dozing off in the sunroom and ending up staying for tea, which is dinner, not another cup of tea), or sometimes she just stayed over. Beth did not want her on the roads after dark, for the safety of everyone!

Granny was a great woman, but a terrible driver. Not just bad, or careless, but terrible. So it was a good thing that her inability to change gear on time gave the kids kicking a soccer ball in the street an early warning sign of her imminent arrival. The sound of the roaring engine approaching provided precious seconds to grab bikes or tennis racquets from the street before Granny's purple car hurtled uncontrollably round the corner. Granny would park (abandon) her car either across the driveway or a few feet either side of the low kerbs. One day she crashed into the McCallion's pear tree, taking a shortcut through the hedge. The neighbours weren't too happy, but didn't make a huge deal out of it in case Granny stopped bringing them her treasured chocolate fudge cake. Once, on her way to whist, (a card game with her pals) she gave me a ride home. After that terrifying trip I decided not to get in the car with her again. It had been like a death defying ride at a theme park. Not Barry's but Six Flags!

Family get-togethers and her regular visits to the house aside, Granny and I had a lunch date, whenever possible, over my vacation. On the days that Patrick was busy sorting out his university hassles, we'd sit in her house, or beautiful garden if it was nice out, and she talked me through the family tree. Today was no different. She made me a snack while I was waiting for lunch, then lunch, and then a second lunch, (I nervously joked with her that early Alzheimer's was setting in, when she forgot that I had eaten one lunch already, but actually I think she is just a 'feeder'!).

Sometimes we weeded or harvested vegetables from her garden, played cards, or looked through old home videos and photographs. Other days we went into town to have a 'juke' around the shops where we searched for new clothes and old gig posters, badges and other antiques that we thought Granda would have loved.

We also worked our way through Granda's huge collection of LPs and a treasured songbook they had written together. It was a songwriter's dream and she granted me copyright on some of his lyrics. Granda's band were on the verge of big things when he called it quits. Today, as she made lunch, Granny played on her old turntable the last LP The Forevers had made. I never tired of listening to Granda's soulful voice. Granny also taught me a lot about how to fix things around her house, such as her wheelbarrow, the wonky shelf in the bathroom and a leaky tap in her utility room.

Every time I left her house she would slip a £20 note into my hand, or if I refused to take it, she shoved it into one of my pockets. We had the same friendly 'take it/no I can't' argument every time and every time I walked away with the cashola. With the money burning a hole in my chinos, I usually

209

called by the University Quarter to explore the little book and antique shops round about.

At the start of the date crazy week I brought Tabitha around to Granny's house. Despite Beth telling me not to get into something serious, Granny was very interested in helping me get things right with Tabitha and gave me plenty of words of wisdom about girls and 'courting'. In fact, before my first date, I was honoured to receive the first text Granny ever sent on the smartphone I helped set up for her. 'Goodluckgrannyx'. She hadn't quite mastered the space button. Then, while I was having lunch at Granny's soon after, she asked me to go on BookFace to show her some pictures of Tabitha.

'She's a pretty young thing so she is.'

Note: a lot of people in Northern Ireland use the following expressions at the end of their sentences: 'so it is' 'so we did', 'so they did', or a particular favourite, 'so I did, so I did'. These phrases have no real purpose except maybe to underline a point. You'll hear residents of Norn Iron saying things like, 'It's a sunny day so it is' or 'They are really lovely, so they are'. Charming, I guess, but really frustrating when you are:

(a) Struggling to pick up people's accents

(b) Trying to decipher whether people are making statements or asking questions. As it is, all sentences go up at the end, so you can understand my confusion!

Anyway, back to the story! My times with Granny were precious times. My formative childhood years had seriously lacked playing card games in her house on rainy afternoons and running around her garden playing airplanes. I was lucky enough to have spent so much time with my Italian grandparents in New York, and don't get me wrong, I loved growing up with them around, but I had still missed hanging out with Granny and Granda in Ireland. So I was determined to make the most of our lunches and any other time we could grab together.

Granny also let me into the family secrets and shortcomings and recalled her life's highlights and disappointments. She regretted putting off travelling outside of the UK until her late 50s and being too hard on her colleagues in work. She described Uncle David as having 'destructive tendencies', but didn't go into details. I quizzed her on it, but thinking back to some of the off-the-cuff comments Mom had made about David over the years, I began to link him and Patrick. The one thing that was hard to hear was how much she missed my Mom. Granny never got over Mom's decision to move away from Northern Ireland, but she knew her decision to follow her heart was what she had to do. Besides, the 80s were a difficult time for all who stayed in Northern Ireland. Not just The Troubles, but the lack of decent job opportunities for someone like Mom.

The time spent in Granny's meticulously arranged and freakishly clean house, counting her collection of strange little animal ornaments, and talking about her life that had been and mine that was still to come, was one of the most treasured experiences of my trip. Our conversations brought an immeasurable, untweetable amount of joy and thankfulness to my soul. Hanging out with Granny was more than a good thing to do; it was the right thing to do and the perfect way to spend part of my summer.

So today, when I told her about my escapades at Graham's, all she did was laugh, call me a loveable idiot, and asked (in song of course) if I wanted 'just one Cornetto!' for my lunch-time dessert. (I later found out that Cornettos are a UK brand of ice cream cone, which had an Italian themed TV advertisement) notorious for its operatic jingle. So much for the advice!

THE KINGDOM

Patrick:	*Bro wer r u?*
Tyler:	*@ Grannys*
Patrick:	*Did u forget bout camping?*
Tyler:	*Yup. Trying 2 fix a tap.*
Patrick:	*Random. Get bak asap. Leaving in 2 hrs.*
	And call a plumber.

All day I had been expecting the call from Pat telling me how his meeting went.

Tyler:	*KK. How was panel?*
Patrick:	*Will tell u when u get bak. Think it went*
	well. Just wanna get outta here 4 a while.

I gave Granny a peck on the cheek goodbye and promised

to give the tap another try on my next visit. On my bike ride home I thought through a packing list for the trip, but forgot it all when I arrived at the house and spotted a postcard from Mom and Dad waiting for me.

Having a blast in Brasil! Our days here have been the most surreal we have ever experienced. Two seasoned Manhattanites, in the Amazon rainforest for a home-stay visit. We started in Manaus. Caught an opera in Teatro Amazonas and had time to explore the town before we joined our tour group and spent the next couple of nights checking our beds for snakes, spiders and everything else that could kill you! Even some of the caterpillars are poisonous here! The jungle was noisy with animal sounds and steamy but we saw some beautiful birds and met the nicest people ever.

Dad here! First day in Rio. Spending it chilling at the beach with the beautiful people! Going to Cristo Redentor tomorrow - the statue up on the peak. Will take selfies as proof we made it. Then getting our samba on. Onto Iguassu Falls next. You been to the Belfast Falls yet? I'm sure they are similar ;0 Have you settled in? Hope you are having fun. Say hi to the gang for us.

Miss you xx

Mom & Dad

It was great to hear from them, but before I could send a reply on Facebook, Patrick summoned me to the garage, where two backpacks and various other camping gear, including our old faithful pop up tent, stood waiting. 'Come on Mayor Bloomberg. We need to pack asap.'

While I stuffed items into Richard's old backpack, Patrick filled me in on his panel experience. All his preparation had been necessary as they 'grilled my ass' - Patrick's words not mine! He talked me through the process, from waiting in the hall with the other students, to the stern, stoic expressions on the faces of the panel. He told me he nearly lost it as he had to recount some of his darkest days from the year. It had been even tougher than he had anticipated, but he felt, despite the formality of the panel, that they were generally sympathetic and supportive.

'Plus my tutor is really going to bat for me. She is a star. But I don't wanna think about this anymore. I wanna party on the mountain!'

We grabbed a microwave snack and got changed into outdoor clothes, as Patrick filled me in on the next 48 hours of my life. Finally, we chucked our bags 'n' stuff into Pat's car and, for the first time that summer, left the house on time.

Sure I was excited about the camping trip, but let's get something clear, discovering the great outdoors wasn't part of my plan for the summer.

My family tried camping.

Once.

Who knew a groundsheet was so important? Right?

It was a terrible trip – a time before pop up tents, edible camping food, LED lights, wind up mobile chargers, apps of camping spots and walking routes. Thank the Lord for glamping* - that's my scene.

Prior to this trip to Ireland, anything other than my comfy

bed was a scary environment, but having spent a few nights in hostels, one night in a car, 3 nights in a tent and only a handful of sleeps in a bed to call my own, I think someone is trying to teach me that I need to 'catch a grip', as they like to say around these parts. Sleeping in a different bed most nights hasn't been as bad as I thought it would be. But maybe that's because the weather has been kind to us and dreams have been easy to come by in Ireland. Well, apart from the night in the Dublin hostel - that was a different story!

When we turned into Conor's driveway he was sitting like a boss in his dad's SUV. He gave us a huge grin.

'Yeah boys. What a ride!' he shouted over the music that was blasting from the stereo.

'Unbelievable', Patrick remarked, quickly followed by a huge call of 'SHOTGUNNNNNN.'

Rick rolled into the driveway so three became four, which became five when Conor's dad, Michael, emerged from the house and kicked Patrick out of the front seat. Conor had been put on the insurance for our trip - a bold move by his dad! We were dropping Michael off at the gym en route, so on our way, Michael gave his son strict instructions about how to look after and drive the vehicle and told me stories about his frequent business trips to NYC. He even gave me a few new diners to check out. In return, I gave him one to check out in Belfast: #connectioneconomy

Our destination was about an hour from Belfast, so I had time to flick through my Ireland book and see what Rodriguez had written about The Mourne Mountains, or The Kingdom as the area is affectionately known:

> *The Mourne Mountains are the main mountain range in Northern Ireland. Slieve Donard is the highest peak, the 19th highest in Ireland, and stands 853 metres above sea level. Newcastle, the town at the foot of the Mournes, is 31 miles from Belfast and 62 miles from Dublin, making it very accessible for east coast daytrippers. The stone Mourne Wall was built by hand between 1904 and 1922. It's a beauty, as far as walls go.*

Rodriguez's helpful stats and taken-off-the-internet photos, including a photoshopped one of himself sitting on the stone wall in his prom tuxedo, failed to prepare me for the sheer beauty in every corner of The Kingdom of Mourne. As we drove into Newcastle, the tower of an historic hotel beside the miles-long curve of beach was like a scene from one of those movies about Victorian times, or something out of *Downton Abbey*. There's nothing like that in the Big Apple! And I was blown away to see the dark Mountains of Mourne *'sweep down to the sea'*, just like in the song Mom sings now and then. Epic.

Through town and we continued driving along the coast road, then uphill through vivid green countryside of small fields surrounded by stone walls, then woods and moorland towards the Silent Valley. When we reached the lonely midst of the mountain range, an almost spiritual feeling came over me. The feeling stayed with me the whole trip as I walked through empty heathery boglands criss-crossed by walls made of piled up rocks and scaled dramatic side trails to the peaks.

But before the farmland ended and the mountains began,

217

we stopped in a farmyard that belonged to Conor's friend's neighbour's uncle's cousin. Yeah work that connection out! We used the facilities, filled our water bottles and flasks before we jumped back into the SUV and took an off-road track up into an open treeless landscape of moorlands, peaks and sheep. We parked, grabbed our backpacks, tightened the laces on our walking boots and began hiking into the High Mournes range. Goodbye civilization!

Because it was early evening already and stomachs were growling, we only walked for a few miles before we found a good place to set up camp and pitch tents. The boys lit a fire and we sat around it, munching snack foods and talking for hours. Patrick fessed up to the boys about his panel experience. Turns out Conor had faced a similar panel the previous year! My turn: so I told them about my 'pinging windees' experience and the boys 'raked' me about it all night. It was just the pick-me-up that Pat needed after his stressful week.

The next morning the boys had to wake me up. Writing songs until the early hours of Friday morning was a good idea at the time but I was wrecked. As we chowed down on a couple of cereal bars, Rick explained the route, and boy he wasn't joking when he said we were out for a good walk. Seventeen breathtaking (literally) miles later and we had conquered the peaks of Bearnagh, Commedagh and Donard. *'Get her climbed'* was the cry of the day from the guys. I got through the trek focusing on three things:

1. Capturing scenes that would energise me in times of deepest winter when I was in boring college lectures.

2. Making sure I didn't fall off the track into sheep droppings, a squelchy boghole or bunches of heather.

3. Keeping up. These guys showed blatant disregard to the golden rule of walking at the pace of the slowest member!

The view from the summit of Donard was out of this world. After drinking it all in, we followed a long, long wall made of stones down the mountain – I was wondering why it was even built! I'm sure this was the one from Rodriguez's guide, so maybe he knew the answer. Soon we came to a sheltered place where Conor, Patrick and I set up camp while Rick prepared a one-pan feast. He's a sous-chef in a top restaurant in Belfast. Screw the below-average boil in the bags; we dined on food fit for kings. For the rest of the night we sang all the worst, cheesiest songs we could think of and swapped more stories. I hadn't heard from Tabitha since our bust up and asked the boys for some advice. They told me not to worry, but I couldn't help it. Despite what she had said in her house a few nights back, I really liked her and I knew it was all my fault anyway.

After our moment in the North Coast, Patrick had agreed to keep me more in the loop about how he was doing with Jess and everything else in his life. And so far, he was keeping to it, which was more than I could say about the promise I had made to myself at the start of the trip about noting down a highlight of my day!

I didn't ask him if he was OK everyday or about medical school. He had his mom for that. But he did tell me that one of his Christian friends, Matt, had taught him about an old centering prayer as a way of helping him to process his day. Writing down the good things, the difficult things, the things that made him stop, the things he knew he had missed through worry, the things that made him smile, the things that made him thankful. Although he wasn't a believer, Patrick felt it was a great way for him to review his feelings and make sense of what he was going through. It seemed to be doing him good. From our campsite, we could see lights twinkling far below from scattered farms. Pat and I walked a few yards to the wall to brush our teeth.

'Hope I am not being out of line, but you've seemed more yourself lately. Matt's prayer must be doing its thing.'

'Aye. I'm just so glad the panel is finished. Now I can move on and enjoy the rest of your trip before getting stuck into the books - if they allow me to do my resits. And being up here has been great. Good to get the head showered.' (It's another NI expression that is really really useful. Sort of means clearing the head.)

We started walking back to camp when Pat opened up.

'Things with Jess were so hard. I'd come off the most brilliant summer. Best of my life.'

'Europe?'

'Yeah.'

'That sounded like an awesome trip.'

'It was unbelievable. Italy, Slovenia, Croatia, Hungary, Slovakia, Czech Republic, Poland, Germany, Netherlands and a lot of cool places in between. You need to do more of Europe bro.'

'I think Ireland will do me this summer. Maybe next year.'

'Part of the reason I had such a blast was because Jess and I had gotten back together and it was great. It was like having the old Jess back; someone I knew and liked. And I had matured.'

I gave Pat the 'raised eyebrow look'.

'OK I had matured a bit. Anyway, we were loving our new fresh start. Probably too giddy about it really. But it didn't last. 30 seconds later and it was all different again. When I got back, I knew something had happened by the tone of her voice. Jess had waited until I was home to tell me. First there was this overwhelming fear. Then shame as we told our parents. The embarrassment, but a lot of that eventually was replaced with excitement. Well I was still scared, I didn't have a clue how to be in a serious, permanent relationship, let alone be a father, but I was starting to deal with it and was actually getting excited until-' he paused. 'That morning.'

I let him talk.

'Jess called. But it wasn't Jess. It was her mum on her mobile. I knew something was seriously wrong. By this stage in the pregnancy it should have been smooth sailing. Anyway I was on my way to a job interview. Most students were earning money to piss against a wall. I was earning money to pay for nappies and baby food. I nearly didn't answer the call.'

'Get to The Royal. We think she's losing the baby!'

'I was beyond scared. I broke land speed records to get over there. When I arrived on the maternity ward Jess was in bed. She was so pale. She was crying. She was hooked up to various bleeping monitors and some kind of drip. Her parents were there too. Nurses came and did checks and I heard 'heartbeat' mentioned. At one point Jess was wheeled away, for a scan I guess. We just waited, not knowing what to say or do. It seemed like we were there for hours, but probably not.

'Then a doctor came up. He recognised me from our first ante-natal hospital appointment. He briefed us on what was happening. They had hoped to save the baby, but it had become clear there was no chance. There had been a faint heartbeat when Jess arrived, but now, no trace. He explained the baby had a congenital condition that hadn't been picked up on any scan. Jess would need to be brought to the operating theatre. Then, as they moved Jess out of the ward, the doctor walked with us through the double doors into the corridor. Jess gripped my hand so tightly. I managed a few seconds alone with her before they wheeled her off.' Pat couldn't finish. Just broke down. I must have been really affected too, because Patrick comforted me, instead of the other way round. Like a big brother, he put his arm round my shoulder.

When we had been on our trip Up North Patrick hadn't given me any details about that day at the hospital. Now he told me how he could not forget the fear in Jess's eyes and how uncomfortable he felt around her parents, who probably could not help blaming him for the whole situation.

'When Mum told me you were coming over in June, to be honest, it gave me a target. I was going to be OK by the summer. But I don't think I'll ever get over this. I don't know if you're supposed to. It's an ache inside, or an emptiness that I can feel everyday. I get better, then regress, then get stronger, then it hits me like a tidal wave and wipes me out for a few days. I know it does happen that people lose babies. I'm a medic, or trying to be. But … but it's the guilt. I put Jess through this. It was Jess, not me, Jess alone who had to go through so much in the hospital. Who had the complications afterwards. Who had to wonder, at age 19, if she could ever have kids again. And it was all my fault. I should have been more careful when, you know, we hooked up. I still have nightmares of her being wheeled away down the corridor. It's horrible.'

'How has Jess been about it all?' I asked.

'Pretty quiet man. She's OK now, no lasting medical issues, which is great, but she went through so much. I know she's pushing her feelings way down. She won't tell me how she feels and it's driving me crazy. She'll tell me to stop going on about it and get on with my life. She'll say that's what she wants. Some days I think she blames me for this whole thing happening, then other days she just acts like it didn't happen.'

'That's tough man.'

'Yeah. It's like she has moved on. She even started dating some other guy earlier this year, but then split up with him. Maybe realised she still wanted something with me. I dunno. But now she won't talk to me properly. I just wish it was two years ago and I was carefree and didn't have any of this stuff going on in my head.'

'You have other people to talk to don't you?'

'Yeah I do. But you're somewhat removed from it all. Like you're family, but you've got a funny accent.'

'I can't even imagine what that day would have been like. It sounds like hell.'

'I just felt numb. Jess and I had made great commitments to each other. One minute we were getting together, finding out what love was about, and then we were thrown together with this lifelong bond. Not just the thought of many more years together, but another person in our lives who was going to have her own personality, grow up, have dreams, love us, do stuff with us. Then it all changed as that future was ripped away from us. We had a reason that brought us together and now ... the hurt is lasting so much longer than I ever imagined.'

Patrick talked about how Jess and he had tried and failed to comfort each other through the grieving process.

'Everyone grieves in their own way. I've learned that.' he said. 'And there is so much more to it than I ever realised.' But he did not finish. I got a sense of unsaid stuff. This might not be everything.

Instead Pat stared out at the perfect night. From our perch high up in the hills, past foothills and fields, the reflection of the full moon shimmered like a silver coin on the distant sea. Mist was creeping along the mountainside into the valleys. I stared up at the stars and realised the carefree thing I had with Tabitha was a blessing and any issues stupidly simple. At most I was struggling to figure out three things:

1. How has she not noticed how much of a dork I am?

2. Am I falling in love? (And can it really happen that quick?)

3. How do I resolve our situation?

Pat broke the silence. 'We better get to bed.'

'Sure.'

'Don't worry, the rest of the lads know. Conor had even started buying baby presents! And I have been doing a lot better over the last few months. I'm getting there, bro!'

I distracted him on the walk back to the tent by getting him to tell me stories about his European roadtrip. He laughed pretty hard when he told me about a night he spent in a Croatian hostel. A Canadian guy was really drunk and started waking people up in the hostel to make porridge for them. Needless to say it was a 'you had to be there moment.'

Patrick was unzipping the door of the tent when I announced, 'Oh gotta pee cuz'.

'Cool. Make sure you wash your hands before you come back in!'

I didn't need to really; instead I knew I needed to text Tabitha. I knew it was on her to make the first move, but after listening to Patrick's girl problems I realised I didn't have the time to be stubborn. Not contacting her was stupid and I needed to see where I stood with her. Plus I wanted to talk to her about how we could get Pat and Jess back together, for good. I just hoped I could get some sort of network way up here.

> *Tyler:* *Hey. Am camping in The Mournes. I know*
> *u might not wanna hear from me but I think we*
> *should talk? Lunch Monday?*

I managed to get a few hours sleep before the morning sun peeked its way through the misty duvet of cloud that enveloped our campsite. Then it was business as usual, despite my aching legs! Thanks to Rick we enjoyed an amazing breakfast of porridge and toast (cooked on sticks over the fire) which helped us capture Slieve Binian by lunchtime.

On our descent I picked out a miniscule shiny box like a toy car, far below. Our SUV. I wondered why we had abandoned our vehicle in such a remote spot, but all was explained when we came to a river, then a lagoon that was hidden on the far side of the 4x4. We dumped our bags by the vehicle and couldn't lose our muddy clothes quick enough. Carrying our towels we ran to a rocky ledge where I watched, and then followed as the guys jumped into the coldest lagoon known to man, entering the icy water with yells and screams. Damn it was Arctic. (Or '*Baltic*' as they say in Belfast.) We swam frantically to keep the blood circulating, before passing round a bar of soap to wash the dirt of the Mournes from our smelly armpits and grubby fingernails. As I dried off, I knew the memories we had created, and the secrets Patrick and I had shared in The Kingdom of Mourne, would stay with me for a lifetime.

* glamping (glamorous camping) is an upmarket version of camping. When you go glamping you try and bring as many modern conveniences as possible to make your camping trip comfortable and even slightly opulent. Velvet pillow anyone?

EGG ON MY FACE

Monday morning. Day One of our week of waiting.

Waiting for Patrick's panel result and waiting for Tabitha to text me back. Pat and I went out for a morning run. When I came back I was relieved/nervous to see a text from Tabitha.

> Tabitha: *Hey Tyler. Yeah let's talk. Bread and Banjo*
> *Ormeau Road 12.30.*

YUSSSS! After I got ready I messaged Mom and Dad. *Got your postcard! Looks like you guys are having an amazing time. Have been having a blast here too. Non stop since I arrived. We took the long way home from Dublin – via Cork, Ring of Kerry and Galway! Have been camping Up North and in the Mournes. We swam in a lagoon – 'Baltic'! Ireland is so beautiful. And don't freak out, but I have met a girl. She's called Tabitha.*

Mom was online

> *LOL I know you have met a girl. Just because I'm in S. America doesn't mean that I don't know what's going on with my baby! She looks lovely. Be good! Your dad says hi. Say hi to the family and give Granny a hug for me xx*
> *Love you*

My fingers hovered over the keyboard. I was tempted to ask Mom about the whole Patrick thing. But I didn't have the guts.

Bread and Banjo it was for our showdown lunch in this up and coming part of the city. That is if she even turned up! It was 12.45 and I thought I had been stood up when Tabitha came into view.

'You probably think I was late on purpose. But I had to cover in work for a couple of hours. And my phone battery went!' Her chair scraped loudly as she pulled it out.

'Oh that old one! Don't worry I knew you would be here.' I said with a veil of confidence.

The café she had chosen was really neat. While waiting, I had been staring at the giant cookies and the cinnamon rolls - I needed some American comfort food. Being the guitar playing son of a Belfast born/American residing pâtisserie store owning lady, I couldn't help but feel that Tabitha had put some effort into thinking about the spot where we were having lunch.

She mustn't have been that angry at me. Well that's what I hoped.

Since arriving in Ireland I had developed an obsession for anything old school and antiquated - including my granny! So I thought we might have a quick convo, make up and then browse the vintage stores I had spotted along the Ormeau Road. But when we sat at the table I could tell Tabitha was not in a shopping mood. So we made small talk and avoided the window-smashing topic. I told her about my trip to The Mournes. She seemed semi-interested and told me she had been part of the cast for a film set in those parts. *How serious had her acting been?* I quizzed her about it but she didn't bite. I made a note to ask her friends about it, if I ever got the chance to meet any of them again, that is!

'What about Pat and the panel?' she asked.

'He feels pretty positive about it. I'll be so glad when he finds out the result. The house has been stress city. But he had a good time in the mountains.'

'Yeah I can imagine.'

'Plus the stuff with Jess. I mean the guy has had a horrible year.'

'True. But he brought a lot of it on himself.' Tabitha noted. Her words jarred with me.

'What!?'

'I mean, come on, he got a girl pregnant.' I couldn't believe what Tabitha was saying.

'Well junior high science taught me that it takes two.'

'Yeah. But he should have been more careful. And now he

keeps trying to make it work with Jess. But-'

'But what?' I asked.

'But he needs to realise that it's not going to work. Just leave her alone and move on.'

I hadn't even thought about this scenario. I always assumed Patrick and Jess would just settle things and get back together.

'Seriously Tabitha. You think they should just split up?'

'Obviously.'

'But they were high school sweethearts.'

'You are such a hopeless romantic,' Tabitha swirled the remains of her cup of tea. 'Not everything's like the movies. People change. Break up and learn from the experience. Grow up. Meet other people and one day, with a bit of luck they do meet their soul mate. They are both hanging on for something that's not gonna work. It's making them miserable and keeping them from meeting the right someone who might actually make them happy.'

'But it could. They met up a couple of nights ago and Patrick was in a good mood when he came back.' I pointed out.

'Look Tyler, I have been watching this happen for months, years actually. Even before the pregnancy. It's never going to work and they need to realise that.'

'But-'

'That's the point Tyler. The whole relationship is based on their emotions. Hot and cold. Even if they still had a child together that pair would not have stayed the course.'

Wow. Harsh. I was a bit shocked by her vision for their relationship. But Tabitha was sold on it. I was sold on mine.

No point discussing it any longer.

The wait staff came over and brought a much-welcomed break to our dispute. We hadn't even talked about the whole window thing. I ordered another soft drink.

'Well we can't agree on everything.' Tabitha said.

'Yes. But I can't believe that you don't even give them a chance.' I didn't mean for that to come out. This conversation was meant to be O-ver!

'Tyler you haven't been here all year. You have no idea about this. Considering Patrick hadn't even told you about the baby, well that shows how much he trusts you.'

That made me mad and I was about to push back when I realised, what's the point? At this rate we'll end up shouting. 'I guess-' I stared hard out the window but everything beyond the glass was a blur.

'You guess what?' Her tone made me want to shrivel up.

'I guess we'll have to agree to disagree.'

Tabitha padded her eyes with the sleeve of her jumper. 'No we won't,' she declared before she grabbed her bag and stormed out of the café.

BANDSTAND-OFF

I could have chased her, some would say I should have chased her, but right then, what I needed most was advice. I sat on in the café and FaceTimed a sleepy Rodriguez who was in his Fresh & Juicy uniform, ready to head out for his morning shift.

'Hey Tyler! 8 DAYS! I'm stoked about seeing you! How's your day going?'

'Oh it's going,' I said, before Alex came on screen wearing a furry crocodile suit.

'What the heck are you wearing?' Suddenly I missed those guys and my simple 'pre-Ireland' life so much, it was like a punch in the gut.

'I got a job helping at kids parties. This thing is hot!' Alex said it like it was perfectly natural. 'And I got another piercing.' Alex brought his right ear towards the screen and showed me a new addition to what was now a constellation of piercings. It looked pretty cool.

'Why are you two together? It must only be just after 9 there?' I asked.

'Alex stayed over last night and we watched a few movies.'

'Sounds cool.'

'How's Belfast?' Rodriguez asked.

'Well. Your book's been really useful. I've been to a lot of the places and-'

'Yes?' Alex cut in.

'I've met a girl.'

'EHHHOOOOOOOO' Rodriguez shouted.

'She's called Tabitha.'

'Is that the girl you went on a date with?'

'Yeah. Sorry I've been terrible at keeping in touch. I've been so busy. But she's awesome. Though I think it might be over now. I tried to serenade her a few nights back and I ended up smashing her window, long story, and we just had a huge fight, well two actually, and it's all a giant mess at the minute. She stormed out of the café just now. And now I don't know what's going on really. Like I only have another week left here and I don't want to ruin it thinking about a girl. Plus there's this whole thing with Patrick failing his exams, and-'

Rodriguez and Alex stared blankly back at me as the last two week's worth of events gushed out. I really needed my bros to say something, if I stopped talking long enough to give them a chance. But they looked somewhat shell-shocked so to fill the silence, I filled them in on our dates and the time Tabs and I had spent together over the summer.

At last Alex spoke up. I could tell he had been thinking. His attire was making the whole conversation easier to take. He told me straight.

'You need to go and talk to her bro. Go get her. Tell her how you feel. You're clearly into her.' And I always thought Alex was the goofy one!

'There's probably a reason you don't even know why she is acting all crazy like this. It might have nothing to do with you at all. Look at it from her point of view. If you were that into someone and they were about to fly out of your life, well, a big fight or three can make the saying goodbye bit a little easier.'

'Alex, you are a genius!' Just like that I exited FaceTime, threw a twenty onto the table and ran outside.

Dark, rain-filled clouds had arrived. It was still warm and humid, or muggy as they say over here, but the morning's 'mizzle' (mist meets drizzle) had turned into a heavy downpour. As I unlocked my bike the heavens started chucking it down. (There are hundreds of expressions here for the different varieties of rain and how it behaves!)

I called Tabitha to see where she was. No answer. She would either be in her car or heading back on foot into the city centre. I started to cycle up and down the streets around the Ormeau to try and find her car. Then I remembered something she had said to me on our first date. She had a favourite spot in Ormeau Park. It was her 'go-to' place during her teenage years when her parents were fighting. Maybe she was there? I began to cycle like a crazy person into Ormeau Park. Then I saw a coat I recognised. She was sheltering under a bandstand.

'Tabitha.'

'Tabitha!' I yelled again. She turned round.

'Tabitha we need to talk.'

I cycled towards her, stopping in a squeal of brakes. There was a stubborn silence. Neither of us apologised. No one was in a hurry to, even in this rain. But somebody had to go first!

'Tyler, I'm sorry that the last few days have been a mess, but I can't apologise for having a different opinion. But I am not going to go into all that again. Plus, about the window-'

I was going to reply, but she beat me to it. 'I need to tell you something.'

I had that feeling it was a Susan moment all over again. I stared at the dripping trees in the park and the ceiling of the decorative bandstand as I braced myself for her revelation.

'I have had so much fun with you. It's been amazing. I feel like I'm finding myself again. But there are reasons why I simply can never agree with you on this point. And if it means it tears us apart that's the way it has to be.'

'Tab-' I began, but she spoke over me.

'I am Ella.'

'What?' I replied.

'I'm Ella. My parents are Jess and Patrick. I guess you could say my brother Jack is Ella too. My parents found out my mum was expecting him when she was 19 and they had only been going out a few months. They stayed together because of my brother. Got married and right from the start it wasn't particularly happy. Then they had me, thinking if their family was complete that would help. For a lot of years they kept trying to make things work. But they just weren't compatible. Never had been really. Mum and Dad had a plan to stay together until Jack and I both finished school, but they didn't get there. So I know what it's like to see two people try and stay together for the sake of a kid and it's horrible. The atmosphere was pure poison and there was always this feeling that the kids are to blame, or have to take sides or make things better in some way. It doesn't work and it hurts everyone more than you know.'

'That's why you can't let this drop,' I realised.

'Yeah. Plus I know Jess and Pat and I've seen this type of situation and they can't be together. It's not *When Harry Met Sally*. It's real life and painful to watch.'

'Oh. OK.'

'I mean you can keep trying to force it. But all Patrick needs is for you to be honest with him. That's all.'

'But I have been honest with him, and I think they should keep trying.'

'Urghhh! You just don't get it do you?'

'Clearly not.'

'Look. Patrick is hanging on because he feels guilty about Jess. Jess keeps going back to him because she feels guilty about him - worries about his state of mind if she ends it. But she is starting to resent it. And so is Patrick if he really looks hard at himself. But that's all their relationship has left. Guilt.'

'I don't believe that. I think it's more than guilt that is keeping them together,' I said stubbornly.

Tabitha heaved a big, impatient sigh. 'They need their

freedom, Tyler.' She put her hood up. 'I can't say any more. You're gonna have to figure this one out for yourself.'

I stood up beside her. My phone buzzed. It was Patrick. I silenced his call.

'Take some time to figure out what you'll say to him. But Tyler-' Tabitha put her hand on my arm. 'There's another thing.'

Uh oh.

'About the other night. What you did was-'

'Embarrassing? Stupid? Romantic?' I said.

'Well a mixture of all of those things. And the sweetest daftest thing anyone has done for me, ever. But you must realise that my dad and I look out for each other, maybe more than the usual.'

I could have just sat there and listened but it was time for me to stick up for myself. 'I get all that, but you have to admit you over-reacted just a teeny tiny bit?'

'OK, confession.' She put her hands up. 'Something happened the day I blew off with you. You know how my mum cut me off, and my brother too. Well, as a result, none of us have had much of a clue what has been going on in her life. Nor did we want to know. But yesterday Dad and I found out she is with someone else. Has been for some time. In fact we discovered Mum started seeing this guy even before she walked out on us. So we all feel betrayed. Turns out she is living with him up in Limavady or somewhere. My Gran ran into someone who has a house up the road.'

'Oh. I understand.' Sort of.

'So yeah I was annoyed at you smashing my window. Obvs. And I'm sorry for venting like that.'

'No. Don't apologise. I was stupid. And your mum ... I wouldn't have come round if I had have known.'

'You weren't to know. Don't feel bad Tyler.'

I leaned against the rail of the bandstand. Tabitha stood in the middle of the shelter.

'So are we cool?' I asked.

'I need a day to process this. Be with Dad. Plus you need to get your skates on paying him back. I've had to sleep in the box room because of the air conditioning you installed in my room!'

There was so much I wanted to say, but I didn't get the chance to tell Tabitha the many things I had worked out in my mind as I'd cycled down to meet her. I wanted to pour my heart out to her. But this was her time, she had her own problems to sort out and I needed to give her a few days, even though it was something that I knew I didn't exactly have. We hugged, parted ways and due to the bi-polar Northern Irish weather left the park to bright sunshine splitting the clouds.

£39 AND CHANGE

July 1st already! No time to waste! So I was up and out of the house early and set up near Victoria Square - just out of earshot of the opera singer girl on Ann Street and a carrot-topped (they call it ginger over here) dude who had been on TV. Not much to set up really. Just me, my guitar, a hat for money and a raincoat, for just in case.

Halfway through my day of busking I was drowned out by an overly enthusiastic Christian street preacher, complete with blaring boombox and loudspeaker. Under the weight of her judgment I packed up my case and set up shop outside a preppy looking store, where I serenaded students and teenagers who had just spent a lot of their parents' cash.

A few hours and £39 later, I packed up my case and cycled over to Tabitha's house. With an ice cream carton filled with cash in one hand (topped up with one of Granny's £20s) and a peace offering of chocolates and beer in the other, (the panniers on Richard's bike came in handy) I stood repentant on Graham's doorstep. He answered the doorbell.

'He uses the bell! He's housetrained!' laughed Graham who actually seemed pleased to see me. 'You here to pay your debt?'

'Yes sir.' I even wiped my feet on the mat!

'Come on on on on in!' Turns out this is a really old joke from some comedian when Graham was a 'kiddiewinkle'.

'This is for you.' I handed him the heavy jingling ice cream tub filled with change.

Graham prised open the lid and chuckled at the mass of copper coins. 'Tyler you can give the money to a local charity.'

'What? But what about the window?'

'A friend who owns a building firm said he would come and fit a new window for free.'

'That's awesome,' I responded. 'But I am still really sorry for the other night. So you pick the charity.'

Another chuckle from Graham, as he set the tub on a side table. 'Not to worry Tyler. Have you recovered from the ordeal?'

'Just about. This is all so new. Girls. Romance. Breaking windows.'

I knew Tabitha was out at yoga. But I also knew it was a dangerous move to visit the house of your 'casual-summer-friend-possibly-girlfriend' if it weren't for the whole 'I live in America and you live in Ireland situation'. Especially when she wasn't around and especially after a still semi-unresolved argument with said possible girlfriend! Opening up to her dad could be another dumb move. But here I was.

'Grab a seat.' Graham pointed to the sunroom. When he joined me, he handed me a beer. Not one of mine which probably was all shook up from the bike ride and would have exploded all over the nice cane sofa. Graham paused the soccer game on the TV and turned to me. 'Young love is hard to figure out, son. I had a girlfriend when I was your age and I thought I was going to marry her. And I did.'

I pretended to know nothing.

'What happened?' I asked.

'We just grew apart but ... Tyler,' he took a long sip of his beer. 'I don't know what you kids are doing, but I do know that I haven't seen Tabby this happy in a long time. She probably mentioned about her mum and I. Well, how much she's told you is neither here nor there, but she had to grow up a lot faster than a wean, sorry, little one, should. Childhood should be carefree don't you think?'

He paused. I was unsure if I was supposed to comment.

'There are two sides to any story but the bottom line is that her mum walked out on her family for that French polisher from Limavady. I know I'm better without her, and that's fine, but it hurts because I know what cutting off the kids did to Tabitha and our Jack.'

NOT AGAIN I thought. *First Patrick, then Tabitha and now Big Graham's dumping his inner burdens onto me. I didn't know his wife ran off with someone from France, though! Wow. It all keeps getting weirder.*

Graham was still talking. 'I've been so worried about her. Her spark hasn't been the same lately. Probably because her mum has been messing her about. Gets in touch and never follows up. But your arrival seems to have really helped.'

I nodded like those dogs on a dashboard.

'And sure, I was ready to blow my top the other night,' conceded Graham. 'But that's because I was wondering what you were playing at? Tabitha is my little angel and I won't stand for anyone treating her without respect. But now that I know that you're just a wee romantic fool it's all OK!'

Graham laughed softly, probably at the idea of me being such an epic fail at the Romeo bit! He leaned forward to take a closer look at me. 'Is it true you're half Italian?'

I nodded again and he nodded too as if that explained and excused everything.

'You're only young once,' he said and raised his beer bottle in a salute to daft lovers.

'I never meant any harm.'

'Of course you didn't, and Tabs should not have kicked off like that the other night. She knows it. But we had some difficult news that day.'

More nods and sips.

'Which I won't go into. And really it's not important anyway, because these past couple of weeks my wee girl has been positively glowing. Growing with confidence everyday and she's even talking about pushing on with her acting again,' Graham smiled.

I was so relieved that got us off the subject of yours truly and onto the topic of Tab's interest in acting and her real potential. I had no idea she had won awards, played lead roles and been part of acclaimed youth groups that did touring shows. She played it down when she talked about it with me. A plan began to formulate in my mind.

'Anyway, don't feel under pressure.' I was so absorbed in my idea that I didn't know what Graham was referring to.

I made some guttural noise in reply.

'You never know what will happen when you head back to America, so just enjoy what you have with her. But I know that she likes you a lot.' He looked me in the eyes when he said 'A lot.'

But Graham wasn't done yet. 'Aye, she's a different girl since she met you. That last boyfriend? Waste of space! But you seem to be sound as a pound and I'll trust you with her if you forget about crazy stunts, be honest at all times and finish things with her the moment one, or the other, or both of you stop feeling the magic. Lecture over!'

All sounds good I thought. I nodded again, not sure if my voice even worked anymore after so much sitting and listening.

'And if all it turns out to be is the best summer romance you ever have, then we'll always have the memory of #windowgate! Isn't that what you cool kids say? Hashtags before everything. Gate after everything?' Tab's dad laughed at his own coolness. Big Graham was beginning to grow on me.

'Ehhh yeah. Something like that.'

We chatted for a while longer as we finished our beers; you know the type of small talk you make with the father of the girl you're kissing. Then I made some excuse about meeting Patrick. I knew I needed to get out of the house before Tabitha came back from yoga. We still hadn't properly made up and with the weight of what her dad had just said hanging around my neck, I needed to think about what it meant to gain the trust of a girl who lives on the other side of the Atlantic.

I cycled home, grabbed Patrick's skateboard, caught a bus to the other side of town and hung out for the rest of the night in one of the city's outdoor skate parks. For one of the handful of times since I had touched down in Ireland I enjoyed spending a few hours in my own company. (Us only kids probably need more of that than most people!) For the first time too, I thought seriously about what a future might look like with Tabitha. That is, if we resolved our immediate future! Something I knew just might be possible if I gave her the space she wanted.

Up until that point it just felt like Tabs and I were writing a few lyrics together. Catchy, light and flirtatious. But now, without her, I couldn't believe how much I missed her. That empty feeling actually ached. So with the scarily dawning realisation of whatever we now had, or might have, developing into an album, I filled the rest of the night with pop-shovits, alpha flips and the mind-spinning twists and turns that are my thoughts about love and commitment.

JOY STREET

Respecting boundaries is all well and good, I decided as I woke suddenly the next morning. But with only 6 days left, I really needed to tell Tabs how I felt. Like pronto!

Tyler: *Meet me @ St Malachy's. 1pm. I need to do some serious repentance! Tyler x*

Tabitha: *Make it 2. Thanks 4 bringing the $ round 4 dad. Cu l8r. BTW that's a totally random place to meet. Tabs x*

Tyler: *I saw it on a walk and thought it was pre ty! Have missed u xx*

Tabitha: *Me 2. Can't wait 2 cu xx*

From her text I figured Tabitha was OK with me, maybe partly 'cos I made things right with the No. 1 guy in her life.

But I was still nervous when Patrick dropped me off. We were late, and when I couldn't see her, Patrick asked me *what* St Malachy's I had told her to go to. Apparently there are two St Malachy's in Belfast! I called Tabitha. She was already on her way to the wrong one and it would take her twenty minutes to get across the city. Not a promising start. Patrick kicked me out of the car - he was eager to get to the gym and sculpt his guns, so I stood and waited for Tabitha to arrive. My nerves vanished when I saw her little car appear around the corner of Alfred Street. She walked through the green gates of the church and my heart gave a happy little leap as she called my name.

'Tyler.'

'Tabitha. So sorry for sending you to the wrong place.'

She rolled her eyes at me. We hugged and then spoke at the same time.

'I-'

'We-'

'You go,' I said.

'No you,' she replied.

'Look. I didn't say it the other day, but I can't help that my life has been pretty easy so far. I can't help that I'm a dreamer or busk in the subway or spend way too much time thinking up tweets. I can't help that I'm gonna leave soon and I don't know what will become of us.'

'Tyler.'

'I can't-' I said.

'Tyler.' Tabitha interrupted me again. 'Listen to me. I'm sorry that you didn't expect to meet me over the summer. And

I'm sorry for shouting at you. I feel bad too that we have this dilemma.' She twisted the rings on her fingers. 'I didn't mean all that stuff I said the other night. I just feel that I can trust you with anything, so you get the good stuff and the rubbish. Take it as a compliment that you're getting to know the real me!' She smiled.

I couldn't help grinning at that. We walked inside and settled into a pew in the hushed silence. My voice echoed as I tried to explain myself.

'I'll be honest. This summer was not exactly the carefree party-time vacation I had in mind. It's been intense, listening to Patrick everyday and all the stuff you're going through. Even my aunt has been coming to me with her problems about Patrick. Is there something about my face or do people actually think I have it all together?'

'Maybe! But I'm not fooled,' Tabitha joked.

'The reality is - I just have less experience of the bad things that happen.'

'Be thankful for that,' she commented.

'Anyway it's hard to just listen. 'Cos then I worry about people and I'm not really able to do much to help. I don't know how. It's not the listening. It's the worrying.'

'I'm sure it is. But you're so good at listening. And listening is enough. It does help. More than you know. And just think, a year from now you could make millions writing songs about all of our dramas!'

I laughed. 'True. I wrote a song called *One Strange Irish Girl* last night. It's epic.'

'I'm flattered.' Tabitha put on a jokey voice as she gave me a friendly slap on the arm.

'I've been thinking too; I shouldn't have landed at your house in the middle of the night. I could have just texted you to tell you how I felt. But I got carried away and my cell battery died. You're the first girl to make me feel this way, well, apart from Susan.'

'Susan?' Tabitha said.

Stupid, stupid, stupid! 'Whoops! I mean ... er ... All you need to know is that it was for the food and the money.' *Worse and worse.*

Tabitha just stared at me so I feigned interest in the icons on the walls and the intricate ceiling high above my head.

'I'll explain later. Anyway - can we start again?' I asked.

'Well we can't start again. But we can start from where we're at. Tyler, I thought this was a summer thing. I thought it was two people with spare time who realised they liked hanging out with each other.'

In typical Tyler Hollywood (or Holywood!) teen movie style I jumped in! 'Yeah, like it's boy meets girl. It's milkshakes and kisses. It's late night drives and movies. Not-'

'Not what?' Tabitha asked.

'Not something lovely,' I answered.

'Lovely?' she frowned, puzzled.

'Yeah, this is lovely.'

'For a guy who loves to write, that's a weird word to use to describe us!'

'You're right.' I played with my hat brim.

'So are we OK?' I asked.

'Yeah.' Tabitha fixed my hat. 'I just want you to stay here in Belfast and we can figure this all out. Part of the reason I got mad was 'cos even though you have only been in my life for 5 minutes, I know how much I'm gonna miss you when you leave.'

'Hey, let's not think about that for now. Hug?'

'You bet!'

We stood. Tabitha rested her head on my shoulder and we bear-hugged.

'Now let's go get some lunch. I'm starving.' Tabitha announced.

We cut off from Alfred Street and found ourselves on Joy Street, chatting as we walked into town. After all, we had what felt like a week's worth of conversations to catch up on. Tabitha was in the middle of telling me a story from work when a little lady interrupted us.

'Alright love.'

I caught her eye as she blew smoke into the air. 'Eh afternoon ma'am.'

A small fat woman stared at me as Tabitha tried to make her way round an obstacle blocking the footpath.

'Here, yer nat from round here, so you're nat,' she remarked. (People were very good at pointing this out during my vacation.)

'Sure not,' I smiled at the little old lady.

We were about to walk on by when she asked, 'Here, a strong wee lad like you with big arms like that wouldn't wait a minute and help me inside with this? I near broke my back trailing it out here.'

The back-breaking object in question was sitting on the sidewalk. An old-fashioned school desk. The woman started rubbing my arms. Tabitha tried not to laugh at the growing affection this wee woman had for me.

'Ehhh yeah sure,' I replied. I didn't have any other option.

'God he's a good looking big thing so he is, so he is?' she stared at Tabitha, waiting for a reaction.

I remained quiet, not knowing whether she was asking a question or making an astute observation. It was so embarrassing. She nudged Tabitha in the arm and told her she was a *lucky duck*. I laughed at her silly phrase and chuckled to myself as our new acquaintance added another example to my *so it is so it is* observations.

Then the lady piped up. 'Hold on, son! Don't lift her yet! I just need to finish this and then finish that.'

She pointed to her cigarette and then to the sandpaper, polishing cloth and probably highly flammable tub of oil that sat on top of the desk. Tabitha and I perched on the windowsill of her house, where we made 2x King Size cigarettes worth of chat, while Theresa smoked and did her finishing touches to the sanding and oiling and polishing.

'You been writing naughty words on the desk?' Tabitha enquired. Realising she may have sounded a bit cheeky, she tumbled out a few more words to our small dumpy acquaintance, 'I mean, that's a lovely desk. Where did you get it?'

Ignoring Tabitha's question Theresa took the conversation

in her own direction. 'So how long are you here for, son?'

'Well I've been over for nearly three weeks. I just have 6 days left.'

In between draws on her 'feg', she repeated the words *three weeks* to herself. 'What the heck have you been doing for that length of time? There's only so many times you can dander up to the Giants Causeway.'

I laughed, as I had already been there and was going again at the weekend!

'Well my cousin and I did a quick tour down south, went camping in a few places, and I met Tabitha.' I nudged Tabitha in the ribs, hoping she would add to the conversation.

'Yeah he met me,' she chipped in as she pointed to herself with two thumbs up and made a goofy face.

'Girl with legs like that would make any trip to Belfast worthwhile,' Theresa noted.

Embarrassed, Tabitha looked at her feet and crossed her legs.

'This is my first love you know,' the wee woman went on, smoothing the surface of the desk lovingly with the palm of her hand.

I spluttered out some of the take-out coffee I had been swirling round my mouth as I tried to figure out a reply to Theresa's statement.

'Sorry?' I asked.

Sensing she had caught us off guard, Theresa laughed. 'Hah! Scundered! I take it youz haven't talked about that yet? Call me The Titanic and consider the ice broken! I was talking about the desk. This was my desk the whole way through primary school. I loved it.'

She nodded in the direction of a building across the road. I could see from the carving on the stonework that it used to be a Catholic school.

'Used to be my school. And see where that there car park is?'

'Yeah.'

'Used to play hap skatch there.'

'Hap Skatch?'

'Aye. Hap Skatch. Happiest time of my life.'

I was bewildered.

'Hop Scotch,' Tabitha translated.

'Oh! Got it now.'

'And there's my name right here on this desk.' Theresa pointed out two scrawled and scratched signatures. 'And my best friend, here. Rosie sat right beside me all the way up through school. She lives in Australia now.'

'So how did you get the desk?'

'Oh when *they* (she said the word *they* with real menace) were closing the school *they* piled up all the desks and were gonna take them to the depot. But I sneaked over one night and nabbed one, well actually four, but I sold the rest on eBay. I wanted to give my own desk a wee summer makeover so I spotted a gap in the rain and brought it outside to clean it up.'

'Awhhh that's such a pretty story,' said Tabitha the actress.

'Thanks love.' Theresa disappeared into the house and a few minutes later brought out three cups of tea and a plate of biscuits. For the next fifteen minutes we chatted to her about her family, her desk, what she was having for tea and where she was going on holiday. Turns out she was going to Benidorm in Spain and then in October, to Las Vegas. Paid for by 'thon desks' which turned out to be antiques and in demand. Proudly, Theresa gave the top of the desk a final once-over with sandpaper. I wiped the grains away and soon found myself covering a rag with oil and rubbing it into the wood for her. After that she sent me up the stairs of her 'wee two up two down' house to make space for the desk by moving four hamster cages from her spare room onto the landing. Being overly careful not to mark her new purple floral wallpaper, I hauled the desk up the stairs and into the bedroom.

I lingered on the landing as I heard Theresa giving Tabitha some relationship advice. Parts of the conversation floated up the stairs. 'When you know you know . . . Love beats distance . . . It's a good sign that you missed him when you fell out.'

I could hear their chat coming to an end and made my way down the stairs. Honestly, I tried not to listen in, but Theresa was just so loud.

'Well you know where I am if you ever want a natter,' Theresa patted Tabs on the shoulder, with a cigarette still smouldering between her fingers.

'Thanks so much. That's really kind of you,' Tabitha wheezed.

'There's the big fella!' Theresa gave me a hug and shoved a tenner into my hand.

'That's for your troubles. Go take her for a wee cocktail or a coffee or something. I'm partial to a Sex on the Beach myself. D'you know if they put rum in it?'

'Thanks Theresa.' I was blushing. 'But you don't have to do that. I was happy to-'

'Oh I know I don't have to, son, but I want to, so I do.'

We said our goodbyes, left Joy Street in a fit of the giggles, and made for a city centre shopping mall.

Tabitha and I spent the rest of the afternoon going from shop to shop trying on the latest trends. She picked me out a whole new outfit, having a better eye than me. To say thanks for her fashion tips I returned the favour and bought her a pretty frock, handbag, nail varnish and gutties. US translation: dress, handbag, nail polish and sneakers. £84 later I realised that dating can be expensive! Even in the summer sales. Tabs refused to let me pay for any of our bargains, but I was too fast for her.

In between watching Tabitha try on outfit after outfit and trying to get my legs out of super skinny jeans, I had one thing in my mind. The L-bomb Theresa had dropped into our conversation on Joy Street. Tabitha didn't have her mom to talk to about all of this stuff. Was our relationship going to be guided by a woman we had only met for half an hour? Would a once in a lifetime encounter with a wee fat eccentric woman from Belfast change the direction of my life?

IT'S ALL GOOD!

For the second morning in a row I woke with a start. But this time I was jolted awake by a strange howling, which at first, I thought was part of the weird dream I had been having. But then I realised it was Pat bellowing 'Yeooowwwwww!'

What the-? I couldn't finish the thought because he burst in the door of the bedroom and began doing a celebration dance in the middle of the floor singing: 'It's good. It's good, it's all so good!'

I sat up. Was it something to do with Jess? They seemed back on track the other night.

'What's all good?'

'My course! The University sent me a letter. They were really understanding and accepted that . . .' Patrick began to read the paper clasped in his hand: '. . . *your recent life experiences have greatly hindered your ability to focus on your course. Therefore the Univer-*

sity permits you to conduct your resits and, on the condition of passing these exams, to enter third year Medicine.' I have a second chance! Way hay!' He jumped up and down.

'I'm so happy and relieved for you dude! That's awesome news.' First things with Jess are looking up and now this. 'We can get our summer back on track!' I jumped up and down too.

'Summer of revision, here we come! But first a celebration! And I have an amazing idea.'

'Uh oh.' Did my voice give away a bit of anxiety?

'No need for fear, mon ami. I feel bad, summer so far has been a bit of a bummer for you. The house hasn't been the happiest of places. So let's get out of it!'

'I'm up for that!'

'How's about a day trip to some of my favourite happy places?'

'Anytime!' I was just happy and relieved the letter had arrived before the weekend trip up north with the family.

Singing, 'It's all good', we switched on the laptop and booked ourselves into a *Game of Thrones* tour of many of the locations featured in the incredible TV series. Yes, the soggier kingdoms are actually filmed here! Then we planned to meet up with the rest of the lads for a night on the town. That was Thursday sorted. But I was sensible and didn't stay out too late, because Tabitha had a July Fourth surprise organised just for me, and it was going to involve an early start!

INDEPENDENCE DAY AND NIGHT

'Oh what an adorable log cabin!' Tabitha gasped as she tugged my arm, pulling me towards an American frontier house complete with porch and rocking chair. 'Wouldn't it be amazing to have a house like this? A porch to sit on, a rope swing from a big old shade tree in the front garden, a craft table for me, fresh sweetcorn growing out the back, a flower garden, an old barn full of hay, two hound dogs. Though we would have to have electricity! And a shower.'

As for me, I was sitting in the rocking chair, lulling myself into a nice daydream thanks to the bluegrass music that was drifting in from another part of the village. It just added to my reverie, when Tabitha's voice drifted into my daydream. The word 'we' woke me up with start.

We?

C'mon Tyler, you were thinking 'we' too!

I didn't know how to react, because I was imagining the same thing, so I laughed it off. She was kidding around; it was a slip of the tongue. But for a moment my heart was racing and I had an answer to the questions I had asked myself during my skateboarding sess! To be sure, I knew I needed to ask the other lady in my life about this - Mom - and fast! Is this how girls think? Is this how I should think? I'm only 18. Maybe Tabitha realised I was acting like the rabbit caught in the headlights because she gave me a 'cheeky' wink and instantly calmed my nerves.

'Don't get too comfortable, we have so much more to see,' she said pulling me up from the rocker. Staying in the mischievous spirit I winked back at her.

As a surprise treat for US Independence Day, Tabitha had brought me to the Ulster American Folk Park in County Tyrone, an hour or so west of Belfast, to help me experience life as it had been for the immigrants and early settlers who made the journey from Ulster to the Land of The Free. The Park was having its annual July Fourth celebrations, so that bluegrass music wafting across the field was no fantasy.

Tabitha ran ahead of me towards a weathered clapboard farmhouse set in the fields and enclosed by a beautiful white wooden fence. Minutes later, under the duress of a tour guide, I found myself re-enacting the daily tasks of a settler farmer – at this house the duty was to hand grind corn. You gotta start somewhere I guess.

But it sure was different from Independence Day back Stateside. Every Fourth of July we usually travel for a break by the lakes and watch the fireworks with our vacation families – the same people from our Christmas ski trip. So today was the first time I'd been a little bit homesick. I had made it three weeks and a day before I wanted a hug from my Mom and Dad. But, if there is anywhere else in the world, outside the US, that you want to be on this day, it's Ireland. We do St Patrick's day even better than the Irish and they return the favour with 4th July celebrations that, OK, aren't better than ours, but score a solid B+.

After a day filled with exhibits, real life enactments, old fashioned costumes, burgers, banjos, fiddles, marching bands and even root beer, we high tailed it to the other side of the country (remember you can do that in Northern Ireland in a matter of hours!) and spent the evening in the coastal village of Groomsport – about twenty miles east of Belfast. Their annual 4th of July firework display lights up the sky with an abundance of red, white and blue. We were joined by an entourage consisting of Beth, Richard, two of their neighbours and their kids, plus Patrick and Jess (who were still getting on pretty well, for now. Patrick hadn't had an animated phone call with Jess in a while, so fingers crossed!).

The little village was buzzing with a real party atmosphere. Everyone was so friendly. Patrick being Patrick made his way to the stage steps and told one of the organisers that 'a real live American' was in attendance. I was thrust on stage and forced to be US ambassador as I brought impromptu unofficial greetings from my homeland. Now I know what feeling Presidential means!

Beth won a fluffy 'cuddly toy' at the amusements and Paul, their neighbour, came second in the arm-wrestling contest. After Patrick made an embarrassing attempt at the hotdog eating competition, we oooohed and aaaahed at the fireworks display. All in all, the perfect cure for my homesickness.

I would have been 100% happy, except for that grey cloud growing bigger by the minute in my mind. I could not stop thinking about how soon I would be leaving, saying goodbye to everyone, especially Tabs. Just like that - whoosh! - I had run out of time!

As I had done many times before, I went through my mental calendar, which of course included all my opportunities for spending time with Tabitha before I had to leave. Every day was precious.

So today - that's nearly over - then the weekend with the family up north. That would be the big 'send-off' from Pat's crew. Which left Monday July 7th. My last day for everything else, 'cos 5am July 8 I was outta here! So, packing, gift shopping and Tabitha. I was trying to work out the how and where of saying farewell to Tabitha. A plan was half formed: a meal in her favourite restaurant of course (had that booked already), but no goodbye gift as yet. And no idea what to buy her. Panic! I felt far from ready. Too much to do and not enough days!

Tabitha was off somewhere with the girls to get food and I was on my own at one of the 'shoot-em-up' stalls, my head a million miles away thinking about goodbyes, while trying to aim my toy rifle and hit some plastic bottles lined up at the back of the stall.

Then Patrick pounced. He was giddy with excitement which usually means another plan is brewing. And it was.

Grabbing my arm, he said in his most urgent voice: 'Tyler. You need to stay for another fortnight.' I looked puzzled until he rephrased it. 'Two weeks.'

At that moment, the pellet gun fired, my aim was miles off and the stallholder yelped and jumped clear. I had nearly hit him with my shot, which instead wounded one of the toy penguins displayed as prizes.

'What?' I stared at Patrick, then at the toppling penguin, then at the shocked stallholder. 'Hang on a mo-'

I apologized profusely to the stallholder, and Pat joined in, even offering to buy the injured penguin, which he then bestowed on me, after pushing the stuffing back into the injured critter's tummy and putting a happy face sticker over the wound to seal the deal.

'I'm serious. With all my college stuff going on and me being so preoccupied, it's like our summer never got started properly. I haven't given you the summer you expected. And besides, things with Tabitha seem to be hotting up. This is so not the time to go. Stay.'

'But I can't. I told Fresh & Juicy I'd be back in work for most of July and August. Plus I should spend time with my folks and my friends before leaving for college. And what about packing?'

Pat gave me a look. 'Packing. Are you for real? Like you've got, what, 6 weeks? It will take you a couple of hours to pack for college. A day tops. And you still will have a lot of summer left for all your friends. As for the money – hey, you didn't do too badly busking. Besides, if you leave, you'll miss the festival, and you'd def-o be paid for gigging at that. Far more than you'd get rearranging the mangos.'

I scratched my head. Never thought of that. It did all make sense. Festival experience! Any musician would be crazy to pass that up. And the money could maybe cover the cost of changing flights and a bit more besides? Besides there was Pat, and Tabitha . . . When I looked at it that way – no brainer really. I had to stay!

I spotted the girls returning.

'Look, no hugs or PDAs, but you've sold me, I'm staying. But say nothing to the girls. I want it to be a surprise. Plus we need to clear it with both our parents.'

'Oh don't worry. They're in. It's one of the first times they have agreed with one of my cray ideas!' Patrick answered with a wink.

I looked across at Beth and Richard chatting with friends at a food stall, impressed at their ability to keep such a good secret. Would I be able to hide the huge grin all over my face as successfully? 'Maybe it's not so cray! Cover me while I go make a call.'

I darted off, penguin tucked under my arm, to a quieter place to phone my folks. Please let them be somewhere with civilization and mobile network coverage!

'Happy Fourth!' we called out simultaneously.

'Just a quick one. The university are letting Pat do his resits. I've been invited to play at a festival next week, I've fallen bigtime for Tabitha, and Beth and Richard want me to stay on another couple of weeks. But I don't know what to do because I promised Fresh & Juicy and I miss you guys and home and all my friends. Rodriguez and Alex are gonna be mad too. Did you know Alex works as an alligator?' I stopped for air.

'Well hello there Tyler,' Mom said as an announcement in Spanish blared in the background.

'Listen we can't talk long - just about to get on the plane.' Mom said.

'But what do I do?' I asked.

'Stay. Change the flights. No, wait, Dad will do it when we get home.'

Instantly all worries lifted. 'Are you sure? But-'

'It's not everyday your little boy falls in love (*I'd never even said the word but now Mom was dropping the L-bomb too!*) for the first time. You need to figure this out. So why not talk to me about her tomorrow? And it's true Pat needs some downtime with you before he starts hitting the books. Beth said he's been a different guy because of you, so I know she would love you to stay on.'

'That's cool Mom! And I promise to pay you back for the flight changes. You'll send on my flight details and we'll talk tomorrow? We're going up north, but I'm reachable.'

'The Giant's Causeway again?' Mom asked.

'Lol, that's what Theresa said.'

'Who's Theresa?'

'A wee fat woman with a desk fetish.'

'We *really* need to catch up. And wee? Our boy is even going native! Will call you! Gotta go.'

I went back and found the crew. The neighbours' kids were like little sleepy zombies with balloons tied to their wrists. They headed home, but we stayed on and danced for hours to the sounds of East Coast rock and roll. I was in a little fog of dance-happiness, just thinking about the wonderful surprise I was going to spring on Tabs and how to do it.

But it lifted when I noticed Pat was acting goofy and flirty, like he does when he is happy, and it was really getting on Jess' nerves. There seemed to be post-spat tension going on, 'cos they were dancing with other people and clearly avoiding each other. I crossed my fingers it would blow over. But Tabitha gave me a meaningful 'see?' look which made me doubt it.

Maybe it was the prospect of staying on a bit longer that added to my homesickness - it would be an extra couple of weeks before I saw my parents again - so when they played the US national anthem as a signal that the night's events were over I felt a twinge of homesickness.

The twinge turned into concern. On the way home, Jess was sulking. Pat was stony silent. Who had said what to who? It was going to be a long drive and confirmed my need to stay. This Jess business was far from over and before I left, had to be sorted out for once and for all. And Pat was gonna need my support if he was going to get his head right for studying and exams. These fireworks needed to end.

When we got home, Beth and Richard were still up, getting stuff together for the weekend away. Both hugged me and told me how much they wanted me to stay on for awhile longer and how thrilled they were that it was going to happen.

Next morning, the email with my flight changes made it official. Friday July 25. So I guess I was here for another couple of weeks and then some! And when I contacted James Marcus with my plan and reasons, his reply was typical JM!

'Sup T-man! Nps. Not surprised you have romantically conned a beautiful girl into loving you, or r u exploiting a gap in the market and bringing your smoothie A-game to the streets of Belfast? Roddy is proving to be a supertastic replacement. So chill & enjoy bro.'

Possibly I'd given him too much info?

NORTH COAST AND BACK AGAIN

Tabitha should have been the first person I told. But I made the family promise not to say a word. I wanted to make it a surprise. As if. For the next two days we would not be anywhere near Tabitha.

On our way up to the North Coast I texted Rodriguez and Alex the news. They wouldn't be awake yet, so I expected their emoji filled response later in the day. Hope they would not be too mad.

This trip to the Causeway Coast was the opposite of the fly-by-the-seat-of-your-pants-snooze-in-a-tent-surf-in-the-morning-rush-around-the countryside tour that Patrick had brought me on, and more of a relax-on-the-beach-stroll-on-the-prom-plenty-of-dinner-at-that-fab-restaurant-with-the-me-ga-desserts time. With added precipitation. Beth had told me she wanted the mini mini break to be the nearest thing to a family holiday before Patrick had to 'get seriously stuck into the revision'. Summer job this year, forget it!

Uncle Richard's family joined us for the weekend, which meant there were 9 people in a caravan constructed for 6, so Patrick and I slept outside, in a tent. In a shoddily constructed tent. In the rain. We basically snoozed in a puddle in a field just outside Portstewart. #irishsummer

The whole gang ate in a new restaurant, The Port, before the 'young guns' went to the local nightclub and the old guns, well, went to the local nightclub. Where else? It was that kind of place, but still pretty weird to boogie with Beth and watch Richard get involved in a dance-off with a hen party from Newcastle. I swear the speakers in the club were larger than our caravan, which made for an interesting ringing noise as I tried to get to sleep later that night.

The revelry came to an end about 2 am, when we gathered round the chip van and swapped greasy food and groovy dancing stories. Back home you only dance if you've got moves, but here they 'throw shapes' like they're kids in a kindergarten class. Even the oldsters!

Eventually, at 5am the sound of rain bouncing off the metal roof of the caravan replaced the nightclub induced ringing in our ears. I was tired! We spent our last day playing golf, in the rain, before we walked the length of Portstewart Prom, in the rain, and ate (more) chips in the car as we sheltered from, yes, the rain. We decided to give the Causeway a miss after all – slippery stones!

Pat dropped me off at Granny's for afternoon tea, before he met Jess for an 'I'm sorry' coffee.

'Keep it light,' I advised him, not really sure if that was the right guidance or not!

Granny was delighted I would be staying on a 'fortnight' longer and had already planned out all the things she was going to bake for me that were 'a wee taste of Norn Iron'. Bakewell tart, treacle tart, strawberry flan, pavlova. Starting with a super-amazing lemon curd cake.

Then she asked if Tabitha had anything to do with this change of heart and pumped me for details of all our dates. Of course I didn't spill everything, like the windees episode! Strictly 'need to know' info.

Granny was her usual upbeat self. 'It's going to be the best thing for our Patrick, and, you never know where things with you and Tabitha will go. Oh this is such an exciting time for you! But just be careful. Don't be reckless with her heart. Take it handy.'

The conversation moved on to Patrick and his situation. Of course she knew about wee Ella and 'was gutted, absolutely gutted'. Then she told me just how low Patrick had been for ages. I had no idea! Things were 'desperate' right after the loss of the baby, but he had Jess to support and that kept him going. But, when the date when Ella would have been born came round - that would be early March - Patrick hit a new low. Granny told me that by then Jess could not be anywhere near Patrick at all. She could understand, in a way. Everyone copes differently with loss. I had to wonder if it all reminded her of a terrible time in her own life?

Granny said Patrick had a few weeks there when he struggled even to get out of bed. He missed quite a lot of classes and lab work (which had to explain the exam results).

But my mind was still back in March. That would have been right around the time I had the bad Oscar haircut and I had that puzzling Skype with Pat!

'I was heartsick the lad might do something silly,' Granny admitted.

Then she started talking about the time he told his mom he thought about committing suicide. He confessed to her his feelings that he was a disappointment and a burden to everyone and that it was better if he weren't around. He felt everything he touched turned to disaster.

I felt sick. I knew he had been down, but I couldn't believe he had thought about doing something like that! To my relief, Granny did not say if Pat ever got beyond talking or made any actual attempts. But the suicidal thoughts, or whatever happened, quickly led to getting a therapist involved.

Granny asked me to watch over him. 'I know he seems fine now and I am just over the moon about the panel decision. But he still has all those exams ahead and the lad is like a roller coaster over that girl. I worry constantly that the slightest wee knock could send our Pat right back down again. The lad is like that. I can see it.'

Granny, with all her life experience, would know. She asked me to keep an eye on him over the next couple of weeks.

I had to wonder if she and Beth were 'in cahoots', but I

owed them my support. It scared me though. Being his cousin and friend was one thing, but acting as his guardian angel was a whole other level of responsibility I didn't think I could handle.

Patrick picked me up from Granny's. He breezed in, grabbed a slice of the cake and gave her his usual charming banter about her new hair colour and the freshly dusted flying ornamental ducks on the wall. He seemed more chipper, but I know he's a great actor. Patrick didn't say much about his date with Jess, except that it helped him to clarify a few things. Namely that he definitely didn't like mochas and that even the best cake shops could not top Granny's creations!

'Here Granny, any seconds going?' Pat asked, reaching for another piece.

Granny's revelations about suicide were all I could think about as I brushed my teeth and put on the zit cream before bed. Four weeks ago my deepest thoughts were about starting college and meeting girls. And two days ago about flight tickets. Now this. Talk about the deep end . . . and being totally underwater!

I wanted to talk to Patrick about it, but now did not seem the time. He seemed happier that night and I was wary of putting 'those thoughts' back into his mind. Maybe the relationship with Jess was looking up for him at last. Maybe not. Either way, I knew Tabitha and I had to hatch a plan to put things right - for good.

LOCH CUAN

The stately home was a hive of activity. Servants and maids were in a frenzy as they dashed through the hallways of the manor house, endeavouring to complete their last orders in time for the 11am pre-banquet inspection.

The bright rays of a beautiful summer's sunrise burst into the bedroom and awakened the Lord of the manor earlier than usual. After his manservant helped him select his morning attire, he strolled around his colourfully blooming gardens to ensure every plant was to perfection, and watched the peacocks, pheasants and squirrels as they scurried between their hiding places in the vast woods and the vibrant blossoming shrubs lining the manicured green lawns of the country estate. Swans and ducks bobbed on the private lake.

Walk complete, he settled down to a breakfast of champions. Buoyed by the arrival of spectacular weather, the Lord raced through the three-course meal, eager to enjoy more of the morning sunshine and check on preparations for the gala event.

Everything had to be perfect for his distinguished guests. Friends and noted dignitaries were arriving from all parts of Ireland, London and Scotland. Special notice was reserved for Lady Elise Le Bain, who had travelled from her summerhouse in Monaco to join in the night's antics. The front lawn had been marked out for the polo match that afternoon, with the lawns of the walled garden perfectly trimmed and rolled for the evening soiree. This year the famed topiary display included a family of squirrels, a horse, crown, chess piece and an extravagant throne.

The polo match was destined to be the most competitive in years – the perfect hors d'oeuvre for the twilight revelry. Alongside the topiary and the afternoon's match, the tiaras, gowns and summer plans of those in attendance would provide ample conversation starters during the pre-dinner drinks gathering.

The Lord wore a smile as natural as the sea that lapped the boundary of the estate. He stood in his white tuxedo beside the triple height front doors, sipping a dry martini as he personally greeted each guest. By mid-afternoon the circular drive was a parking lot, crammed with the headlamps of *Schacht and Columbus Roadsters, Mitchells, Auburn Coupes, Four-30's* and *Overlands.* The deep grunt of finely tuned engines crunching over the gravel added another layer to the symphony of sounds that rose into the azure sky.

Clinking of glasses, chatter and playful laughter, alongside the melodies of the ragtime band, dictated the mood and pace of the party. After a sumptuous dinner, prepared by celebrity chef of the day, John McGuire, and his team, the Lord and his elegant Lady strolled arm in arm through the crowd. They moved to the pace of the music, smiling and extending good-will to all the guests from their bouquet of charm. His Lady was stunning. Dressed in the finest *Lucile* gown from London, the last word in chic this year, 1911, she rolled flirtatious words into his enchanted ears as they walked.

The final rays of sunshine glinted off the lake. Soon the flickering candles would be the only light for the rest of the en-chanted night, until the fireworks brought the party to a close. Boom!

I came to with a start. I had closed my eyes for a split second and allowed my imagination to run away with me. Tabitha grabbed my hand and dragged me out of my dreamlike state, through the double doors and into the next room. The tour guide winked at me. He knew I was carried away by the history of the house - carried away right into 1911!

But he didn't know that I was lying to Tabitha. For, as far she knew, I was leaving the country in 24 hours and this was to be our last day together. While I was up north, I worked it all out with the help of Richard and Beth. They suggested I invite Tabitha out for a special last day out and recommended the area around Strangford Lough - a huge sea inlet - as it is particularly rich in things to do and places to see.

When I told Tabs, she was delighted, but wondered when

and how I would find the time to pack and do all my last minute stuff. So I told her not to worry – it was all under control – and made up a tall tale about going shopping with Pat after he got his letter and being half packed already. As if! Plus, it was easier having a day away with Tabs because it reduced the danger of Pat or any of his family spilling the beans.

So anytime Tabitha brought up the subject of us, or leaving or the future, I could distract her by suddenly pointing and exclaiming 'Wow, look at that castle. It's so cool all the old stuff you have over here! I can't get over how everything is like a thousand years old!' Yakety yak. Yep, the tried and tested enthusiastic Yank spiel. Or by telling her 'Let's not talk about that now and just enjoy our time together.' Both worked.

We left the drawing room of Mount Stewart and entered the elegant hallway of this impressive 18th century mansion. History whispered from the ornately decorated rooms. The faces of the portraits that covered the walls blushed due to the sins and sights they had cast their eyes on through the years of parties the house had hosted. Privy to the comings and goings of decorated war veterans, the revealing stories of royalty, the secrets of statesmen and the seductive glances of scandalous socialites. And now they were looking down at us!

Tabitha and I were halfway through our whirlwind tour. The day was all about escaping city hassles, travelling through quaint villages and uploading beautifully framed and filtered pictures to Instagram.

Vowing to make the most of my last day in Ireland (well that's what Tabs thought!), we rose with the dawn, packed up the car and soon found ourselves munching on breakfast in a little village near the site of Nendrum monastery - haunting early Christian ruins (1400 years old possibly!) on the shores of Strangford Lough. The mist of the morning had cleared and brought us a glorious summer's day.

Throughout the morning we stopped at different sites along St Patrick's Trail which follows the route taken by Ireland's patron saint. To stand near the site of his landing, his first church and the place where it's claimed he performed a few miracles, brought a real sense of meaning to our adventure. It was not all that long ago that I had skipped school on St Patrick's Day to hang out at the parade. Seeing his rumoured burial spot - marked by a large boulder in a old-world churchyard high up on a hill beside a church that had to be a couple of hundred years old, at least - was such a contrast to the ticker tape parade and green plastic leprechaun hats.

Next stop, a pretty little seaside town where we boarded a ferry that would take us across to the Ards Peninsula. Not just any ferry, but the smallest car ferry known to man! OK, I'm making a slight exaggeration, but we drove the car onto a 'totey wee' boat that took all of ten minutes to cross the narrowest point of Strangford lough. Such a great mini-adventure; I just had to grab some awesome snaps of the sea views and of the boat, before Tabs dragged me to the front where we acted out *that* scene from *Titanic*. Of course I found it totally embarrassing, and on a level of cheesiness only my dad could reach, but when you're crazy about an aspiring actress, this is the kind of thing a guy has to do to support her career. And it was kind of a laugh.

The sense of history everywhere was striking as we travelled over the winding roads and through the villages that dotted the shores of Loch Cuan – the Irish name for Strangford Lough. I pictured the terrifying ships of the Vikings as they sailed through the waters they named, and the desperate faces of fleeing local farmers and fishermen, falling on their swords rather than fall victim to the plans of rape and pillage from the invading foreign foe. History rises from the shallow bed of the island-studded lough.

The whole culture of the area has been formed through the historic tales and myths handed down by centuries of colourful storytelling. And through the landscape itself, which has been said to inspire the *Narnia* books, and probably has featured in *Game of Thrones* too. It's that gorgeous!

The Lough dictates the lives and invades the souls of the people who inhabit the hamlets and quiet villages that hug the shore, and even the folk who live on the many tiny islands out in the middle of the shallow Lough. When the tide is out, it's even possible (if a tad risky!) to walk to them. All under the backdrop of the imposing Scrabo tower high on its hill. I thought it was a bit spooky, like something out of *Dracula*, but Scrabo was actually built in Victorian times by the owner of Mount Stewart who wanted a romantic and stirring view across the Lough from his property. Who knew?! Another ingredient to add to my daydream.

After our wonderful tour of the house and gardens at Mount Stewart, led by a guide who was full of fascinating stories and gossip, we backtracked a couple of miles to Greyabbey, where we rooted around the antique shops and searched the medicinal herb garden in the monastery for some love potion! And at last we made our way up to our final stop, Groomsport, back on the North Down coast. Call it a scenic detour, but looking out over Belfast Lough was a good place to munch a late lunch of fish and chips eaten straight from soggy newspaper wrappers.

Funny to think just a couple of days back I had been on a stage in this town offering greetings on behalf of approximately 317 million people, but today I was just another anonymous soul, enjoying the peace and quiet and the ice cream the village had to offer on a sunny Monday in July. We sat on the beach in the tiny fishing village, with the sun casting our shadows onto the sand and its heat warming our backs. The tide brought the water close to our feet. I had 24 hours left with the most beautiful girl I had ever known. She had been quiet.

'Tyler.'

Having finished my ice cream I used the half-munched cone as a beak, covered my nose with it and began to peck at her arm. I was using one of Patrick's tactics, humour, to avoid the truth. I didn't want to have another conversation about us.

She laughed when I started to peck her arm.

'Take that off your ninny. Now you've got a blob of chocolate on the end of your nose!'

Knowing that she was going to launch into the us conversation I grabbed her arm and pulled her up from the sand.

'Come on. I have a surprise for you. One last date night. We've gotta be glammed up and ready to go by 7.30!'

DINNER

The surprise was dinner in a wannabe NYC-style restaurant. Though I couldn't make it a total total surprise, or we would have turned up in our shorts and sandy sneakers. So when Tabs dropped me off at home, I told her she had one hour to get gorgeous because the taxi would not wait!

She had shown me her city and I wanted to show her something of mine, albeit minus the cityscape and post-dinner stroll in Central Park. So it was great to hear about this place from Rick, who knew his food and seemed to know every restaurant and chef in town.

During the drive back to Belfast we reminisced about the day trips and date nights we had shared. She only brought up that window smashing incident once. There were a couple of long pauses in our conversation where doubt, heartfelt lingering glances and sweet memories threatened to invade the conversation. Thank goodness Tabitha had to keep her eyes on the road and hands on the steering wheel. And we had a table reservation to keep, so no unscheduled stops allowed!

Now, as the taxi turned the last corner for Tabitha's house, I couldn't believe I had made it this far through our supposed last day together and hadn't let the news of my extended stay slip! Of course there were a couple of close calls. In Tab's car, when we were talking about plans for the evening I nearly blurted out I didn't have to be up early for an 11am flight after all. And I caught myself in the nick of time before I invited Tabitha to hear me play at the festival.

But I couldn't keep it in another minute! Tabitha was going to love the news!

I knocked on her door and big Graham answered it.

'Thanks for keeping this a secret Graham.'

'No probs Tyler. You're a good lad!'

'She'll not be a minute. Here, wait till you see this.'

Graham walked out to the driveway and pointed out the new window. We chatted about it for way too long until Tabitha emerged from the house. Wow. Simply stunning. I couldn't hide how blown away I was by her beauty. I think Old Graham was pretty proud too. The dress she was wearing – the colour, the style – brought out the green in her eyes, and showed off her great legs too. And her hair. I'd never seen it curly before and was mesmerized. The summer sun had turned it gold. The curls bounced as she walked. Of course I did not hear Graham tell us to 'be good and have a great time' before he went into the house.

I opened the door of the taxi for her, in disbelief that this fantastic looking woman was my date. I don't think the taxi driver could believe it either. He left us at the door of the restaurant, which was in one of the streets near the back of City Hall. A few suited types who must have been doing overtime in the busy offices nearby were still leaving their buildings. I'd been nervous since I got home that I had messed up the booking and the place would be closed. It was Monday after all and most places would be. Even chefs gotta rest! But I guess this place was so popular, or maybe it is a NYC thing. You know – the city that never sleeps. Or closes!

Anyway I had the right day and the right place. The vibe was a mixture of classy and out and out busy. Black and white photos of iconic places in NYC and Broadway stars decorated the walls. I knew them all and missed them a little bit too, but what's another two weeks?

I chose the grilled salmon on a bed of vegetables. Tabitha ordered something involving a mysterious vegetable known as mangetouts, which actually turned out to be what we call snow peas back in the Village.

Then she gave me the opening to spring my big surprise. 'This time tomorrow you'll be seeing all these places again,' she said, indicating the Brooklyn Bridge with her fork-speared mangetout. 'You must be so excited.'

'Actually,' I began.

'So I guess you might hook up with Susan once you're back? If she's free?' Tabitha was acting like she was all casual and did not really care, and was doing a pretty good job of it too.

Another guy might be fooled, but I know she's better than your average drama student.

I was about to answer, but my mouth was full and she followed up with more comments about how things might still work out with Susan.

'Actually', I started over again. 'I'm glad things never happened with Susan because-'.

Just then the waiter appeared asking if everything was OK. The second he was gone, Tabitha started in again. 'I'm only winding you up. You've avoided talking about us for too long. What are we gonna do when you fly away tomorrow?'

'Well. I've kinda got something to tell you about that.'

She just stared at me with her mouth open, forehead scrunched up.

'What? I guess you're going to make some lame joke about not going back to New York?'

'Ermm, what if it wasn't a joke?'

'Tyler don't even mess about with this. I need you to be serious tonight.'

'Well I need you to have an imagination for a second,' was my comeback.

'You know I would love you to stay for longer. But you gotta go back and get ready for college.'

'That's six weeks away. Actually-' This time I got to finish! ' I kinda changed my flights on the 4th of July. That night.'

'No!!! If you're having me on I'm going to kick your bum up and down Royal Avenue.'

'For real. Patrick felt bad that he was so distracted with

exams and stuff for nearly the whole of my time over here and he told me I needed to hang out with you more too. So I took his advice and Dad was able to change my flights. I'm staying until the 25th.'

This gorgeous girl was speechless. Winner.

'That's the sweetest thing anyone has ever done for me. I . . . I . . .'

Sensing she was about to drop the L-bomb, I interrupted her, 'are you having dessert?'

The waiter brought our dessert to the table (chocolate-orange bombe, I kid you not) and moved away. That's when I just blurted out what I was feeling. Which turned out to be quite a speech. My Americano coffee was cold by the time I was through.

'Tabitha it's like this. I really like you. We have been on what, 12½ dates. Maybe more. It would have been more if I hadn't have been a total dork and broken your window. But . . . I don't . . . I don't know what love is. And for once I'm not quoting a lyric at you. I really like the whole hanging out, kissing, eating food and laughing at each other's terrible jokes thing we have. But I'm not sure about the L word. Does love have a zip code? Can love exist beyond international borders and across 3000 miles of ocean? What will we do when I'm on the plane home and I hear, 'In preparation for take off the captain has indicated the fasten seatbelt sign'? I just don't know how I feel. This, us, it's awesome. But there are so many challenges to what we've got becoming more than a summer romance. I mean in little over a month I'll be heading off to college for 4 years.'

Silence.

What had I just said?

Had I made a huge mistake?

Tabitha appeared to be intensely absorbed in rearranging the strawberries on her dish. Too late, I could sense that she couldn't take another person kicking her in the teeth, and walking in and then out of her life. But I had to be true to my heart.

'Are you quite finished?' Tabitha demanded, looking directly at me.

Then suddenly she flashed me the eyes to look at the table next to us. Just at the edge of my vision, I caught a very nosy couple staring right in our direction.

Tabitha set her knife and fork very firmly beside her plate and started in: 'But what about the kids? Are you just going to leave me to bring up our babies, while you go hang out on the other side of the Atlantic and entertain your fantasy of being the world's leading underwater aerobics teacher? I mean how is that going to pay for our dinners and nappies?'

She kicked me under the table.

I was startled but took a deep breath and got it together. 'Listen. I told you it was a mistake. A massive mistake. Giving up an Ivy League school for the diving course. Of course I regret it. But (pause for a sec to come up with a ridiculous name) Henrietta, I need to follow my dreams. Maybe I will find pirate treasure on my virtual dives and we can skip off to a desert island, just you and me … and the kids.' I winged it.

'You really do live in a fantasy world,' she stood. 'I can't believe you don't care about us! How could you do that?'

Tabitha burst into tears. The couple at the next table were loving every minute.

'I've had enough!' I stormed out of the restaurant and hid around the corner. Sorry Tabs, but I'd run out of improv ideas! The future Oscar-nominated Tabitha emerged a few minutes later, red eyed and blowing her nose, having been comforted by the restaurant manager and given a complimentary meal. It was the first time I had witnessed Tabitha's acting skills, and they were incredible!

'Do I really look like a Henrietta?' she demanded, fake offended, as soon as we both were safely outside.

I put my hands up. 'OK, maybe a Myrtle.'

Of course I slunk back, and pretending to be very apologetic and hen-pecked, I paid the bill and left a decent tip. Tipping is in our DNA in the Big Apple. Then I ran outta there before the laughter exploded out of me.

For a few blocks we couldn't do anything but laugh until we bumped into a guy selling tickets for a gig. I hadn't heard of the band he was flogging the tickets for, so after listening to one of their songs on Youtube, we bought the cut price tickets and made our way, alongside countless dudes with buttoned up shirts and very styled short at the sides, 'quiffed' at the top hair cuts, to the gig. The lyrics the band punched into the air were dramatic and explosive. Even better, during the final song, Tabitha turned to me and threw her arms around my neck.

'Tyler I don't know what this is. I don't know where it's going. I know you might not want to see me when you go back to America, but I don't care if we are wasting our time on this, because today was so much fun, yesterday was so much fun and the tomorrows, whether we have one or one hundred thousand, will be perfect, because they will be with you. Plus you know you love me. You changed your flights! So tonight, don't think about all that other stuff. And *don't* write a song about it when you go home.' She touched my nose. 'Promise.'

So we did a pinky promise with our little fingers.

'I'll write a song about Henrietta instead,' I vowed, before we both collapsed into giggles.

I had to give it to the girl. Tabitha had only known me for three weeks and could already predict my behaviour patterns. For the rest of the night I held her as tightly as I could and tried not to think beyond our summer together.

'Where u for?' Pat's house was closest, so the taxi driver dropped me off first. Maybe not the most chivalrous, I thought later. But before I got out of the car I kissed Tabitha, then I kissed her some more. Until the taxi driver began clearing his throat and made a remark about fogging up his windees. When we stopped kissing, Patrick's face was pressed against the passenger window and his fist was knocking excitedly. Too weird. He opened the door and bundled me out of the car.

'You've had him for too long! Good surprise ehh?'

Tabitha just smiled at Patrick, gave him a hug as she whispered 'thanks' in his ear.

I waved goodbye and ran inside with Patrick where we talked about our days. After a pretty productive day of studying, he was feeling optimistic. Understatement. He was on a high.

In typical Patrick fashion he was already on to the next thing and hurriedly began explaining to me the financial structure of a fantastic micro-business he had dreamt up whilst trying to study infectious diseases. This one involved bringing a lunch cart over from NYC and starting a New York style sandwich cart in Belfast. From bacteria to burgers, hmmm. Patrick has books of ideas. Most of which are below average, but this one had legs, or wheels.

I allowed him to finish his description before I had the chance to share a few details about my day. He laughed hard at our restaurant antics before we talked through our agenda for the rest of my stay. Suddenly we had oceans of time to enjoy! We had a couple of day trips to cram in so we could finish more of the places on Pat's list, and then a lot of 'let's see what happens.'

Later, I ignored Tabitha's advice and, inspired by the lyrics we had whispered to each other that night, I wrote a few words on my phone. *'It's not love. It's boy meets girl. It's milkshakes and kisses. It's late night drives and movies. It's all good.'*

Amazing that in just four weeks I had learned so much about life and now I guess I was learning about love. Thanks to the promptings of Theresa, her use of the L word, and the lyrics from an Indie band, once again I knew I was brought here for a purpose. I had been struck by Tabitha's acting in the restaurant. It had to be professional standard. Going to bed that night, I knew my dreams were going to be interesting - a mash up of early twentieth century parties and 21st century scuba diving sessions.

ATTIC

People say silly things at breakfast time. This morning we made up some Belfast inspired urban legends.

'Legend has it David and Goliath actually fought on the grounds of Harland and Wolff shipyards.'

'Legend has it that Narnia is actually reached through one of the caves in The Cavehill.'

'Legend has it you can experience all four seasons in one summer's day in Belfast.'

It is widely accepted that one of these urban legends is true. I'll give you a clue. Golfball-sized winter hailstones, followed by blazing summer sunshine, with a gust or two of autumnal winds and a light spring shower thrown in for good measure - in July.

Today it wasn't so much four seasons, but two. Dry, then ridiculously wet. Over an early morning cuppa, Beth exaggerated that some summer days in Ireland could be as wet as the monsoon season in Bangladesh. If she were to experience the weather our Bangladeshi cousins endure, I think she would alter her statement. I stared blankly at her.

Then she started a mini-lesson about some word. It sounded like she was hawking up a piece of toast from the back of her throat, but she assured me that it was a word.

They have some bizarre expressions over here. The wonderful mixture of English, Irish and Ulster-Scots has created accents, dialects and strange, strange sounds, like this morning's word of the day - *dreek*. Aunt Beth said people from the countryside, or *culchies* as they are known, would use the word dreek to describe today's weather. Even Patrick had never heard of the word. It confused me all breakfast, so before I threw on my work clothes I looked at the slang expressions tea towel I had bought Rodriguez's mom, and, sure enough, dreek was on it. So there you go. Useful word as it turned out.

The night before, after I finished explaining interesting historical facts about the Ards Peninsula to Beth, and Patrick had told his mom how much revision he had got through after his first day back at the books, Beth reminded us we had let our list of summer chores slide – off a cliff! Most of the tasks were light, like cleaning, painting the garage floor and doing some yard work - hedges, lawnmowing etc. (which materialised into a bit of a money spinner for Patrick after I went back home in August.) So today we tackled the most taxing job – finishing laying a floor in the attic, which we hoped we could do in a day.

For twenty-three years, precious family heirlooms, old

school notebooks and Christmas decorations had balanced precariously on the insulation-stuffed beams and floor joists of the attic. This summer it was time to give them a solid, safe resting place. Richard had started the task over the Easter break, but ran out of time. Why Patrick and I had been given this important job I will never know. I can't tell a hammer from a hand crank and Patrick pretends, but definitely doesn't know, the difference between a corkscrew and a floorboard screw. Maybe it would be character-building. Go up into the attic boys and come down the ladder men.

Richard had given us a pretty serious safety lecture last night as well as the necessary instructions and vital measurements. After showing us what to do, he spoke in great detail of the importance to our manhood (literally), of avoiding putting our feet through the ceiling, (don't be fooled by the insulation – it's not terra firma) the electric wires and plumbing pipes, as we fixed the chipboard panels to the rafters. In his final bid to deter us from having a life-altering experience, he showed us a Youtube video of the consequences of someone incorrectly laying floorboards. The final clip was of some hairy guy falling through the ceiling and landing in the middle of the stair banister. More than just his pride crushed in the process. Oooooooch! We watched that video at least nine times with the same grimacing reaction. Though without the banister to stop his fall, that guy would have been kaput.

Today's *dreeksoon* was certainly the right day to get round to this mammoth task. Wisely, Aunt Beth decided to get out of the way and was taking Granny to see her sister in Dungannon.

Feeling like proper tradesmen we woke at 6.30, gobbled breakfast, threw on old clothes and brought the last of the boxes, lampshades and toys (fondly remembering happy times with that old Fisher Price Garage, pieces of car track from a racing game and loads of Ninja Turtles!) down from the attic.

'Here Tyler, take these. I think that's the last of it. We can shift anything else that's left onto the parts of the attic that are already floored. Besides some of the boxes say *valuable* on them and I don't wanna be responsible for breaking them!' Patrick instructed.

I was standing at the bottom of the ladder when Patrick reached down two dusty leather suitcases. One of the cases fell open and out fell a whole pile of old clothes. Patrick began to laugh as one of Beth's 80s dresses covered me like a scarf. Instead of helping me, Pat gave an impish grin and said, 'I have an idea!'

At the start of the summer Patrick had the local car mechanic fix a towbar to his car. He'd had big plans to buy a second-hand jetski in August, when the season would be nearly over and he could get it cheaper. But that was before the epic exam fails wiped out his plans to get a summer job and some extra cash. Uncle Richard told me the whole thing was just another mad Patrick brainwave anyway. Did he know how much those things cost? Where would they keep it? What about his college expenses? The towbar had been a good idea though – handy for the bike rack and the neighbour's trailer. For 10 minutes we tried to connect the neighbour's trailer to the towbar - in the rain. Finally attached!

Then, soaked, we headed for the local hardware superstore where we picked up the boards. In our polo shirts and multi pocketed khakis we were incognito amongst the other real men. Following Richard's instructions, we picked out the correct screws and board sizes and then played Tetris as we tried to fit them into the world's smallest trailer. Turns out only half would fit.

By lunchtime we had made surprisingly great progress. Getting out of the sack early paid off; by 1 o'clock, we had completed more than half of our task. OK, so it did help that Richard had already fitted the more complex part around the hatch (and some rows of flooring.) Hard graft, teamwork, cream buns and sausage rolls had been a winning combination. And while Patrick raced over to the DIY warehouse to pick up the rest of the board, I kept on working.

'Patrick! Pass me the saw.' He failed to respond to my request.

'Patrick! The saw!' I called again. I turned round to see why I got no answer. He was kneeling over a box.

'I forgot about this.'

'What is it?' I pulled down my dust mask to speak.

'When I found out about Ella - that we were expecting a little girl - I started to buy her some little bits and pieces. I thought I had given everything away. Mum must have saved this box up here.'

'Look how tiny this stuff is.' He passed over a minuscule pair of socks, each about two inches long. His eyes were glistening with unshed tears.

'You know,' Pat began, as he took out a miniature fuzzy rabbit, 'originally Jess had wanted to bring the baby up by herself, but I convinced her that we had to be together for the sake of the child.'

Tabitha's words about Patrick trying to force the relationship instantly came into my mind.

'She said we didn't have to be together to be parents, but I knew she appreciated that I wanted to stand by her and be a proper dad. Anyway.' Patrick went silent as he folded a little sweater back into the box, on top of some teeny weeny sneakers. 'Doesn't matter now.' He put the lid back on and shoved the box behind a couple of others.

I was still holding the micro socks and stuffed them into my pocket. 'I'm sorry Pat. What with all my own stuff, I have forgotten to ask how you have been lately. I guess I just figured with the panel over-'

'Don't worry cuz. I've been good.'

'You telling me the truth?' I asked.

'Kinda. Mostly good. Since July 4th of course, Jess has been doing her own thing. As she does. Again. Right after I found out about the results of the panel, I was so excited cos' I thought things could start again. But we had that row and then when we met for coffee to try and resolve stuff and maybe get back together again, she was having none of it.'

'Hang on. Again, again, again, you mean!'

'Well when you put it like that, true. And it does get old, month after month of not knowing.'

Remembering the reality check Tabitha had given me, I had to ask, 'Pat, do you *really* want to be with Jess? Or do you just feel like you have to be with her? 'Cos of guilt or whatever. Or do you even know?'

'Honestly?' He sighed with relief when he saw my face, which I hope was wearing it's best 'I'm not going to judge you bro, whatever you say' expression. 'I want to move on. I'm just scared of what it would be like without her. But maybe we need to just be apart. For good. It's complicated though.'

Then, typical of Patrick, he turned the subject round in the next sentence.

'Enough about me. What about you? I mean it's difficult enough trying to be with someone when they live up the road. Just think what it's gonna be like when they're hundreds, correction, thousands of miles away.'

'Tell me about it. But your advice at the start of the summer not to overthink it has helped.'

'Yeah right,' Patrick was skeptical.

'No, serious man. You have given me all this advice over the summer. 90% wise. You're like a Northern Irish Buddha.'

'Who happens to fail his university exams,' Patrick joked.

'Well that's karma for you!'

Patrick shook his head and turned back to the box of baby keepsakes. He tucked it further away behind one of the beams in the attic.

'Pass me the box of screws behind you?'

I reached for the box and before I could hand them to Pat he said, 'We better crack on bigtime if we're gonna get this finished, especially if we want to make my idea happen,' he said.

'What's this great idea?' I asked.

'Laters,' Pat was being mysterious. 'I'll explain in the car.' Then he lowered his mask and got back to work like someone who'd OD-ed on energy drinks.

The final few hours of our afternoon were madcap. And that's an understatement. Flooring done, we raced to the local thrift store, loaded up the trailer with a few items of really dated freebie furniture and vintage rugs even the charity shop couldn't sell or give away, then we shifted most of the visible contents of Pat's front hall and living room into the garage. All this stuff we replaced with our tasteful 70s finds from the secondhand shop. That includes some of the artwork in the living room and dining room. We did a switcheroo with old photos and pictures from the attic and some truly 'tasteful' art we picked up at the thrift store. But we didn't dare touch Beth's prized Terry Bradley original - we knew our lives wouldn't be worth living if we damaged that big money investment during our retro-inspired transformation of the house.

Rubix cubes replaced iPads, an Atari games console replaced the PS4. We ran out of time and only managed to place a few sun-bleached books on the shelves and vinyl albums and videocassettes where the CDs and iPod dock usually lived. We also had wanted to replace the flatscreen with an old black and white TV and the CD player with a big old stereo system, but that was probably too ambitious, so we just hid the modern technology upstairs and stuck the small portable TV in the dining room. But we did grab a transistor radio and an avocado 70s shag rug!

We finished the transformation just as Pat's parents pulled into the driveway. Patrick and I were waiting in the living room. He was wearing his dad's old school blazer and sports shorts - hidden treasures from the attic. I was sporting Aunt Beth's multi-coloured noisy nylon shell suit, complete with wrist and headbands. The door opened and we tried to act cool lounging on the 70s flower power couch. One of Granda's old records was playing in the background.

'Yo lads we're-' Uncle Richard couldn't finish his sentence as he sank in shock onto the new, yet old orange brocade telephone seat in the hall. His eyes widened in horror as they took in the lava lamp and the brown swirly patterned lampshade just inside the living room door. Aunt Beth walked in behind him, dropped the shopping to the floor and started laughing.

'You boys,' they both said.

'I hope you got the-' Richard began.

'Of course we finished the attic!' Pat and I said together. Quality workmanship? That was another story.

'And with time to spare for redecoration I see,' laughed Beth.

After Beth and Pat made sure their TV and good furniture were somewhere safe, we spent the rest of the night enjoying a 70s night, even down to the dinner Patrick and I cooked up - gammon steak grilled with pineapple rings (from a can) on top, followed by Angel Delight – a totally chemical sweet confection made from mysterious powder mixed up with milk. Actually pretty tasty. And amazingly, after Richard played about with it, that old 'telly' still worked; well, one channel anyway, but every scene looked like a blizzard was going on.

While we were on a roll, Patrick and I spent another hour after dinner on our attic project, bringing the last of the boxes back up the ladder, rearranging them in the newly floored section and, while we were at it, having a look through some of the family history. It was better to keep busy so Patrick wouldn't have time to brood about the box of baby clothes.

At last, downstairs, after a shower and change, we flicked through some old family photo albums and I was given a history lesson about my ancestry. It was fascinating to discover that Patrick and I bore a striking resemblance to our Granda during his teenage years. On our travels around Ireland, people were always asking if we were brothers.

Then the doorbell rang.

SUMMER MOM

'Who's this at this hour of the night?' Beth asked, consulting her watch. It was after ten so it could only be a friend of Pat's.

I was actually relieved to see that Tabitha had arrived with Jess. It was one of the first times Jess had been over at Pat's crib this summer. I caught the look on Patrick's face as he opened the door. I think he was relieved to see they had arrived together. Maybe this was the last step in trying to figure it all out.

The girls were impressed by our experiment in time travel back to the 70s. But Beth had had enough of this blast from the past, so while there was a crowd of us in the house, she enlisted us all to put things back the way they were before bed. 'It would be nice to be 15 again, but I do want to wake up back in the 21st century!'

So all four of us got busy packing away the vintage furnishings, putting the 21st century stuff back in its proper places, and reloading the trailer with the old furniture. Well, most of it - Uncle Richard wanted to keep the Belfast sink we had brought home as a patio planter. Before the girls rearranged the living room they marvelled at our talent for set design. Jess said her granny's house still looked just like that. In no time the trailer was full to the brim.

Job done, I scurried upstairs to grab a hoody. Aunt Beth came into my room. She was holding the little pair of baby socks.

'I was throwing your work gear in the washing machine,' she said.

'Patrick found a box of Ella's stuff in the attic,' I explained.

'Oh Tyler. I'm so sorry we have burdened you with this since the day you arrived.' Beth sat on the edge of my bed.

'Really, don't worry,' I said.

'Oh but I do.' Then she looked right at me. The kind of gentle, concerned focus only a mom, or summer mom in this case, who really loves you, can master.

'Listen, I haven't really said to you yet, but we are so grateful to you for changing your flights. Esther will kill me for stealing her baby for another couple of weeks! The least we can do is pay the difference for you.'

'Don't be silly,' I said.

'Your presence has been so important for him. We didn't know what way he was going to go, but Pat's really come on these past few weeks and has managed to get through the worst of the whole exams business. Without you here . . . it doesn't bear thinking about.' Beth shook her head and I knew exactly what she was referring to, though I couldn't say. 'We were so frightened. But now his old self is back. Tonight was pure Patrick.' She laughed.

'I haven't done much for him.'

'You've done more than you'll ever know. When I walked through the door and saw that hideous orange phone table, my heart gave a happy little leap. That would not have happened without you.'

Suddenly I had a James Marcus moment. 'Well that's just what frousins are for.'

'Frousins?'

'Yeah, friends and cousins. My boss back in the States has a thing about mash-up words. I miss him and his crazy words.' A thought struck me. 'I could go one better. Frebrosins!'

'What on earth?!'

'Friends, brothers, cousins.'

Her eyes welled up. 'So that makes me a mothant I guess!"

'Or a momauntie'

She giggled as she walked to the doorway. 'You know you're not here to fix Patrick, or Tabitha.'

'What do you mean?'

'All summer you've had the weight of Patrick's problems on you. And I know about Tabitha and her mum. Let your feelings out. Be honest with yourself. Be honest with her.'

'I know. But-'

'What?'

'What if being honest with her has makes me feel even more mixed up? We've had our fights and she's said some stuff that really hurt. Honest stuff. But it feels like it would hurt so much more not to have her in my life. And I think I love her. Like every time I spend time with her I feel. . . something I don't feel around anyone else. But what do we do about the Atlantic Ocean?'

'Tell her that. Tell her exactly how you feel.'

'I did.'

'And?'

'And she told me to not write a song about it. It's kind of a habit I have.'

Aunt Beth laughed at me. 'Clever girl! Now go downstairs and hang out with the rest of them.' But she stopped again. 'One last thing. I'm being good and staying out of the way, but how are Pat and Jess, you know, together, like, this evening.'

'No sparks flying,' I reported. 'Of the good or bad kind. We're keeping them busy!'

Aunt Beth pondered this before putting the tiny socks in her cardigan pocket and patting me on the shoulder.

Patrick and Jess were in the sunroom. To give them some time alone, Tabitha and I were watching a mindless rom-com in the living room. I can't remember even watching the movie, and before I knew it Jess had popped her head round the door and coughed. 'It's gone midnight Tabs. We need to go if you want to be in any state for Dublin tomorrow. Plus these boys need their beauty sleep.'

I was too tired to give a witty response so just stared sleepily at Jess. She's a 'say it like it is' person! I could tell she felt a little awkward being in the house and wanted to split. Jess probably was aware that my aunt would prefer they saw less of each other while Patrick had his resits to deal with. The girls grabbed the bags that Aunt Beth had given them, filled with some of her old costume jewellery and a few pieces of clothing she discovered in our attic boxes, including a skirt that Tabitha hadn't been able to take her eyes off all night. Aunt Beth told her my mom used to wear the skirt to the discos.

'See you bright and early tomorrow at the train station!' Tabs reminded me on the way out. How could I forget! Once I knew I was staying on, I had planned a day in Dublin with Tabs and I could not wait. But right now, I could not stay awake. Did I *really* have to be at Central Station 7 hours from now?

Bed. Exhausted. My sawing arm was starting to ache. But I was happy. Monsoon 'dreek' Tuesday had been a blast. A thousand times more fun than sitting on a plane 35,000 feet above the Atlantic. But it left me with a gnawing feeling in my gut too. I worked out that it was fear. But not a fear of the contents of the attic crashing down through the ceiling due to our dodgy workmanship. Going through all the boxes of memories in that attic, I realised that time waits for no man. Life changes. Styles evolve. Reminiscences fade, but we all get older. Some of us get wiser, some more eccentric, some chase their dreams and others settle. Some people accept they will never be anything more than what they were in their teens, or what other people have told them they can be.

What were the tales of my attic? I thought about the photos of Beth and Richard's old sweethearts and best friends; people who were once pals, but were now strangers. Pictures of holidays and family days floated through my mind, and made me realise that I didn't want to miss any of these opportunities to live my life to the full. I didn't want to lose contact with my buddies from high school or my new friends in Ireland. (I heart Skype!)

Today I found a life's worth of meaning, stored in an attic. And this summer I was making more memories of my own. I was filling the attic of my life with people and experiences that would shape and change me. I vowed to take this life-affirming-new-day-grabbing-memory-making-moment-seizing philosophy and put it into practice. Starting with tomorrow in Dublin with Tabitha.

DUBLIN TAKE TWO

After our infamous Monday night dinner, when I sprung my big surprise on Tabs, the two of us decided 'what the heck?' and planned a day-trip to Dublin on her next day off, which happened to be Wednesday. Short notice I know, but it still gave me time to cook up a further surprise for Tabs; of which more later.

So I left slumbering Patrick to another revision day and Uncle Richard left me at the train station for 7.30am. Of course Tabitha was already there, looking far more lively and wide-awake than me.

'Well sleepyhead. You going to share your sweets with me?' Tabitha asked as we settled into our seats and the train pulled out of the station.

She waited for an answer as I rolled a few toffees in my hand. I was still ¾ asleep.

I jumped. 'Oh sorry, what did you say?'

'I said can I have a share of your toffee for breakfast?'

'Oh yeah. Here take as much as you want.' Like a zombie I handed her the candy.

'What's up Tyler? You don't seem especially excited about this trip.'

I gave a huge yawn and stretch in explanation. 'You know. My life is so boring I can't keep my eyes open, especially since I met you.'

'Ha ha. You're getting funnier! My humour is rubbing off on you!'

Even with the excitement of the trip, and an ache in my lower back and legs from the hard labour in the attic, I just couldn't stay awake. Tabitha took pity on me and only interrupted my slumbers as we stopped in Newry and to bring me some OJ while I snored and drifted in and out of dreamland for 100 miles, missing lots of scenery, until we pulled into Dublin Connolly station.

We snapped a few selfies with a statue of James Joyce (the famous writer), crossed the Liffey river and enjoyed breakfast in Bewley's. It's one of the few Irish institutions people trust in anymore. Guinness is probably the other. There we people-watched as we sampled a delicious breakfast in this ornate café and attempted to come up with a once and for all plan to sort out the mess of Patrick and Jess' relationship.

But mostly we spent the day connecting the dots between the stores and the tourist attractions. First on the list was Dublinia at Christ Church Cathedral where we learned about the Viking and Medieval history of the city. On our way back to the shopping streets, we stopped into Dublin Castle and then took the long way round to St. Stephen's Green where we lay on the grass, watched the ducks bob on the water of the ornamental lakes and we slurped ice cream. Then we window-shopped down Grafton Street before we toured the illustrious grounds of Trinity College (which got me buzzed for freshman year).

Standing in Library Square I felt a tap on my shoulder, followed by a raspy old voice that called my name. I turned round. It was Old Man Chris from Ohio! He seemed to be with a tour group. I wrapped my arms around him and then introduced him to Tabitha. We chatted for a few minutes. He was keen to hear about my time in Ireland and to hear about how I had hooked up with a girl! Finally I got to ask him about his trip.

'How was Dongle?'

'Awhhh. It's a special place. You mean to say you haven't visited there yet?'

'Nope. But-'

Chris offered lots of great suggestions for places to eat, stay, fish and surf all along the Dongle coast. His enthusiasm was infectious.

'Thanks Chris. You're awesome. I'm really glad you're having such a great trip.'

'You know me, son. You only live once so make the most of it. Make sure you get to Glenveagh or your Irish trip won't be complete.'

We chatted for a few more minutes before his tour guide

came and Old Man Chris shuffled on his way. Would I ever see him again? Maybe on the plane back? Anything is possible.

'You *should* go to Donegal before you go.' Tabitha said. 'Seriously. You, me, some friends. Pat. Have a little holiday. It's a magical place.'

Inspiration struck. 'Do you think it could work its magic on Pat and Jess if they both come?'

Tab's face said 'doubtful' but her voice was a little more positive. 'Anything's possible in Dongle.'

The rest of the day passed by in a blissful, relaxing blur. Dublin is one of those wonderful cities that dares you to lose yourself in the history and the hustle and bustle of its crowded streets and alleyways. After dinner in a pop-up restaurant I had found on Twitter, we made our way through Temple Bar and onto the Ha'penny Bridge. Tabitha was anxious to get to the train station, convinced the big day out was over, but I had other plans.

'Come on Tyler, don't dawdle, we need to make the train.'

'What if I didn't want to get the train home?' I had fibbed and told her I bought return tickets to throw her off the scent. We were never getting on that train. Plus her dad was in on the surprise as well - he thought my idea was a great way to inspire Tabitha about her acting. But at this stage she didn't know any of this, so I let her question me.

'Tyler. We need to get on this train. It's the last one. And you know how my dad can get if I'm not home on time. You're still not totally out of his bad books.'

'But look at this view!' I stopped mid-bridge and looked

across at the Spire - a huge, gleaming polished steel needle stretching up into the still-bright sky.

'Now's not the time to be all wistful about the cobbled streets and beautiful bridges of Dublin or to try and figure out how the spire doesn't fall over. Skates on!'

'How did you know that's what I was thinking? Like seriously that spire is an engineering marvel. How'd they do it? I don't think we have anything like it in NYC.'

'You know the locals call it The Stiffy by the Liffey or The Stiletto in the Ghetto.' Tabitha remarked.

'ROFL,' I stayed stopped on the bridge. Tabitha began to walk on. 'What if I had a surprise for you?' I asked.

'A surprise. For me?'

'No for the other girl I'm talking to.' (I was finally getting the hang of sarcasm.)

'Go on, tell.'

'But, with the surprise - there would be one condition. You know the train we're supposedly rushing to catch?'

'Yeah.' Guarded but curious.

'Well the surprise means we won't make it.'

'Mmmmmm. I'll make that decision when you tell me what my surprise is!' She smiled, pleased with herself about her negotiation tactics. 'It better be good if I'm missing the last train.'

'So you want to know what the surprise is?' I asked.

'Obviously.' She folded her arms across her chest, waiting.

'Maybe I will keep it to myself. I don't think you seem too excited. Your old man was though.'

'OK, OK, I'm excited! Tell me!' She pulled on my arm

and started to search my pockets. 'Where is it? What is it?'

'Can't tell you until you get more excited about it.'

So Tabitha gave a big *'men, you've got to humour them'* sigh before she pulled out her best acting job. 'Tell me. Tell me. Tell me!!', she squealed like an 8 year old kid who had eaten way too many candy bars. People stopped and stared. She made such a scene that I was embarrassed into submission. That's what I get for trying to create a little drama with an actress I guess.

'OK, you win. Stop!' I brought my wallet out from my chinos pocket, told her to close her eyes and hold out her hands.

'This better not be a joke, Tyler.'

Praying a breeze would not pick up at that exact instant, I placed two crumpled tickets into her hands. She looked down.

'Wicked. Wicked. WICKED!' she shouted closing her fists over the precious tickets before any gusts could blow them out of her grasp and over the railing into the Liffey.

'And I got *great* seats!'

'Are we actually going to see *Wicked*?'

'Well if we get our walk on and make it to the theatre in time, then yeah! Or do you still want to get the train home?'

She looked at me and her eyes welled up. Turns out the most thoughtful thing her ex boyfriend had ever done for her was a bunch of convenience store flowers on her birthday. I had just scored mega points with my last-minute tickets.

Then, standing on the Ha'penny Bridge, Tabitha did the most important thing that had happened in our 'relationship' to date. As her eyes shone with tears, she reached over and held my hand. It may sound childish, but the innocence of youth won the day. Holding hands may seem like kids' stuff, but it brought a lot of things into focus. I felt accepted. Secure. Happy. Peaceful. Kissing is kissing, hugging is pretty cool, but interlocking fingers with another person brings a sense of togetherness. Instead of over-reacting and intensely analysing the hand holding event as another game changer, I allowed Tabitha to smile and lace her fingers through mine. It was hard to believe that we hadn't held hands until that point.

Now I know that if you were to compare our antics with those from *Fifty Shades*, they would be classed as whiter than white, but that misses the point. Sure we're teenagers, but not everything's about scoring and sleeping around. We are still innocent. We are becoming. We have had encounters, but we're not yet cynical about love. We carry a hope that one day real intimacy can happen with someone special and when it does we hope the experience is pure, inspirational, real, and much more than meaningless sex.

As we stood on the bridge I realised something. I overthink. I try and have everything figured out before I make any decisions. But now - I felt it was time to trust my instincts, close my eyes and leap. So I asked Tabitha something I had never asked a girl before, 'Tabitha, will you be my girlfriend?'

She laughed at me. 'I've been your girlfriend all along you big eejit!' Her laughter turned into a contented sigh as she nestled into my chest. I like to think that one exhalation released the years of hurt she had experienced at the hands of her unfaithful mother and waster of an ex-boyfriend, as she realised that here at last was one other person, other than her dad, in whom she could trust completely.

After a while Tabitha spoke. 'You came along at just the right time. But I hate you too 'cos you'll be away home so soon. And I don't know what's gonna happen to us. So weird how a person can feel their happiest and saddest all at the same time. Love is so kind but love is so cruel.'

'Look at you over-thinking things!' I smiled and touched the tip of her nose. 'That's my speciality.'

'I guess I have been hanging around with you too much,' she smiled.

'We'll figure it all out.'

'You promise?'

'Pinky promise.'

Tabitha stuck out her little finger and on the Ha'penny Bridge in Dublin we gave our summer love another fighting chance to last through the fall. Still holding her pinky finger I spoke, 'I don't want to be the moment-wrecker, but we should get a move on to the theatre before The Wicked Witch flies out of town on her broomstick.'

The musical was off the scale. Tabitha had been listening to the soundtrack all summer so I was able to sing along to a lot of the songs. By the time we enjoyed a post-theatre drink and strolled back into the city centre the last train home had long since pulled out of the station. I hadn't thought of a back up plan. I just assumed there would be another train.

As we stood on the sidewalk, at midnight, wondering what to do next, I realised this was a classic case of underthinking! Sharp as the spike on O'Connell Street, Tabitha figured out that we could get home by catching the Aircoach back to Belfast via the airport. And the stop was only a couple of blocks away. The girl is a genius!

Tyler:	*Missed train. Taking Aircoach.*
Patrick:	*Leaving the country early? Have I been that bad a host? Only messing! Will tell mum. Call me when you get to Belfast and I'll pick u lovebirds up. How was theatre? Did it work?*
Tyler:	A+. *We are now boyfriend and girlfriend*
Patrick:	*What are you? 12? Weren't you always?*
Tyler:	*Haha that's what Tabitha said*
Patrick:	*Pleased for you. Tabs is a catch*
Tyler:	*Thanks. C u soon*
Patrick:	*BTW I told Gareth u changed ur flights - he still wants u 4 festival THIS weekend. U keen?*
Tyler:	*WHAT! Of course I am. Holey moley, I totally 4got about that! Need to get practicing.*
Patrick:	*Lol. L8rs*

By the time I finished texting Patrick, Tabs had fallen asleep on my shoulder. She snuggled her head into my chest. I put my arm around her and wondered how I had arrived at this point. After staring at toffee-coloured hair for a few minutes, all I knew was today would go down in history as a massive leap forward in the love life of Tyler Sontoro. Thank you Dublin.

AFTERNOON TEA

In New York we have our fair share of plush hotels that double as luxury celebrity hangouts. The hotel scene is crammed with trendy rooftop bars, world-class restaurants and day spas housed in elegant buildings with stunning views of Central Park, or nestled in the next up and coming 'hood. The city is chock-a-block with iconic landmark hotels that ooze glamour and sophistication.

Often I use the need for an emergency men's room stop as an excuse to sneak a peek inside the gleaming lobbies of some of my hometown's finest. The bellboys know I'm not a guest, but they usually let it slide. One of my classmates had her Sweet Sixteen Party in one of the hippest hotels on the Upper East Side. Her uncle's wife's brother's husband owns the hotel. It was totally awesome. But mostly my knowledge of the NYC hotel scene comes, like just about everyone's, through movies and TV shows.

In my very experienced view, Belfast's Merchant Hotel would be right at home with some of the best places in The Big Apple - with its attentive staff that spoil you and the opulent décor with plush fringed furniture and huge sparkling chandeliers. On its website, it describes itself as *'a harmonious blend of Victorian grandeur and Art Deco inspired sleek modernity'*, but I would describe it in one word: sensational!

Round the block from The Merchant is a little NYC themed eatery, where you can, in local lingo, 'tuck into' the best patty melts this side of the Atlantic. Diving into one of their melts, then washing it down at a nearby coffee joint means, that, for the length of a lunch break, you can pretend you're in Manhattan. The hotel, the coffee and the sandwich are all a solid 10/10.

After a few too many egg and onion sandwiches (sorry Granny, but urrrgggghhh) at my Granny's house, I decided to return the favour and spoil her with Afternoon Tea at The Merchant. It's rated as one of the best things to do in Belfast, and I have wanted an excuse to go ever since Uncle Richard recommended it for my first date with Tabitha. So, I took my other sweetheart into the city centre, (I insisted we take the bus), and we realised that, yeah, this *is* actually one of the best things to do in Belfast. But first, I booked Granny in for a hand and face massage in the spa (yes I did join her in the same treatment!). After our pampering session, we made our way to The Great Room and sampled sumptuous scones and scrumptious sandwiches.

The Great Room is OTT luxury and elegance. To the max. It's like being smothered in red velvet until you look up and see the soaring ornate ceiling. The cream cakes and fine china are works of art too, but that didn't stop me from eating my share and half of Granny's as the wait-staff in their fancy uniforms looked on. They kept the dainty teacups filled as Granny and I talked about the tea dances she used to go to as a teenager and the hotels she had visited over the years.

She wore a smile as wide as the Lagan as she described the fantastic dances she and Granda used to go to. She also told me about the grand hotels in Bangkok, Kuala Lumpur and Hong Kong that she stayed in when they took their retirement trip to Asia. And she shook her head when she remembered 'the dodgiest place I have ever rested my head' - the primitive Bali beach shack they slept in for one night only.

'Your Granda booked that one. He thought it would be an experience. It was an experience all right!'

Granny is getting a little forgetful, and if she told me once, she told me five times that 'a cousin of mine used to work in this very room, many moons ago. You know, when it was a bank. They were proper banks back then. They knew your name and everything.'

In between enjoying our Afternoon Tea and chatting about yesteryear and family history, I filled her in on my day in Dublin.

'Well, hasn't this been wonderful!' Granny enthused as she popped the last bite of an eclair into her mouth. (It had been her last bite for the last few bites!) Success! The Merchant passed the test of one of Belfast's finest home bakers with flying colours.

With my eyes fixed on a little pink macaroon I said, 'Mom would love this place!'

Granny agreed and added, 'I remember you always did like the finer things in life Tyler, even as a wean.'

'What do you mean?' I asked before biting into the macaroon, which had a surprising burst of zestyness thanks to the passion fruit cream in the centre.

'Well your mum used to tell me she would feed you little bits of salmon and steak, topped with gourmet French sauces when you were a toddler. And you couldn't get enough.'

'That's not normal?' I teased, then proceeded to wipe macaroon crumbs from my chin with an oversized linen napkin.

Job done, I looked across the table for a response from Granny, but she had vanished! I scanned the room and caught the attention of one of the staff. She pointed to the other side of my table. I lifted up the tablecloth, put my head under the table and there was Granny, rooting through her massive handbag.

'Won't be a minute,' she said as if everything was normal.

'What are you doing?'

'Getting you something.' Out came all sorts of strange stuff from the depths of the handbag – emergency toilet paper, a lemon, breath mints, a spare watch, tickets for a play next week, 3 lipsticks, about 50 keys, recipes cut from magazines, measuring spoons and a small fabric elephant, for luck. And was that one of the Merchant's Battenburg slices wrapped up in a hanky for a wee nibble later on?'

'Granny you better not try and pay for this. It's my treat.'

'Oh no, don't worry. This one's definitely on you kid.' She laughed.

'Then what are you doing? People are looking at us. This is a fancy place.'

'Let them look. Don't be so impatient. Sit up. I'll come up for air in a minute.' Yes, this entire conversation had been taking place underneath a table in Belfast's grandest hotel.

Granny motioned for me to sit back up at the table. From my seat I could hear keys jingling, papers rustling, coins, candy wrappers and other mysterious sounds. I made eye contact with the waitress. She gave me a puzzled 'what is your Granny doing?' look. I gave her the same look back! Twenty seconds later Granny sat back up at the table, with an envelope in her right hand and a small box in her left hand. She placed both on the tablecloth and looked right at me.

'Tyler. I- we want you to have these.' She pushed the envelope and then the old battered box across the table. On the front of the envelope was my name, in Granda's writing.

My Granda had passed away when I was thirteen, seven months after he had made a trip out to New York to see us. Now Granny told me that when he found out his diagnosis and the short time he had left, he wrote each of his grandkids a letter filled with observations and life advice. Granny was under strict instructions to pass the letters onto us when we were 'of age'. Today was my turn.

'Open the box first,' Granny urged me.

So I did. Granda had given me the capo he used during his showband days. For non-musos, the capo is a small device you can clip on the neck of an acoustic guitar to change the pitch.

'That is from me. But I know your Granda would have wanted you, of all his grandchildren, to have it.' Granny explained.

Too moved for words, I reached for the letter, but Granny stopped me with a hand on my arm.

'Just read it when you feel ready. And know that your Granda would be so proud of how you've turned out. I'm sure he's smiling down at you today for treating me like this. He loved the finer things as well.' She threw her scarf over her shampoo and set (just done this morning specially for our outing). 'You know, he'd have given anything to see you play at that festival this weekend, even if it meant he was the oldest one there by a few decades.'

Granny grabbed her handbag and made for the restroom. I sat in silence, trying to fight back the tears. Years of missing out on playing soccer with Granda, being taught DIY and all the other things that Grandas do flashed before my eyes. For a brief second I resented my Mom for not moving back to Ireland, but I couldn't hold it against her. You gotta make decisions in life and live with how they settle.

And speaking of the festival, I needed to get home and get practicing some more. I only had today left!

I settled the bill and tipped the wait staff. When my date for the day returned from the restroom we snapped a few selfies and posed for a formal photo on the main steps of the hotel, taken by the doorman. I'd planned a 'juke' round the shops, but we'd lingered over the cakes and I was starting to feel antsy about the festival, so we caught the bus back to Granny's. I gave her a bear hug goodbye, climbed onto my bike and burned rubber home. Halfway back, I had a great urge to stop and read the letter, even just take a sneak peek at the first few lines, but the feeling passed as I realised the memory of the day belonged with Granny.

THE RED WOLF

Pat set the alarm for 7.30 and the two of us were up and at 'em on Friday morning. We had to make the most of the day. Pat was determined to squeeze in a few hours studying before we had to get our stuff together for the festival. We planned to head off to Fermanagh first thing on Saturday and that was a couple of hours away (about as far away as anyone can get in Northern Ireland).

I had decided to kill two birds with one stone by going busking again. I needed some pre-festival performance practice; plus with staying on longer, some extra cashola for presents for friends and family and for going out was pretty necessary. The last couple of days had not been cheap! I had dropped way too much money in Dublin.

Pat said town should be busy because it was the last day before a four-day national holiday when most people clear out of the city for some R&R. He was right. The place was bustling with last-minute shoppers in a happy, holiday mood. Perfect! I set up at Cornmarket again. People came and went, dropped coins; some even stayed and bought my EP! After lunch the ginger fella I had met on my last busking trip came over and we played a few songs together. He was raising cash to get to the festival too.

The day was great craic - I met a few more cool people and it gave me time to test out some of Granda's numbers on the public. I'd revamped them in a more current style and I thought the effect was pretty cool. And I had dropped the rapping from my songs - my attempt that night in The Bike Factory was definitely a 'cringe' moment in my music career! Ditto the falsetto.

I hadn't spent much time with Patrick since Tuesday, but we did see each other enough to have an awkward moment. Pretty much all week he had been hiding away in the library. I know he has to study, but he does have 6 weeks to do it in, so his level of enthusiasm did seem a bit OTT. But what do I know? I've only finished High School.

Anyway, from his texts to me I could tell he was super excited to hang out, not just in Fermanagh, but after that in Dongle! Yes, he thought Tab's and my plan was a solid A+ and felt only a little bit mad at himself that he hadn't come up with the idea. Maybe that was why he was putting in so many study hours?

But, later that night, as we were packing for our weekend trip, he left his cellphone open on my bed and it started chirping. Maybe I thought it was my phone, or that it was his phone ringing and I should answer it. I don't know. But, acting on auto-pilot I picked it up and saw this text:

> M: *Ur such a laff. This week has been class. Who knew revision would be so much fun. Can't wait to 'revise' again next week. Have fun at the lakes. M xx*

I could tell from the smileys and emoticons it was from a girl. My heart sank; I guess I was still sold on the idea that he was going to get back with Jess. And now some other girl – the mysterious M - was texting him. Patrick emerged from the bathroom and saw me holding the phone. I dropped it, shocked, but I knew I was busted. But so was he.

'So that's why you're so into the studying!' I accused him.

Pat turned red and muttered evasively that nothing was going on, they were just in the same revision group. But going by his reaction, I didn't buy it.

For now, I let him off the hook because there was too much to get done before the big gig and I did not want to give Patrick a hard time. He was so stoked to get away for the weekend and had arranged lots of fun stuff.

'Anything to escape the desk and the structure and function of the pancreas,' Pat flustered and I didn't comment.

Traveling to the venue was like uncoiling a spring. Endless twists and turns, up, down and round hilly Irish countryside that made us wonder if we were going in continuous circles, or best case scenario, spiralling our way to Mordor. We left at 7am, which seemed pretty extreme, but Patrick had good reason. He had arranged a 9am cruise on Lough Erne round the lake's many wooded islands, some of which had Stone Age ruins and perfect early Christian towers. Incredible, but even more amazing, our next stop: an underground boat tour of the awesome Marble Arch caves. Everything around County Fermanagh involves water it seems.

Then we took a power nap in the car before we got lost, or errrr took a creative direction, which did happen about four times. Once we got off the main roads, there are as many signposts as there are snowmen in the Sahara. So we were very grateful when we began to see Red Wolf Festival signs and banners with arrows pointing the way.

Gareth had warned me that this was not your usual 'big muddy mosh-pit field' festival, but something just 'a wee bit more . . .' He searched for a word, 'homespun'. But nothing prepared me for the actual venue, an old working family farm. After I caught a glimpse of the homemade streamers that fluttered from the apple trees in the garden and sensed the hive of activity in the campsite, I realised that, after my time at this wonderful little festival, a wee bit more of my heart was going to remain in Ireland.

Two girls, dressed in their finest glamping/festival chic, sat at a makeshift entrance office/hut/garden shed. On approach Patrick gave me a nudge in the right nipple.

'No funny stuff,' I whispered. 'Remember, Gareth is doing me a favour.'

'I know, but that energy drink is beginning to work on me.'
The guy was antsy.

'I can see that! Behave.'

'Chill! I know these girls.'

Patrick used this phrase a lot. He genuinely did know a lot
of people. This usually got us out of a few scrapes, but sometimes into more awkward situations than I cared for. The girls
turned out to be cashiers, ticket administrators, bouncers and
parking lot attendants all rolled into one amazing double act.
I sheepishly raised my sunglasses and announced my arrival.

'Hey I'm Ty-'

Before I could finish the first syllable Patrick interrupted.
'Ladyeeez! Looking gorgeous! I'm the manager for this Yan-
kee artist. So we get any special perks? Free drinks, food, your
phone numbers?'

I rolled my eyes trying to give an 'I'm not responsible for
him' impression.

The blonde to our left stared at Patrick, just long enough
for us to realise she wasn't impressed. 'Paddy. What sort of
establishment do you think this is? It didn't work two years
ago, so why do you think I would fall for your so-called charm
this year?'

'Listen Christy, the fact that a girl with your fine looks and
personality is talking to a guy with an ego like mine, means I
can only live in hope that one day you will understand me, if
you know what I mean? I mean we are Facebook friends, Twitter and Instagram buddies.' Patrick concluded his spiel with a
bumbling comment to the girl with dark curls. 'Nice hat, Emily.

Where did you get it?'

'Not falling for it Patrick. My granny warned me about guys like you. Handsome and gift of the gab = trouble.'

Patrick was grinning like a fat cat. Emily shook her head, rose from her seat, walked to her 4x4 and grabbed a picnic basket from the trunk.

'Your granny's a wise girl. I'll settle for a dance later,' Patrick laughed. 'No roving hands, scout's honour!' He held both hands up and put on a 'who me?' innocent face. Then winked.

Somehow the old Pat charisma worked! He should bottle it.

Christy gave Paddy a wry smile and waved one of her pigtails at him. 'See you later boy . . . if you're good.'

'I'm always good.'

I couldn't believe that Patrick was flirting like this and said so. But he reassured me that this blonde was a friend he knew from college and this was the way they bantered with each other round these parts. Well he is young and single, or single-ish?

'Here. Catch.' Patrick tossed me the car keys and walked off towards the main venue.

Was he a bit annoyed that I had mentioned his flirting? Possibly. Was I cramping his style? Probably. Anyway I didn't see him for another few hours.

Emily returned to the table. She was pouring a steaming cup of tea from her flowery flask. I was now at the mercy of these two girls who chatted at a ridiculously fast pace or a 'mile a minute' as Uncle Richard would say.

'Here, you must be the Canadian cousin Gareth told us about.'

'Bryan Bieber!?' This was humiliating.

'Only winding you up!' Emily ruffled some papers, pretending to be all official. 'Yes you're down to play a four minute set in the chicken run? Hope you are OK with feathers and being henpecked, Bryan?' The pair collapsed into laughter.

'No I'm Tyler Sontoro from New York. Playing a thirty-minute set in the Farmhouse. And not Canadian. Obviously.' I could have explained that 'Farmhouse' was the giveaway. Canadians pronounce it 'Farmhoose'.

The girls winked at each other enjoying how I was taking their prank seriously.

'Not even a little bit Canadian?'

'I'm actually Half Irish.'

'Oh you're 'Half Irish?'' Emily did the inverted comma thing with her fingers when she said 'Half Irish'. 'Sure you are!'

Christy piped up, 'Let me guess how you're Half Irish. You've seen *The Quiet Man* fifty times. You wear green on St Patrick's Day. You have a Guinness keyring. You believe in leprechauns. No wait, you know the difference between craic and crack? You have an Irish wolfhound?'

Having lived here for a month I should have been used to the sarcasm and slagging, but I definitely walked into that one. They stared at me. Then looked at each other. Then burst out laughing. Again.

'Yeah we know who you are! We're only messing with your head!' Emily sort of apologised.

Christy jumped in. 'Actually you're the first New Yorker to play here and we are well excited about that! So here's your official artist's access all areas wristband. Ryan will take you to the venue for sound-check, and Tyler-' She let her hand linger on my arm as she fastened the wristband.

'Yeah?'

'Remember to get your undercrackers out of that twist before you perform?'

Did I really look that nervous? I nodded in agreement as Christy handed me my pass, fumbled for her radio and summoned Ryan to the welcome desk (if you can call an old scuffed table outside a garden hut that). I wanted to jump into my guitar case and stay there until my set started. They must have thought I was a complete pompous dork. Waiting for Ryan to arrive, I hid behind my dark sunglasses and thought about what it would be like to be Canadian. I'm glad Ryan arrived quickly. Canadian thoughts are scary. I'm not into moose and fir trees, but I do dig some country music.

The embarrassing entrance booth experience felt like a lifetime away once Ryan gave me the tour of the intimate, magical venue. A stone-built traditional farmhouse, complete with white-washed outhouses, stables and cattle sheds, a big barn and a spotlessly clean old fashioned cobbled farmyard was the setting. And huge tents had been set up in a couple of the fields.

When I'd heard I was playing in a farmyard, I was expecting to wade through piles of pig dung, chicken feed and ankle-attacking hens on the loose. I didn't know farmyards could look as quaint, be so clean and feel so romantic. But then again I was in Ireland. And anything's possible on this wonderful island. Gotta say though, I was relieved that my venue was going to be the farm*house* rather than the farm*yard* after all.

Still smiling at the freshly painted bright red windowsills with their pots of flowering plants I entered my performance area, *Anyone for Tea?* It made me think of one of my first nights in Belfast when Granny asked if I'd be back for tea - which I thought was a cup of tea - but she really meant dinner. I had two dinners that night!

I was led up to the first floor of the farmhouse. This used to be the family house, but whenever the festival took off they transformed the downstairs into a makeshift café and the upstairs was an open plan performance area. Unique was the only word for it. Climbing up the wooden stairs I suddenly stopped, as I caught a glimpse of some awesome traybakes. Such a Northern Irish word, but something the world needs to experience. Allow me to digress.

Traybakes – Tray-bake (noun)

They are everywhere and Patrick tells me they are a typically Northern Irish sweet treat. (I didn't have the heart to tell him we have them in the US too, but different varieties and under a different name). Sort of a cookie, cake, brownie and gooey sweet-treat all rolled into one. Called traybakes because they are baked in a shallow pan slightly deeper than a baking tray and then, when smelling like heaven, cut into squares. This homemade delicacy makes storebought, factory production line cookies and cakes sweat nervously in their plastic wrappers. Made with as much love that can be crammed into a 3 x 3 inch delicacy, the average traybake contains

as many calories as a hearty meal. Best washed down with a cup
of tea, coffee or a glass of ice-cold milk.

As I stared longingly down at this huge array of beauties I
made a mental note to remind Mom of a new line for her store.
We may have 'bar cookies' in the US, but the flavours I was
looking at were like a whole new world to me. Diet-conscious
Villagers might have a heart attack just looking at all that chocolate and coconut, but I knew resistance would be impossible.
But I was dawdling - nerves I guess.

After listening to my instructions from Ryan, I tuned up and
scanned the room. Definitely old school with a few bashed
old couches, rugs and cushions strewn around. The floor must
have been there at least a hundred years, made of beautiful
aged and distressed timber. There was no stage. No pretence.
No distraction. Music was the focus. The sound engineer was
scratching his beard. I glanced out the window at the rolling
hills of green countryside and arrow straight ploughed fields.
A glimpse of forest and lake in the distance. As I lost myself
in the view, I caught a glimpse of the future. Me, semi-retired,
sitting on a porch, drinking some mid grade bourbon on a
Wednesday evening, sharing travel stories with buddies. I knew
my time at this festival was something I would always reminisce
about. I could just feel it.

I was going to be first up, so I had time for a quick run-
through before I gave myself an essential energy boost, courtesy of a lemon and coconut square, and made my way back
upstairs. The crowd began to settle into the space. As unfa-

miliar faces filed in, I began to think of all the gigs I had played since that afternoon when I wandered the streets of The Village scrounging for an opportunity. I was amazed that I had made it so far and realised I had achieved a heck of a lot over the last few months.

The audience stared at me waiting for something to happen. This part's always weird. You want to say something funny to break the ice, but you can never tell if the joke will be an epic fail or raise a laugh. And NI crowds are tough when it comes to humour.

Some days the best tactic is just to launch into song, but at other times the audience expects a little interaction. Around 140 Northern Irish eyes stared at me. Pat was there too. With Emily. Waiting. You bet I was tense. I hadn't practiced half as much as I would have liked. So I summoned up a flashback of Susan's nana dancing to my cover of Michael Jackson's *Beat It* on that snowy day in Chinatown. It calmed my nerves and put a smile on my mug. Before the panic could take over again, I just started in:

'Hey I'm Tyler. From New York. I was told I'm the first person from NYC to play here. It's an honour. So on behalf of the 8.4 million residents of my city, hello! And a big thankyou to Gareth for inviting me to play. I'm going to play a few covers, a few of my own tracks and a few covers from a band called The Forevers. Your parents or grandparents might have danced to their music back in the day, as you say over here. My Granda was their lead singer during the Showband era and wrote the songs I am hoping to do justice to today. *The Forevers*

329

even played the Silver Sandal Ballroom in Enniskillen. So I hope my Granda will appreciate the twist (no, not *Twist and Shout!*) I've put on his music, and that you will too. And if you have any requests, please just shout them out and I probably won't be able to play them . . .'

A bit feeble but it got them on my side.

We sat down by the river . . .

For forty minutes applause rolled and song after song seeped out from the cracks in the wooden window frames in *Anyone for Tea?* I went over my allotted thirty minutes, but the crowd were enjoying themselves so it didn't seem to matter until the smell of champ and sausages wafted up the stairs and I started to get pretty hungry. So did the crowd. I launched into my penultimate song, *Holding You.*

Holding you
Holding you
Is all I want to do

Holding you
Holding you
Is all I want to do

So come home quickly
Don't even pack your bags
I'll buy you new gowns and shoes with expensive tags

I see you every time I close my eyes
But I need to feel you again
I need to feel you again . . .

The crowd gave me a huge round of applause.

'Thank you, thank you. You're too generous. Oh and to the guy holding up the sign saying, 'Marry me so I can get a Green Card?' I'm flattered but no. But I know someone who would!' As the laughter died down, I went for a change of mood:

'I have one more song and this is the first time I've played it. I have been in Ireland for 4 weeks and have just under 2 weeks left. It's been totes emosh (most of the crowd laughed, some rolled their eyes). It's literally been the best summer of my life. Being on your island has changed me a lot. I have fallen in love with the places, the people, the craic and I think with a girl. I say I think because I have never been in love before, and maybe I'm crazy, but I can't stop thinking about her so I guess I am either really into her or I need to get more friends and hobbies and she is too nice to tell me. Anyway, enough of my personal stuff. You have been the best crowd. Seriously. On two continents. Thanks again to Gareth and the rest of the crew for having me. If you are ever in New York, look me up on Facebook or something like that and I will show you the real NYC. And finally, before I get on the plane, I have some EPs for sale - *Songs From The Mountain* and another one you can pre-order - it's called *Songs From The Island*. See what I did there?!' The whole crowd laughed.

I reached for my Granda's capo. My eyes connected with someone in the audience. A girl was standing in the corner of the room, face half hidden by a man's trilby hat. My heart stopped. I didn't recognise the hat, but I knew those eyes. I stared as she scribbled something on the back of a clipboard she had grabbed from a steward. The rest of the room stared at me wondering why I was just standing there doing nothing. They looked round to see what had caught my eye. She held up a sign.

'You're not crazy.'

She put the clipboard on the arm of a nearby chair and brought her hands together to make a heart shape. I hoped beyond hope that I would never forget the feeling I experienced in those few seconds, as a traveller who, in a moment, had just passed from one stage of love to the next.

Someone sensitively shouted out, 'Is that the bird you were talking about?'

'It better be!' his pal yelled back.

The crowd laughed, and waited for my response. I smiled and nodded, to which the audience gave a stoked round of applause and high-pitched whoops.

The same guy urged, 'Give her a kiss then!'

I blushed.

Tabs and I walked towards each other. I took Tabitha in my arms, looked her in the eyes and before I gave her a kiss, said those three words everyone wanted to hear, 'I love you'. Then, knees a tad wobbly, I assumed position at the front of the room, lifted my guitar and started plucking on the chords of my last song.

'That would have been awkward if I hadn't said those three

little words!'

My comment received the loudest laugh of the day.

'This is for you and your lover, whoever they may be. It's called *A Traveller Passing Through*. Cheers.'

Discovering you
Discovering new
A wondrous way of life

Your hair, your eyes, so beautiful
This feeling, these thoughts, so magical
Am I foolish?
Am I crazy?
Will it pass or will it stay stay stay . . .

We wrapped a plaid rug around us as we shared a plate of fries and a homemade lentil burger. Tabitha had tricked me into believing she couldn't make it to the gig. We replayed our public declaration of the L word, and the ramifications it would have.

'We should go and tell Theresa,' Tabitha said.

'Ha ha she would love it.'

After some talking and some kissing, we came to the conclusion that we didn't just want to wait and see what would happen; instead, we wanted to make a go of it. The hows were for another night, tonight I simply had to get her to stop stealing my fries. Stealing my heart was enough criminality for one day.

For the rest of the night, and most of the next day too, we listened to top quality music from some incredible artists. From scremo to folk, rock to pumping indie dance. Eclectic just about sums it up. Simply put - it was one of, if not *the*, best nights of my trip. I chatted to strangers, laughed nonstop and made new friends, including that ginger guy. Gareth told me his parents were huuuuuuuggggge fans of *The Forevers* and he loved how I had updated their music. We agreed my Granda had been a genius songsmith.

And after watching Patrick flirting, grooving his toosh off and working the room (indoors and out), I was beginning to understand what Tabitha had been trying to tell me all along about Pat. Yes, he needed closure from the whole thing. To be young and unattached again. And maybe, finally, Patrick was beginning to know this too. Watching him use his chat-up-lines on Emily and her friends gave me seriously mixed feelings. A little worried. A lot relieved. He seemed happy and free. And why shouldn't he be?

But it also meant a doubt began to take root and grow in my mind about the 'intervention' Tabitha and I had planned as a last chance saloon for Patrick and Jess to sort out their relationship. Was it really such a good idea for us all to be heading off to Donegal in a couple of days? To force them together? But it seemed too late now. Tabitha had already found a place for us to stay in Donegal, gotten a great deal with people she knew and paid the deposit. We couldn't back out now.

My doubt grew even bigger later on that night at Red Wolf, when Tabitha headed off to the campsite with her friends and I had to go on the hunt for the elusive Patrick. When I did find him, he was a little worse for wear. He also confessed he never got round to putting up our tent and he was now in no shape to do so. I was going to give it a try, but on the way there, we bumped into Gareth who took pity on us. He gave us the keys to *Anyone for Tea?* where we crashed on a couple of couches and ate traybakes for breakfast. So much for bringing along the tent and sleeping bags. At least it meant we did not have to lose any partying time packing the car!

Sunday was a big day for a lot of the open air acts, so more space for trying out our off the wall dancing, which Patrick is an expert at. It all wrapped up around five, giving Tabitha, Pat and me time to finalise our Donegal arrangements before goodbye kisses and high fives. I'll let you guess who kissed who and who high-fived who.

On our drive home, Paddy and I sat in contented silence. Taking the stage at The Red Wolf had been a marking moment. From playing some of Granda's songs to publicly declaring my love for Tabitha it brought closure to the songs that had been born during my winter vacation and brought another layer of meaning to my time in Ireland. I didn't bother Paddy with my wistful thoughts, or my mixed feelings about his behaviour and our 'Donegal Plan'. He was perplexed enough as he tried to figure out how to get us home.

CRISP SANDWICH DAY

Everyone needs a lazy day sometime, and Monday was it.

It was a holiday weekend for everyone in Northern Ireland, but for us festival fatigued guys, Monday was movie day! Well what else are you going to do when you're off work and it has done nothing but rain since 9am?

Beth, Richard, Granny, Patrick and I all hung out – we'd had very few chill-out family days. During the breaks in our movie marathon, Pat and I packed for Donegal (no tents required this time, way hey!) and Beth and Richard did some research into the vacation they were taking after Pat's resits.

Junk food and movie days go together like pastrami and rye bread so we had crisp sandwiches for lunch. Maybe you have to grow up eating them, but I couldn't really see the attraction of potato chips between slices of buttered white bread. Then Alex Skyped mid-lunch and was weirded out by the bread and crisp combo too. Maybe it is a NYC thing, but what is it with the sandwiches in this place? Bananas? Potato chips? Chutney, whatever that was? Butter and mayo together on the same sandwich? And so much mayonnaise, on everything! I just don't get it. Though one cheese and ham toastie later and all was forgiven!

After talking to Alex (who was dressed in normal clothes this time round), I called Mom to fish for tips on what to do with Tabitha on our last night together and ideas for a special gift for her. Hard to believe but my departure was only 10 days away - already! I wanted to come up with a plan and start getting organised before we left for Donegal.

DONGLE

Welcome to a land of long golden beaches, peat bogs, dramatic headlands, rocky mountains, towering cliffs and quaint whitewashed villages tucked into the landscape; totally unlike anywhere else I had been so far in Ireland. Donegal, or Dongle as I like to call it, was even better than Old Man Chris' descriptions. But then how can words capture this wild and enchanting place? The sea was an ever-changing palette of colours - morning azure, afternoon ultramarine, and indigo in the evening. And those sunsets!

Most of the time we played on the deserted beaches dodging huge crashing waves, or building sandcastle cities in tiny bays scooped out from between the rocks. A toe in the 'refreshing' Atlantic water and you know instantly this has to be the last stop before Iceland, Greenland and North America.

Tabitha scored A++++++ for finding such a great base

for our 5 days away, a vacation home that belonged to one of her amigos. So early on Tuesday morning Patrick, Jess, Conor, Tabitha, Kaitlin and I were feeling optimistic as we hit the road. The sun was out and the forecast for the next few days was looking good! A few other mates were coming up for days here and there too.

Only one itty bitty cloud, but it was a dark one. I had a feeling our final, probably not too smart, attempt at helping Patrick and Jess get back together for good was not going to go to plan. Tabs had told me Jess still seemed indifferent to their relationship and Patrick was clearly finding the taste of freedom pretty sweet.

We got off to an iffy start when Jess suggested the girls drive together in Tabitha's car and the boys travel separately in Pat's. But it did mean there was no tension on the two-hour journey.

Patrick brought his lecture notes, a few textbooks and his laptop which contained more coursework, all neatly packed in his small backpack, but 'he hadn't a mission' of getting any work done, predicted Conor. 'Maybe if it rains,' was Patrick's answer.

But no chance of that, with one warm, dry and sunny day after the next. The whole time the weather was incredible. The locals kept telling us how lucky we were and how this sun was not usual at all, at all!

Anyway, to backtrack to the roadtrip there. It was pretty eventful. Part of the Glenshane Pass was closed for roadworks, so we journeyed over the twisty, bumpy back roads across the lonely Sperrin Mountains to Derry/Londonderry, or Stroke

City as it is affectionately known. The city dates back to the 6th century, and is the only completely walled city in the British Isles, so of course I insisted (coming from a country too new for castles, ramparts and fortified cities) that we stop for a look-see. We did the whole circuit of the old town, walking along the top of the amazingly preserved 400-year-old walls, complete with canons pointing down at the peeps below.

After lunch, our little convoy hit the road again, only to get stuck behind a vintage tractor cavalcade between Letterkenny and Creeslough. Patrick didn't even try and weave between the tractors and just accepted the traffic. If it's not tractors, then it's going to be sheep in the road. #wheninDonegal

Our week in Donegal was amazing! We passed our time doing all my favourite stuff (I have a lot of favourite stuff BTW) eating, laughing, playing cards, making up beach games and surfing. Trying, in my case – again. Cowabunga! I was so amped to spend a few days in the water. But that was my problem. 90% of my time in the water and only 10% on the board! Tabitha was soooo much better than me. The surfer dudes said she was a natural and called her 'The Tabster'. Jess was 'The Jesster' of course. I had visions of catching barrels and hanging ten, but, despite my skateboarding skills, my city feet did nothing but slip off the carefully waxed board into the chilly Atlantic. Whoops! Getting ahead of myself again.

So, from Day One, Tabs and I knew our plan was probably gonna be, to use another surfing term, a total wipeout. We noticed it that first night at dinner in a fish and chip café. Jess and Pat were both making a conscious effort not to sit by each

other. And later that night in the pub when the music and craic really got going and Pat was being Pat – in high spirits and
goofing off and being the life of the party, Jess would shoot him
these 'behave yourself' looks, which would certainly cramp my
style. Then Tabs would give me one of her 'see what I mean?'
glances.

Next morning even I had to admit, 'I don't think our intervention is going to work out, Tabs.'

She smiled and patted my shoulder pityingly. 'You think?'

At least the weather was fantastic, so we weren't all stuck
together in the house and could get out and spend hour after
hour on the beach and on the waves.

And astonishingly, Pat seemed to be making progress with
his studying. For a couple of hours at least.

Kaitlin had a resit too and had brought her notes, so she was
going to find a quiet place while the rest of us stocked up at the
supermarket that first day. 'With the exams so close, five days
not studying can make a big difference,' Kaitlin said. 'If I do a
couple of hours most mornings, I'll feel more able to relax and
have a good time later.'

Pat also went off to find a quiet place, but when I looked for
him after we got back from the store, there he was on his bed
playing *GTA* on his tablet. He had that sheepish look that said
it all.

'Just can't focus right now,' he confessed before we went off
to get 'our heads showered' in the Atlantic surf.

Over the next few days, Patrick continued to steal away,
supposedly to study, but I wasn't fooled. He just needed to get

away. Sure he enjoyed the surfing and touring around Dongle as much as the rest of us, but in the quieter moments I could see something was eating at him. And at night he was just a little too 'out there' which concerned me and annoyed Jess. I think too she was giving him grief about not studying enough, if she spoke to him at all! So Tabs and I stuck by him because Jess certainly had no plans to. She seemed to have made friends with some of the surfer people who we'd started hanging out with.

Even if Pat and Jess weren't talking to each other, they were talking to us about their *is it or isn't it?* relationship. By Day Two, Wednesday, Pat seemed pretty sure one of them just needed to make the first move and it would be game over. It was pretty clear P&J had reached the end of the road. Simple. Only Pat wasn't the one who was going to do it. Then Tabitha informed me that Jess didn't know how to tell Patrick they were through, in case, well, in case he did anything stupid. So the week was a bit of a merry go round of conversations between Tabitha and me and Jess and Patrick, but never between the couple at the centre of the whirl.

Oh, and we also discussed Jess flirting with one of the surf instructors which had led to a couple of awkward dinner time remarks from Patrick.

I was torn between keeping watch over Pat, spending every possible minute with Tabs and enjoying seeing as much as I could of this wild, windswept county.

We camped for a night on the Inishowen peninsula (so much for not camping again!) and walked around the headland that is the most northerly point of the Emerald Isle. Another day we hung out at the castle and its gardens at the remote and beautiful Glenveagh National Park. An American from Philadelphia, Henry McIlhenny, purchased the estate and castle in 1937 and devoted many years to restoring the place. His clan made a fortune in industry, but Henry devoted his life to hosting parties, collecting fine art and decorating his Donegal party pad – even in plaid wallpaper! After selling the estate in 1975 he gifted the castle and its gardens to Ireland in 1983. I would have loved to have met that guy and gone to his parties. The guests included Greta Garbo and Clark Gable. Hard to imagine such glamorous celebs in this lonely spot. I wanted to climb Mount Errigal on the way back from visiting his castle but was outvoted. Everyone just wanted to eat then hit the beach.

Before we knew it, we'd reached the last day of our Dongle dream. Donegal is like that. So easy to lose track of time and even what day of the week it is! And had we made any progress with Jess and Pat? Not really. I wish I could say I had made more progress with my surfing, but at least I had a blast. After the waves carried and barrelled me for the final time, our surf instructor summed up my progress. An A for effort, but I was still a Barney and needed 'a lot more board time to make Kelly Slater wigged out.' I was happy to settle for that.

We ate most of our meals outdoors and our final day was no different. We sheltered behind a poorly erected windbreaker and ravaged the standard post-surf Donegal lunch picnic of ham and cheese baguettes with a side of potato chips. Finishing off our sandy baguettes we watched as pasty white locals and holidaymakers soaked up the uncharacteristically warm sunshine. Then we washed down the last of Conor's mom's homemade cookies with lukewarm cups of tea. After lunch we played frisbee on Marble Hill Beach, before we all stampeded back into the sea one last time, splashing into the water simultaneously in a chorus of screams and yells. Then finally, we brought a wonderful few days surf-side to an artistic end as we transformed a snoozing Patrick into a sand-mermaid. McIlhenny would have been proud of our efforts.

Patrick managed to get all the sand out of his ears, hair and from between his toes in time for the night's mega cookout. Having scrimped on a few meals during our stay, we put our spare Euros to good use and raided the butchers that morning, picking up a Texas-sized haul of meat. Steaks as thick as doorsteps, five racks of ribs, burgers, sausages, chicken kebabs and veggie skewers too, to balance the cholesterol scales. Even though a couple of friends from Belfast, plus some of the surfer crew, were there for the party, our eyes were probably bigger than our stomachs! It was a monster of a feast and a perfect last supper to celebrate our time in beautiful, beautiful Donegal.

Sitting down alongside our surf instructor friends (including Jess' 'buddy') I took in the view at the table and was so thankful for the experience. An unbelievable view was before me: new friends, girlfriend, stunning scenery and a banquet of awesome chow! All the ingredients for great memories.

But that Saturday night would linger in my mind for many other reasons too. Not least because it was the night I opened

Granda's letter. Patrick read his when he traveled round Europe. Whenever he talked about his letter, his eyes lit up as he remembered the insights and encouragement Granda had given him. As the meal wound down, I told the rest of the gang what I was going to do. I had expected sympathetic glances and words, but it led to a loud story swap, as we all recalled our grandparents; their eccentricities, eyebrow raising tales (probably totally exaggerated) from their wild young days, and the way they mispronounce modern technology: wiffie instead of wifi, The Goggle instead of Google, shelfies instead of selfies, or my personal favourite - YouTube for U2.

'I'll meet you at the pub,' I announced to the gang. I had delayed for long enough.

Patrick was inside washing the dishes, probably escaping the sight of Jess getting friendly with her surfer friend with the perfect tan and the beach hair. Apparently the dude was a semi-pro and went off to Hawaii and Portugal in search of The Big One, paid for by some big board manufacturer.

I stopped in the kitchen en route from my room to find my letter and trainers and kick off my flip-flops (note: thongs are something totally different over here. I learned that yesterday when I shouted, 'Anyone seen my thongs?' when we were on the beach, and got funny looks from just about everyone). Pat was standing still looking out at the incredible sunset lighting up the beach. Something about the look in his eyes . . . I paused and laid a hand on his shoulder then kept it there. In an instant, Pat turned, mischief back in his face, and he flicked a handful of soapsuds right at me. I ran out of there before it turned into a full-scale water fight, with Pat chasing me and throwing bubbles. But soon I was on my own.

The sky had laid out a pink and orange blanket for the sleepy sun, tired from a productive day's work making freckles and turning a tasty profit for ice cream companies up and down the island. My left hand played with the reeds that flanked the weathered boardwalk. My right held the letter safe. When the boardwalk ended, a worn grassy track guided me to the beach. The setting sun glinted off a nearby rock face. Nature was guiding my way. At first the leaden waves of the Atlantic lapped onto the golden shore, but this soothing sound came to a near silence as I rounded a corner and a deserted cove came into sight. As I approached the cove, the blue sky that had entertained us throughout our Donegal holiday played its final scene. Entering from stage right was a thick glowering cloud, still a few miles off, but promising rain.

I eased into the sand, took a deep breath and opened the envelope. Once again the waves caught my attention and cast their spell. Had it really been five weeks? My mind drifted through the movie scenes of conversations, coffees, cake and cuddles from my time in Ireland. A whirlwind of summer stories flashed before my eyes. It had been an adventure for my mind, my body and my spirit. A journey into friendship, love and self-discovery, yet I knew that Ireland hadn't finished having her way with me just yet. Front and centre was the love of a girl that had awakened my soul to a whole new world of thoughts and feelings. Something told me there was plenty more for me to experience before I boarded the plane home.

Donegal is a remarkable place. So relaxed it's almost sleeping. Being from New York, my baseline for silence is at best a muffled background noise. I hadn't experienced this tranquil sensation since our New Year's ski trip in the mountains. On the night we camped out I fell asleep to the sound of silence, well, in between bleating sheep and the whistle of the wind. Now the lulling waves provided the background track as I began to read the letter.

My American lad,

I have thought long and hard about what I would say to you, but it's always best to write from the heart.

We didn't see a lot of each other while you were growing up and I regret not spending more time in New York. But the 3 months your granny and I enjoyed in The Big Apple just before you turned a teenager were some of the most precious memories I have. During that trip you reminded an old man about the fullness available in each and every day and the importance of new experiences. Remember the time you put me on a skateboard in Washington Square Park?

If life is anything, it's a journey. Central to this journey is an inescapable longing to experience all of the forms and expressions of love. I have realised that no matter what you fill your heart with, it will be empty if you don't feel alive in love. But be warned. If you open yourself up to love, you will be filled with the danger of hope, and an all-consuming passion to see those people you love and the dreams you hold dear come to flourish in the fullness of life. True love will cost you everything.

I loved a lot of women. Your granny, my two sisters, my daughters, my mum, my nana - and when I was 5, Katherine, the girl from next door! Spread your love as wide as you can, but hold your devotion for those who love you back. Like family.

I grew up in a world far different from yours. But some things remain the same. You need to work. You're never too good for any job. Pay your bills. Don't rack up debts, and, whatever you do, don't live beyond your means. You have been blessed with talents. Use them. New and shiny soon becomes old, tried and tested, and then the latest thing again; so don't place a lot of importance on gathering up a whole pile of stuff.

Find the things you are willing to die for – then live for them. When you find the woman who heightens every emotion and sense in your being, the girl who is your missing piece, I urge you to marry her everyday. Be meticulous in your love and inspirational in your expressions of love and commitment.

Dance. In the kitchen. In the supermarket. In the ballroom, in the disco or whatever new fad arises.

Sing. In the shower. In the street, with the dawn and the dusk. Listen before you comment.

Discover. Explore your city, explore new ideas, new lands and always explore your heart. Don't ignore your heart. Guard it, protect it, don't give it away without due care. It's one of the most precious things you have.

Be generous. With your love and with your life, with your time and your thoughts, your possessions and your bank account.

Laugh everyday. Have fun. Build your life on the things that bring you happiness and real joy.

When you stand on the brink of the unknown, fearful of where the next step will take you, know that angels watch over you. You will have to make decisions that bring you to a bridge of tears, where the future is painful because the past haunts and holds you and the thought of what lies ahead is so overwhelming, that it paralyses you.

Let go of your fear.

Walk over the bridge.

Walk into the arms of the future.

Walk into the fullness of life.

You may not be able to choose what lies round the corner but you can choose the attitude you walk with. Round the corner could be cancer or cake, some days it's both. But you have control over your attitude.

Share your passion for life with everyone you meet. Be mindful of eternity.

And finally – what you don't currently know about yourself you will learn if you keep a teachable heart.

Thank you for reading the rambles of an old man.

Love always,

Granda

P.S. Every day I am glad you got the musical genes. Never lose your love of music.

I could do nothing but smile and well up as I stared at the sea and then back at the paper in my hand. Written in fountain pen, his script alone was a work of art. His f's flickered with feeling, his d's danced on the page but his s's stole the show. As I mulled over his words, the air grew chilly, the leaden clouds began to empty and the skies whipped up a storm of emotion that washed over my face. My tears joined with those from the heavens. I rolled the letter up, pulled my hood over my hair, ran back up the path and along the boardwalk. I could hear Granda's voice as I gripped his letter in my hand. *Never give up the music!*

I was so soaked by the time I got back to the house that I had to stop and change. Which meant I was late getting to the pub. I knew instantly I had missed something, and not just some fantastic Irish tunes. But when I walked through the stone archway of The Old Barn, I had no idea what was brewing. There was standing room only. It was the final night of the imaginatively named Old Barn Music Festival. The gang had scored a table near the stage in this cosy traditional pub. The smell of peat from the open fire filled the air. Patrick had a pint of black waiting for me.

We didn't need to say anything about my letter. But then nobody was talking. That could have just been because of the music - or something else. Our whole gang took up several tables and I noticed Jess and some of our group were over with the surfers.

Tabs was beside me though, tapping her feet, ready for dancing. So tonight we let our eyes, the music and the dancing do the talking. And dance we did, until it was closing time and all hell broke loose.

ADRIFT

Seriously.

Drama follows this guy everywhere he goes.

I know now Tabitha was right about this Donegal plan being risky. But she'd gone along because she cared for me, wanted me to have my time in Dongle and because she thought we could manage the situation. She clearly has the smarts in our relationship. Just when we had made it through to the last day and thought we could relax, fold up our guardian angels' wings and focus on each other . . . well.

We decided that we wanted to make our final night of fun last as long as possible, so after the pub, we raced through the rain across the road to the local disco. Now the place might have looked, from the outside, like your small town hick venue with bad country-western music. But remember, we were staying in a surf mecca and surfers like their beats. The DJ was spinning some pumping tunes and everyone seemed to be having a great time. Maybe too much of a great time. Pat was not the only one to have a few too many drinks. One of his friends up from Belfast was challenging a few of the guys to a shots competition and Pat was determined to win. How could I stop them without sounding like a killjoy?

Meanwhile Jess was doing what looked like dirty dancing to me with the surf hunk. In Tab's words – nightmare!

Next thing all of us knew Pat launched across the dance floor and nailed the surf instructor in the jaw with a right hook. Bam! The guy was on the floor, trying to get up. Pat went to smash him in the nose. But he was too drunk, missed by a mile and even though he looked about to keel over, tried to have another shot at it. The surf dudes grabbed Pat and hauled him off their pal. But Pat shook them off with a few more punches and ran out the door, out into the rainy night.

Leaving Conor and the surfers to calm down the situation, I raced out after Pat. Tabs followed me. The village was no more than a few pubs, a grocery store, some souvenir and surf stores, a gas station, two fast food joints and the church. There were a couple of homes on the street, but I think more people live in my apartment building than in the village. There was also a small harbour and pier a little bit further away. My initial thoughts were that Pat couldn't have ventured too far. I had been straight out the door after him. But walking up and down the street and around some of the side lanes and back behind the houses, I started to panic. If I had been calmer, maybe I would have been more methodical in my hunt, like trying the fast food places for a start. But the rain was hammering down and the wind had picked up. Visibility was close to zero.

We trudged back to the nightclub where the barman was holding a bag of ice to the surfer's jaw. Jess was in tears and being comforted by Kaitlin. The place was about to close. The lights were on full, the DJ was packing up and the dancers were starting to move towards the exits, throwing concerned looks back at the surf guy.

'He's gone.' I announced.

I tried Pat's phone, only to hear ringing coming from one of the booths near the dance floor. Pat's jacket lay on the seat.

'We'll have to split up,' said Conor.

So we agreed on who would search in which direction. The barmen promised to check all around the dancehall. Conor, Kaitlin, Tabitha and our Belfast friends would take the town. Maybe Patrick had just gone to buy some late night fish and chips at a take-away? I'd seen two places still open, full of people from the disco. Or candy at the all-night petrol station? Or did he run back to the house?

Jess and I walked towards the beach and the pier. We picked our way carefully along the concrete dock, as we weren't sure what was underfoot. Moss or algae or oil was making it slippery. But we soon found ourselves standing on the edge of the pier in the pouring rain and wind. Fishing boats tied up for the night bobbed in the oily water beneath us; all taking shelter from the storm and packed tight up against the harbour wall. There was a strong smell of fish.

'Tyler, I'm so fed up with this. He needs to grow up.'

'He's just drunk. And embarrassed.' I tried, then, 'and this running off. It's probably one of his pranks. You know Pat likes to joke around.'

'No Tyler. This is no joke. And I'm fed up with his idiocy.' When I said nothing, she continued. 'Now I hope you can understand why I wanted to raise Ella myself.'

'You did?' I pretended I didn't know that, figuring Jess was more likely to open up.

'Yeah. Pat and I should never have got back together. It was stupid. We're too different. We can't work. I have told him so many times that we can't be together but he just doesn't get the message. I'm trying to do the whole friends thing but it's killing me. He won't listen. I don't understand why. I'm only here 'cos Tabitha pestered me to come.' She stopped talking for a minute and kicked a shell into the water, narrowly missing a small wooden rowing boat that was rubbing up against a larger vessel and making a squeaking noise.

Again I was silent, knowing it was not my place to speak for Pat. What did I know?

'And I accept I'm partly to blame. We had a fight earlier, while you weren't around. And Pat made me infuriated, well, I was deliberately trying to wind him up, to let him know it was over. But flirting with a guy in front of him? That was so wrong. I am so ashamed of myself. Why couldn't I have just told him it was over?' Jess was crying but the rain masked the tears. 'The pair of us. We're just a disaster zone aren't we?'

'Don't be so hard on yourself. Everyone makes mistakes.'

'Aye. Not just Patrick, seemingly.' She stopped and thought

for a long time. 'But when he does something stupid, he doesn't hold back.'

'Oh?' I knew there was more to come.

'But tonight. This is the last straw for me.' Jess slapped the pier railing in anger.

Jess turned to me. 'You know he has done this before?'

'This particular type of thing?' I asked. I couldn't believe what I was hearing.

'Yep. The disappearing act. It was the day of the memorial service for Ella,' Jess said. 'He ran out of the service. It was only supposed to be a short thing to remember our little girl. But he made it all about him-'

I had to jump in and defend Patrick. 'Now come on. I'm sure he was as torn up as you were. Maybe that is how he deals with stuff. You know what guys are like. Be tough, don't show any tears.'

She shrugged, not buying my explanation for a second. 'Whatever. He disappeared, it upset us all and no one could find him for a few hours. As if the day weren't difficult enough.'

'Oh.' I looked at my waterlogged shoes.

'It's not so easy trying to grieve properly when you're busy searching high and low for some idiot!' A gust of wind blew Jess' hood back and strands of hair whipped her face.

'Don't worry. He *will* turn up,' I said just for something to say. 'I'm sorry you both have had such a hard time. I guess all this is making it tough for you to move on with your life too.'

'See what I mean? It's all about Pat. His failed exams, his problems. While I have just put my head down and got on with things. That's what you have to do. But I suppose that's my way of coping. We're just chalk and cheese, Pat and I.'

I tried getting my head around that expression as Jess kicked a stone off the end of the pier into the water. Then she was back apologising again. 'And don't think I'm not to blame for to-night. I know I am. Anyway.' She heaved a big sigh and pulled the hood of her raincoat more tightly round her face. 'We better keep looking. This weather is getting worse.'

I put a hand on her arm to stop her. 'Jess, I take some of the blame too. All this time I have been pushing Pat to make the relationship work, without really knowing what was actually going on. Tabs has been trying and trying to tell me to get real, but I guess I am a hopeless romantic who is always looking for the happily ever after no matter what. We wouldn't be here now if Pat had a smarter cousin.'

Jess smiled at me, hair plastered to her forehead. 'Don't beat yourself up. We'll find him, and give him the telling off of his life!'

We continued the search for another half an hour, with help from the surf guys who knew the town well. Unsuccessful, everyone reconvened back at the late night fish & chips takea-way - the only place still open in the village - to consider what next. Police? The lifeboats rescue people? What if Pat had walked down to the sea, slipped on the rocks and banged his head? What if he tried to walk home or hitch-hike to Belfast and stumbled into the path of an oncoming car? Finally we decided we would give it one last try before alerting the police. After all, he was a 20-year-old supposedly grown-up guy. We figured out where he could have walked to in the time we had been looking for him. The only place we hadn't searched yet were the beaches backed by large sand dunes – a lot of land to cover. One of the surfers said he would grab his board and meet us over there, so we made our way, fighting the strong wind every step there.

By now we were beyond soaked, beyond cold, beyond tired. My legs in the sodden jeans were like lead. I only hoped Granda's letter could stay dry in the inside pocket of my rain jacket.

Then we heard a shout. One of the guys at the front of our group had spotted, through the gusts, the dark and the rain, the shape of a small boat being tossed about on the breakers a couple of hundred yards from shore.

'That dinghy's heading right for the rocks,' one of the surfers called out. 'Gonna hit in a minute!'

His friend yelled back over the crashing waves. 'How did it get out there? Some headcase must have taken it out.'

That's when I got that sinking feeling.

'They could still be on it!' The first guy roared.

And the next thing we knew, the guy with the surfboard was on it and paddling hard across the dark waves towards the struggling boat. I held my breath. Would anyone come back alive? The sea was determined not to let the board make any headway and equally determined to swallow the tiny boat and spit it out right at those black jagged rocks.

Tabitha must have sensed my thoughts because she grabbed my hand and squeezed as if her life depended on it. Conor was holding Jess tight. She was biting her fingertips in terror.

It had to be Pat.

Seconds dragged by. Sets of monster foamy white breakers crashed against the shore endlessly. In the distance a swell had kicked in and the boat was being tossed about as if it was a bathtub toy.

'Shouldn't we call the coast guard or something?' Jess asked. 'Suppose that surfer gets in difficulties too.'

But Conor stalled. 'If that does turn out to be Pat, he will get in so much trouble if we get the law involved.'

'Who cares? At least he will be alive!' Jess insisted.

At that point I didn't care either; his life was at stake. I had never been so terrified, ever!

'Look, these local boys seem to know what they are doing,' Conor said.

And sure enough one of them was on his phone, a second guy was now out on his board following his friend, and seconds later, just around the bay a jet ski was coming, fast! The jet ski reached the troubled boat and I could barely make out what was happening - lots of confused activity and shouts. My heart was still pounding.

Minutes later, the jet ski was zooming towards shore towing the two boards behind it. Sitting on the boards were the surfers – and Patrick. Far in the distance, a final huge wave chucked the tiny boat at the rock wall and it splintered into matchsticks.

The jet ski hit sand and stopped. We all let out a yell. And as soon as Patrick stepped, with wobbly legs, onto shore, hoisting his backpack after him, we waded through the surf and pounced on him. Well some of us.

Jess stood back. 'Don't even talk to me Patrick,' she shouted against the wind before she stormed towards the boardwalk.

'Jess. Wait!' Patrick called out. 'I'm sorry!'

She turned round. 'Don't! I'm glad you're safe but we are done. O-ver.'

Tabitha and Kaitlin followed Jess. Conor and I stood with Patrick. Something in me clicked. What had Patrick been thinking? It was so out of character. So . . . selfish! The red mist rose. Furious, I grabbed Patrick by the collar, 'Don't ever do that to us again man!'

Conor split us up.

Patrick broke down.

'I'm sorry. I'm so sorry.' His teeth were chattering too hard to talk. 'S-s-s-s-sorry.'

I had dealt with Patrick's story all summer, but tonight it was too much for me to handle. Plus we now had the small matter of a destroyed boat to deal with.

One of the surfers elbowed in and threw a blanket over Pat. 'Let's get you home, dude. Hot tea with sugar and bed!'

We were all so exhausted, we were happy to let the more experienced surfers take over. They had dealt with this kind of thing plenty of times before and knew all the signs of hypothermia and how to prevent the after-effects of unplanned boating trips in Atlantic storms in the middle of the night. Fast action, they told us.

'He'll be right as rain tomorrow. This happens at least once every summer round here!' they laughed before giving us care and feeding instructions and signs to watch out for, which would mean we had to call in the medics.

'He *is* a medic,' I said, pointing to the blanket-covered figure lying on top of the surfboard which 4 burly guys were now carrying back to our cottage. (Including the guy Pat had decked just two hours before!)

Pat was now installed in bed and the rest of us were sitting shell-shocked in the living room, too stunned and worn out to speak or speculate. It looked like the truth of what had really happened that night would have to wait until the next day.

THE RETURN

Sunday breakfast was a quiet one, and late. But at least Patrick seemed OK. I didn't get the best sleep though. All night I kept thinking Pat was going to die from exposure to the cold, so I lay there listening out for reassuring sniffles and movements.

The girls left early. Jess needed to be out of there so we volunteered to do all the cleaning chores.

Patrick said nothing; just looked about as remorseful and embarrassed as a person could get, so we didn't bother him. He'd surfaced (sorry!) later than the rest of us, so while he munched toast forlornly, we busied ourselves packing and cleaning the cottage top to bottom.

I was glad to have some mindless busywork because the thought of what I might have to do – tell Beth and Richard that their only child had stolen a boat and tried to kill himself while I was supposed to be keeping watch over him - was just

361

too much to get my head around. I knew Conor was feeling the same way, so at least we could be doing something constructive by cleaning the toilet.

The surfers paid a visit and helped us track down the owner of the small rowing boat. It turns out the local newsagent knew everyone and everything around here. And sure enough, the guy was already at the pier, discussing the whereabouts of his boat with another salty seadog. They were puzzling over a piece of broken rope, one end still firmly tied to a ring in the pier wall.

'Are you the fellas missing a boat?' Conor asked.

'Aye, that would be me,' a bearded guy answered.

'We're still not sure what happened exactly, but I think our friend may have taken it,' Conor began to apologise.

'Looks more to me like it took him,' the man replied with a chuckle. 'See this here rope? Nobody untied it, that's defintootly. It frayed and it broke. Nobody's fault but my own. Sure that rope was so old, what did I expect?'

'I told you to replace that oul' rope a dozen times if I told you once, Michael,' his companion chided him.

'The fact remains,' cut in Conor, in his best law student voice. 'Our friend was on that dinghy and it's now been smashed into smithereens on the rocks. So we owe you a boat.'

The two men looked horrified, but Conor held up a hand. 'It's OK. Our friend is safe. But we feel terrible about the destroyed boat, and we'd like to reimburse you.'

'And apologise,' I chimed in.

But the two men were not having it.

'Are you off your head? Sure that boat was even more ancient and decrepit than the rope! And it nearly killed your mate by the sounds of things. If anything we're to blame.'

We argued back and forth about who was at fault, but got nowhere, partly because we still did not know exactly what had happened on that boat, or if Patrick had even intended to go on a sea voyage in the middle of last night's storm. Eventually the whole thing was settled with a handshake and a 'no harm done in the end up thanks be to God.' The two guys seemed pretty pleased as they headed off back towards the coffee shop muttering about insurance and replacement boats.

'Money for old rope,' chuckled Conor as we walked back to the house, but I really had no idea what he was talking about.

When we arrived back at the house Patrick was busy checking his small backpack, which had survived the boat trip with him. Why he had it with him last night I had no idea! And I was not about to ask.

Pat was still looking pretty weedy, so Conor offered to drive. No arguments there. We packed up and hit the road. The car was silent nearly the whole way. Pat was sleeping, or pretending to be, so Conor and I didn't talk much. Except to decide when to pull over for gas, and to ask if anyone wanted a coffee or a sandwich.

All the way back I realised I just could not process what had happened. For starters, I still didn't even know what had gone down (terrible choice of words, Tyler) last night, or what was going through Pat's head. Was it a suicide attempt, or Pat running away, or a mad adventure? How could I begin to know?

Pat had never told me the whole story, or Beth even. Only Granny had come close.

Pat and I didn't exchange words until we had dropped Conor off at his house. Pat pulled the car round the corner, killed the engine and looked straight at me.

'Tyler I have never been so sorry for anything in my whole life, but please please please don't tell Mum and Dad.' He gripped my arm, squeezed tight.

'I won't! Let go!' I said. Pat didn't know his own strength.

'Sorry,' he released his grip. 'Sorry man.'

'I don't want to hear sorry again. And I'm not going to tell.' This was kind of a white lie. If Pat had been about to jump off the pier, or sail out to Greenland, then it was my duty to let his parents know. But for now, the truth would do. 'I just want an explanation,' I answered honestly.

'I'm sure Jess had plenty to say,' Pat observed bitterly. 'This is the kind of thing she hates about me.'

'Well it would be hard to live with. And I gotta admit Jess said some pretty difficult things to me last night when we were searching for you,' I said.

'I know.'

'What you mean you know?'

'I was in the boat at the end of the pier, hiding under a blanket. I heard everything she said,' Patrick stared into the rear view mirror.

I was speechless. Infuriated that Patrick hadn't made himself known but somewhat relieved that he had been able to hear what Jess had said.

'What?! Why didn't you come out of the boat? You could have finished things with her. What do you remember?' I asked.

'Everything man. But that made it final. And then I took the hump because she didn't tell you the whole truth about Ella's thanksgiving service. The days up until the service were really tough. I felt Jess had excluded me from everything, like the mourning was hers alone. She had totally closed herself off from me. And I had zero role in that service. Nothing. How else was I to react? And yeah, if I had stood up in that boat and said 'we're finished', I would have spared a lot of people from unbelievable worry and hassle and everything else but-'

'But what?'

'First off, I never expected the rope to break and me to go floating out to sea. That was not part of my plan. And second, there was something I needed to do first.'

'What something?' I was too curious to be mad anymore.

'It had nothing to do with Jess. It had to do with me. Didn't you wonder why I was lugging that bag loaded with all my books and gear round the pub and disco last night?'

'I never even noticed.' That was the truth.

'My plan all along, even before I lost the plot and hit that guy – for which I feel really terrible, especially after he went and saved my life – well, my plan was . . . I was going to throw my backpack off the pier.'

'What!?' I was horrified, but at least it wasn't suicide.

'Aye, quit medicine. I've been thinking about packing it in for months, but I just couldn't bring myself to tell Mum and Dad, or my tutor or anyone. They had such high hopes for me.'

'Was the course too hard?'

'Nah. I could manage fine. But after Ella died, I started thinking, here are all these medics and not one of them could save my little girl. I was told she had a serious condition and never would have survived. And I thought, what's the point? How can I face doing this job, seeing people dying every day and not being able to do anything about it? So I started skipping lectures, daydreaming through labs. I did get it together for the panel, but only 'cos you were here and for Mum and Dad. All that time in the library when I was meant to be studying? Mostly I was chatting up girls, but the last couple of days I just couldn't face going. I couldn't even face looking at anything medical. That's when I decided, OK, chuck the whole lot – books, notes, everything into the water. Wait until the last night and heave ho.'

'So you weren't trying to, you know . . . 'cos . . .' I could not finish the terrible thought.

'Never!' Pat so adamant that I had to believe him. 'No way! My plan went up the left 'cos I got too drunk and then jealous and then hit the guy and then I had to run. You might have noticed the pier is like a skating rink. But I thought, 'run out here, toss the backpack over', head back, face the music. But I lost my footing when I went to throw the bag, and me plus backpack landed up in that boat.'

I finished the story. 'Then me and Jess came along so you laid low and listened. And sometime after that, the rope broke and off you sailed.'

'Exactly.'

I heaved a sigh. In some ways the story was worse than I imagined and in other ways better.

'I won't tell your folks, scouts honour.' I promised. 'But first thing you have to do, tell Jess what happened and end it with her, for all our sakes. And I am really really sorry for pushing you guys together ever since I came here. That was not on.'

'You weren't to know.'

'As for medical school-' I shook my head. I really did not know what to tell him at that stage.

Pat smiled. 'We'll sleep on it. Funny thing though – all my books, my laptop, everything survived. Can you believe it?' He opened his backpack and showed me the laptop, safe and intact in its case. 'And all because Mum was insisting I order this super-duper everything proof case when I bought the laptop last year.'

'How are we gonna play this with your parents? Think you will ever tell them?'

'Probably at some stage. Maybe when they are in zimmer-frames. For now, nobody got hurt, nobody needs to know.'

'Your call.'

'And Tyler, don't be worrying. Last night was a once off.'

It looked like it was time to lighten the mood and the car was starting to fog up too. What would Conor's neighbours think? 'Trust you to decide to commandeer the first boat you see just 'cos you've got some sort of weird pirate fantasy going on, Patrick Silverhook McGaw.'

'Arrrrrrr, nothing like piracy on the high seas to float my

boat!' Pat started busting a gut laughing.

But before we drove off, I did have to remind him even though I was making a holiday related joke I was still a little pissed with him.

I figured Pat needed some alone time to sort stuff out in his head and with Jess, and he owed Conor an explanation too, so I asked him to drop me at Granny's. He zoomed off, obviously in a hurry to get somewhere.

Granny was delighted that I had read Granda's letter (amazingly it had survived the storm) and blew loudly into a hankie when I read some of it to her. #totesemosh.

While she was warming the apple pie, I made a quick call to Tabitha.

'How was the trip back and Jess?'

'Quiet, but she'll be OK. She feels bad about last night. Blames herself.'

'Don't we all? But Pat has probably been in touch with her by now.'

'So did you find out what actually happened?' Tabs asked.

I told her quickly, listening out the whole time for Granny returning.

For the first time, Tabitha showed sympathy for Pat. 'Gosh. The poor guy. And all this time we had no idea.'

'I feel responsible. I should have kept a better eye on him.'

'Even guardian angels need a night off. And besides, we make our choices and learn from the consequences. Patrick chose to drink those shots. And they made him crazy. He'll never do that again, we hope!'

We talked a little more about whether to say anything to Beth and Richard, even about Pat's course. Tabitha was more clued-in than me about this kind of stuff, so I was happy to take her advice. She thought I should try and persuade Pat to talk to his folks, or someone, about his career doubts, but since suicide did not seem to be in his thoughts, to say nothing to his parents about the Donegal shipwreck.

'Look, I better go. I'm at Granny's. Talk to you tonight?'

'Of course!'

'Laters Tabster!' I could imagine her smile at the other end of the phone.

Pie demolished, Granny and I listened to a few of Granda's old records and I gave her a live performance of a few tracks from my EP and one of the songs I had written during my vacation. And we worked on our surprise for my leaving party. We had so much to talk about Granny never had the chance to ask about Dongle. Nice work Tyler!

Patrick wasn't around when I got back to his house, so I found myself kicking about the empty rooms pondering a really significant question, *'What to do with a girl called Tabitha?'* I had asked myself that question so many times this summer. At the start it was more of a whimsical thought along the lines of, *'Imagine if I had a girlfriend who lived on the other side of the Atlantic. People at college would think I was so cool and mysterious.'* Then, as Tabitha and I grew closer and our stomachs housed enough butterflies to open a butterfly farm, the thought changed to *'Imagine if I had a girlfriend who lived on the other side of the Atlantic. Hmmmmm how would that work? No seriously, how would that work?'*

Reality hit, quickly followed by a thousand questions. For the last five weeks, my overactive imagination directed the serious thoughts of love and destiny, the playfulness of being 18, and the mystery of the future into my now wall-to-wall scribbled songbook. But still the question remained, *'What to do with a girl called Tabitha?'* Like how do I end our time in Ireland together? It was coming up so fast. I could not believe my extra time was nearly over. But it was. Today was the 20th and I flew back home on the 25th, leaving just four precious days.

One thing was sure, I had to do something utterly unforgettably romantic.

I had thought of an idea before Donegal and Mom had given me some pointers. So, excited by the prospect of one last romantic night, I started serious planning. That involved a quick bike ride and a few phone calls. I needed to follow up on them, but that could wait until tomorrow. Beth and Richard would be home soon from their own weekend away and would want to hear all our news. Well, all the news Pat and I had agreed to tell.

I must admit, Pat's happy-go-lucky acting job with his folks that night was practically in Tabitha's league.

CHECKLIST

Patrick took off to the library early. Or was it a pretend trip/ delaying tactic to keep his parents from knowing? While he got ready I faked sleep. But as soon as I heard his car shoot out of the street, I got up, grabbed a shower and overthought the weekend's events over a bowl of soggy cereal.

After breakfast I made a couple of piles on my bed of the stuff I needed to pack. There was way too much, but just to be sure, I hauled out my suitcase from under the bed. And I found something else under there beside the dust bunnies. It was *Patrick's In No Particular Order Top 3̶0̶ 31ish Things To Do In Northern Ireland* list. I gulped hard, then scanned over it to see the things that would have to wait until my next trip - like Rathlin, a couple of castles and some of the other museums.

I called Tabitha. She had a couple of hours before work, which she said gave us just enough time to hit Carrickfergus

Castle. CC is just a little ways further down Belfast Lough, literally in a suburb of Belfast, and she assured me it is one of the most impressive castles in Northern Ireland, having been a fortification since the 12th century or something insane. She was right. The castle was totally dope, but my head wasn't with it, churning over thoughts of Patrick.

As we leaned against the castle parapet looking across at the other side of the Lough towards the North Down coast and maybe Groomsport, Patrick dominated the discussion. That was never the plan. I wanted to talk about *us*, but how could we? I couldn't help feeling down, knowing that my staying on an extra couple of weeks, in fact my being here at all, had not helped Pat one tiny bit.

Tabitha wasn't buying that and insisted he'd have never gotten through the panel without me. Ok, true, that was one thing. But what good had it done if the guy hated medicine and was still miserable?

'I'm not sure Patrick actually does hate medicine,' pondered Tabitha, tracing a line on the mossy stones. 'Although he might be hating himself.'

'That makes sense.'

Then Tabitha had a lightbulb moment. 'I just realised something! Maybe all along we've been asking the wrong question. All year it's been 'When are Patrick and Jess going to sort out their relationship?', when really it should be 'When is Patrick going to forgive himself for everything?'

It was a 10,000 watt lightbulb moment! 'Of course!' I shouted out at the seagulls and gave Tabitha the biggest hug ever! Didn't I tell you she was the wise one in our relationship?

'But you're the only one who can ask him that question,' Tabitha said as we made our way to the car.

We talked more about how to approach it with Pat on the drive home. Tabitha had to hurry into work, but she gave me a big kiss and a 'Go easy on him' reminder before I got out of the car. Pat's hunk of junk car was in the drive.

'Text me and let me know how things are,' Tabitha shouted.

I took a deep breath before I opened the door. Everyone was in the garden. I popped my head around and said hello before telling them I had to call Mom.

I needed some more advice. Mom and I talked for 45 minutes. I swore her to secrecy about what had happened with Patrick in Donegal. I didn't want one stupid night to define the summer and mess up his relationship with his parents.

'I don't get it Mom. There was so much going on in Pat's life that nobody ever told me. Not Beth, not Richard and especially not Granny. How could I help him when I didn't have the whole story?'

Mom was silent for too long.

'Did you know about his thoughts in March?'

'Tyler. I couldn't tell you. It wasn't my business to tell. Beth begged me not to. I feel so bad about that, but I promised her. And I hoped Pat, since you guys were so close . . .' she trailed off.

At last I could vent. 'He's his own worst enemy. Puts on this happy dappy act, never really opens up completely. Or just does this big cover-up job with lies and joking around. He is impossible!'

'No he's not. He's a 20-year-old guy. In his shoes, you might be just the same.'

'Maybe. Whatever. I dunno. But I have been pretty worthless as a guardian angel and I have to wonder what I was even doing here all these weeks,' I muttered. 'I feel like a bystander.'

'You were seeing the country, making new friends, gaining independence, having a wonderful time, becoming a musician, reconnecting with Granny and your roots, and don't forget - falling in love. So many new experiences to last a lifetime. This summer wasn't just about Pat, you dork! It was about *you*!'

Another 10,000 watt moment. Mom was almost as smart as Tabitha. They'd probably really hit it off.

And just like that, I was happy! So for the rest of the call Mom and I talked about the surprise I had planned for Tabs and what would happen next.

Before she hung up, Mom counselled, 'don't ever feel you can sort out all Patrick's problems. He and his folks have to do that themselves. But you can encourage him to open up and talk. It could be the best help of all!'

Despite the advice from Tabs and Mom, I just couldn't face discussing anything serious with Patrick that night. And the opportunity didn't come up. He was going out 'to the library', so I spent the evening watching a movie with Beth and Richard. I don't think they thought anything was suspicious - I told them I had a stomach ache - and blamed it on the mountain of spring onions (must tell James Marcus they call them scallions over here) that had been in my champ.

NEW JEWELS

Another early start as I made my way into the city centre, while Pat snored on back at the house. To be honest I was glad to get away from him. I knew we had to talk it out, but I was feeling too resentful towards the guy. OK, so I was brought over to Belfast to help see him through a rough patch, but did his problems have to take over quite so much of my time and my thoughts? I only had a few days left for Tabs and hardly any room left in my brain to think about what she and me had going on. So I wanted to devote at least part of my day to the Tabster.

By now I knew the city well enough to go without a map and felt somewhat at home as I wandered through the streets and side lanes.

I was on the hunt for jewellery. When I was about 12, I bought a twenty-day 'girlfriend' a bracelet decorated with trinkets and oddly shaped semi-shiny plastic jewels. So much bling for less than $15! I knew cheap trinkets wouldn't cut it for Tabitha, so I decided to take a leaf out of my Dad's book and go slightly high end. But when I looked at my bank account I had to tone my thoughts down - a lot. Even slightly is pricey. Dad always buys Mom some sort of jewellery for Christmas. Every December they take a trip to 5th Ave and she picks something sparkly to decorate her hands, neck or wrist. Last year she deviated and picked a beautiful pearl brooch that *Ariel* from *The Little Mermaid* would have adored.

Tabitha has loads of earrings. Her style is so unpredictable. Some days you want to call the fashion police as she mixes patterns and stripes with funny cuts and shapes. Other days she seems to be bang on the smart-casual, preppy-with-a-twist trend. She is a fashion blogger's dream 'cos she looks awesome in everything she wears. Her jewellery taste isn't as unpredictable. She wears a small signet ring given to her by her dad and a cross necklace. They are her two staples. Of course she has costume jewellery - pearls aplenty and rings with massive fake stones on them, but they are always in addition to her two classic, timeless pieces.

Today, wearing boat shoes, chinos and a striped shirt, I decided to enter one of the smartest jewellery stores in Belfast. I made small talk about my 'jewellery needs', her words not mine, with the blonde sales assistant who had way too much blusher on (they wear a lot of make-up over here I noticed and was glad Tabitha was the exception. She never tried to hide those cute freckles.). The shop was filled with sparkling rocks, fancy earrings, pretty pendants, necklaces with mega price-tags and some striking watches. I was interested in the antique 'estate' jewellery, and as she showed me some fantastic pieces I realised I needed to thank her for the time she had spent with me and get on my way, as I couldn't afford even the smallest item in the store.

By now some of the guys in the little antique shops round about knew me. So I ended up chatting with them and they sorted me out with a 1930's pocket watch with chain for Dad. It was pretty battered, and needed some TLC, but he would love the challenge. After that I pointed to a ring for Tabitha. Don't worry, not *The ring*, just *A ring*. A single real pearl formed the centrepiece of a rose gold flower arrangement. I knew Tabitha would love it. The velvet box was slightly battered, torn on one side. I told the guys I was leaving in a few days and they knocked a couple of quid off the price.

On previous trips into town, I had already bought most of my gifts, but these two had been the most important and probably the trickiest to find. So it was a huge weight off my mind, to have this job done, and all before 10.30am!

All along, I was determined to avoid buying the generic touristy Irish gifts and had quickly discovered my fave place for local handmade crafts, St. George's Market. I tried to visit the market as much as possible during my stay. The Victorian market is a hub of creative energy, filled with a friendly community of cake makers, artisan butchers, bag stitchers, screen printers, silversmiths and antique dealers specialising in recycled, upcycled, hand-made, time-worn, freshly-cooked, lovingly crafted vintage goodies of all shapes, styles and tastes. Tabitha took me one morning for pastries and live music, and I left this soul of the city laden with presents for pretty much everyone in my phone book, including Mom! But today, being Tuesday, it was closed. Bummer!

My bum had barely landed in the booth of my favourite coffee hangout before Sam (blonde/24/funky bandana/fairy dust tattoo on her hand) had an extra shot caramel latte on the table. Her boss was on a break and she lingered to catch a glimpse of my purchases. She ooohed and ahhhhd at the watch and ring and brought them behind the counter to show the rest of the staff. And all the girls tried on the ring, because I was slightly worried in case it did not fit Tabs! One of the guys was so impressed with my taste that he asked me to go shopping for an anniversary present for his wife when his shift finished. Had to say no though, but I gave him some places to visit! Man this place is so friendly. As I sipped on my latte I made a couple more calls to confirm the surprise I was planning with Tabitha.

But how was the surprise even going to work without Pat on board? (Ever since the boat adventure these nautical terms kept popping into my head.) As if Pat were reading my thoughts, he texted at that moment.

Patrick:	*The crew want to say goodbye 2 u 2nite - dinner in Cathedral Quarter @ 7 then onwards*
Tyler:	*Sure*
Patrick:	*Wer r u?*
Tyler:	*In town - getting last minute gifts.*

Patrick:	*I'll pick u up. Smithfield in 30 mins*
Tyler:	*OK*
Patrick:	*BTW sorry again bout Donegal and that we*
	haven't caught up. Been getting stuff sorted etc
Tyler:	*Cool. CU soon*

While waiting for Pat, I had time to think about what I would say to him. Tabitha's wisdom about forgiving himself had stayed in my head, but how would I get around to bringing that up? Especially because I wasn't feeling very forgiving myself at that moment and was still kinda p'd with the guy.

I was determined to jump straight in, but Pat beat me to it. He was in a very chipper mood.

'Happy days! Jess and I are history. We had the best talk we've probably ever had. We also agreed we're probably two of the biggest eejits going – we don't even have a clue when to know it's over and how to break up properly!'

'I never thought a breakup would be the best news ever, but it is!' I laughed.

'Aye. Such a huge load off.'

Now it was my turn. 'Pat, I don't understand why you couldn't have been straight with me about everything that has been going on with you all year. Your course, how things really were with Jess, (I couldn't say the S word), how worried your family has been. I feel like I've been in a fog or something.'

'Hey, that's just my way. You're on your hols. We should be having the craic. Why should I go round burdening people with all this heavy stuff?'

'But that's not the way to deal with problems! Being the king of banter, the joking around. Covering up. That's running away!'

'In my book, that's coping.' Pat was trying to shut me down.

'I'd get a different book.' This conversation was going all wrong. We were starting to get annoyed with each other. That wasn't supposed to happen. I tried to shift direction and only made things worse. 'And med school?'

Pat's voice strained to hide his anger. 'Look Tyler, I can only cope with one thing at a time, OK? So just let me be happy.' He clicked on the turn signal and made a brisk right into his street. 'Anyway, we don't have time to talk about all this right now. We're meeting the lads in half an hour for five-a-side footie.'

Now what was I going to do about Tab's surprise? Pat was vital for the whole thing to come off!

The rest of that day, things were still semi-awkward between us. I was more aggressive than usual on the field; Pat and I were on opposite teams and I did tackle harder than I should have a couple of times. Conor noticed and called out 'Go easy!'

And as we got ready for our big night 'doyne the toyne', the only topic of conversation was about what to wear, due to the unusually balmy weather. It had been warm in Belfast, like NYC warm. Which is strange for this part of the world. It's even stranger that they use a different system for measuring temperature over here. At breakfast Richard had got so excited that it was going to be 26 that day. I just scratched my head until he translated for me: 26 C = 79 F

Hair shaped, shaving complete (when you're 18 it doesn't take long!), we were looking slick and Patrick seemed more upbeat. All the unsaid stuff hovered in the room like an overdose of cheap aftershave, but we couldn't bring ourselves to it. Did Beth and Richard notice something was up? That I was probably more subdued, while Patrick being Patrick was bouncy and full of himself? He made the first step towards making up, when he announced to the room that he was going to pay for my dinner before ruffling my hair that I had spent ages trying to get just right. Let's just say my hair is not the most co-operative. We gave each other a half smile. For tonight we would forget about everything, except having fun.

Destination: Cathedral Quarter.

Meal: Chicken & fries.

Peeps: An APB to anyone I had met during my time in Ireland.

Purpose: BANTER.

Tabitha and some of her friends were there, the guys from camping, and most of the Botanic crew - the notable absentee was Jess. Pat was really relaxed the whole night, and I noticed with relief, was sticking strictly to beer! Walking through the cobbled streets of this happening area of Belfast with some of the guys and gals who I had met during my trip was so cool. After dinner we danced in a pop up DJ venue before we hit the dance floor of a nightclub and threw shapes and moves that resembled a baby giraffe trying to take its first steps.

FREBROSINS FOREVER

I crashed into bed about 2. Patrick came in ten minutes later. We didn't talk before we hit the lights, but the humidity kept me from nodding off to a much-needed sleep. My body blamed the sticky warmth, but my mind blamed the still unresolved situation between Patrick and me. I lay there for over an hour before I came up with a plan. *There's still a few things on the list we haven't checked off yet.*

'Patrick,' I whispered. He didn't respond.

I whispered a little louder, 'Patrick.' Still didn't budge.

So I got up and tapped his arm. He moaned a little.

'Patrick'.

He grunted. I looked at the glass of water on his bedside table and considered throwing it over him to startle him out of his sleep. Better not.

'Patrick.' I repeated.

'What?'

'Just checking if you're awake.'

He rubbed his eyes and grunted again.

'Is it morning time already Captain America?'

'Well it's morning time somewhere, but just not here.' I paused. 'Wanna go for a bike ride?'

'A what?'

'A cycle. Like get the bikes and hit the streets.'

He shook his head. 'You're cray. Like proper cray.'

I smiled to myself. I knew it was daft. But I guess Patrick's spontaneity had rubbed off on me.

'If it's not morning time, then what time is it?' he asked.

I reached for my phone as he rubbed his eyes again.

'Just after 3.'

'In the morning?'

'No the afternoon you idiot.'

'Call me at 3 in the afternoon then.' He rolled over and I threw a sock at him.

'OK, OK!' Pat sat up, yawned, sighed and rubbed his bed-head. 'Where do you wanna go?' he asked. Before I could give a reply he answered his own question, 'No wait, don't answer that. I have an idea.'

Five minutes later, wearing makeshift cycling clothes, Patrick and I were poking our noses into the fridge, looking for a snack. What do you eat at 3am?

'Sit down at the table and I'll get you some grub.' I told Patrick, feeling slightly bad that I had brought him out of a deep sleep and was making him cycle round the streets of Belfast for no other purpose than because we could. Grub consisted of left over cheesecake, orange juice, hot coffee and a lot of hummus and breadsticks. Uncle Richard appeared and scared the hummus out of us. He had been in the living room catching up on *Breaking Bad*. The dude had a terrible sleep pattern.

'Hey Dad. Want some cheesecake?

'Sure.'

'Are you guys going out?'

'Yeah. The American wants to go for a cycle.'

'Oh. A cycle,' he repeated. He looked at us with raised eyebrows. 'Late night bootie call more like? I remember those days.'

Patrick cringed. 'No you don't Dad.'

'Oh, the things you don't know about me son.'

'Dad, urghhhh, that's just urghhhhh. You had sex once. To have me, and that's all I need to know. Seriously the American wants to go for a cycle. Can he use your ride?'

'Of course. He's used it all summer. Just fill it up with gas when you're finished.' He laughed to himself, grabbed the plate of cheesecake and went back to finish his show.

Patrick lifted a few bottles of water from the fridge and came into the garage. The bikes were propped up against a tea chest filled with old plant pots. The month before I had arrived in Ireland, Patrick and his dad bought two 'new to them' rides from a local bike store. Patrick described the store as a home brewery for bikes. They stocked every colour of handle-bar tape imaginable and spring-loaded seats that 'your toosh thanked you for.' In reality it was a fix-em-up shop, but to call it that cheapened the craftsmanship, art and love that went into their beautifully restored bikes. My ride all summer had been an olive green number, with tanned handlebar tape. A little beauty.

Dawn was hovering at the edge of the horizon as I wheeled my bike out of the garage. There was no route and no agenda. Cycling through the tree-lined streets of Malone and Stranmillis, we made our way over the embankment and meandered through East Belfast, stopping at a few of the blue plaques dotted around the city. They mark the birthplaces of important historic people. I imagined what life was like for them 'back in the day'. Patrick gave me some more local knowledge about the streets we were cycling on.

I can't describe Belfast pre-dawn. It's something special. I'm never out at this time in NYC. It's usually too busy. We had the roads to ourselves and passed sleeping windows hiding dreaming angels. I began to think about how interesting it would be if the windows of houses turned into TVs at night and showed the dreams of those who slept in the rooms. Watching *Hunger Games* with Tabitha last week had definitely influenced my imagination.

We had been roaming around the streets of the city for around an hour, taking selfies at George Best's old house (a global soccer hero) and CS Lewis' grade school (he wrote *The Chronicles of Narnia*), when we were pulled over by a police vehicle. I think they were bored and probably checking that we weren't out robbing! After the cops figured out we were just two random students they chatted with us for a while. One of the officers was going on holiday to Boston so I recommended a few places to eat. When we asked them where we could get an early early breakfast they unanimously replied, 'Sunrise Fry' at Gina's in the north of the city. The NYPD know their doughnuts and pies. Over here, for the boys in blue, (or is it dark green?) it's all about the Ulster Fry.

We rode through the Docks and with the water at our backs and the mountain in full view, Patrick challenged us to cycle up to Belfast's best vantage point, near the top of the Cavehill, to see the sun cast its early morning rays on the city. We pedalled like crazy people from the shore to the turn in the hill just in time to witness the first drops of gold sign their name on the rooftops. The entire city was at our feet.

Breathless and exhausted, we propped our bikes up against a rusty railing and walked into a field.

'Wow!' was all I could pant as I climbed onto a wall and rested my toosh.

'Do you think God gets bored of the sunrise?' I asked when my lungs had recovered.

'I don't think so, but I think we do. Maybe that's why there's cloudy days,' Pat replied.

'Uh?'

'You know, too much of a good thing,' he said.

'Yeah.'

'Why do you ask?'

'No reason, just think it's pretty cool.'

I think my sentimental, over analytical side had rubbed off

on my cousin over the last few weeks. I looked over at Patrick. His eyes were squeezed closed and his face pointed towards the sun like a cat enjoying the heat of the early morning sun. I uploaded a picture of the view to Instagram and sent the boys from camping a picture of Patrick's face.

Enough delaying. Time to address the thing that had been hanging over us for days.

'I don't know if this is the right time or not,' I began.

With his eyes still closed Patrick interrupted me. 'Yeah. We really need to do this.' He breathed deeply.

I continued. 'It's been really awesome. I mean the summer. I can't begin to describe how good it's been.'

'I know man. You came along at just the right time. I can't believe so much time has passed. I don't want you to leave, dude. I mean you have to, but you don't know what it's meant to have had you here this summer. The roadtrips, the banter, the late night food detours. And let's not forget about your love life!'

'My love life. More like our love lives.'

'True. It's been a journey. Bumpy in parts.' He paused and looked across at Belfast Lough and the shipyards gleaming in the rising sun. 'I might come and do this more often.'

'It's pretty good all right,' I agreed.

'There's something about coming away and just staring at the city or being in nature. It connects me to something. Like it lifts me. Sometimes it makes me feel so insignificant, that this is all just here for me to look at. But it also makes me feel pretty special that something so beautiful is here for me. It's nice to know I can just come and do this, anytime I need it. I'm making a hash of explaining this, but it's great to be able to get so much joy from something so simple. It's like a gift.'

I had expected we'd talk, but not for this to be a time of self-realisation. Had Patrick found meaning and even happiness in the beauty and the mystery of an early morning sunrise? On the side of a mountain had God given Patrick the glimmers of hope; a marking moment in what had been a really difficult year? I don't think it was as clear as that, but maybe something in his soul had shifted. Patrick continued to talk, so, as I had all summer, I listened.

'When I was sitting in that crappy boat heading for those rocks, well I knew, that was it. Couple of minutes, then the end. And suddenly all this-' He held out his arms to indicate the vista in front of us and the wooded mountain at our backs. 'The world. Life. Well, it seemed so fragile and fleeting. Like it could be gone in an instant and I had never properly even appreciated it. Same goes for my family and my friends, and everything. But now I can. Appreciate it and make my life worthwhile. I am so grateful to whoever or whatever gave me a second chance.'

'Maybe there's a reason, bro. Some people say He works in mysterious ways.'

'True dat.'

'Haha. Do you think God understands teenage slang?' I asked.

'I hope so. If not I'm in big trouble.'

We took in the vista. The Mournes were a distant dark silhouette. The rising sun highlighted the coastal road that had brought us on so many adventures. Belfast Lough shimmered like gold, with the docks and city centre buildings lining the waterfront like shiny toys. At this moment Belfast became a miniature model of silhouettes changing colour as the basin of black turned into a bowl of deep yellow sunshine. A new day had arrived, along with an endless world of possibilities. The city had another chance to craft its future. And so did we.

'Thanks for the girl advice over the summer. I don't think Tabitha and I would have worked out without your help!'

'Yeah you would have. You're a smokin', exotic, song-writing, trilby wearing American,' he teased. 'Girls here love that sort of thing.'

'When you put it that way I suppose you're right!'

'I'm really sorry about all the hassle over the summer, and … and especially about Donegal. I feel like all my problems have kind of hijacked the good times we should have been having, and your thing with Tabitha too.'

'There's no need for that. You've had a rough ride 'cuz. We all just hope you are through it now. For good. But I'll tell you, I have never been so scared in my life.'

We both stared out at the city.

'Remember that day you Skyped me when you were back home?' Pat said as he broke the silence.

'Patrick, we have chatted every week since last November!'

'Oh yeah! But I'm thinking of *the* time. After Oscar cut your hair? When you were into that Susan girl.'

'Ha ha. Yeah. Susan! I have to tell you a funny story about

that.'

'Well, you don't know what that conversation meant to me. It was my darkest time. I hadn't been out of bed in a couple of days. It was coming up to the time when little Ella would have had her due date, if she had lived. I was starting to have some really dark thoughts. Like why was I here and why hadn't she survived? Why did I deserve to be alive? All I did was mess things up and wreck people's lives. Thinking that way can lead to some very very dark places. My counsellor calls it 'circling the drain'. Nowhere to go but down. And I went down . . . to the point where I was seriously considering suicide. I even had it all planned out. In fact that day, if I could manage to get it together enough to put some clothes on, I was just about to leave the house and go drive somewhere and-'

Patrick took a deep breath. I thought of the two of us standing at the edge of the Cliffs of Moher; I had been so afraid to look down.

'Then you popped up on screen and all I saw was the speed stripes in your hair and I could do nothing but laugh. I hadn't laughed in months. And then you just ranted for like five minutes straight.' He laughed again at the memory.

'So that crazy haircut did have a purpose!'

'It saved my life. Like all I could do was laugh! It reminded me that there are good things in life. Even the smallest things. Well, like this.' He reached out and his gesture took in the dawn-drenched city below. 'And suddenly I had something to look forward to again. You coming over and visiting me. That meant everything. It also made me realise I had been lying to so many people. Telling them that I was OK. And lying to myself. After that I realised I needed help. I told Mum and Dad. I had to. And I agreed to go to some counselling sessions. It's taken a while, but I now know that things are gonna be different. Good different.'

'Jess is a start,' I ventured.

'You bet.'

'So now you know why I was so scared my parents would find out I went AWOL in Donegal. Absolutely no way. Even the biggest lie was better than Mum and Dad imagining the worst. Which they would have done. That day we drove home, I was really worried someone was going to tell them. Especially Jess because, of course, she found out about my thoughts back in the spring. I'm pretty sure she imagined I was taking that boat to my death. So as soon as I dropped you at Granny's, I was over to her place like a shot. Jess wasn't going to let me in and I had to camp on her front step, in the rain, for about an hour, just so she'd know I meant it. I've had some pretty terrible hours over the last year and that was one of them. Finally her dad made her let me in.'

'I'm glad it's all OK now.'

'I suppose there was some sort of silver lining, in that it did force me to realise that I needed to call it a day with Jess and do something about it. Now we both feel so much better for being honest with ourselves,' Pat talked on. 'She was right all along. It was never going to work. I think for months we had been fooling ourselves – or maybe just I was – making ourselves miserable instead of facing the truth. All my friends had been telling me to call it quits. In her own way, Jess was trying too. But she had the same guilt I had for so long – about leaving the other person on their own to grieve.'

I nodded. I'd had a lot of practice this past 6 weeks. 'I can understand you feeling guilty about Jess going through so much.'

Pat turned and faced me. 'But that's just it. I could live with the guilt about Jess, but it was the other guilt . . . the guilt about Ella.'

I took a deep breath.

'I tried to run away from it, all this time. But I kept being reminded – I'm here, I'm alive, enjoying life, getting on with stuff. Having a future. And the more fun I had, the worse I felt, 'cos I was free, young, not a dad. A whole world out there just waiting for me. But not Ella. Why did she have to die? Why did she have to have a medical condition nobody, even with the most modern tests, could fix? The medics told me she never had a chance. What did Ella ever do to deserve that?' Pat stared out at the gleaming Lough waters, eyes glistening. 'I thought God wanted us to be happy and to make others happy.'

I considered for a while, picking at the grass. 'I guess . . . maybe . . . if everything was perfect in this world and nobody had any sorrows, well then . . . we'd all be shallow and selfish. Nobody would have any compassion.'

Pat did not react so I hurried on. 'Take you. Medical student, maybe. What kind of doctor would you be if you had never experienced what you have gone through? But you've had a huge loss, you've seen someone you love die. And stood by helpless. Don't you think that understanding would actually make you a better doctor, probably better than a lot of the people you're studying with right now, or even your profs, because you've been there?'

'I guess so,' Pat continued to be absorbed in the dawn.

'I mean empathy has to be at least as important as the spleen.'

'Spleen isn't that vital,' Pat had the trace of a smile.

'OK then, the appendix.'

You can live without that.' The grin grew bigger.

'You know what I mean. As important as knowing when a person has appendicitis!'

'So you're telling me to stop feeling sorry for myself and start using what I know to help others?'

'You said it buddy, not me. I was just going to tell you to stop taking the blame all the time and start to forgive yourself.'

Pat pulled his knees up to his chin and chewed this one over for another while. There was beginning to be real warmth in the sun's rays. 'Wow, I never even knew I was doing that.'

'Bigtime.'

'I suppose it is OK to feel free. Now that Jess and I have ended it, it will be nice to have that feeling back again. Not that I'll ever forget what happened with Jess, or Ella, but-'

'You're not supposed to.' I interrupted. 'No one our age should have to face that.'

'I guess I forgot that Jess has been grieving as well. I've been so up my own arse dragging things out and having her have to worry about me on top of everything else. And then leaving it until the last minute before you fly off to start wising up. But you know me!'

'There you go, blaming yourself again! Change the subject!'

Patrick laughed. 'I'm just glad you're getting your hustle on with Tabitha. If you really want it you'll make it happen. And if it's not meant to be, you still had this incredible time together. Win. Win.' He stood and stretched out his legs and arms. 'Did I tell you Jess thinks you and Tabs could go the distance?'

'Check us out with our love lives sorted!' I said.

I stood too and stretched out my legs. After that huge cycle up the hill and sitting on the wall, they were starting to cramp up. 'Don't forget that I'm always here for you, Patrick. Like always. You can call me whenever. And I'll try and have a regular supply of bad haircuts for you to laugh at.'

'Hope they won't be needed!'

'Frebrosins forever.'

'Frebrosins forever,' he echoed. We fist-bumped and Patrick squeezed me as tight as the orange juicer at Fresh & Juicy. As we stood and hugged it out at the most beautiful place in Belfast, I knew that if my saving, gigging and working had been for this moment, it had all been more than worth it. Because of this summer Pat and I would never look at ourselves in the same way again. In such a short space of time we had both journeyed so far and we had each gained a brother.

'Now I need some breakfast, and a favour,' I said.

'If you're lucky. Race you to the café,' Patrick said as he ran towards the bikes.

On our way down The Crum we stopped and sampled that famous Sunrise Fry, the choice of the coppers, and I filled Pat in on his supporting role in my romantic surprise that night. Sitting alongside other bright-eyed people fuelling up for a busy day we felt a real sense of satisfaction at achieving something so awesome by the time most people were figuring out what to wear to work. Our early morning cycle was another precious experience to add to our summer adventure.

As Pat put his knife and fork together on the greasy plate he suddenly asked, 'Frebrosins?'

BOTANIC

It was our last night together. Tabitha and I would see each other at a final family good-bye shindig the next night, but there would be no chance for any alone time. History would record this night as one of the most romantic nights in the history of romantic surprise date nights. Urban legends would be created about this night that would travel from Tralee to Magilligan. People would make memes about it, but for now all you need to know is that Tabitha was late (standard) and I really didn't want to go home. Yeah, can you believe it? This from the guy who is smitten with every little thing about the Big Apple. Now I didn't wanna leave Belfast.

I leant against the gates of Botanic Park, took my journal from my pocket and began to write:

'I don't want to go to home and I certainly don't want to be the star guest at tomorrow's party. It's my party and yeah I'll cry if I want

to. College will be a blast – a new, welcome chapter of my life, filled with countless opportunities and a bucketload of stories that I'll swap with my high-school classmates when we all meet up at spring break. But I just don't want to leave Ireland yet. I know I will have to learn to live on the memories.

On dark November days I will have my travel pictures and souvenirs to lift my spirits, and of course all the Patrick-inspired escapades (the fun ones that is!) to keep me chuckling through February. I hope the memories of young love, now part of me, will endure the passing of time.

But still, I hate the thought of leaving the people with their dark, yet life-bringing humour, or saying goodbye to the fields and flowers that clothe the cliffs. And the stone walls, the tiny villages, the endless coastline that gives a ruggedly defiant answer to the waves that crash against the towering cliffs and rocky bays.

But I know I have to board that plane, and, as Granda wrote:
Let go of your fear.
Walk over the bridge.
Walk into the arms of the future.
Walk into the fullness of life.

My heart belongs to this Island, but my soul belongs to NYC. Maybe that's what it means to be Half Irish?

I shoved my journal into the back pocket of my jeans. The whirlwind romance with Tabitha was one part of the journey I didn't plan for. I thought I was coming over to hang out with my hero of a cousin and be a tourist, not have an encounter with The Belle of Belfast City. I'm still figuring out what love is. In many ways I hope I always will. I have questions. Many, many questions. Will we call each other between classes or as night falls? Will we long for vacation time when we get to see each other for real? Will we realise the Atlantic is too much of a barrier? I knew one thing for sure; I treasured this nervous, love inspired, destiny-searching feeling of thankfulness. That's so mushy it's unreal - isn't it?

This summer I got to know three people really well in a short space of time. Patrick, Tabitha and myself. Like a thirteen-year-old BFF I know all of Tabitha's favourites – food, colour, music and so many other factoids only an interested boyfriend would want to know. Topping the trivia tree; I can recite all the countries she has travelled to and all the places she wants to see – as well as knowing way too much about her love for red pandas and Japanese snow monkeys. I even know the pizza toppings she likes - which vary according to her mood. Hawaiian on a sunny day and Chilli Bonkers on a wet day. And her dad's No.1 micro-brew ale.

But I wonder if this heartfelt encounter should be measured with facts and figures. What if love has a different scale? What if love is measured in shared dreams and late night cups of tea, unexpected gifts and lazy romantic meals full of flirtatious glances that make your head spin? And yes, I now feel guilty about all the times I left Patrick so I could go on dates with Tabitha, but it is very very hard to regret one minute of the time I spent with Tabs. I couldn't believe it had been 5 weeks since we spent a lazy sunny afternoon in the park and Tabitha walked into my life through the misguided flick of a wrist. Thanks for that Patrick – I'll owe you forever!

So what better place to have our last night together? I told her to come for nine and wear a pretty dress. At ten after we caught eyes as she walked down Stranmillis Road. She was gorgeous and glamorous as always. I locked my phone and checked my hair in the reflection. Now we had made eye contact, we had that awkward thirty-yard interchange to play out. If you keep constant eye contact you look like a weirdo, but if you stare at other things you look like you don't care. It's a tricky one that I hadn't quite mastered. Seconds later she stood before me, threw her arms around my neck, gave me a little kiss and then placed her hands on my chest.

'So handsome man, why's a girl all dressed up at this hour? It's a bit late for a meal.'

'I'm not so sure about that,' I answered before I took her hand and walked towards Botanic Park as we chit-chatted about her day. She had been working, while I told her I had one last date with Granny and had packed a little. Untrue, but hey! She tugged my arm and began to pull me in a different direction.

'Tyler, the park's closing soon.' It was still light out but the sun had set and dusk was not far off.

'That's what you think, my love,' I said in a terrible Cockney accent. My acting skills were nowhere near as convincing as Tabitha's!

She turned her puzzled face towards mine and caught a glimpse of the grin that had worked its way across my face.

'Come on. I have a surprise for you.'

Hand in hand we strolled through the gates and the tree-lined entrance to the park. The path led us to the historic Victorian Palm House. I pushed open the door (yes not locked yet thanks to the Park connections I made!) to a tropical wonderland and ushered Tabitha through. She marvelled at the exotic, colourful foliage and flowers that filled the inside of this lush piece of the city's history.

'Incredible, but I've never been in here', she whispered in awe.

'Seriously?! You've been missing out.'

'It's beautiful in here. And warm. Thanks for the wonderful surprise.' She spoke with real sincerity, as if her visit to The Palm House was the sum of the surprise.

I chuckled to myself as Tabitha began to tour the jungle.

'What's so funny?'

Still walking, she turned to look at me and bumped her head on something. She stopped to see what it was. Hanging by a ribbon from a lemon tree laden with ripe aromatic fruit was a small gift box. Delight spread across her face even before she unhooked the gift from the tree. Then laughter when she saw the tag read: *For Henrietta*. It seemed like a million years as she untied the ribbon, opened the box and with a cry of delight, placed the antique ring on her finger. Perfect fit! She loved it! Then she hugged me tight.

'That's not the end of the surprises,' I said. 'If you will allow me . . . for this next part . . .' I quickly popped a blindfold over her eyes which were still shining.

'Tyler, what are you doing?' Tabitha was always asking questions. But tonight, I always had an answer.

'Trust me, you'll find out soon.'

I tried to contain her excitement as we left The Palm House and walked the few hundred yards over the main lawn of the park. On the way, I asked her loads of 'Would you rather' questions. Like, 'Would you rather have hair for teeth or teeth for hair?' and 'Would you rather have burgers for ears or ears for burgers?' I noted, for future blindfold-related surprises that the distance we were walking was actually maybe just a tad too far away, especially when the person I was leading was so intent on finding out her destination.

Just as I had planned, while we were exploring The Palm House, twilight fell, the Park emptied and the Park wardens had locked the gates and were now closing up all the greenhouses too. I waved to the guy who was hurrying to shut The Palm House after us for the night and he gave me a big double thumbs up.

'Where are you taking me?' Tabitha repeatedly chirped as I guided her.

'I can't spoil it. Nearly there,' I said.

We stopped. I removed the blindfold from Tabitha's eyes and what came into focus was a dainty table for two, decorated with lots of pretty things: candleholders, flowers, picture frames with snaps from our dates and a birdcage with flickering tealights inside. On top of the table were two lace doilies and on top of them, two pretty old fashioned china flowered dinner plates she had spotted when we had been antique shopping a few weeks earlier. A fire crackled within a chiminea a few yards from the table.

'Tyler, wow. What's all this?'

'It's more of your surprise.' I beamed, so happy she was happy. 'I thought we wouldn't be able to be together much tomorrow night at the family party, so we're having one last date night.'

I'd been hard at work most of the evening setting everything up and the guys from The Gardens had kindly kept an eye on it all while we were in The Palm House. I showed her to her seat, put a wrap (Irish handwoven wool so fine it was like a cobweb in a gorgeous shade of Donegal Mountains Blue) that was hanging over the back of a chair round her shoulders and cracked open a bottle of bubbly. We stared into each other's eyes as only two giggly young lovers are allowed to.

Then a guy (Patrick in a penguin suit – an actual penguin suit – he had clearly taken the literal interpretation of the term 'penguin suit') bundled a trolley cart across the grass. He placed some of Tabitha's favourite nibbles from a gourmet deli she loves to visit onto the table.

'There you go Madam. Sir.'

'Thank you,' we said, me trying very hard not to burst out laughing.

'Enjoy.'

He bowed to us and then realised he didn't need to be there so, with a final 'Bon appetite!' waddled off to his late night date with a local takeaway. The next hour flew past, as we reminisced about the highs and highs of the summer, talked about movies and music, and Tabitha suggested some Youtube videos for me to watch. It was bliss to have the entire Botanic Gardens, usually so busy and crowded, just to ourselves.

After dinner I walked Tabitha from our wee table to another section of the park, where a plaid rug and a picnic basket were laid out.

'Pudding' I announced, flipping open the basket which contained fresh strawberries and cream and a scrumptious lemon meringue pie made by Granny especially for tonight. There was another bottle of bubbly and two glasses tucked in there too.

Gareth from the festival had pulled in a few million favours for me, and Joseph Richardson, an up and coming local musician, played a 25-minute private set for us. It was amazing. Tabitha beamed the whole time. Later she told me she had a face ache from smiling. At the end of his set Joseph had a drink with us and we repeatedly thanked him for coming to play; he even signed a few napkins for Tabitha and her friends before he left. Could he be the next big thing? I told Joseph he was a saint and gave him a copy of my EP before he left us.

Then we lay on the rug and shared more stories of the once in a lifetime summer vacation that was now drawing to an end. All the complex questions remained unasked. Talking about our memories brought a surprising peace. Tabitha snuggled in.

We must have dozed off, as just after the stroke of midnight raindrops awakened me. Tabitha was nestled into my chest, she rubbed her eyes and before the heavens opened we grabbed our rug and ran hand in hand from the park. As we scurried,

I knew two things:

1. My old romantic Dad would be beaming with pride.

2. At last I have experienced love and I can truly say I now know what all the songs and poems are about. Love is good. Love is here. Love will come alive when we hold it in our hearts and take time to shape it with careful hands and open souls. Love will always blossom from the seeds of hope that we plant, especially if we are willing to deal with the weeds.

The caretaker of the park was waiting for us on the other side of the railings. I had paid him to take his wife to a local restaurant and have a three-course meal on me. He was swinging his keys as he unlocked the heavy iron gates. I thanked him and did an extra #moneyhandshake for letting Pat and Conor come in and tidy up after us. He gave me a wink.

Tabs and I took shelter in a doorway and waited for the shower to pass.

'It's been perfect,' sighed Tabitha, leaning into me. 'Except for one thing . . .'

I froze and felt ill. What on earth could I have overlooked?

'You forgot the frisbee.'

COOKOUT

I spent the morning finishing my laundry, then sorting through and packing up my stuff.

Tacky souvenirs.

Cool gifts.

New clothes.

Then I tried to cram the memories from my trip into my suitcase.

I sat on my bed, failing at packing, flailing at dealing with my emotions of the trip.

My iPad. It was Rodriguez wanting FaceTime.

Rodriguez:	*'TYLER!'*
Tyler:	*'Dude! How have you been?'*
Rodriguez:	*'Yeah. Great! Fresh and Juicy is still fresh and juicy! The crew can't wait to see you - and you*

	better not be changing your flights again!'
Tyler:	*'No, I'm definitely coming home tomorrow!' I said, with a sense of finality.*
Rodriguez:	*'How was last night?'*
Tyler:	*'It was special man! We chatted for hours and I had a few surprises planned which were a huuuuuge hit. One more day to wait and I'll tell you all about it. Anyway, what about everyone at home? What's been going on with the guys? I've been missing you!'*

Then we caught up on Rodriguez's life. His Dad had returned to work part-time.

Rodriguez:	*'Can't wait to see you bro.'*
Tyler:	*'Tomorrow!'*
Rodriguez:	*'YESSSSS!'*
Tyler:	*'Gotta go. I'm helping my Granny with the pudding for the big family send-off party tonight.'*
Rodriguez:	*'Pudding? You're getting the accent man.'*
Tyler:	*'That's another thing I'll explain when I see you.'*

Granny and I spent the afternoon together, with me as sous pastry chef. We also recorded a wee video to show to Mom when I got home, including a couple of songs Granda had written which I performed on my guitar. I was going to play the songs that night at the family party too, just to surprise everyone. To get Granny and her cakes to the party, I was forced to break my vow to never get in the car with her again. I'll tell you - it was hard work preventing the meringue pavlovas she had baked for the cookout from turning into some form of Eton Mess (It's a dessert you get a lot over here, cream, meringue pieces and fresh fruit all mashed up together. Looks messy, tastes incredible) as she hurtled round corners in her little car.

Richard and Uncle David had grilled up a feast for all the extended family. I had eaten so much good food over the summer, even if a lot of it was American food, but there were some things that I still, and would probably never, get used to. Like calling fries 'chips' or the fact you get some form of potato with most meals! I loved the variety of desserts I had experienced, including amazing new ones like trifle and fresh strawberry flan. And Sunday Lunch – not actually lunch but a huge meal in the middle of the day involving a large roast of some kind of meat, gravy, veg and especially the roast potatoes. Gotta be designed with guys my age in mind.

And you already know about the traybakes and fries. But I have never seen a bigger selection of sweets (candy) anywhere! And the breads. Mmmmmm. I was gonna miss the wheaten, the soda bread, and that dark molassass-y Veda topped with marmalade and cheese! And the fish and chips. I can't say I'd miss all those 'salads' though, which seemed to be mostly carbs drowned in mayo, or those sandwiches with grey, mushy bananas in the middle that Pat loved so much. As for NYC foods I missed the most? No contest. Big Apple deli sandwiches and real Mexican food. Nothing compared to Cosalá's or my favourite sandwich haunt in The Village.

But that final night's cookout had to be the most satisfying meal of my whole summer. Maybe because Pat seemed happier than I had ever seen him. I soon found out why. For the first time ever, he was actually talking to his parents about his course. So did that mean-? I caught snippets as he talked about a programme at Queen's where med students can go off and work in the developing world for a few months as volunteers, using what they have learned to help others.

'Now that I'm free, single and willing, there's nothing to stop me,' he explained.

Of course before he could go, he'd have to fundraise hard. Beth suggested enlisting Granny's help. Much as they loved her baking, Beth and Richard 'hadn't a mission' of being trim and slim, no matter how much Pilates they tried, as long as Granny was bringing baked goods over very other day. But a bake sale for Pat's work in Africa? Genius!

I guess he'd been doing a bit of research back in the library while I was getting ready for Tab's surprise yesterday and cooking with Granny today. Pat also said he had started reading up on the condition that ended Ella's life so soon.

'Did you know they are doing loads of research into it and in maybe twenty years time, babies will no longer die from it? There are already some things which doctors can fix while the baby is still in the womb.' He seemed excited by the idea of these medical advances and sounded like he wanted to be part of it.

I had never seen my summer parents happier either.

We sat round the table and recounted stories of the summer and spun old family tales into the small hours of the night.

They sure know how to tell a good yarn on the Emerald Isle. The highlight of the night was when Granny and I burst out of the sunroom doors into the garden and began to perform to the crowd. I was wearing one of Granda's old suits. Granny had donned one of her showbiz gowns and we sang two songs - one that Granda had written and another classic from the Showband days. There wasn't a dry eye in the house. I played a few more tunes, the neighbours' dogs joined in, and after that we had a big sing song that probably woke the whole street.

The hardest part was when people began leaving, but I took comfort in knowing that all the tears were happy tears. Tabitha and I had said our goodbyes the previous night. Even so, giving her one last hug and kiss and watching her drive away from the house that final time brought a lump to my throat. When would I see her again?

Aunt Beth and Uncle Richard had tried to put into words what the summer had meant for them. When I went up to bed, I found their note on top of my packed suitcase.

Having you as our second son was a pleasure.
We will do our best to enjoy our Merchant Afternoon Tea voucher!
Thanks for everything and have a brilliant time at Uni.
Much love
Beth & Richard
xx

T'ESSAY

Most nights (with the exception of that time we weren't talking!) Tabitha and I exchanged text messages before shuteye. You might have noticed my slight tendency to go on and on and get all lyrical and to, at times, get all whimsical with my words?! Tabs calls our pre-bed-exchanges T'essays. Tyler essay, text essay, whatever!

Sometimes our pre bed message would be a picture of an animal wearing human clothes or a ridiculous selfie. Other messages would be a photo of the sunset as we made our way home or a cup of tea with 'I miss you' written over it. Tonight, instead of a picture, I planned to send her another T'essay. As I was composing it, I imagined this as my pre-credits end scene. I'm riding a motorcycle into the sunset, or in my case, cycling down Broadway in NYC with a guitar strapped over my back. So, as if I hadn't expressed my love for her enough, tonight I took one more opportunity to put it down in words. But before I could press *send*, Tabitha beat me to it.

Hey Tyler, I'm playing u at ur own game.
I hope the neighbours' dogs have stopped howling!
Before I knew u I didn't know how 2 trust because I couldn't put my confidence or hope in most of the people we r told we can. I had just about given up on falling in love, but then I found u. And now u know my story.
We have the hope of a love that will endure time and distance.
But even if I never see u again, thank u for what we have shared.
But, I know I'll see your ugly bake again! Thanks for making me smile a thousand smiles every time I see u or think about u.
Love was but a word until we brought it to life.
I love you.
And before you say it … I love you more.
Night
T
x

I must have read her T'essay four times before I scrolled through some of the other messages she had sent me this summer. After reading them for half an hour I smiled, looked across at Pat crashed out on the opposite bed, switched off the light and laid my head on the pillow. You bet I was still clutching my phone.

And now you're wondering what I wrote to her.

Well … I can't tell you everything!

THE CAPTAIN HAS TURNED ON THE FASTEN SEAT BELT SIGN

Richard, Beth, Patrick and Granny all came to the airport. Granny cried. I cried. We all cried! 90% happy tears. I checked in, weighed my bag (one ounce over so they let me off) and lingered with my family before I heard a boarding call for my flight and gave them one last hug.

As I was joining the line for security I recognised the hat six people ahead. I was tempted to take a photo and send it to Tabitha. 'Someone's wearing your hat!'

A few seconds later the owner of the hat turned around.

I recognised those eyes.

I recognised that smile.

And the freckles.

My heart gave a little happy leap.

She waved her ticket at me.

Tabitha was NYC bound!

I had to hand it to her.

This was the best surprise ever and absolutely trumped my night in the park. For the first time that summer I was totally speechless and couldn't wait to show my beautiful girl my wonderful city. And vice versa!

Welcome to New York Tabs.